It
Was
Her

MARK HILL

sphere

SPHERE

First published in Great Britain as a paperback original in 2018 by Sphere

1 3 5 7 9 10 8 6 4 2

A CIP catalogue record for this book is available from the British Library.

ISBN 978-0-7515-6324-5

Typeset in Adobe Caslon Pro by Palimpsest Book Production Ltd,
Falkirk, Stirlingshire
Printed and bound in Great Britain by Clays Ltd, St Ives plc

Papers used by Sphere are from well-managed forests
and other responsible sources.

MIX
Paper from
responsible sources
FSC® C104740

Sphere
An imprint of
Little, Brown Book Group
Carmelite House
50 Victoria Embankment
London
EC4Y 0DZ

An Hachette UK Company
www.hachette.co.uk

www.littlebrown.co.uk

For Pete and Doreen

I Years had been from Home
And now before the Door
I dared not enter, lest a Face
I never saw before
Stare stolid into mine
And ask my Business there
'My Business but a Life I left
Was such remaining there?'

EMILY DICKINSON

After Will:

One moment Will was there, and the next – he was gone.

Clumps of grass trembled on the lip of the chalk cliff. An armada of cloud scudded across the thick line of the horizon where the sky met the ocean. But all that was left of Will was a ghost of a movement. An absence in the empty space where he had been, above the quivering tufts of grass and the white stone, and now – in the blink of an eye – wasn't.

Joel's parents ran down the slope. Their screams and shouts were muffled in the rattle of the wind in his ears. His mum's eyes bulged with terror as she stumbled over the uneven ground. His father roared for them to get back, step away from the edge, for god's sake, get back. Joel saw Poppy run back towards them, in floods of tears.

But Sarah was leaning over the edge, where the cliff dropped away to the waves lashing angrily against the jagged rock hundreds of feet below. Hands planted hard on her knees to stop her toppling, the fierce gale making her hair twist and tumble around her pretty face.

His dad's voice was hoarse: 'Get away, get back!'

'Will! Will!' shrieked his mum.

And then Sarah glanced over her shoulder at all the commotion, and her eyes fell on Joel.

And she was smiling.
This big smile on her face.

One moment Will was there, and the next—

2

This, she decided, was her favourite room in all the world.

There were so many beautiful things. Sitting at the antique dressing table, she touched the bottles and containers of all shapes and sizes – magenta, turquoise, jade, every colour of the rainbow – which glimmered in the gentle light of the bulbs decorating the mirror. The bed was the biggest she'd ever seen, and piled high with pillows and cushions and throws. It was a delight to scrunch her toes into the delicate weave of the soft carpet.

The woman walked to the wardrobe, which was set into a wall so that you hardly noticed it was there. And when the door slid open – with a sound as faint as a whisper – neat rows of dresses and skirts and blouses were revealed, and neatly stacked racks of pretty shoes: heels, flats, pumps, sandals. Hangers clacked when she took out a summer dress imprinted with pale blue flowers.

Holding it to her body, she twirled before the dappled rocking horse in the bay window. The creature's silver mane fell across one ear. Polished stirrups and buckles sparkled on its leather saddle. She saw approval in its painted eye.

Yes, that one.

If anything, this room with its gleaming walls and silver

3

trinkets spilling from the jewellery box on the dressing table, the sparkling chandelier, and the heavy antique wall mirror with aged black spots on its faded surface, was even more lovely than the others.

Earlier, she had soaked in the oval tub in the bathroom, relaxed in flickering candlelight, enjoying the scent of pomegranate and blueberry and winter spices from the salts and soaps and creams. Let the steaming heat lift the cares and worries from her muscle and bone.

But then a sudden, terrible image of that *poor man* came out of nowhere, making her gasp and jerk upright. Water surged over the side of the bath to slap angrily on the chequered tiles.

And just like that, her composure was shattered.

Tension knotting her shoulders, the woman reached for the plump towel of Egyptian cotton warming on the heated handrail, avoiding her nakedness in the mirror – the pendulous breasts and heavy thighs, the sagging stomach, the thick threads of scar tissue snaking down her shoulders and back – and wrapping it around her, opened the cabinet to choose from all the lotions. The face cream she selected was cool against her flushed cheeks.

Now, she placed the dress on the bed, careful not to crease it, to apply make-up from golden tubes and black compacts which snapped closed between her fingers. Her face, usually pale and careworn, burst into colour. Finally, there was just a lipstick to choose. Her fingers hesitated over the different shades and settled on a bright red infused with a faint sparkle, to the admiration of the rocking horse.

Yes, it said. *That one.*

The woman picked up an ivory hairbrush, its milky surface

4

inlaid with pretty curlicues and loops, and pulled it through her hair. The brush crackled against her scalp, the static charge kinking her tangle of curls.

'It's ready,' called a voice.

She winced again at the thought of that *man*, just left there like that. It was no good, the whole night would be ruined if she didn't do something about it, so she went to her cargo shorts balled on the floor and took out a phone with a screen as big as her hand.

The woman hesitated. What she was about to do was a dangerous thing. But when she pressed the power button and the keypad appeared, she had no idea of the passcode.

'Come on down!'

The voice flustered her and she pressed random numbers on the screen. The phone buzzed tersely. She tried again, but it was pointless. The woman turned it off, replaced it in the pocket of the shorts.

Walking past the horse on its bow rocker, she inched the curtain aside. In the early hours of the morning the road seemed abandoned beneath the wash of streetlight. And yet inside all those big, handsome houses, she knew, people were safely tucked up in bed, and the thought comforted her. The roar of a car receded into the distance. She wished the driver god speed and hoped they would be reunited soon with family, with the people they loved.

'It'll get cold!' shouted the voice.

The dress she had chosen was too tight – she'd never be able to zip it up – but there was no time to choose another, and she went downstairs.

The kitchen at the rear of the house was vast. A skylight ran its entire length. This room, like all the others, was a bright, happy place in daylight, and at night was infused with a cosy glow from all the hidden lighting. Sleek appliances covered every surface. A silver range cooker was set into a converted fireplace. The cabinets were the type that popped open at a touch, and the long island unit was topped with a shining granite surface. But pots and pans had been dumped in the sink, and the tap, its neck as long and graceful as a swan's, seemed to recoil from the mess.

Her companion was hunched over a table, forking food into his mouth, and when she sat he squeezed her hand, gazing at her in adoration.

It was late; they were both weary, both hungry.

'Eat,' she told him.

The prongs of his fork rang against the china whenever he speared a shell of pasta on his plate. She prodded at it, but the food was burned, rubbery. Popping a piece into her mouth, the woman tried to enjoy the ambience of the lovely kitchen, and ignore the ugly chewing sounds of her companion.

She considered once again the twisted path that had brought her to this man, to this place.

And then a noise made them both look up sharply . . .

The door opening at the front of the house.

They heard anxious voices in the hallway. The front door slammed. A fragment of urgent conversation. Wheels fluttered along the floorboards.

Seconds later, the kitchen door swung open and a tanned woman in bright, loose-fitting clothes stood in the doorway. She cried out, and then a man pushed past her, dropping the handle of his case. His face was bronzed beneath steel-grey hair, but his arms, the skin on his neck, were sunburned.

For one stunned moment, the two couples looked at each other, and then the man in the doorway demanded angrily: 'What are you doing in our house?'

The woman at the table felt a terrible sadness.

She scraped back her chair to stand, its legs screeching on the tiles in the fierce silence. Beside her, the man's fork clattered to the plate. His chair tipped backwards. He jumped to his feet, the tendons in his wrists jerking taut.

The woman thought of this house, made into a wonderful home thanks to the care and attention, the *love*, of the couple in front of them.

Tatia wished it didn't have to end this way.

Stepping over the body was out of the question. It stretched along the hallway, one arm flung over the face, the other reaching for the stairs, fingertips pressed against the bottom step like a swimmer grasping for the edge of a pool. Simon Harrow's pink shirt rode up over his belly, which was mottled purple. His shock of grey hair was plastered by blood to the tiled floor. One leg, the bone snapped, rested heel-up against the wall. Teeth were scattered like dice along the skirting.

Harrow's body caused a bottleneck. If police and crime scene examiners wanted to reach the dining room at the rear of the house, where Melinda Harrow's body lay curled beneath the baby grand, they had to go through the living room to the left.

'I don't want to pre-empt the autopsy,' said Detective Constable Millie Steiner. The young black officer stepped back to consider the fire poker, matted with hair and gristle, and sticky with blood, dropped at the victim's feet. 'But I'm guessing they were beaten to death.'

Eddie Upson winked. 'Top-notch detective work, Millie.'

She shoved an elbow into Eddie's ribs just as Detective Inspector Ray Drake stooped over the body.

The skin on Harrow's leg was ruptured, torn apart beneath the force of the poker like the flesh of a dropped peach. Muscle and tendon bulged from the tear; there was a glimpse of arcing white bone. Bruises, imprinted from the killer's footwear, crisscrossed the edge of the wound.

'He was brought down hard with a stamp on the lower leg.' Tugging at the knees of his scene suit, Drake crouched to look at the victim's crooked fingers, the lacerations and lesions across his arms and shoulders. Most likely defensive wounds from where he lay on the floor trying to protect himself. 'And hit repeatedly with the poker.'

Millie Steiner watched Drake examine the corpse, fascinated by his hard face, the sharp, jagged cheeks, the straight nose and tapered jaw, those pale blue eyes from which the colour seemed to drain the longer you gazed into them. Not that Ray Drake ever let you meet his eye for very long. He was a shy man, it seemed to Millie, who kept a healthy distance from his team.

'The crime scene people are happy bunnies,' she said. 'They're picking up plenty of fingerprints all over the house, forensic samples galore, and some new words, too. One of them told me there's a *cornucopia* of evidence.'

'I went to a restaurant called Cornucopia,' said Eddie. 'It was very pricey.'

'And plenty of footprints.'

A faint footprint yielded the best results. Bloody prints were often difficult to read. The liquid poured into the pattern, obliterating the unique signature of the tread caused by wear and tear. Every sole on every shoe was different, in the same way as every fingerprint was unique, or every gun barrel.

'It's good to have you back, boss,' Millie said.

'Thank you.' Drake smiled, but his eyes didn't lift from Simon Harrow's cruel injuries. 'This . . . is not your usual.'

'No,' agreed Millie. 'Not your usual.'

Drake considered the victim's cotton shirt, his shorts and the boating shoes flung across the hallway. Next door, Melinda Harrow's body was barely a foot from the phone, sat in its cradle on a cabinet shelf. Like her husband, she had almost certainly been bludgeoned to death, suffering fatal blunt force trauma, multiple blows to the head and body. Melinda was dressed in a fitted shirt and silk skirt. A single espadrille hung off one tanned foot – sky-blue nails glistened in the light – and the other was kicked against a piano leg.

A trolley-case was on its side in the kitchen doorway, a baggage claim tag tied to the handle. A larger case – the companion part of a matching set – stood inside the front door, along with Mrs Harrow's Hermès handbag. Two passports were tucked into a pocket, and a pair of airline boarding passes.

Everyone knew the relief of getting home from holiday. It was good to go away, but there was a special kind of pleasure in returning home. Boiling water in your own kettle, brushing your teeth at your sink. Curling up beneath a crisp duvet, surrounded by beloved things accrued over a lifetime. But the Harrows had instead arrived home to find themselves plunged into a life-or-death struggle.

The confrontation was swift, catastrophic.

Two plates on the kitchen table contained half-eaten pasta. The lights were on upstairs. A dress was dumped on the floor in the bedroom. A tideline in the bathtub and a damp towel suggested someone had used it.

Someone was here, in the Harrows' comfortable home. Someone they knew, perhaps, minding the house. Friends,

10

neighbours, or people they had found on Airbnb. But that didn't explain the forced window at the side of the house.

'How much do you think a place like this is worth?' asked Millie. This was a four-floor, six-bedroomed detached home in a sought-after area in Tottenham. All the rooms were bright, spacious and immaculately decorated.

Eddie Upson scratched at the collar of his scene suit. Sweat filmed his forehead. The spring morning was warming up. The bodies would have to be moved soon.

'A pretty penny, although the asking price is plummeting by the second.'

'I never thought I'd say it, Eddie,' said Drake. 'But I've missed your repartee.'

Eddie winked at Millie. Loud voices disturbed Drake. A pair of officers stood at the front door in animated conversation about rugby with the arriving pathologist. Then the fabric of the tent erected outside lifted – Drake glimpsed squad cars and support vans parked in the street – and a small woman pushed through the men. The protective hood that framed her wide face rose unnaturally high around her head and her foot coverings were stretched tight over heavy boots. Deeply engrossed in her phone, thumbs dabbing at the screen, she barely glanced at the body sprawled in the hallway, and walked upstairs.

'Who is that?' said Drake.

She wore a lanyard, at least. A lot of people came and went from a crime scene. It would be nigh-on impossible for anyone unauthorised to breach two cordons, but he didn't like the idea of people wandering about checking their lottery numbers.

'Who's what?' Eddie looked up, but the woman had already gone.

11

'Never mind.' Drake was irritated by the braying laughter of the men at the door. 'Do me a favour, Eddie. Tell them to take the conversation outside.'

'Sure thing.'

Drake stood, rolling his shoulder. The wound he had sustained several months ago had healed, but the muscle stiffened easily.

'Where's DS Crowley?' he asked Millie.

She gestured over Drake's shoulder. 'In the garden.'

Through the kitchen window, he saw Flick Crowley on the lawn with a police search advisor. He watched her for a moment, his anxiety building. When he turned back to the body, DC Vix Moore was standing beside him.

'I spoke to the cab driver,' she said.

'Hold on.' Eddie had joined the conversation at the front and it was even louder than before. Drake could hardly hear himself think. 'Next door.'

In the living room, tasteful abstract art provided splashes of colour on the brilliant white walls. A charcoal-grey sofa and matching chair sat at right angles to an antique fireplace. The long neck of a floor lamp reached across the room.

Pride of place on the mantelpiece was a framed photo of Simon and Melinda Harrow on a beach of white sand. A handsome couple in their fifties, they looked relaxed and happy at a table in the surf, silver water lapping over their feet. A glorious sunset flared off the rims of their lifted champagne flutes. Simon was tanned and trim in tennis linens. Melinda's white teeth flashed between full lips. Her scooped top was edged with sequins which glimmered in the red dusk.

The circular mirror above the fireplace gave the room a

sense of space and light, despite the tent erected across the front of the house. A rattan rug was rolled up on the painted floorboards so that crime scene examiners could collect samples – prints, fluids, stains. In the dining room next door Melinda Harrow's body was partially hidden beneath the piano.

'I spoke to the cab driver,' repeated Vix. 'He picked up Mr and Mrs Harrow from Gatwick at 12.45 a.m.'

'And they were alone?' asked Drake.

'Yes, they chatted with him about their holiday – the food and the weather.'

'Neither of them made any calls, or sent texts?' asked Drake. 'Or mentioned anyone would be here when they got back?'

'They were tired, but in good spirits,' said Vix. 'Mr Harrow told him they had come home because of a work emergency.'

'They speak to anyone on the phone?' Drake asked again, and Vix blinked. 'You didn't ask.'

Her cheeks reddened. 'No.'

Drake stepped back into the kitchen, careful to keep to the transparent footplates laid on the floor. The atmosphere was stuffy as the sun pulled across the roof of the house.

The fridge was a giant Smeg. Using a single finger of his gloved hand, he tugged open the door. The chill air cooled his face. Inside, it was mostly empty. The Harrows had binned most perishables before their holiday. There were jars of pickles and olives on a top shelf; a tub of butter; a lonely bulb of garlic. A carton of milk from Quartley's Supermarket was forgotten on a shelf in the door. The curdled contents slopped lazily when Drake tilted it.

13

'I've the driver's details,' Vix said. 'I'll get back onto him, and do a background check.'

'Thanks, Vix,' said Drake. 'We'll go over the rest later.'

'Yes.' The tips of the young detective's fierce blonde bob twitched like the antennae of an anxious insect. 'I'm so glad you're back, sir. I've already learned so much from you.'

Fishing for compliments, she waited for his reply. But Drake's attention kept returning to the garden, and to Flick.

It was good to be back on the job, doing what he did best. This was his life. But it could all be ripped from him at any moment. And not just his career – everything. His family, his good name – maybe his freedom.

It was all in Flick's hands now.

Ray Drake took a deep breath and stepped outside.

4

He stood on the decking beside a wooden table and chairs, among numerous terracotta tubs of plants and herbs. The sun nosed over the roof, chasing shadows up the long, lush lawn. The Harrows should have been sitting here this morning, rested after a sunny holiday, enjoying coffee and toast, surrounded by fragrant sweet peas and magnolias, dianthus and laurentias, watching bees buzz around the purple lavender. Instead, a PolSa – Police Search Advisor – team swarmed across the grass looking for evidence, and CSEs photographed the broken lock on the garden gate.

Next to the garage, beside the nose of a silver Audi series 6, Detective Sergeant Flick Crowley spoke to a uniformed officer.

'Anything?' asked Drake.

Flick walked over, arms folded across her chest as if it was cold, and nodded down the lawn. 'There are a couple of partials in one of the beds down by the gate.'

'And there are plenty of prints inside. I'm sure we'll get a suspect soon.' Drake turned to the officer. 'Excuse us for a moment, will you?'

Flick reluctantly followed Drake beneath a magnolia tree. Its curling white flowers opened to the sky; the shade beneath its crooked branches was a welcome relief.

He tried not to betray his agitation. 'How are you feeling this morning?'

Flick's hand instinctively went to her waist where she had been stabbed months ago. She had undergone an emergency operation for the haemothorax, and weeks of physical rehabilitation. The wound had healed, but Drake knew the psychological fallout of the attack still lingered.

'Good,' she said. 'I'm good.'

She watched the PolSa officers at work, and he studied her in profile: her angular face and cheekbones; her brown hair, lately grown long, and the fringe that fell across her almond eyes; the strong shoulders tapering into a long, lean body and slender arms.

'Flick.' Conscious of the officers nearby, Drake spoke quietly. 'We haven't had much time to talk since—'

'Let's not.' She held up a hand. 'Let's just . . . get on with the job.'

'You're right, it's not the right time.' He hesitated. 'But we're going to have to speak about it soon.'

'Why?' She turned away. 'Why do we have to?'

'I need to know you're doing well.' Drake moved so that they were face to face, trying to get her to engage.

They were in this together, whether she liked it or not, in the aftermath of that terrible night when they had been attacked by an associate of the man who called himself the Two O'Clock Boy.

Drake wanted Flick to know that he understood the risk she took by supporting his version of those violent events. They had told the Specialist Investigations team from the Met's Directorate of Professional Standards that the killer had targeted officers investigating his murder of former

16

residents of a long-closed children's home. Drake's mother had been attacked, a crime scene manager killed; his own daughter had been used as bait to lure him into a deadly trap.

But if the whole story of that evening ever came out, Drake's reputation would be left in tatters.

Because Flick knew the truth about Ray Drake. A lifetime ago he was somebody else, a disturbed teenager called Connor Laird who took a dead boy's identity as his own. Took Ray Drake's name, his home, even his family.

Lies were toxic. Ray Drake had lived a lie for so long that he barely knew any more what was truth and what was falsehood. But Flick was isolated, vulnerable. She was hurting. And if she changed her statement, his whole world – everything he had painstakingly built for himself over a lifetime – would collapse. Drake wanted to help her to a better place. For her own good, but also for his own survival. But to do that, she had to let him in.

'Let's not talk about it here,' she said. 'Not with two people dead inside.'

Drake could tell she was thinking again about that catastrophic night. The murderous confrontation in Drake's home, and that isolated cottage in the countryside. The blood pouring from her wound as he stood among the carnage.

A muscle ticked in her jaw, and he *knew* – the shock was like a punch to the gut – that she was keeping something from him.

'We're good, aren't we, Flick?' he asked softly.

She watched the search team comb the lawn. 'I don't know if I can do this. The counsellor—'

'What about her?' He kept his voice calm. 'What have you said?'

'I haven't told her anything.' She shook her head. 'Not yet.'

He understood the implication. She wanted to unburden herself of what she knew about Drake – and about Connor Laird, and his deadly connection to a string of murders. But if Flick told just one person, sooner or later everything would be revealed. Assigned by the Met to deal with Flick's trauma in the aftermath of the incident, the counsellor was bound by patient confidentiality – but only up to a point. She would do everything in her power to get Flick to reveal the truth. Drake's secret history would unravel.

And perhaps the most dangerous secret of all would be revealed. *Elliot*.

'Tell me how I can help.' He wanted to reassure her that the terrible guilt she felt – the loneliness – was temporary. She would heal and together they would move on. He wanted to assure her they were both good people, blameless people, who had become embroiled in a shocking series of events beyond their control.

But he couldn't.

Because Drake once again forced himself to consider what else Flick had seen that night . . .

'It's over now, it's the past, and we have a job to do.' He nodded at the house. 'Those victims inside need us to focus now. I promise I will do anything to help you—'

She blurted out, 'I'm going to tell her.'

Despite the dread he felt, Drake kept his voice steady. 'Tell her what?'

She met his pale eyes for the first time – and her look was defiant.

'Boss,' said a voice.

'Flick—'

'Boss!'

Distracted, Drake turned to see Eddie Upson at the door. 'The digital forensics lady wants a word.'

Drake tried to collect his thoughts. 'Sorry, Eddie, who?'

'The Digital Forensic Specialist. She's in the attic.'

'Give me a minute.'

'Sure thing.' Eddie lingered at the door.

'*A minute*, Eddie.'

When DC Upson had disappeared inside, Flick said: 'Every week I sit in my session and I say nothing. I talk about everything but what happened that night, the one thing I need to talk about. But I can't . . . keep it inside any more.'

'You're not alone. What happened that night happened to both of us.'

'You don't understand, Ray,' she said. 'You're not the solution, you're the problem. People have no idea who you are. But I do. I know who you are.'

'Yes,' Drake said. 'You do.'

'And I don't think I can handle that burden. Of knowing about you and . . . what happened.'

And he knew then, with a terrible certainty, that she saw. Saw what he did.

Flick walked off towards the search team and Drake gathered his thoughts. Then he walked back into the house, trying not reveal the fear that simmered inside him.

That the world would soon know the truth about Ray Drake.

But he couldn't do anything about that now. There was

work to do. A crime scene to attend to, an investigation to launch. For now, at least, he was back doing what he was put on this earth to do.

5

Climbing the stairs, Drake tried to focus on the crime scene. He looked inside the door of the spacious bathroom where somebody had used the tub last night. Luminol had been sprayed on the walls and bath but no blood traces had been found. Towels and the contents of the cabinet had been bagged up and taken away for examination.

In the bay window of the main bedroom, a rocking horse sightlessly watched Drake. Behind it, the heavy curtains were drawn. A CSE knelt in front of a long wardrobe, lifting prints off the sliding door.

Drake climbed the stairs to an attic office. The conversation with Flick repeating in his head, he tried to make sense of the enormous implications of it.

Ray.

Drake stopped on the stairs, called over the bannisters. 'Hello?'

The forensics guy came out of the bedroom below. 'Sir?'

'Did you call?'

'Not me,' said the examiner, and went back inside.

Drake was at the door to the attic room when he realised he was looking at the broad back of the woman he had seen come into the house earlier, the hood of her scene suit oddly bulbous around her head. She was still hunched over her phone, her fingers swiping fluidly over its surface.

Unlike the other rooms, this one, hidden safely out of sight in the roof, was a messy, comfortable space. There were shelves and cabinets filled with books about art, music and travel; a poster tacked to the wall beneath a rose window advertised an opera in Berlin; box files and papers were piled on a small sofa, bills, receipts and documents spilling to the floor. Two desks were pushed together to allow the Harrows to work facing each other. A MacBook sat on one desk, a PC laptop on the other.

'Look at this,' said the woman, looking up.

'I can't see what it is,' said Drake.

The woman presented the phone. The screen wobbled so he steadied her wrist. Drake saw her chipped black nail polish and a twisting henna tattoo along a forefinger, and realised she wasn't wearing gloves. 'I hope this phone isn't evidence.'

'Oh, don't worry, it's mine.' She lifted a lanyard from inside her protective clothing. 'I'm Grace Beer. I'm your Digital Forensic Specialist.'

With people increasingly living their lives online via a variety of smart devices, the DFS was responsible for recovering digital data. It wouldn't be long, Drake was reliably informed, before every household utility and device would communicate wirelessly with everything else. Fridges talking to toasters talking to music systems, the water mains discussing the weather with the garden sprinkler system. And everything run remotely from an app on a tablet or smart phone. The day would soon arrive when experts like Grace Beer, who could make sense of the deluge of digital information, would be given priority access at every crime scene.

'Nice to meet you,' said Drake. 'Why are we looking at your phone?'

'The apps.'

There were rows of icons on the screen. None of them made the slightest bit of sense to him.

'The one with the little Viking helmet?' he asked.

'That's a Thrash Metal Lyric Generator,' she said. 'The one next to it.'

Drake saw a logo shaped like an antenna, surrounded by crackling waves of sound. He recognised it as the branding of a major telecoms company.

'You're going to like this.' She held the mobile at her shoulder like a tech guru addressing a convention of acolytes.

'So basically, a lot of public places – cafes, restaurants, airports, libraries, yeah? – have Wi-Fi hotspots. Wait, you know what a Wi-Fi hotspot is, right?'

'Yes,' said Drake patiently. 'I know what a Wi-Fi hotspot is.'

She pulled down her hood to reveal a huge pair of head-phones clamped around a complicated milkmaid plait. Piercings ran up and down her ears and tattooed angel wings disappeared into her hairline at the neck. Her eye make-up was dark and heavy. To Ray Drake's mind, Grace Beer didn't look older than twelve.

'It's a space where you can log onto the internet. To use a public hotspot you're usually asked to connect from a web page. But if you have a special app that allows you to log on . . .' She dabbed at the telecoms app, opening it. 'It'll happen automatically, the phone will communicate with the hotspot and say –' the phone danced in her hand as if speaking '– *I'm here, let me onto the internet, good sir.* And the hotspot will reply, *welcome, friend, please partake of all my pleasures*. And then they hook up. Follow me?'

'Yes,' said Drake, who could live without the funny voices.

'Well, this house has a private Wi-Fi account, used by the householders. We all have them. You'll need a password to connect with that. But there's also a hidden portion in the router which is used to boost the local public hotspot signal.'

She made a face – ta da! – and waited for him to reply, but he didn't know what he was meant to say.

'So,' she continued, unfazed, 'the service provider uses it as a hotspot for anybody who wants to log on in this area using their paid Wi-Fi service. You'll probably find a similar thing in many homes in this neighbourhood. And guess what, when I walked into the house the service provider's app on my android,' she waggled the phone, 'allowed me to log on automatically to the public hotspot.'

Drake frowned, trying to get his head around it all. 'And that helps us how?'

'Maybe it doesn't. But if the router communicated with my phone, then it could have communicated with other mobiles that came into this house. If, and only if, they had that app. If they did, then the phone owner will have needed an email address to register with the service, and that mail address will lead us to an IP address.'

'What are the chances of that happening?' asked Vix Moore, who had appeared behind Drake.

Grace shrugged. 'It's a long shot, but if I logged on automatically when I came in, I'm sure there'll be other people walking around this house right now who regularly use that public Wi-Fi provider.'

'As long as they have the app,' repeated Drake, intrigued by the possibility.

'Yes,' said Grace. 'And as long as the phone was turned on.'

Vix, who believed it was every woman's sworn duty to aspire to the glamour of Grace Kelly rather than the emo sensibilities of Grace Beer, stared grimly at the investigator's hair and make-up. 'What does it all mean?'

Drake pondered the idea. 'We can apply to the service provider to find out if any IP addresses logged on to this router last night.'

'Boom! If they came into this house the service provider will be able to trace it to the owner.' Grace turned to the computers. 'I'd better get this stuff back to the office so I can have a good root around their social media.'

'What are those for?' Vix nodded at the chunky headphones. 'Listening to phone messages and audio files and suchlike?'

'These? Oh no.' Grace tugged at one of the 'phones and it snapped back against her neck. 'They're for my tunes.'

'Let's do it,' Drake said. 'What have we got to lose?'

6

It was Ray Drake's experience that sometimes, just sometimes, long shots paid off – and this was one of those times.

Someone had taken a smart phone into that house. At some point it was switched on, because the device auto-connected with the public portion of the router in the early hours. A legal request was sent to the service provider, and an IP address identified. They had a name, and they had an address in East Finchley.

Drake dared to hope they would make an early arrest for the murder of Simon and Melinda Harrow, leading swiftly to charges. The phone belonged to a man called Gareth Walker, whose details appeared in the CrimInt database for a minor public disorder offence at a demo years back.

His home in a quiet street was put under observation. Nobody went in or out for twenty-four hours, and because it was shuttered front and back, it was impossible to tell if anybody was holed up inside. Discreet inquiries on the street revealed nobody knew much about Walker. Not long ago, neighbours complained, there was a sense of community – an annual street party, a book group – but not any more. These days, everybody kept themselves to themselves. In many cases, the owners didn't even live there. The buildings were investments or corporate leases and left empty, or let by agencies or absentee landlords.

Drake's DCI applied to a magistrate for a warrant to enter the premises and – calculating the level of risk: they had no idea what they would encounter inside – arranged to send in C020, the Territorial Support Group, the Met unit assigned to deal with potentially dangerous situations. Drake and his Murder Investigation Team gathered in the incident room, far above the noise and traffic of Tottenham High Road, to watch the raid.

Usually one of the news channels played silently on the television fixed to the wall, the sound only turned up if there was a major incident in the capital. Often, at the end of the day, DS Dudley Kendrick, one of the older detectives on Drake's team, and an enthusiastic pub quiz moderator, watched ancient quiz shows on Challenge. This afternoon, however, a live feed would be broadcast from a camera attached to the shoulder of a sergeant in the TSG.

Drake's team rolled chairs across the room to face the blank screen and waited, unwrapping sandwiches, drinking coffee. Others perched on the side of desks, fiddling with their phones.

Drake was tense, preoccupied by Flick's intention to reveal his secret to the counsellor. He felt his future hanging by a thread. At the other end of the office, she was on the phone to Millie Steiner, who was at the scene. If she felt Drake's attention on her, she didn't show it.

His spine juddered as something hit his armrest. Vix Moore smiled sweetly as she forced her chair into the tight space beside his. Sitting at his desk, Eddie Upson dug something unspecific from a nostril.

Kendrick was beneath the TV, pointing a bewildering array of remote controls at the screen and pressing random buttons. He got a round of ironic applause when he finally managed to get a picture. An image of sorts appeared, but no sound. Movement in the claustrophobic gloom of a police carrier. Indistinct figures shifted in the dark, from the point of view of a camera on the shoulder of a sergeant. Drake caught a glimpse of legs and kit bags, and a thumbs-up from an officer as the image swept across a row of men.

'Do we have sound?'

Kendrick skated a finger over the trackpad of a laptop. 'Nearly there.'

Unpeeling a lid from a Tupperware box to reveal a fruit salad, Vix speared a chunk of pineapple onto a plastic fork and offered it to Drake, who politely declined.

'Any moment now,' said Kendrick, and then explosive static tore from the speaker. Loud sounds accompanied the images. They heard the tear of Velcro; the snap of buckles as the men adjusted their chainmail MetVests; their banter as they pulled on helmets. This team knew each other well. Every day they travelled together miles across the city, ready at a moment's notice to attend major incidents – riots, violent attacks, any number of unstable situations. Kendrick lifted a remote to adjust the volume.

There was a thump on the outside of the carrier and the camera tilted to the door. A whirl of light pierced the gloom. On the road, Millie was framed against the glare, speaking into her phone. The team jumped out – toe-capped boots rang on the steel step – and into the blinding sunshine.

'Yes, we can see you, Millie,' said Flick into the phone.

The camera moved across the road, jerking up and down with the sergeant's every step. Drake saw trees lining the pavement; well-tended front gardens and spacious driveways;

tall, detached houses; recycling bins squared neatly against fences. It didn't look like the kind of street a homicidal maniac would call home, but in the light of the ferocity of the attack on the Harrows, nobody was taking any chances.

'They're going in now,' Flick said, a moment after Millie said the same thing off-mic.

Three officers swung away from the group, towards a side gate leading to the garden. The end of an enforcer, a kettle drum used to smash open doors, could be seen at the bottom of the screen. The sergeant turned to his team. One of his men tapped his helmet with his knuckles, a good-luck gesture. Then another officer stepped forward to pull the enforcer behind his body, ready to swing it. A radio burbled, the men at the rear confirming they were in position. The unit stood ready. Focused, like actors waiting to step onstage.

Vix Moore replaced the lid on her Tupperware box and slid it beneath her chair.

More radio communication, then the sergeant's hand sliced the air. 'Rear team, we're going in!'

The enforcer was swung forward. It smashed into the door, which flew open. The men poured inside, shouting. The camera jerked up and down with every movement of the sergeant's shoulder.

Loud, aggressive declamations: 'Police! Police!'

Officers swooped left and right into the dark hallway. The speakers crackled with shouts. Drake glimpsed colourful walls, the glint of a silver pendant light hanging from the ceiling. At the other end of the corridor, blank white light exploded when the back door was flung open and silhouetted figures raced in.

Heavy boots clattered on wood. The camera whipped left

and right. The sergeant moved into a ground-floor room, his breath rasping. It was dark behind the heavy wooden window shutters, but a torch sent a powerful beam of light whipping across the floor, revealing flashes of scattered magazines and books, upended furniture.

The hoarse shouts of the officers reverberated around the house – short, sharp orders designed to shut down resistance.

'Get down! Police!'

The camera moved left and right, up and down, making the torchlight spin.

'What are those dots?' Vix Moore pointed at the screen. 'Is it interference?'

'Flies,' said Drake. He rubbed his eyes wearily, already suspecting how this scenario was going to play out. Flick picked up a sandwich and immediately dropped it back on the desk, not in the mood.

A phone rang and, rolling his chair backwards, Kendrick leaned over a desk to grab it. 'No,' he said into the receiver, his eyes glued to the screen, 'you'll need to speak to traffic about that.'

Thuds and shouts came from the speaker, the heavy thump of boots on the floor above. Garbled voices squawked on the sergeant's radio.

'Police!' The men shouted again and again. 'Show yourself!'

'Kitchen – clear!'

Voices coming from every which way now.

'Toilet – clear!'

'Bedroom – clear!'

'It's empty in here!'

'There's nobody.'

The camera turned, following the beam of the torch. A flat disc of light illuminated empty shelves and nooks, books thrown on the floor, a stereo upended, a television face down; a glass coffee table was smashed. The room was piled with mess.

'It smells in here,' said the sergeant, 'and it's insanely hot. The heating is on.'

'There are flies.' An officer swung round to the camera, his eyes reflecting in the torchlight. 'Lots of flies.'

'Bathroom!' someone called from upstairs. 'The en suite.'

The camera moved through the door, where officers jostled in the hallway. It went upstairs, jolting with every crash of the sergeant's boots on the steps.

Drake's hand tapped against his thigh in anticipation.

The camera passed officers emerging from rooms, and went into a dark bedroom. Bright light came from an open doorway, a tiled bathroom. And inside was a shape on the floor.

A patterned silk dressing gown, like a kimono, twisted around the naked torso of a bloated body. The skin was darkly mottled, a sickly green. Drake saw clumps of hair on the floor, as if they had tumbled from a barber's chair, and a round, shapeless face, the lips parted by a swollen, leering tongue.

The floor and walls were spattered with dark patches which twisted and pulsed. Flies. Then the camera whipped away. Officers milled about; all the explosive energy of that first entry into the house had subsided.

'The house is clear,' said the sergeant into his radio. 'But there's a body.'

'Yeah,' Flick said on the phone to Millie. 'We got that.'

'Get the sergeant to move in closer,' said someone in the room.

31

'Don't bother.' Drake stood. 'If it's Gareth Walker, and he's been there for a while with the central heating on full blast, he's going to be unrecognisable.'

Kendrick touched a button on the laptop to kill the feed. Three deaths now . . .

7

'. . . In two different homes.'

Uncapping his marker pen, Drake wrote down a name on the whiteboard.

'Gareth Walker was a freelance director of television commercials. A divorcee who lived alone. Mr Walker went to a work meeting at a Wapping production company in the morning and then to lunch with a school friend. This was ten days ago, on the Friday. CCTV picked him up at various points on his journey. Autopsy results suggest Mr Walker died hours later, most likely that evening. Beaten to death with one of his own golf clubs.'

Drake's MIT was gathered in the incident room, trying to concentrate above the noisy blast of the portable air-conditioning units placed at either end of the office. The ancient units made the stuffy room in the old Victorian building just about bearable on hot days, but also made it almost impossible to hear anything. Eddie doodled on his notepad. Millie took notes as if her life depended on getting down every single detail. Kendrick sat with his elbows on the table, hands clasped beneath his chin, ready to mop up any phone calls that came in during the meeting. The blinds, lowered to keep out the glare of the sun and the roar of the traffic on the High Road below, tapped listlessly against the sill.

'And nobody tried to contact him?' asked Flick.

'There are voicemails on his phone. From friends, work colleagues, and his mother who lives in Derby. But Mr Walker was a private man by all accounts. Most Friday nights he travelled alone to a holiday cottage in Norfolk. But he told his friend at lunch that he'd decided to stay home that weekend.'

'So, whoever killed him knew he would be there?'

'We'll get onto that. And then there are our other victims, killed over a week later.' Drake wrote two more names on the board, the nib squeaking faintly on the surface. 'Simon and Melinda Harrow.' He made a quick adjustment to the 'w' to make it more legible and stepped back. 'Mr Harrow headed up an economic think tank and Mrs Harrow was taking a year out from her job in marketing to write a children's book.'

'Young Adult,' corrected Millie Steiner.

'The Harrows lived in a large house in Downhills Park. They came home early from a holiday in Mauritius to discover people – we're now certain intruders who broke in – at their home in the early hours of Monday morning. As with Mr Walker, they were beaten to death with an object improvised at the scene, in this case a fire poker.'

Millie looked up from her notebook. 'Could there be a political angle?'

Drake tapped the marker against his chin. 'It's possible, but Simon Harrow was a policy wonk on the centre-left. It's not exactly radical.'

'Why did they come home early?' asked another detective.

Vix turned in her seat. 'They told the taxi driver a deadline

34

for a project Mr Harrow was working on had been shifted forward.'

'A golf club, a fire poker. Makeshift weapons,' said Flick. 'Are there other similarities between the two murder scenes?'

'Neither homes have alarms,' said Vix.

'Or children,' said Kendrick.

'We know someone made themselves at home at the Harrow house. We have a pubic hair from the bath, hair on a brush, saliva on food, footprints, and fingerprints on windows and doors and bottles and cupboards, on the television remote and make-up compacts.' He held up his hands. 'And just about everywhere else. We're expecting those DNA results any time now.'

Eddie scribbled furiously on the pad. 'Let's hope Goldilocks has an alibi.'

'The Walker house, on the other hand, was a mess,' continued Drake. 'Everything was tipped from the shelves, cabinets overturned and the television smashed. We're still going through the rooms but it's difficult to ascertain whether someone spent time there.'

'If Mr Walker was unexpectedly at home when the intruders entered, they would have got a nasty surprise.'

'And how did they get in?'

'That Friday was even hotter than today. We found a glass of water in the garden, and a book. If Gareth Walker had the back door open or left it unlocked, they could have just walked right in.'

'But our intruders took the trouble to secure the house on the way out, close the shutters, even turn on the central heating to let decomposition take its course.'

Millie had put her finger on it. These break-ins didn't fit

35

the normal pattern. Most burglars were opportunistic. They entered homes as quickly as possible, grabbing as much stuff as they could – portable items that were easy to sell, no questions asked, such as jewellery and electronic devices – and then got the hell out. But in these incidents – two homes invaded, the owners brutally murdered – it was difficult to tell what, besides Gareth Walker's phone, had been taken.

'There'll have been other break-ins with a similar MO. Borough police will have recorded burglaries at upscale homes in which little, if anything, was taken. Or where the house has been left altered in some way. Food eaten, objects disturbed. We're looking for unusual patterns of behaviour.'

'But why would anyone break in and not take anything?' asked Vix.

'Neither set of victims was meant to be there,' said Flick. 'Gareth Walker should have been in Norfolk that weekend and the Harrows on holiday. Seems to me those homes were targeted on specific nights.'

Kendrick looked up from his screen. 'Then the house had been watched.'

'Burglaries, break-ins . . . home invasions leading to murder.' Drake slapped the marker pen against his palm. 'This seems like the end of something, or . . .'

'Or what?' prompted Millie when his voice trailed away.

'Or it's an evolution,' he said quietly. 'An escalation.'

A phone rang at an empty desk. Kendrick diverted the call to his phone.

'Are there any links between the victims?' asked Eddie.

'Our friend Grace is going through their social media

and computer files, but she's found little. The Harrows were tagged on Facebook at occasional work functions, but that's about it, and they're not users of any other social media platforms. They were content to live their lives offline. And they mixed, as far as we can see, in completely different circles to our other victim. But if there's a connection between them, we'll find it.' He held out his hands to his team. 'You'll find it.'

'And if there isn't a connection,' asked Vix, 'what does that mean?'

'It means,' said Flick, 'that the attacks are random and they could happen again. Anywhere, at any time.'

8

That same image looped in his mind, like a home movie flickering on a white sheet.

One moment Will was there, and the next – he was gone. And again –

On, off, in Joel's mind. He was there, and then in the blink of an eye, he wasn't. Leaving the clumps of grass trembling on the lip of the cliff, the white stone, an armada of cloud scudding across the thin brown line where the sky met the ocean.

Joel's weary body swayed listlessly with every shudder of the carriage. He saw, once again, the top of Will's head, his blond hair lift in the wind.

One moment he was at the edge, and the next – Gone.

Over and over. All day, all night.

It was impossible to know how many times Joel had relived this moment. Hundreds, thousands, a million times or more. It was embedded in his mind. A double exposure over the everyday world, twenty-four hours a day.

All the detail – the colour, the texture, the density – was extraordinarily clear, in vivid high definition. But Will, the star of the show, was less tangible. Reduced to a ghost of movement, a flickering phantom – disappeared in the instant just gone.

The train slowed, rolling smoothly over steel. Joel's head lolled to the soothing tempo, oblivious to the other passengers. An explosion of noise – and then the driver's announcement was obliterated by static. Joel could barely follow it.

'Ladies an . . . aligh . . . oors.'

Brakes hissed. The carriage jerked to a stop. Unsteady on his feet, Joel lost his footing and stumbled into the man next to him.

When the carriage doors opened with a pneumatic sigh, he peered at the station sign, reading it several times, lips moving, breaking down each word into syllables before putting it back together. Just to be on the safe side. Until he was absolutely sure the words had sunk in, and he knew where he was.

Caledonian Road.

Caledonian. Road.

Cal-e-do-ni-an Road.

All the platforms and stations, all the names, the people around him, looked the same now. The station announcer said something – the words were an incoherent burble in his head. Joel was jostled as passengers stepped on and off the train. He pressed himself flat against the glass partition and closed his eyes.

One moment Will was there, and then –

The screech of a whistle and the doors trundled shut. The engine growled, the floor groaned beneath his feet. Joel waited for a hiss, and then *Joel!* a jolt as the overground train jerked away from the platform, but nothing happened. *Joel!* In the back of his mind he registered, very dimly, a voice. *Joel!* Then banging.

A man touched his shoulder. 'Someone's trying to get your attention.'

Joel followed the man's gaze to a woman on the platform. She stabbed at the door release button but nothing happened. She was tanned and pretty in a bright summer dress with a scoop neck that accentuated the prominent curve of her collarbone. Versace sunglasses were wedged into her long brown hair.

'Joel!' She smacked her hand against the window. 'It's me!'

He stared.

'Please!' The woman said to a man in a uniform. 'Can you let me in? I need to get—'

But then the engine throbbed – and the carriage shunted forward. The woman kept pace along the platform as the train picked up speed, frantically swerving to avoid the rush of departing commuters. She pulled behind her a small boy who struggled to keep up.

'Call me,' she shouted. 'Please call me!'

The woman slapped the window in frustration one last time as the train accelerated. Joel watched her recede into the distance. She stood on the edge of the platform, clutching the boy's hand, watching the carriage coast from the station. Then it angled away, and the platform slid out of sight.

'She seemed pretty keen to speak to you,' said the man beside him. 'Who was she?'

Joel thought about it for a moment. 'I have no idea.'

One moment Will was there, and in the blink of an eye –

9

'There's a connection between the Harrows and Walker. We just need to identify it.'

As Drake spoke, one of the Met's communication officers moved around the back of the room. Media coverage of the murders was gathering momentum. The investigation still in its early stages, there was little actual information to report. But newspapers were already spinning the story in all kinds of lurid directions. The news – in print, on TV, radio and online – was filled with trigger words intended to make the city uneasy. The victims weren't people who lived in crime-ridden tower blocks or violent sink estates. They were middle-class people, innocent people, slaughtered in the place they should feel most secure. In their own homes, in supposedly respectable streets, safe neighbourhoods.

Nobody knew if or when it would happen again. And anybody could be a potential victim.

Drake was already spending too much time managing the expectations of his superiors, who demanded quick progress in the investigation, and in discussions with rattled press officers.

'What we know,' he said at the whiteboard, 'is that Mr Walker's phone was taken into the Harrow home and switched on long enough for us to trace.'

'Why would they do that?' asked Eddie. 'It doesn't make sense.'

Drake frowned at the elaborate doodles that covered Eddie's notepad. 'Why do you think?'

'Well . . .' Conscious of his DI's attention, Eddie closed the pad. 'It could be . . . I mean to say . . .'

Vix rolled her eyes.

'Gareth Walker's body hadn't been found,' said Flick. 'He lay in his home for more than a week.'

Millie Steiner put up her hand. 'The killer had a change of heart, then, and was trying to tell us about him.'

Drake nodded. 'That's a possibility.'

'Someone will come down shortly,' Kendrick said quietly into a phone.

Eddie had slumped so low in his chair that he had to haul himself back up. 'But why would they do that?'

'Because they want to get caught,' said Drake. 'Or because they're getting brazen.'

Everyone thought about it for a moment. Over the roar of the air conditioners, the blare of car horns and shouts drifted up from the High Road.

Flick sighed. 'Terrific.'

'Look, let's not get downhearted. We have a hell of a lot of evidence on our side.' Drake counted off his fingers with the marker pen. 'Footprints, full and partial, plenty of finger-prints in both homes, any number of DNA samples.'

'A veritable cornucopia,' said Eddie.

'Forensics are confident they'll get a result, and they know this case is a priority.' Drake dropped the pen on a desk. 'Now let's get to work.'

Everyone in the room rolled their chairs back behind their desks. Drake saw Flick shoot out the door.

The communications officer, a red-haired woman named

Charlotte, stepped forward. Drake held up a hand, *give me a minute*, and hurried out after Flick. He saw her go through an internal fire door and followed – and ran straight into Marion Cresswell on the other side.

'My goodness!' she said as the papers she hugged to her chest slipped, one by one, to the floor.

'Let me help you!' Drake watched Flick disappear down the corridor as he crouched to pick up the sheets. He had no idea if he was putting them in the right order.

Plucking at a piece of A4 that had seemingly glued itself to the floor, Marion dropped her car keys. 'Sugar!'

'How's your boy, Marion?'

The Met Human Resources department where Marion worked was now centralised in a building across the city and she only came to Tottenham a couple of times a month, but whenever they met, Drake made a point of asking about her beloved son.

'You should see him! He's a hulk, and much bigger than me.' Her voice dropped to a gruff monotone. 'He talks like this now, and has fluff all over his chin. I miss my little boy, DI Drake. I want my precious boy back.'

Marion finally plucked the final sheet from the floor. Drake, who could never remember her son's name, handed her the documents he'd picked up.

'He's turned into a surly teenager who stays in his bedroom all day. Playing on the Xbox and goodness knows what else. I bought him a dog, a cute little thing, because I thought he'd have to walk it twice a day. But, of course, he does nothing of the sort, so it's down to me. At least Bernie loves me.'

Drake frowned. 'Bernie?'

43

'The dog. Bernie Battenberg, I call him,' she said. 'Because I like the cake.'

To Drake's relief, he saw Flick coming back the other way.

'Are you due your appraisal, DI Drake?' asked Marion.

'I'm sure I am,' he said, smiling.

'We'll book you in, then.' She winked, and disappeared through the door, just as Flick came towards him.

'Got a moment?' Drake went into an empty office and she followed him in reluctantly. He closed the door. There was a meeting table with a hexagonal conference phone in the middle, and a jumble of chairs. Drake lifted a flap on the floor to disconnect the phone. 'Have you decided?'

'Yes.' She crossed her arms across her chest. 'I'm going to tell her.'

'I understand.' Drake felt like a countdown on his future had started ticking. When it reached zero, his life would implode. 'But there'll be consequences for both of us. You lied to the inquiry. You'll be throwing away your career, Flick.'

She edged to the door. 'I'm going now.'

'Flick.' He went to touch her arm but she jerked away.

'I saw what you did.' Her eyes flashed in sudden anger. 'I *saw*.'

His childhood friend choking on his own blood.

Elliot Juniper was dying anyway. He would have survived for only a few minutes more, probably, but the emergency services were on the way. Drake had come so far in life, and Elliot, like Flick now, wanted to tell the truth about the past, about their shared history.

Eyes, red from the ruptured capillaries, staring up in shock.

44

Drake just couldn't take the chance that his secret would be revealed, and while Flick lay unconscious – or so he believed – he killed the man who used to know him as Connor Laird.

Eyes wide with fear, his hands scrabbled weakly at a sleeve.

But when Elliot lay dead at his feet, Drake saw Flick's eyes were open, and she was looking straight at him.

Sirens in the distance.

There was nowhere he could hide now. She knew his secret past. And if she had seen him kill Elliot, then it was over. His life would follow a familiar path for a few days or weeks, but then there would be a knock on his office door, an unexpected visit to his home. The internal investigation would reopen.

And then it would all unravel. Everything he had painstakingly built – the normal life that everyone else took for granted – would be destroyed. He would lose his family, his reputation – and maybe his freedom. He thought of the consequences for his daughter, April, and for Myra Drake, the woman who many years ago had given him a second chance.

'Tell me how Elliot died,' she said.

'You were insensible. Your mind was playing tricks.'

'Just tell me you didn't kill him.'

It should have been the easiest thing in the world to lie to her; Drake had lived a lie all his life. But he couldn't tell her, *no*. Couldn't say it out loud.

They stared at each other for a long moment, and then Flick flung open the door. 'I'd better get back.'

She walked out. Drake ran a trembling hand down the plain brown tie his late wife had given him, letting the familiar feel of the rough fabric calm him.

45

Ray, said a voice. *What are we going to do with you?*

He didn't dare look to his side where the voice seemed to whisper in his ear. He was too terrified to do it. Instead, he followed Flick into the corridor, where he saw Dudley Kendrick standing with her.

'DI Drake, I took a call but you rushed off,' said Kendrick. 'There's a pair of gents downstairs. They say they have information.'

'Take a statement, Dudley.' His heart was pounding; he wanted to get away. 'I've got to speak to that press officer.'

Kendrick blinked at Drake and Flick. 'I think you're going to want to talk to them. They say they discovered people in their house in the dead of night.'

10

Plastic cups of tea sat untouched on the table in front of Douglas Mortimer and Bailey Waghorn, who waited patiently for Drake and Flick to sit.

They were both tall and dignified, like a pair of aged matinee idols. Douglas's hair was an astonishing jet black. A paisley scarf was tied around his neck and he twisted the cloth of a flat cap between his fingers. Bailey wore a plump yellow tie over a mustard waistcoat. One collar of his patterned shirt was turned up, stabbing at the slack wattles beneath his jaw. A heavy overcoat hung neatly over the back of his chair. Drake felt catastrophically hot just looking at the pair of them. When Flick edged her chair away from Drake, Douglas watched with interest, as if sensing the tension between them.

Wrinkles crackled down his cheeks when he smiled. 'We're sorry to bother you.'

'On the contrary,' said Drake. 'Thank you for coming in.'

'It was difficult for us to come. You see, we didn't report anything at the time. In retrospect, that was perhaps a mistake.' Douglas glanced at Bailey, who stared blankly over Flick and Drake's shoulders. 'We saw on the television news about those poor murdered people.'

Flick said, 'Why don't you tell us what happened?'

'We didn't report it because – well, my husband isn't very well.'

'Let's not tiptoe around the subject.' Bailey's voice was a rich baritone. 'I have early onset dementia.'

'It can be difficult for him to remember details.'

Bailey bristled. 'I didn't make it up.'

Douglas touched his hand. 'I know you didn't.'

'Can you tell us what happened?' prompted Flick.

'I found people in our home,' said Bailey. 'This was . . . November.'

'Bailey is sometimes disorientated. He'll get out of bed to pee and forget where he is. He's been known to wander out of the house, leaving the front door open, which is why we were too embarrassed to report it.'

'You think you let people in?'

Bailey shook his head. 'I didn't do that.'

'But it's a possibility,' said Douglas.

'I didn't.'

'Tell us what happened,' said Drake. 'In your own time.'

'I can tell you that.' Bailey knocked his knuckles gently on the table. 'But sometimes, in the telling, it becomes a bit of a muddle. And I suppose it's only going to get worse.'

'Bailey was an actor,' said Douglas. 'Mostly on the stage, although he appeared in several things on television. That drama about the stately home, he was briefly in that. He was so good at learning lines, so his . . . condition frightens him.'

'Do you want me to say what happened or not?' Bailey cleared his throat. 'As Douglas said, I often get up in the night and wander. He usually leads me back to bed and afterwards I'm none the wiser.'

'I usually wake up straight away but I'm afraid we'd been to a party that night, and I had more than usual to drink,' explained Douglas.

'I suppose I went downstairs, and I saw there was a lamp on in the sitting room. And . . . there were people there. A man sitting in my favourite armchair.' He gestured to a chair against the wall, as if a stranger sat there. 'And a woman was with him.'

'A woman?' Flick leaned forward. 'What happened?'

'The most astonishing thing.' Bailey's eyes sparkled. 'We danced.'

'I'm sorry.' Bailey looked around in bewilderment. The room was familiar to him, awfully familiar. And that was his chair, the one the man was sitting in, he was sure of it. There were some items he recognised. The sideboard his mother had bequeathed him, and the table with the puzzle on it. Those infernal puzzles – Douglas insisted they were good for the mind. But Bailey couldn't shake the awful feeling that he had walked into the wrong room, the wrong house – it wouldn't be the first time. It *must* be the wrong place, because those people shouldn't be there.

'Can I help you, sir?' asked the lady.

Bailey tightened the cord of his dressing gown. 'I'm sorry, I . . .'

That was his chair, definitely. He recognised a stain on the arm. But the way the man stared was very frightening. The deep shadows in the room made him look almost demonic. Bailey had a terrible sense he had interrupted something.

'My goodness.' Bailey laughed suddenly. 'Selena, is that you?'

He couldn't believe he had seen her again all these years later, his lost love, and felt happiness swell in his chest.

49

'My darling.' He stepped forward, forgetting about the unpleasant man, and took Selena's soft hands in his. 'Where have you been?'

'What's the matter with him?' The man spoke in a low, urgent tone. 'Why's he talking like that?'

The lady cocked her head. 'Who am I, sir?'

'Why, you're Selena, silly,' said Bailey.

'What's he say—'

'Yes.' The woman lifted a finger to her lips to quieten the man in the chair. 'That is me. I am Selena.'

'But I thought you . . . It's been . . . ' Bailey rubbed his cheek, frustrated at his inability to remember. 'How long has it been?'

'A long time, sir.' The lady took his hands. 'And I have missed you, Mr . . .'

'It's me, Bailey! I hardly dare to believe it. Douglas will want to say hello.' He turned to the door. 'He was here a moment . . . he was . . . somewhere.'

'Oh, I am sure he will be back,' said the woman. When she spoke, there was an odd inflection to her voice that he couldn't place.

'He's seen us,' said the man with a whine. 'He knows what we look like.'

'He is harmless, of course he is. It is good to see you again . . . Bailey.' Selena smiled. He remembered well the way it lit up her face. Of course, when things became . . . difficult, as a coldness grew between them, she hadn't smiled so much.

'And who's this?' If he was with Selena, then the man must be a good soul, but the truth was, Bailey didn't care for the fellow.

'Oh god.' In the gloom, tears glistened in the man's eyes. 'It's all ruined now.'

'What's wrong with him?' Bailey asked Selena, low. 'Why is he so . . . upset?'

'It is late at night,' she said. 'And he is tired, he gets . . . what is the word?'

'Crotchety. I'm the same if I don't sleep well.'

'He's seen us.' The man gripped the worn arms of the chair. Bailey heard the crack of leather beneath his fingers. 'He knows what we look like.'

The woman touched Bailey's cheek. 'He is not well, he is confused.'

'Am I?' Bailey wanted to ask Selena a question – something had happened to her years ago, he was sure of it – but the thought flew from his head like a bird fluttering from an open cage. She was here now, that was the main thing, and he said, 'Do you still dance, Selena?'

'Oh.' Selena lifted the hem of an imaginary gown. 'It is one of my favourite things. Would you like to dance, sir?'

'It's been a long time.' Bailey looked at his threadbare slippers. When he was younger, the young ladies and many of the men watched riveted as he glided imperiously across the dance floor of the Locarno. Back when his legs were strong and his mind was sturdy, and he thought nothing of dancing all night long. All night! 'I'm worried I won't be able to.'

'Show me,' she said. 'Show me what a good dancer you are.'

And when Bailey looked around, to his astonishment, they were back again in the Locarno ballroom, that romantic and glamorous place that was so dear to his heart, the spotlights sweeping across the floor. As the ladies and gentlemen twirled past, he smelled their perfumes and colognes as they drifted close. And the band played – he didn't know how he hadn't noticed before that they were there. Selena let him lead her in small, hesitant circles to the music.

'I'm sorry,' he called above the noise, and she told him he didn't have to shout, she could hear him perfectly. All these years later and quite unexpectedly Selena was here, looking as healthy and happy as when they were young and carefree, and he so desperately didn't want to let her down. He cursed his old legs and poor balance, felt ashamed in his dressing gown and slippers. Once upon a time his footwork was the envy of the ballroom, but now Bailey struggled to remember even simple steps.

But there really was nothing to beat a live orchestra. The conductor flung his baton about, the horn section stepped forward as one and the drummer kept rhythm with an effortless energy. Bailey realised he was quite enjoying himself.

'It's so good to see you again, Selena,' he said as they turned stiffly. 'It's been so very long.'

'I remember now what a lovely dancer you are.'

'I've missed you so much.' He wondered again where Douglas was. He would be thrilled to see Selena again after all these years, despite everything that had happened. Bailey had so many questions – about the accident, for one thing – but he had to concentrate on his footwork, conscious of the ladies and gentlemen watching from the balcony.

'The children miss you,' he told her. 'We don't see them much, they're down in Devon now. And they have their own children – we're grandparents, Selena, imagine that!'

'I am very pleased.'

Bailey was relieved when the music ended; he felt exhausted. Selena stepped away, the soft lights tumbling down her face and gown.

'You've made an old man very happy.' His throat ached with emotion. 'I never dared to hope we would meet again.'

When she gave him a peck on the cheek, Bailey saw the man in the chair scowl. Bailey had quite forgotten he was there.

'Why did you do that?' the man said. 'Why did you kiss him?'

'Who is that chap? He looks . . .' Bailey's happiness was fading along with the whirling lights. 'Upset.'

'He is jealous because I am dancing with such a handsome man.'

'I'm afraid I've lost my looks.' Bailey had been very good-looking when he was younger, everyone said it, but age was a terrible thing.

'You are very distinguished, sir. And I am a lucky person to have danced with you.'

There was a noise from above and they all looked up at the ceiling. The man jumped from the chair.

'That's Douglas,' said Bailey, hearing the soft thud of feet in the bedroom.

'It was good to meet you, sir.'

'Will you stay for another dance?'

'It is not going to be possible,' said Selena.

Bailey saw the man moving around the room, putting things in his pocket. Familiar keepsakes and cherished mementoes, items he and Douglas had collected together. And when he looked again at the woman, he didn't recognise her at all. 'You're not Selena, are you?'

'I am not.' She curtseyed. 'But it was an honour to have danced with you.'

Bailey bowed. 'You are most kind.'

'We've got to go.' The man took the woman's arm. 'Right now!'

'He's uncouth,' remarked Bailey, as the man stuffed an ornament in his pocket.

The woman smiled sadly. 'He is not as fine a gentleman as you.'

'Take care on the roads. When I arrived it was very wet, very slippery.' Bailey felt anxious. 'You will be careful, won't you?'

'Goodbye, Bailey.' Her fingertips brushed his cheek as she passed – and when he turned, the room was empty. A moment later, Douglas appeared in the doorway.

'Where have you been?' he asked. 'The front door is open.'

Bailey touched his cheek. His dead wife's favourite perfume still lingered in his nostrils.

'You danced with the woman,' said Drake.

'She was very good, actually,' said Bailey. 'Very patient and gentle.'

Douglas squeezed his husband's hand. 'Bailey won trophies for his dancing.'

'But you saw no one in the house?' Flick said.

'No,' said Douglas. 'Bailey's voice woke me up. My goodness, you can hear it across the borough. But when I got downstairs he was alone in his jimjams.'

Bailey lifted his chin. 'I didn't imagine it.'

'I know you didn't,' Douglas said, and turned to Drake.

'There were items missing. Small things, ornaments. Sentimental tat, really.'

'Can you tell me what they looked like?' Flick asked Bailey. 'The man and woman?'

Bailey blew out his cheeks. 'I can give you a description, but it will probably be one of Selena. The man was very nervous. He was very big, a brute, but mostly he was sat in the shadows. There were . . . so many shadows.'

'The woman,' said Drake. 'Can you try?'

'Shoulder-length curly hair . . . straight, glossy . . . no, wait, that's wrong.' He shook his head. 'I remember she had a lovely smile.'

Flick wrote in a pad. 'This is all very helpful.'

'Will we be much longer?' Bailey's voice lifted in frustration. 'I have a matinee performance in a few minutes.'

Douglas smiled sadly at Flick and Drake.

'We're finished,' said Drake. 'Thank you for coming in.'

The two men stood. Douglas helped Bailey into his overcoat.

'Selena was an awful bitch to him,' he whispered to Flick. 'Left him for a used-car dealer. He was terribly upset about it. I was left to pick up the pieces. We became close and – well, you know the rest.'

'Did they stay in touch?' asked Flick, curious.

'Selena died in 1974. Car crash. One of her lover's second-hand motors skidded off the road in treacherous weather. We went to the funeral, for old times' sake.'

'It was good of you to go, in the circumstances.'

'Oh, I didn't have much choice. Selena was my sister.' Douglas raised an eyebrow. 'We weren't close, she was a difficult woman to say the least, but I have her to thank for

55

Bailey.' He looped an arm through his husband's. 'Come on, let's get you home, you silly old fool.'

'Less of the old,' said Bailey.

11

'I love her. I love her, I love her, and if anything happened to her . . . I'll go to pieces, I swear I will.'

Crouched at Joel's side in the dark room, Carl waited for a response. But Joel barely heard what he said. His mind was filled with that familiar image, of the last wisps of Will's hair disappearing over the edge of the cliff.

And laid over that, like a double exposure, he saw something else. A woman running along a train platform, desperately trying to reach him.

Joel! Joel!

'So we've got to keep her safe. Because Tatia's done bad things, some *very* bad things. You haven't seen what she's capable of, not really, but I have. And all it takes is for you to have an accident or get lost, and for a busybody to ask awkward questions, and you're going to bring down a load of trouble on her head. A *lot* of trouble, Joel. You might want to think about that before you go wandering off.'

Carl's voice was thick with emotion. Beside him, Joel was slumped against the wall, his thin legs almost lost in the garish diamond pattern of the threadbare carpet.

'You'll never understand. When you find that special person – your anchor, your rock – it's like you're blessed. It's a precious thing, Joel, and the thought that I could lose her . . .' He shook his head at the terrible thought of it. 'Just doesn't bear thinking about.'

It had been a mistake to go out, Joel knew that, but sometimes it was so difficult to remember all Carl's rules, and they changed so quickly. Every day, Carl gave him a new instruction to follow. He couldn't open the curtains or go near the window or answer the door – not that anybody ever came.

All he knew was, it was difficult to stay in this hot, cramped room where there was just enough space for a bed and sofa. Every surface was piled with clutter and the floor littered with rubbish. The only other place to go was a tiny bathroom, barely bigger than a cubicle, with a grimy sink and broken toilet, a shower that produced a trickle of water and an extractor fan that rattled noisily for hours after the light was turned off.

Joel sat here all day beneath the naked bulb that threw sallow light barely as far as the net curtain. He knew every pattern of damp on the ceiling tile – sometimes he looked at them for so long that the stains writhed in his vision like snakes in a pit – and how shadows crept across the walls to consume the day. Sometimes all he wanted was to get outside, feel the sun on his skin. And he didn't understand why he couldn't do it.

'I'm going to marry her. That's what I'm going to do. It'll be me and Tatia together for ever.' Carl glanced sharply at Joel. 'Just the two of us. I'll be able to protect her, I'll stop them taking her away.'

His face, the cheeks cratered by pockmarks from ferocious childhood acne, was so close to Joel's that the stale musk of his body odour overpowered even the heavy stench of takeaway food. Because the window was shut day and night, the smell of grease and sweat was trapped inside. 'And besides everything else, she told me . . .' In the dark, Joel dimly registered the tears in the big man's eyes, felt Carl's hot breath in his ear. 'She told me what happened to your little brother, she told me what she *did* to him.'

If he had been better able to stay in the moment, maybe he would have recognised the sly look on Carl's face, the way his darting tongue slid quickly across his lips, but Joel's mind turned once again to that empty space on the cliff where Will had been.

'And I don't want to put ideas in your head, mate, but maybe it would be for the best if you slung your hook and left us alone, me and Tatia, because maybe it'll be you next. Maybe she'll get tired of you, yeah, and she'll want to do *you* in.' Carl cracked the joints in his fingers. 'Because between you and me, I think she's capable of anything.'

The sharp crack of a woman's hand on the doors of the carriage as a train shunted forward. Joel! Joel!

And the name of the woman he saw today was . . .

But then there was a metal tap at the door. Carl raised a warning finger quickly to his mouth.

He stood as a key turned in the lock, and Tatia stood silhouetted in the dim light.

'What is going on?'

Carl stepped away. 'I found him on the floor.'

Throwing down her rucksack, she immediately dropped to her knees to gather Joel in her arms and rearrange him. Joel was used to it now, the way she moved him about. Touched him, petted him fussed over him. Pulled him upright so that his spine was flush to the wall, arranging his spindly legs in front of him as if he was a doll.

Carl hovered. 'I was trying to help him.'

'Stand over there.' When Carl hesitated, she shouted. 'Over there!'

His feet ploughing through a tumbling collection of plastic bags and takeaway boxes, Carl moved behind the bed.

'I am here now.' Tatia pressed Joel's head to her chest. His cheek rubbed against the rough fabric of her rugby shirt. 'I am here.'

'He went out.' Tears burst from Carl's eyes. 'If he meets someone he used to know, if he tells them about us—'

'He would never do that,' Tatia snapped.

'Everything started going wrong when he came.'

'What did he say to you?' she demanded of Joel. 'What did he do?'

Joel shook his head. Already, the details of what Carl had said were slipping away. Something about his brother, about Will – that he was in danger. It was so difficult to keep thoughts in his head these days.

Tatia stood and beckoned to Carl. 'Come here.'

'Please don't be angry.' Tears and snot gathered between Carl's lips. 'I don't like it when you're angry with me.'

'I said come here!'

Sweaty palms rubbing miserably against his thighs, Carl shuffled forward, his left foot tangling in a plastic bag. His big arms enveloping her completely, he buried his head into the nape of Tatia's neck and wept.

'I cannot be here all day,' she told him quietly. 'I must work. It is the only money we have. If you love me—'

'I can't live without you.' Carl squeezed her tight, staring resentfully over her shoulder at Joel. 'I'd die!'

'Then you must . . .' When she stepped back, Joel saw Carl's dismal gaze drop to the floor like a guilty child. 'You must love my brother, too. Because he is my only family.'

He took her face in his big hands, pulling his thumbs down her cheeks. 'Anything. I love you. Do you love me?'

She took him by the wrists and lowered his hands, which could crush her skull as if it were an egg, and said, 'We should go out again.'

His mood brightened in an instant. 'Can we?'

'One last time, Carl, and then it is over.'

'Yes.' He nodded eagerly. 'One last time.'

'But we must not . . . make any more mistakes.'

'I know somewhere!'

He ran across the room and picked up clothes and clutter, throwing them across the room, looking for something. Chicken bones flew from a takeaway box and dropped between Joel's legs. Knick-knacks Carl had taken from the homes, keepsakes and trinkets, scattered across the floor. He fell to his hands and knees to reach beneath the bed, slamming against the mattress and making the cheap frame shudder. Jumping to his feet, he fumbled with the pages of a small red notebook. 'Here!'

He tapped at an address and postcode – just one of many on the page. Every line was filled with Tatia's small, precise handwriting.

'It's empty,' Carl explained quickly, as if he were sure she would change her mind. 'I've done my homework, like you said we should.'

Joel watched them huddle over the book, which contained the details of so many homes, so many lives, as if it was a treasure map.

'I do not recognise it,' said Tatia. 'I do not remember it.'

'I've been careful.' Carl blinked. 'Very careful.'

She gazed at him steadily. 'If you have planned correctly, if you have taken precautions, we will be alone.'

'We won't hurt anybody, not this time. Please let's not hurt anybody.' Carl's face dropped. 'You and me, we've done things. Things people wouldn't understand.'

Her voice was a bitter whisper. 'Yes.'

'But we'll always have each other.'

She smiled over her shoulder. 'And Joel.'

'Yeah.' Carl shot a sour smile in his direction. 'We'll get our own place. It doesn't have to be flash. Somewhere quiet, out in the country. A two-up, two-down. A small garden, maybe. A patio, a square of lawn. The main thing is, I've got you and you've got me.'

'It is a dream.'

'It doesn't have to be,' he insisted.

Joel couldn't bear to stay in this dark room a moment longer. He was trapped here. Forced to listen all day to the burble of the market on the street below, the endless shouts of the stallholders, and at night the brap of passing mopeds, Carl's noisy snores.

'Take me with you,' Joel said. 'Tonight.'

'No,' Tatia told him. 'You cannot come.'

Maybe if the home they went to was quiet and comfortable he would even be able to sleep, just for a short while.

His voice was a tired croak. 'Please.'

There was a glint in Carl's eyes. 'We'll take him. What harm could it do?'

'And then it is over, Carl,' Tatia said. 'And we are finished.'

'If you want.' Carl didn't look pleased about it, but he said, 'I just want you to be happy.'

She looked around the cluttered bedsit. 'Take a shower before we go.'

'Do you love me? You didn't say it earlier, when I asked you.'

'I do.'

'Say it, then.' He gazed anxiously at her. 'Tell me you love me.'

'I love you, Carl.' Joel saw her fingers were crossed behind her back when she said it. 'But perhaps not when you smell so bad.'

Carl went into the bathroom, and air conditioner rattled into life behind the closed door.

Tatia stared at the door. Her face was a blank mask. Joel, who found it so difficult to read expressions now, had no idea what it meant. But then she must have felt his eyes on her, because she turned and smiled.

That big smile, jagged like a scar.

12

The counsellor crossed her legs. 'So here we are again.'

Flick shifted on the seat. She could never get comfortable in this chair. The fabric, worn rough by the backs of many clients before her, was like a bed of nails against her spine.

The best thing would be to say it immediately. Get it over with. Tell the truth about what happened that night, the truth about Ray Drake.

And she would be free.

Flick knew that once she had told just one person the truth she could do it again and again. It would mean the end of her police career – but also a new beginning.

The room was on the first floor of a building off Euston Road, where long lanes of traffic burst from one set of traffic lights to another in a canyon of glass and concrete. The double glazing reduced the traffic noise to an infuriating buzz. Flick took in all the usual furnishings. The low table where a tissue fanned from a silver box, a watercolour of a Cornish harbour, the teak sculpture of an African warrior in the empty fireplace. And she saw once again that kinked bristle of a brush sealed beneath the paint at the edge of the skirting. Every week she vowed to prise the bristle free from its painted prison with a thumbnail.

'Okay.' Flick cleared her throat and nodded at Sunita, a

small, middle-aged woman dressed in a white collarless shirt and black trousers. 'I have something to say.'

Sunita tried to conceal her excitement, but Flick was too good a detective not to sense the eagerness beneath her placid smile.

All their meetings so far had been punctuated by long periods of silence. Sunita didn't mind: she seemed to have a patient expectation that Flick would open her heart in her own good time. Occasionally she glanced at a clock, but mostly the counsellor watched and waited. Sometimes Flick would discuss work stuff, or her family – talk about her dad, and the loneliness she felt now her sister's family had moved to Australia – but never anything about Ray Drake or the night she was almost killed. At the end of every session Sunita would click her pen closed and say encouragingly, 'See you next week.'

But today Flick was determined to tell her the truth she had withheld from the DPS inquiry. Ray Drake was a bloody good detective, with – she had always believed – a strong moral drive. But she knew too much now about his secret. About who he had been many years ago . . . a troubled boy called Connor Laird.

And it was a secret she suspected he had killed to keep hidden.

That night in the cottage she had been stabbed three times, had drifted in and out of consciousness – but she was convinced she had seen Drake suffocate Elliot Juniper.

Just say it, she told herself now. Tell her everything.

Sunita sensed her anxiety. 'What would you like to tell me?'

Flick liked the woman's gentle demeanour. She thought of the investigation team who had snarled and snapped during the internal inquiry into the Two O'Clock Boy's murderous spree. If they had listened to her as calmly, if they had treated her with as much respect, maybe she would have told them her suspicions. But for reasons that Flick didn't understand, she felt a bond to Ray Drake – a loyalty to him that made her risk everything.

Now, in this small bare room, with its drab watercolour and ethnic sculpture, its curling bristle entombed in the skirting, she would tell the truth.

'What was it you wanted to say?' prompted Sunita.

Flick opened her mouth.

'No.' She stood and grabbed her bag from beneath the chair. 'I can't do this.'

'We don't have to talk about anything, we can sit here and enjoy the silence.'

There was enough silence in Flick's life; she was sick of all the silence.

'Thank you for everything,' she said. 'I won't be coming back.'

'Wait . . .'

By the time Sunita had jumped up from her chair, Flick was already through the door and striding down the corridor. She kept her head down, determined not to respond if the counsellor followed her out, and barged straight into someone coming the other way.

'Whoa!'

'Excuse me.' She went to the lift and jabbed the button.

'What's the hurry?' It was a man's voice. 'You're as white as a sheet.'

'I'm fine.' She stared at the lift door, willing it to open. 'Thank you.'

'Sunita been telling you her dirty jokes?' The door finally trundled open. 'Her limericks would make you blush.'

When the lift door began to close again, the man lunged forward to grab it. She saw he wore a shirt and a knitted tie beneath a leather jacket, and an old pair of jeans slung so low they just about managed to cover his groin. The trainers on his feet were filthy, the rubber sole of the left one almost separated from the shoe. His baby face was hidden behind several days' worth of patchy beard, and he kept scraping hair out of his eyes. He looked like an art teacher desperate to get down with the kids.

The door shunted impatiently against his hand.

'After you.'

Flick stepped into the lift and pressed the ground-floor button, and the man followed her in. Leaning his head against the wall, he closed his eyes. There was a fusty smell in the small space as the lift dropped. Flick suspected it was the jacket.

'I think I'm in after you.' His eyes opened and he held out his hand. 'I'm also a patient . . . client . . . whatever the proper term is. Sam Wylie.'

'Flick Crowley.' His shake was as strong and firm as hers was weak and unwilling. 'Shouldn't you be seeing her now?'

'Not for a while. You came out super early.'

The lift eased to a stop and she was conscious of him following her to the door. 'She'd be upset if I walked out of a session. I'm a model patient. I tell her everything she wants to hear.' He leaned around her to palm a green button on the wall, and the street door unlocked with a buzz. 'I tell her about my emotional breakdowns, my fucked marriage, my anxiety attacks and crying jags, the week-long benders.

And we haven't even got round to my shitty childhood. As far as Sunita is concerned, I'm a fascinating vessel of unquenchable pain. Honestly, she gets cramp writing it all down.' When Flick stared, he grinned. 'Don't worry, it's all made up.'

'You lie to her?'

'All of it. Oh, wait.' He made a face. 'My marriage really is fucked.'

She started walking towards Euston station, where she'd left her car, and he kept pace at her side.

'You seem kind of jolly to me.'

'I can't help it, I'm a people pleaser. I give her plenty of things to scribble down and I get to have a little fun. People like it when you make them feel like they're doing a good job.' He stopped in the middle of the pavement. 'Would you like to go for a coffee with me?'

Flick stepped back to allow people past. 'You're married.'

'Barely, and anyway, we're just talking coffee.'

'You don't know me.' Flick didn't understand. 'Why would you want to do that?'

'Because it's all been me, me, me, but I know nothing about you, and you strike me as an interesting and, dare I say, attractive woman. I think it's only fair that we discuss you, just for a little bit, before the conversation inevitably returns to me.' He took out a coffee chain loyalty card. 'One more stamp and I get a free one.'

She reached into her bag. 'I've got a card somewhere.'

'Just write it here.' He held out the top of his hand. She avoided looking at the gold band on his finger as she wrote down her number. After writing three digits she stopped.

'Changed your mind already?' he asked.

What she needed was to step out of her own head, to forget everything for a short while. Flick had met this man, this stranger, only a few minutes ago, but she didn't know who else to call, so she said, 'Let's go for a proper drink.'

'Sure.' He grinned. 'When?'

'After your session.'

He considered the offer. 'Let's go now.'

'What about your appointment?'

He shrugged. 'I'm all out of lies today.'

13

Sitting against the skirting, Tatia took Joel's cold hand in hers and rubbed it. He dearly wished she could warm the blood that moved listlessly in his tired veins, bring colour back to his slack features. If she could do that, then perhaps one day she could help him become once again the person he knew he used to be.

'I have done a terrible thing to you and I hope you can forgive me.'

Joel was slumped against the wall like a marionette with its strings cut, the faintest of outlines in the dark, barely a mass in the darkness. On the other side of the bathroom door, the shower groaned into life – he heard spray patter on the shallow plastic tray.

Carl's shadow moved in the bright strip beneath the door. He wouldn't be able to run the shower for long – the drain was blocked, the tray would quickly fill with water, its swirling surface scummed by cheap soap – and he would be out soon.

'It has been my dearest wish for us to be together, little bear. The thought of seeing you again is the only thing that has kept me going all these years. You must understand that it has never been my intention to hurt you, but I have placed you in an unacceptable position. I am guilty.' Tatia's eyes flashed wildly in the dark. 'I am responsible, and I will go to hell.'

She squeezed his cold hand and he thought his tired bones would crumble in her grip. He knew the thought of prison terrified her. When she came out – months, years, or even decades later – she would be deported. Everything she had done to return to this city, all the sacrifices she had made to get back, would have been in vain. All those years of planning wasted.

All she wanted was for both of them to be happy, he knew, and yet . . . death, violence, seemed to follow her everywhere. First Will, who fell from a cliff many years ago, and then the people in those homes. She didn't talk to him about what had happened at those addresses, but Carl was all too eager to tell him in terrible detail. Three people killed, he said – slaughtered where they stood.

He saw the slash of her smile in the darkness, and realised how little he knew about his sister . . .

Before she had come into his life, before Will had died, he had been a happy child, full of energy and hope for the future. And now look what he had become all these years later.

A hollow man, a husk.

'It is too late for me,' she said quietly. 'I am cursed. Sooner or later, the police will come for me.' Her thumb rubbed across the top of his hand, stretching the blue skin taut. 'But you are innocent, little bear, and we must get you to safety, somewhere you will be able to get well.'

And yet since his breakdown all the people he knew who could give him shelter had faded one by one from his life, and it had been left to her to care for him. She was a woman who crept into other people's homes in the dead of night

71

in order to feed a terrible fantasy that she led a normal life, that she was just like everybody else – and three people had died.

She was damaged. And very possibly a killer. She was hardly a fit and proper person.

But there *was* someone else.

The woman's palms banged on the window of the carriage. Joel! Joel!

As if she had read his mind, Tatia took his jaw in her fingers to turn his face towards hers, her eyes points of faint light in the dark. 'Joel, listen to me. We are going to contact Poppy. She will help you.'

'It was her.'

Tatia thought she'd misheard. 'What did you say, my darling?'

'I saw Poppy.'

'Oh, Joel, it is a *sign*.' Tatia clasped her hands together, barely able to believe it. 'Did you speak?'

He shook his head.

'We are going to find her, and she will look after you.'

'And you . . . Sarah,' Joel said, calling her by the family name she had briefly taken a lifetime ago.

'It has always been my dream that I could be Sarah again. And that we could once again be a family, a proper family.' She shuddered with pleasure at the thought of it. 'You, me and Poppy – back together! It is all I have ever wanted.'

Next door, the shower shut off. Joel heard Carl noisily clear his throat as he dried himself on a scratchy square of towel. When he came out, the three of them would venture into the night to grab a few, short hours of pleasure in a stranger's house – for one final time.

72

'But what if she does not want to see me . . . after what happened?'

The events on that clifftop all those years ago still haunted them all. Will had been killed – and Tatia was responsible. They both knew Poppy could never forgive her for what happened to their brother.

'But she will look after you,' Tatia said. 'She will want to do that. There is something I have not told you. I have her telephone number. I got it from work, just in case there should come a time like this.' She scrabbled in her pocket and took out a piece of paper. 'And you are going to call it. Whatever becomes of me, we are going to get you home.'

She yawned and leaned her head back against the wall. Every night Tatia stayed awake with Joel for as long as she could. But her job was exhausting and he knew she found it a struggle to sit with him into the early hours. Her saw her eyelids flutter.

'Maybe she will find it in her heart to . . . like me. I have gotten you something.' She unzipped the rucksack, took out a fistful of chocolate bars and placed them in his lap. 'Eat. You will need to keep your strength up.'

His hands plucked uselessly at a foil wrapper. She took it from him and ripped it open, snapped the chocolate into segments. Then she took a can of fizzy cola from the bag and pulled the tab. The bubbles popped faintly on the top of his hand as she wrapped his cold fingers around it. Joel's weary body craved sugar day and night.

'We will be leaving soon.' She rested her head against the wall. 'And I have to . . . get some . . .'

'Ring a ring o' roses,' he whispered.

'A pocket full of . . . so sorry.'

73

Closing her eyes, she sank into sleep.

Carl would return any minute now. The ambient noise of the street at night filled Joel's head. He heard the distant traffic, the bark of a restless dog. This was the only time of day when he was able to get a sense of who he was.

Joel watched Tatia. Head thrown back, her eyes whipped restlessly back and forth beneath trembling lids, her mouth twitched. He wondered if she saw in her dreams the faces of those people who were killed. He longed to dream. Even a terrible one would be better than the nightmare he lived now. She could never comprehend his total exhaustion after months of being awake, his sense of dislocation, as his body lost energy, as it slowed a little bit more every day, like the hands of a watch losing time.

Joel Bliss was a man who had once had the ability to sleep just like everybody else – but had inexplicably lost it.

He was sure that at some point in the long hours before dawn he must sleep. Sometimes several hours disappeared in an instant, like sand slipping off a riverbank – or a little boy falling from a cliff. But he had no idea where those hours went. Doctors had told him he dropped into several hours of light sleep, otherwise he would be dead already. But when he woke, if he even did sleep, he was as exhausted and disorientated as before. Those missing hours were never enough. Deep sleep was what he craved: the type that obliterated the world completely.

Joel looked towards the bathroom – the light winked off beneath the door, Carl was about to step out – and then at the woman beside him. Her name was Tatia, but she would always be Sarah to him. Sarah, his sister.

His mind was filled with the memory of that day when

she walked back into his life after many years away – the very last day when he was still the man he was always meant to be.

14

18 years after Will:

This is what was meant to happen: Joel would give the pitch and then maybe, just maybe, they could make a real difference to the lives of millions of people.

There wasn't a curveball question the investors could throw that he hadn't anticipated. Because Joel knew that if he wanted to do something good, if he wanted to carry people with him, then he had to practise the pitch again and again, run it through a kind of simulator in his head, the way a fighter pilot practised dangerous manoeuvres. He had repeated that ten-minute pitch endlessly in his mind, broken it down sentence by sentence to maximise its effectiveness. Because if he wanted to help people, he had to *make* success happen.

It's called PMA. Positive Mental Attitude. Sports people, CEOs, that's what they did. They imagined the finishing line, the gaping net, the big takeover; they saw themselves flying past that tape, converting the penalty, signing the deal. And Joel, who was determined to save lives, was no different. He and his friends had worked on this water irrigation project for months – it was a low-cost, hi-tech project that had the potential to transform parts of Africa. Give people access to water and you give them a chance not only to live, but to prosper. They can run farms, rear cattle, grow their own food. It gives them a future. And with proper backing, with the kind of money that these investors could provide, it could be just the beginning.

Joel was ready. This was his moment to make a difference. His mother, his father – they would have been so proud of him.

So they slammed through the swing doors into the reception of the fancy hotel, with its dark panelling and silver flock wallpaper and long, sleek sofas. His whole team was energised, focused, adrenaline crackling through their veins like atoms shooting around the Hadron Collider.

The investors would be arriving within minutes. Denise would shuttle back and forth between reception and the conference room to ensure nobody got mislaid on the way.

Outside the room, Joel gathered his people. The manager, the designer, the financial guy, the marketeer. 'Who's meeting and greeting?'

Hermeet, who put the financial package together, dabbed at the screen of his phone. 'That's me.'

'Make sure they've everything they need. Tea, coffee, juice.' Joel frowned when he didn't look up. 'Mate, are you listening?'

'Just gotta send this mail.'

'Do it later.' He held up his palms. 'Please, people, we're so close. Let's concentrate.'

'Joel,' said Denise softly. 'We're all up to speed.'

She was right, of course. He was sure that no matter how many questions he asked of his team, they'd have the answers. Everything was ready, he knew that. But Joel couldn't help micro-managing, drilling deep down into every detail. He was always two steps ahead of everyone else – not one, *two* – and that's the way he thought he'd always be.

He held out his hand. 'The drive?'

Hermeet said, 'I gave it to Tyrone.'

But Tyrone was already patting his pockets, and everyone watched with concern as he dropped to his knees, pulling everything from his briefcase onto the floor, the panic rising in him. When he looked up, his face was as white as a sheet. There was no flash drive – and the presentation was saved on there. The others groaned. Right about now Joel would have every right to get angry. But he always looked for solutions, not problems.

'Do you still have the printout?' he asked Dylan, who pulled a file from his bag. 'Take it to the office, ask to use the photocopier. We'll need twenty copies. The best paper, in full colour. Use clips, not staples. Place one on every seat.'

Dylan strode away. 'I'm on it.'

Tyrone looked gutted. Joel was disappointed, they'd worked hard on that PowerPoint presentation, but he wasn't going to let it ruin everything. PMA.

'We've got time to fix it.' These were all talented people. Each of them could earn a fortune at FTSE-100 companies, but instead they came aboard Joel's crazy project because they wanted to make the world a better place. Because some things in life were more important than money. 'Whatever happens, I want to thank you all for the hard work you've put in.'

Tyrone and Hermeet had clashed more than once, but Hermeet gave his embarrassed colleague a reassuring pat on the shoulder. If Joel said it was okay, then it was okay. His drive, his vision, had brought them all this far.

Now it all hinged on Joel standing in front of those investors – hedge fund managers, bankers, financial angels – to give

78

the pitch of his life. He was word perfect on long-term strategies, on how to build local economies and boost trade links. The aim was to appeal to the good natures of these immensely rich people, yes, but also to tickle their business instincts.

And there wasn't a shred of doubt in Joel's mind that he would knock it out of the ballpark.

Tyrone pumped his fist. 'We're going to do this!'

'So.' Joel tightened the knot in his red silk tie. He looked handsome in the simple, three-buttoned black suit and white shirt. The look was contemporary but classic. Denise had chosen the suit for him. It wasn't the hand-me-down that he'd worn to his father's funeral. But he felt self-conscious and used a finger to prise some space between the shirt collar and his neck. 'Let's go to work.'

When the others went inside, Joel said to Denise, 'Got a moment?'

'Of course,' she said, and he guided her into an empty room. 'What's up?'

'I just wanted . . . need you . . . to wish me luck.'

Her tongue curled along the edge of her straight, white teeth, considering him. Her vivid green eyes were bright beneath jet-black hair. She pressed her slim body against his, her hips straining forward beneath her tight black skirt. Silver nails touched his cheek as she pulled his face to hers and slipped her tongue into his mouth.

And while he was still momentarily lost in the fragrance of her perfume and the warmth of her body beneath the red silk blouse, she gently pressed her thumb across his lips to remove any glittering trace of lipstick.

'Oh, Joel,' she said. 'You don't need my luck or anybody else's.'

And it was true. He felt like a tuning fork singing along a ley line. Everything that had happened, all the pain and tragedy his family had endured, had led to this moment. For the first time in his life, he felt ready to shake off the ghosts of the past. Will, Mum, Dad – Sarah. He was ready to begin again.

Joel stuck his hand in his pocket to feel the diamond ring. As soon as the presentation was finished, he planned to pop the question. He was going to marry this woman, and they'd have kids, and live wherever in the world his work took him, enjoying a simple life, unencumbered by material need.

He thought of his mother and father and wished they could see him now – doing something good, something worthwhile. And then he thought of Poppy. He couldn't even remember the last time he'd spoken to her, and he felt a twinge of guilt. They were the only Blisses left now. Whatever their different paths in life, he was determined to get in contact, to make things right. He would fix whatever it was that had gone wrong between them.

'Are you ready?'

He smiled. 'I was born ready.'

And Denise was right, he didn't need luck, because he went into that glass room off reception and he stormed the pitch. Absolutely killed it. As soon as the investors were seated, finding glossy printouts of the presentation on their chairs, he held them in the palm of his hand. He paced the room, talking about how the new technology would pull thousands of people out of poverty. He gave them facts and figures; planning strategies; growth projections. He detailed very precisely how their money would be used – and how their companies would benefit.

The fifteen-minute pitch finished – it had gone better than he could possibly have imagined – and Joel told the men and women they could help themselves to the coffee and croissants provided by an artisan bakery across the road, right after he had taken a few questions.

Someone in the front row asked him how much it would cost to expand the irrigation process across three sites. Joel couldn't help but smile – it was an easy one to start with. Whatever happened with the investment, whether or not these people gave him the money, Joel hadn't put a foot wrong.

But then he saw, through the glass window, a woman come into reception. It was someone he hadn't seen for a *will* long, long time.

She looked around quickly – as if looking for someone, as if looking for him. And then her gaze found his through the glass.

Turning back to the man, he cleared his throat. 'Can you repeat the question?'

They were close, so close. They were on the edge *Will* of success now.

On the edge.

The edge.

Will.

He turned once again to the woman in reception, all grown up now, and that familiar smile lit up her face.

And then it happened –

An image popped into his mind for the first time. Joel saw a cliff of white rock, grass swaying on the lip. The thick band of ocean at the horizon, cloud rolling across the sky. And Will disappearing off the edge. Will, who was gone for ever.

'I'm sorry.' His mouth was dry. 'Can you—'

The man in the front row frowned. 'How much would it cost to expand the irrigation process?'

Joel opened his mouth. The answer was on the tip of his tongue.

In the weeks and months following that pitch, when his mind weakened and his personality fell away, he wondered many times about that moment. Part of him was convinced that if he had given that answer, a simple figure, a set of digits as familiar to him as his own shoe size, he would have just carried on with the Q&A, like a stylus slipping back into a groove, and his life would have continued on its way as usual.

But instead he stood, mouth open, and looked around the room. At the investors, and his people – Tyrone and Dylan and Hermeet and Denise – all watching.

And, behind the glass, Sarah. Back in his life after all these years.

They were all waiting for him to say something, anything. And he didn't know how long it took for him to speak. All he knew was that he saw that empty space on the cliff, but not his brother, who had already plummeted over the edge. In the years to come, that image would consume his every moment.

'Yes,' said Joel, and fell to the ground.

And when he regained consciousness, his old life – everything he thought he was, and believed he would be – was ended, and a new one begun.

15

Before she knew it, it was late at night and she was still out on the town and, even more amazing than that, she was still standing.

Flick stood at the sink in the ladies' of a noisy bar in Camden Town, getting jostled by the women queuing for a cubicle, or pushing to get to the mirror, all of them younger than she was. This wasn't the kind of place she would normally be found in. It was achingly trendy and heaving with people. The volume of the music was merciless, the pounding bass of the sound system thumping through the door.

They'd been out all afternoon, wandering from pub to pub and chatting. Flick's face was red from sitting in the sun. But Wylie had this way about him, an easy charm – she couldn't explain it properly – which made you believe you'd known him all your life, and she'd lost track of time. What was intended to be a quick drink had become an afternoon, an evening – virtually a whole day. So when they'd walked past the bar – the pavement was packed with people standing behind a rope, drinking, smoking, laughing – and he'd suggested going in, she'd half-heartedly told him she should go, she had to be in work first thing. If there was one thing Flick was good at, it was saying no to more fun.

But he took her hand – she felt a jolt of electricity at his touch – and she relented immediately. 'Go on, then. But just the one.'

There had been no awkward silences, which was kind of incredible since they'd only met at lunchtime. Wylie, she discovered, was one of those people who liked to talk. Boy, could he chat. He just opened his mouth and all this rubbish came out.

She asked him why he was seeing a counsellor, and he told her he'd had a serious fall a couple of years ago which had left him with a fear of heights. It was inconvenient in his line of work – he was in the building trade, he said, and walking across scaffolding was kind of crucial to the job. He worked cash in hand, mostly, which explained why he carried a thick wad of notes in his pocket. He spoke about his three sons, who were into football and computer games and all the usual stuff boys liked, and he tried to explain to her some fad of the moment, something they were obsessed about, but when he described it she didn't have a clue what he was talking about. They fought like cat and dog day and night, he said.

'They're good kids.' He lifted his bottle of beer to his lips, and nodded. 'They really are. Considering the split and everything.'

'Do you get to see much of them?' she asked, probing for details of his break-up with his wife.

'Anytime I want. Astrid's good like that.'

'Astrid,' she said. 'She sounds very striking.'

He shrugged. 'She's a beauty.'

'And you and . . . Astrid, you've split up for good?'

'You asked me that already.' He laughed, making her blush. 'And the answer is still yes.'

He changed the subject and they talked about her work, and was impressed when she said she was a police detective. Wylie listened gravely, his eyes fixed on hers, when she told him she was working on the so-called Goldilocks Killings. He asked her questions about how you go about investigating something like that, the logistics of such a complex investigation. There were things she couldn't discuss, of course, but she felt on safe ground talking about her work, the investigative process, and her career in the Met.

'That's so cool.' He lifted his bottle of beer in admiration. 'You get on well with the people you work with?'

'Yeah.' She grimaced.

He laughed. 'You don't sound sure.'

She was so close to telling him about the situation with Drake. It was on the tip of her tongue, but her discomfort must have been obvious because he touched her hand and said, 'You tell me in your own good time.'

Then he downed the rest of his drink, slammed the bottle back on the table, said, 'Let's move.'

Which was how they ended up walking up Hampstead Road towards Camden. It wasn't the prettiest of roads: a jumble of unlovely post-war buildings and tower blocks. Lanes of traffic raced past in the opposite direction towards the West End. But it was still warm – the sky was a deep red – and plenty of people were making the most of the long nights and good weather. And as he spoke about some funny thing that had happened to a mate of his, she considered what a crazy day it had been.

Hooking up with some random bloke outside a therapist's office wasn't the usual way to go about things, but she didn't care. It was no less weird than going on a blind date, to her mind, or meeting someone on the internet – both of which she'd done in the past, with disastrous results.

But standing at the mirror now she checked her phone – it was definitely time to go. Flick headed back to the bar. Everyone was packed in close, shouting into the ears of their companions just to be heard, queuing five deep at the bar. Flick didn't so much as walk back to Wylie as bounce off the shoulders of people in the crowd.

And when she got back to the standing table, Wylie was talking to two young women. They wore tight summer dresses and strappy heels and big hair and long eyelashes, and their expensive bags were sat on the table beside them as they gazed at Wylie over the tops of their cocktail straws. He was explaining something, as full of energy now as he'd been hours ago. Flick felt a bit put out, but had learned already that it was something you had to get used to where he was concerned. Wylie had this habit of talking to people whether they desired it or not. The old man nursing his pint in the corner; the young couple on a date; that guy who wanted to be left alone with his phone. It didn't matter; he'd pull them into conversation as if he had a compulsion to charm and dominate everyone in the room.

She drained the rest of her bottle and decided she'd had enough. It was time to go. But then Wylie turned and a big smile lit up his face – he looked genuinely pleased to see her.

'My turn,' he said and momentarily took her face in his hands – she felt a crackle of longing for him – 'but then we'll scoot.'

When he had disappeared to the toilet, one of the women sucked on her cocktail and smiled, giving Flick a leisurely appraisal up and down.

'He's really into you,' she shouted over the deafening music. 'He can't believe how nice you are. He said you'd only met today!'

'Yeah.' Flick was embarrassed. 'We did.'

'Ah.' She wrinkled her nose. 'That's so romantic! It's really nice when older people get together.'

'Thanks.' Flick guessed she probably had only ten years on the women, if that, but dressed in her work trouser suit in this glam place, she probably looked a hell of a lot older.

The woman and her friend drained their drinks, ready to leave. Flick checked her phone, thinking about whether she should get the tube or order a taxi. She didn't know what to do about Wylie. The sensible thing would be to call it a night, but . . .

When she looked up, the two women were anxiously going through a bag, and Flick's instincts kicked in.

'Is there a problem?' she asked, just as the music came to an end and the bell rang for last orders.

'She can't find her purse,' said the friend.

'I don't understand it.' The woman was getting flustered. 'I had it in my bag. My money's in there, and all my credit cards.'

'When did you last have it?'

Pickpockets and thieves thrived in places like this, where people packed together, relaxed and, with a few drinks inside them, took an eye off their things.

'Only half an hour ago,' the woman said. 'I bought some drinks.'

'What's the matter?' asked Wylie when he returned, and Flick told him about the missing purse.

'You mean this one?' He handed it over. The woman

opened it and went through the contents. The cards were there, but no cash. 'I found it dropped in the men's toilets. I was just going to take it to the bar.'

'There's CCTV in here,' said Flick.

'We're in a blind spot.' Wylie pointed to a camera on a wall that was facing the other way. 'Do you need money to get home?'

'I've got some,' said the friend. 'But thank you, anyway.'

Flick felt sorry for them. The women were shaken; it was a sad way to end an enjoyable night. People had been pushing past them all evening, on the way to the bar, the toilet. Anyone could have lifted the purse quickly from her bag. Whoever it was, they'd be long gone by now.

When she and Wylie left, the high street was still busy, despite the fact that its famous fashion shops and body-piercing studios were shuttered, and the market stalls empty.

'Let me ask you something,' said Flick.

Wylie stuck his arm out as a black cab came down the road.

'Go on then,' he said.

'You know a secret about somebody.' She hardly knew where the question came from, but guessed she had wanted to ask him all day. 'It's a terrible secret and if you told anybody it could ruin their life, and maybe yours as well.'

'A secret!' He grinned. 'I love those!'

'What would you do?'

'Wow, okay.' He squeezed her shoulders and she leaned against him gratefully. Her fingers tangled in his. He was perhaps an inch shorter than she was, but she liked his solidity, the warmth of him. 'Do you like this person?'

'Yes, I think so.'

'Are they . . . a bad person?'

She closed her eyes and rested her head against his shoulder. Wylie's hands rested on her waist. 'I don't think so.'

She was mistaken about what she'd seen. Drake was a man with secrets, certainly, but she couldn't believe he was capable of murder. She was projecting onto him all the tensions in her own life – her sister leaving, her loneliness – and he didn't deserve any of that. She didn't want to lose anybody else.

'And is it worth ruining your own life over?' asked Wylie.

She felt very tired all of a sudden, but content, and needed to change the subject. 'Thank you for a great day.'

'You're welcome,' he said, grinning.

The cab swung to the kerb. Wylie opened the door and she climbed in. He stood on the pavement, ready to slam the door, and when he didn't take the hint, she patted the seat beside her.

'Are you sure?' he asked. She leaned out to kiss him hard on the mouth.

'Yeah,' she whispered. 'Right now, right at this moment, I'm very sure. Come home with me.'

Wylie didn't need to be asked twice. He climbed into the back of the cab and took her hand in his. Her heart banged in her chest. She leaned against him. The closeness felt comfortable, natural; it felt good. But a moment later she nearly slipped down the back of the seat when Wylie leaned forward.

'All right, mate?' he said to the driver. 'Busy night?'

16

Two people dead at their feet.

Joel's heart clattered so hard in his chest that he thought it would smash from his brittle ribcage. Blood filled the inside of his skull, it gushed in his ears, in his temples. His hands and legs shook. Giddy with disgust and panic, he thought he would collapse.

Everything had happened so fast – in the blink of an eye. Only moments ago, this room, now so deathly quiet, had been filled with the terrified screams of a man, a woman, fighting for their lives.

They hadn't stood a chance.

Joel's gaze lifted to Tatia and Carl – they stared back, panting for breath, eyes wide in shock – and then moved down to the bodies of the dead man, the dead woman at their feet.

The woman's head was thrown back, and her arms and legs flung wide, her top and sweatpants sodden with blood. Her manicured fingernails curled across the top of Tatia's trainers. The man was slumped face down where his shoulders had crashed to the floor, legs folded beneath his knees, arms at his side, his swollen, bloody face hidden in the weave of the rug.

A sick expression of horror and disbelief twisted across Carl's face. A toneless keening noise came from his throat.

'Stop,' hissed Tatia. 'Do not make that noise. Do not!'

He said something, but it was lost in the smack of the snot and tears filling his nose and mouth.

Her voice was a hoarse crack. 'Again.'

'What have we done?' Carl whispered, incredulous, and his eyes flicked to Tatia and Joel, and then dropped to the bodies, and the bloody ornament that lay between them on the rug.

Tatia stepped back and the woman's hand flopped off her trainer and onto the floor. 'You said the house would be empty.'

Carl whined. 'I'm sorry.'

Her voice rose angrily. 'You said the house was *empty*.'

'I didn't know.' Phlegm popped on his lips. 'They shouldn't be here.'

Sweat raced down Tatia's neck, soaking her collar. Imprinted on her face was the revulsion she felt that Joel had seen what happened to these people. He had watched. She reached forward to touch his fingers, and he felt a jolt of static from the carpet.

Forgive me, her eyes begged him. *For what I have done to you.*

Then Joel listened to Carl and Tatia argue like a bickering married couple – they hurled accusations at each other so quickly that he didn't understand half of what they said – and Carl dropped to his knees to cringe over the body of the woman. His fingers stroked her hair, which was knotted with blood, and pressed at her face, as if he could raise her from the dead. He lifted her in his arms, the dead woman's head tipping back over his elbow. The way her long hair dropped to the floor as Carl pulled his fingers gently along its length made Joel think of the ladies he saw as a kid getting shampoos in the windows of expensive salons.

Tatia told Carl, 'We must go.'

His lips quivered. 'After what we've done?'

'We cannot stay.'

Ignoring her, he put his mouth to the dead woman's ear. 'Wake up.' His mouth trembled. 'Wake up now.'

'There is nothing we can do for them.'

'How can you be so cold?' Spittle flew across the body as Carl shouted. 'These people are dead and you feel nothing!'

'Please,' said Tatia. Only moments earlier the screams of the dead people would have reverberated up and down the empty street. 'Keep your voice down.'

'You're so cold!' he wailed.

'Carl, listen to me.' She glanced quickly again at Joel. 'It is important that we leave now. You are upset at what happened, we both are, but we must go.'

'Are you upset?' Carl's face was a picture of misery. 'Because it doesn't look like it!'

'We will talk when we are away from here.'

She tried to calm the shudders that wracked Joel's body, whispering, 'We are going, little bear. We will get you out of here.'

One moment Will was there, and the next –

'No, we're here now.' Carl gently placed the woman back on the floor and climbed to his feet to look at the impressive collection of records that stretched across an entire wall, and the art deco drinks cabinet in the corner of the room. The bottles crowded on a silver tray crashed together when he stumbled against the cabinet. Carl picked up a bottle and drank.

92

'Carl . . .'

Joel started moving along the wall, trying to find a place where he could curl into a ball until the nightmare was over. Reaching a sofa, his foot kicked the side of a box, which rattled.

A box of toys.

Horrified, Tatia wrenched the sofa away to reveal the box. It was a plastic yellow tub covered in stickers – and full of dolls and games and books, thick wedges of a child's jigsaw, mysterious bits of bright plastic – tidied away out of sight.

'No,' she said. 'It is not possible. It cannot be. There are no photos on the walls, nothing to suggest . . .' Her fear transmitted to Joel. 'If I had known there were children here I would never, *never*, have placed it on the list. We are going.' She grabbed Joel's arm. 'Immediately.'

But then deafening music filled the room.

Tatia shouted at Carl to turn it down but the noise blaring from the sound system, all thrashing guitars and pounding drums, reduced everything to a dumb show. His back was turned as he stood at the shelves, pulling out records and flinging them over his shoulder.

'There are thousands of these things,' Carl shouted. 'But it's all jazz!'

He saw something he liked and tore it from the sleeve, whipped the record off the turntable – it spun across the room into a wall – and replaced it with the one he had found.

'No more music!' barked Tatia, but it was no good.

The room was filled with pops and scratches as the stylus settled in the grooves of the disc. Carl struck a pose, *wait for it*, and a moment later ska music pounded out. Guitar, piano, a blaring horn section.

Carl whooped and twirled, pumping his elbows in tight, jerky movements, lifting his knees high. Tears whipped from his eyes. He hopped around, kicking his legs, thrashing his arms, smashing into the wall, the cabinet, sending bottles crashing to the floor. A vase toppled from a shelf, a picture frame from the wall.

Joel pressed his hands to his ears, scrunched his eyes shut.

The music was deafening, a noisy accompaniment to the terrible images spinning in his head.

A spray of blood soaking into the weave of a rug.

Tatia screamed at Carl to stop, but he didn't hear, or didn't care.

A woman begging for mercy.

She went to the record player and swatted the stylus off the turntable.

A man's head hitting the ground, one open eye gazing sightlessly along the floor.

It made a screeching noise that ripped across the walls, and then there was a jarring silence that was almost as loud and monstrous as the music.

'You will wake the whole street!'

Tatia's fury made Carl cringe. Smearing away his tears, leaving streaks of bloody pink across his face, he gulped from the bottle. 'We're gonna get caught, they're gonna take you away from me. We won't be together!'

'Not if we go now.'

He nodded, forlorn, all his energy gone, and dropped the bottle. The liquid glugged onto the rug. But then they heard something from the hallway that made Carl and Tatia freeze.

Short, angry bursts on the doorbell.

They stared at each other, hardly daring to breathe. Waiting for the bell to stop ringing. After a minute, it did. Tatia pulled Joel to his feet, ready to leave.

And then the bell started again – one long ring that didn't stop.

Carl goggled at Tatia.

'Stay here,' she told them both.

Standing in the gap of the door, Joel watched Tatia slip into the darkness of the hallway. A figure stood on the other side of the frosted glass of the front door, framed in the yellow blur of a street lamp. Edging it open, Tatia was careful to keep as far back in the shadows as she could.

'Where are Bryan and Samantha?' A man in a dressing gown stood on the step, a haze of thin hair swaying on his head. 'I want to talk to them.'

'They are . . . there is a spill.'

'Who are you?'

'I am . . . a friend.'

'Okay, Bryan and Samantha's friend,' said the man sarcastically. 'Do you know what time it is? Do you have *any* idea?'

Looking behind him, Joel saw Carl gawping.

'We are sorry,' Tatia told the man. 'For any noise.'

'It's not good enough.' The man squinted down at his watch, making the fine hair on his scalp tilt. 'It's nearly four in the morning. I've got to get to the airport in an hour, but guess what, I haven't slept because of your bloody racket.'

'The music is finished,' Tatia said. 'We are quiet now.'

'Yes, well.' Now he'd made his point, the neighbour spoke quietly. 'You tell them I expected more of them.'

'We will not trouble you any further.'

'It's too late for that, I'm afraid.' He tightened the belt of his dressing gown. 'I've already called the police. You can explain to them why you've been disturbing all and sundry. Music, shouting!'

When he left, Tatia closed the door and returned to the living room. Joel and Carl stared at her. 'The police are coming.'

She looked down at the woman's body, and then at the rug. Her eyes widened in horror and Joel followed her gaze –

To where the man was crawling very slowly towards the kitchen, moving with great purpose on his hands and knees. He lumbered like some prehistoric creature, each lift of his arms and knees seeming to take enormous effort. Head down, eyes swollen to slits, a long string of drool swung beneath his chin. Joel heard the flapping rasp of his breath. His instinct for survival, his primeval urge to find safety, kept him moving onto the kitchen tile, a trail of smeared blood behind him.

Carl surged to the door, but Tatia held out an arm. 'Not the kitchen!' They watched him inch towards the patio door. Moments later the man collapsed to the floor. He didn't move. 'We have to go.'

She took Joel by the shoulders and pushed him quickly into the dark hallway, to the front door. At that moment, the street lamps up and down the street winked off. But at the door, Joel looked upstairs.

Sitting on the top step, silhouetted against the soft burr of a night light, was a little girl.

Tatia went to the bottom step. 'Go. I will follow you out.'

Carl whined. 'She's seen us.'

She turned and snarled angrily. 'I said go!'

17

'We were good friends once, me and you. I like to think we were friends.'

In the early morning, Ray Drake and Elliot Juniper walked across acres of grass and scrubland, past derelict factories and railway sidings where empty carriages stood on sleepers. Streets where all the homes were abandoned, windows smashed and tiles slipping from the roof, and the broken pavements covered in weeds.

They walked for miles – along a canal path, where the surface of the brown stagnant water twisted slowly below them – towards the tall, silver towers of the city which glittered against a blood-red sky. But despite having walked for a long time, the skyscrapers of glass and steel, the winking roof lights calling them home, never seemed to get any closer, and Ray Drake despaired of ever leaving this desolate place.

But still, it was good to see Elliot again, quite unexpectedly. To Drake's surprise he was happy and talkative. Although every time Drake tried to get a good look at him, Elliot was faced away.

'Yes,' said Drake, 'we were friends.'

Elliot stopped to watch wasps buzz around the rusted frame of a shopping trolley which poked from the canal. Hands thrust deep in his pockets, he saw something in the distance, and pointed. 'He's following us.'

Sure enough, there was a figure walking towards them. Too far away to make out properly. This place, this path, seemed oddly familiar to Drake, but he couldn't say why.

'I'm never going to get back to Rhonda now.'

The foreboding in Elliot's voice made Drake uneasy. They watched as the figure seemed to disappear into the ground. A moment later the top of its head reappeared, the body coming into view over an incline.

'I'll get you home.' Right at that moment he wanted to make it happen more than anything. He wanted to get Elliot home.

'Come on.' Drake took his arm, but Elliot dragged his feet, unable to take his eyes off the figure who followed in the distance, arms and legs pumping with a sinister efficiency.

'I'm not going to make it.' They walked off the path and onto the grass. Elliot's feet stomped loudly on patches of hard mud, sending up puffs of dust. He kept looking back. 'I'm not going to get home.'

'Don't talk like that.' Drake was getting annoyed. Elliot's fear was infectious; he felt it gather about him like a cloak. Neither of them wanted to look behind them now, they just wanted to get to the city, to those bulging buildings shining beneath the red sky that never seemed to get any closer.

'I'm just not one of those people.' Elliot grabbed Drake's arm, making him stop. Drake saw his face clearly for the first time, and there were tears in his eyes. Glancing back, Drake saw the figure adjust its course towards them, arms swinging. Drake felt it – felt *him* – approaching in the pit of his stomach, in his bones. 'But it's okay, Ray. Now I know we were mates.'

'We'll always be friends.'

And Drake meant it, too. They had known each other a lifetime ago, and for a short period, but they had survived a terrible ordeal and were bound together for ever. They were blood brothers.

But then something had happened to Elliot, something bad. Drake couldn't remember what it was; all he knew was that *somebody* was responsible. The sun lifted, pulling jagged light up the side of the tall buildings. The heat was stifling and he dropped his jacket, pulled down his brown tie.

'I'm sorry I let you down.'

'Don't talk like that,' said Drake. 'You don't have to apologise, not to me.'

'Then I forgive you.' Elliot pulled him into a hug. When Ray tried to pull away, the big man held him tight, whispered into his ear, 'You are forgiven.' Then he grabbed Drake's arm. 'We have to go.'

And they ran. Stumbling over weeds and patches of tarmac and treacherous crusts of mud baked hard in the sun.

Drake was unable to see over his shoulder, and what was behind them. 'What's going on?'

'Just don't look back.' Elliot panted as he ran. 'It's you he wants.'

And then they stopped suddenly as a train blipped past. It came out of nowhere with a roar and passed directly in front of their faces on sizzling tracks, lifting Drake's tie, the hair off his forehead. One carriage, two, three, four. A whistle screamed; sparks flew from the wheels, which clacked in a deafening rhythm. Carriages of steel and glass whipping past. Five, six.

'Don't let him get you!' shouted Elliot above the scream

of the train. Panicking, he fell to his knees to find a way past underneath. Clack, clack, clack.

Drake spun round. The figure was near now, walking calmly, arms swinging. Clouds passed across the sun, reducing the figure to a silhouette as he bore down on them.

He experienced a terror he had never felt before. 'Elliot!'

The last carriage finally passed, the noise receding instantly, and Elliot was about to leap across the tracks when he winced. His hands flew to his gut and when they lifted, they were covered with blood.

'I'm sorry.' Drake watched in shock as a dark stain spread across Elliot's stomach. A crimson tide seeped into his jeans, soaking across his shirt.

'It's okay,' said Elliot in surprise. 'It'll be okay.'

He vomited blood onto the tracks. Drake held Elliot as he slumped, his weight pulling them both down. Lying on the ground, Elliot stared up at him in a pool of sticky blood. His voice was a frail whisper. 'Promise me you'll never let him out again.'

'Elliot,' he said. 'I don't—'

'Tell me . . . I'll be the last.'

'Elliot!' But his friend didn't move. Clots of blood spiralled in his eyes, clouding the whites like ink dropped into a glass of water, as he stared at something over Drake's shoulder.

Drake tried to stand, but the shadow man stepped forward. His arm shot out, a knife gleaming in his hand, to stab at Drake's heart.

And then Ray Drake's eyes snapped open in bed, and he tried to scream.

But his arms, his legs, his chest, were useless. He was paralysed, and could only watch as a shadow, much blacker than anything around it, peeled away from the darkness at the end of the bed. Unable to move or make a noise, Drake watched helplessly as the figure slid around the side, the sharp point of the knife snagging in the fabric of the sheets.

The familiar voice in Drake's head said, *I can do things you will never be able to, Ray.*

Drake wanted to say a single word – 'No' – but no sound came out.

I can make all the badness go away. Like I made Elliot go away.

When he leaned towards Drake's face, his features were as black as a starless night, and his breath was warm, odourless.

Because you are weak, and I am strong.

Drake's phone buzzed beside him.

He jerked bolt upright, a scream ripping from his throat, and swiped at the mobile, sending it spinning off the bedside cabinet. Terrified, heart pounding in his chest, Drake stared around his dark bedroom, trying to fit together all the shadows, make sense of the familiar shapes. They shifted momentarily, swirling into inanimate objects. A wardrobe, an armchair, his wife's dressing table. He watched, ignoring the buzz of the phone on the floor, until he was certain there was nothing out of place. There was no intruder, no shadow man.

When he was absolutely sure that he was alone, Ray Drake swung his legs out of bed. Sweat trickled down his back, plastered hair to his slick forehead. His sheets were sopping. He leaned over to pick up the phone. Took a deep breath, answered the call.

'Eddie.'

'Sir?'

'What time is it?'

'Early.'

'What can I do for you?'

'Sorry to disturb you, boss, but we've got another one.'

There was a knock on the bedroom door.

'Raymond?' asked a voice.

'Wait a moment, Eddie.' Drake placed the receiver to his shoulder and called, 'I'm fine, Myra. Go back to bed.'

'You'll wake the street,' she said shortly. 'Have some consideration.'

A moment later he heard her footsteps creep off down the hall. Drake put the phone back to his ear.

'How many?'

'Another two vics.' Drake heard the engine of Eddie's car roar into life. 'But, sir, there were children in the house.'

'Text me the address.' Drake rubbed his eyes. 'I'm on my way.'

18

What a party! But after the party came, inevitably, the pain.

When the sun came up, and the first sliver of light burned the edges of the curtains, Poppy was already awake thanks to a blinding headache. Twice in the night she had to pad downstairs to refill her glass of water, her mouth was so parched. But she had nobody to blame but herself for drinking on a weeknight.

'Are you awake?' she asked Tim quietly, but he was asleep on the other side of the bed.

The time on the alarm said 5.45 a.m. Gabe would be awake soon. Poppy knew she wasn't going to get back to sleep, so she slipped on her silk gown and went downstairs.

The kitchen was a mess. Nearly every surface was covered with plates of half-eaten food. Blinis, olives, cold meats – a green salad, its peppery leaves wilted in the bowl after being left out all night. Tubs of dips were left open. Her heart sank when she saw three empty bottles of red, and another one open, the wine glasses sticky with fingerprints – and the shot glasses, too. A saucer had been used as a makeshift ashtray, and the kitchen stank of smoke. Poppy remembered scrounging a couple of Alexi's menthols, and the thought revolted her. She tried to remember if her cleaner would be coming in later. It didn't matter – she couldn't leave this mess for poor Yasmin to clear up.

The first thing Poppy did was open the windows to let in fresh air, then she put the kettle on. Scraped the uneaten food into the recycling, cleared the table, stacked the dishwasher.

She didn't know what on earth she'd been thinking. The older she got, the more she was terrified of putting on weight. Proud of her slender figure, of her lean arms and legs, her toned stomach, she did yoga, Pilates, a Zumba class. Poppy worked bloody hard to keep in shape, and last night she was piling calories down her throat like there was no tomorrow.

The evening was meant to be low-key and comfortable, but she had gone a little bit mad, just didn't want the party to end, and hoped she hadn't scared poor Bella, or Alexi – her friend's on-off boyfriend, a food photographer for one of the Sunday glossies, who looked like he couldn't get out of the door fast enough at the end of the night. She would message Bella later to apologise.

Poppy, who had tied her hair into a ponytail and wore a dress shirt and a pair of pumps, needed more than anything to be distracted from seeing Joel earlier that day. She was certain it had been him. If it was, he must have lost an awful lot of weight, and his face was ghostly pale behind the glass. The upsetting thing was, when she had tried to get his attention he had just stared, as if she were a stranger. Perhaps that was what they were now – strangers.

Thinking about it, that was what had made her so manic, and she was also anxious because Tim was working late again – his long hours played merry hell with their social life – and somehow it all became a perfect storm in her head, and her one glass of wine became two, became umpteen. After the third or fourth, her mood changed and – oh god, she cringed at the thought – she demanded they all do shots. The others weren't keen – mixing wine and spirits was never a good idea – but Poppy insisted; she could be stubborn when she wanted to. She fetched vodka from the freezer and forced them each to make a toast. Bella did one to some lifestyle guru, Alexi toasted his favourite football team and Poppy, annoyed her husband was missing, toasted Tim. 'To wherever the hell he is!'

'To Tim!' they all intoned gravely. Poppy gulped down her wine and refilled her glass immediately.

It wasn't like she was a habitual drinker – she wasn't one of those women who were in a foul mood all day until wine o'clock rolled round – but when she saw Alexi sneak a look at his watch, she was damned if she was going to let the evening come to an end.

So she put on one of her *Now! Dance* compilations. Turned it up loud.

Bella jumped to her feet as soon as she heard her favourite track. Poppy knew exactly which song would get her in the mood – they had danced to it for two weeks solid in Ibiza years back. Poppy pulled her hair loose, let it toss and swing over her head, and kicked off her shoes. Danced like a maniac until the kitchen door opened and Tim walked in.

'Darling!' she cried. She must have looked like a madwoman with her hair stuck to her sweaty face, and he was as sober as a judge.

'I've got an early start tomorrow,' he said, 'so I'm going to go up.'

'Isn't he mean? What a mean person!' she wailed. The

wine and vodka had knocked her for six. She snatched his wrists, dragged him to her. 'Dance with me!'

The music pounded, another rave anthem from years back. Poppy waved Tim's arms about, trying to get him to join in, but he pulled away.

'You guys have fun,' he said, and left.

'He's mean,' shouted Poppy, finding the word hilarious every single time. 'He won't dance with his beautiful wife. Down with meanies!'

'Flog him!' Bella laughed, but turned to Alexi. 'We should go, too.'

Alexi didn't need to be asked twice, grabbed his coat.

Poppy could kill Tim for spoiling the evening. 'Oh, no, don't!'

'I'm sorry, darling.' Bella hugged her. 'Alexi has a shoot first thing.'

'I'm going to have a proper party soon.' Poppy held onto Bella as the room spun. 'We haven't had one for ages and we deserve it.'

'I'll be the first to arrive and the last to leave,' promised Bella.

Poppy got a lump in her throat at the thought of all her good friends coming: Bella and Ange and Suze and Issy and the others. She'd think about dates, draw up an invite list. Tim's parents John and Tanya would have Gabriel for the night. But it would have to be later in the year. She, Tim and Gabriel were off to Mexico soon, and there was their annual family trip to John and Tanya's place on the Algarve.

'Look after yourself.' Bella kissed her goodbye. 'And if you need to talk about anything . . .'

'He's just grumpy, that's all.' The way Tim had skulked away had been offhand. She didn't understand what had got into him lately. 'Work playing on his mind, probably. He's having to make redundancies.'

Now, this morning, Gabriel walked into the room in his red PJs before she'd had a proper chance to tidy. Just the sight of him took the edge off Poppy's hangover. As usual, he carried the beloved soft toy John and Tanya had bought him for Christmas. Nobody could work out if it was a dragon or a dinosaur, until Gabriel gravely told them it was a dragosaur.

'What a mess!'

'Isn't it!' admitted Poppy. 'Sit yourself down while I tidy up a bit.'

She turned on the television on the wall and he sat, his little body almost consumed by the fat beanbag, ready to watch cartoons. A news channel came on. There had been another of those sickening home invasions – and not so far away either. There were casualties, a policeman told the reporter, which usually meant something worse. And two children were in the house! The last thing Poppy wanted was for Gabriel to be exposed to the insanity of the world, and she quickly flipped the channel to the familiar animated mayhem of *Scooby Doo*.

Her phone rang while she was dropping a chamomile teabag into a mug, but she couldn't find the receiver. It rang and rang – she hoped to god it wasn't Yasmin calling in sick – and she found it eventually under a Jamie cookbook.

'Yes?' she said, but nobody spoke. 'Hello?'

There must be something wrong with the line, she decided. But the intensity of the silence made her hang on. She heard, or imagined she heard, breathing.

'Joel?' She moved deeper among all the plants and shrubs in the conservatory, away from the noisy crashes and whistles from the TV in the kitchen. 'Is that you?'

'Poppy,' said a voice, and she clamped a hand over her mouth in shock.

Hungover, nerves jangling, she lowered herself onto her haunches, barely feeling the cold tile on the soles of her feet. Hardly daring to hope that after all this time they would see each other again.

19

'I should be on a plane right now.' Alistair Judd picked up his cup of coffee. 'In business class with a Bloody Mary in my hand.'

'I'm sorry, Mr Judd.' Flick opened her notebook. 'This must be difficult.'

'I've never known the likes of it.' Judd kept tipping forward to prop cushions behind him, unable to get comfortable on his own sofa. He was a slight middle-aged man with flyblown hair. He wore shorts and loafers without socks, clothes thrown on in the early hours when the street began to pulse with blue light. 'I've lived here fourteen years. The worst thing that's ever happened was when olive oil was poured into the postbox down the road.'

Drake stood behind the sofa. Weary, unsettled, he couldn't help but contemplate the real possibility that Flick had set in motion the sequence of events that would ultimately lead to his disgrace. But the bodies of Samantha and Bryan Langley lay in their house next door, and he tried to focus.

'How well do you know the Langleys?'

'I knew Bryan more than Sam, to be honest,' Judd said over his shoulder. 'We'd sometimes meet as we left for work. And we shared a . . . mouse problem and spoke about that. The kids can get a bit loud, running up and down the stairs screaming, like children do, but I've never had any reason to complain before. As a family they're polite, respectful.' His phone buzzed on the arm of the sofa and he switched off the ringer. 'That's Zurich. They can wait.'

'What time did you go round?'

'It was after four. I was meant to catch a flight, so I was spitting feathers.' Judd took frequent, rapid sips from the mug on the table, and Drake wondered if there was something stronger than caffeine in his coffee. 'I'm not one of those neighbours who holds a glass to the wall, but it was just too much. All that screaming! I was furious.'

'You weren't concerned about hearing screams?'

'I thought they were having some kind of rowdy party. In retrospect, it was . . . out of character. But the husband . . . Bryan sometimes likes to play his music loud. I barely saw the woman who answered the door. The light was off in the hallway, and I was insensible with tiredness.'

'Didn't you think it odd that neither of the Langleys answered their own door?' asked Flick.

'I thought they were having a joke at my expense. I was convinced they were giggling behind the door. I feel terrible about it now.'

'What do you remember about her?'

'She was shorter than Mrs Langley. More . . . fulsome.' He glanced apologetically at Flick. 'Her smile . . . hung there in the darkness, like the smile of the Cheshire Cat.'

'Anything else?'

'I remember thinking that her voice was . . .'

When Judd frowned, Drake prompted, 'Was what?'

'It had an odd inflection to it.'

'An inflection?'

111

'She spoke very precisely, very carefully. Every syllable was enunciated.'

'She was foreign.'

'Possibly. I can't be certain.'

Ray Drake walked around the side of the sofa to face him. 'Were the Langleys intending to travel anywhere to your knowledge, Mr Judd? On holiday, or any kind of trip?'

'They went away at Easter. Cornwall, I think.'

'Do they go away regularly, leaving the house empty?'

'Bryan was a college lecturer so I'd imagine it was difficult for him to holiday during term time. Sam was a full-time mum with two small . . .' He winced. 'I didn't mean to sound rude when I mentioned the children's screaming. They were happy, you see, which was why I never complained.'

'Have you seen anyone hanging around the street lately?' Flick tapped her pen on her knee. 'Any unfamiliar faces?'

'We get a lot of foot traffic along the street. There are shops around the corner, so people use it as a cut-through. My work often takes me away so perhaps I'm not the best person to ask.' Judd placed his mug on a coaster on a low onyx table. 'I'm not a bad neighbour, you know. If I had thought for one second that they were in distress . . .'

He looked down in embarrassment.

'I have to speak to DS Crowley, just for a moment,' said Drake.

The neighbour nodded. Flick followed Drake outside. They stood on the doorstep, watching a familiar scene. Officers moving around the squad cars; support vans parked in the middle of the road; police tape flapping between lamp posts. Behind the tidy exterior of the Langleys' house – with its spacious drive and beds of spring flowers, the street number neatly clipped into the green hedge; beyond the wide gunmetal-grey front door and polished letterbox – lay the bodies of a husband and wife, a mother and father.

'The children are unharmed, at least,' she told him. 'They're being looked after by their grandmother at a neighbour's house. A social worker is there, and a family liaison officer.'

'There's nothing to suggest the Langleys intended to be out of the house last night.' Drake watched a supermarket delivery van pull up at the outer cordon, blocking access to the street. 'If that's the case, it means this isn't about empty homes any more, it's not about intrusion. It's about murder, plain and simple.' He stepped forward to tell an officer to get the van removed – the officer ducked under the tape and headed towards it – then turned back to Flick. 'Can you speak to the children? Their grandmother has given us permission.'

'Sure.' Flick was about to go back into the house. Drake bit his tongue, couldn't bring himself to ask the question he so dearly wanted to. But then she turned back to him. 'Just so you know, I didn't talk to the counsellor, and I'm not going to.'

It took a moment for her words to sink in. 'May I ask why?'

'Because I simply can't believe you would just . . . do something like that.'

He closed his eyes for a moment, allowed the relief to flood through him. That was the end of it. Maybe the shadow man would leave him alone now.

Work was piling up. There was plenty to do in the immediate hours ahead, and he would pour himself into those tasks gratefully. Discussions to be had with the crime scene manager and the pathologist; and there were numerous calls to take, including with the Met communications team, who were ringing constantly.

Press teams and camera crews from across the world were setting up equipment at the bottom of the road, to cover what had been dubbed the Goldilocks Killings. Reporters called out the same questions over and over: *Do you have any leads? Have you made any arrests? Should the public be afraid?* The anxious murmurings in the media had become a loud roar of outrage. The city was spooked. Estate agents reported a steep drop in demand for properties north of the river; security businesses celebrated a stampede for home protection systems.

But Ray Drake had his future back, and would focus all his energy on bringing this investigation to a close as soon as possible. His fingers slipped down his tie. He felt the future expand ahead of him again.

He waited for that familiar voice in his ear – and heard nothing.

When Alistair Judd appeared in the doorway, Flick told him, 'I'm coming now.'

'Thank you,' Drake told her again. He'd climb into a scene suit, pull on overshoes and nitrile gloves, and head back next door. 'I'd better get on.'

Drake was already halfway down the path when Mr Judd said over the top of his coffee mug, 'You're going to watch the video footage, I suppose.'

Drake turned slowly on his heels. 'Excuse me?'

20

Flick saw no fear in the boy's big blue eyes, just bewilderment at being in an unfamiliar house surrounded by strange people. The trauma would come soon enough, and would last a lifetime. Right now, he clung to his grandmother. His older sister sat at the table beside him, her blonde hair shivering furiously as she scribbled on a sheet of paper. Coloured felt-tip pens were lined up neatly at her side. When she finished with one she replaced its cap and put it back in the rainbow line.

Till this morning both these children were loved and protected. They lived in a big, comfortable house – the only home they had ever known in their short lives, which they would likely never go inside again – with a mummy who cared for them all day and a daddy who smothered them with kisses when he came home. Until a few hours ago their young lives were on course to unfurl in a steady, predictable rhythm. After their Montessori nursery, they'd go to a good private school and during the Christmas break learn to ski. Long summer holidays would be spent at a villa in Tuscany with friends and family. When they were older Emily and George would attend two of the better universities, likely become lawyers or doctors or academics, and one day they'd have children of their own. Samantha and Bryan Langley would have been so proud of what they achieved.

But that destiny had been taken from them. Replaced by an uncertain future, shaped by hardship and heartache.

'That's a lovely picture,' Flick told Emily. The drawing was of a lady with an explosion of curly yellow hair, red lips and a triangular dress, matchstick legs protruding from feet shaped like bricks. 'How old are you?'

The girl didn't look up from the drawing. 'Five.'

'Do you mind if I ask you some questions?'

Emily's grandmother glanced anxiously at the social worker. 'A couple, perhaps.'

Pressed tightly together, Sylvia Langley's lips were drained of colour. Her face was grey. Every molecule inside her was screaming with despair at the murder of her son and daughter-in-law. She controlled her agony and incomprehension by doing the only thing she could: remaining focused on the well-being of her grandchildren. But as more details emerged about the awful circumstances of the deaths, her health would unravel like thread from a spool. The murder of a child was devastating for anyone, but for an elderly widow devoted to her only son and his family, it could mark the beginning of the end. Flick wondered if there was anyone – an aunt, an uncle, devoted godparents, family friends – who could take in Emily and George and offer them a future. She hoped to god there was, or these two children would drop into the system.

'Did your mummy and daddy have visitors last night, Emily?'

'They were shouting and playing noisy music. I heard Mummy . . .'

'What did you hear?' asked Flick.

The girl didn't answer. Her hand moved up and down

116

like a seismograph, the squeak of the pen as loud as a screech in the quiet room.

It was bad enough speaking to adult relatives of murder victims, but these kids, carried from the crime scene in their pyjamas before the sun even rose, didn't understand what was happening. Perhaps they never would.

'How many—' Flick's phone rang in her bag. She thought it had been turned to silent already, and she muted it quickly. She felt a momentary excitement when she wondered if it was Wylie, and then a sickening guilt. 'Do you know how many people were with Mummy and Daddy downstairs last night?'

'There was a man.' The girl placed a felt tip under her nose. 'He was very noisy, and a lady and another man.'

Flick leaned forward. 'Two men, Emily?' Are you sure?'

'That's enough now.' Sylvia Langley hugged George to her. 'Both the children have been very good, I think you'll agree, and Emily has been very helpful.'

'Very helpful,' agreed Flick. 'But I just wanted to ask one more thing. Did you get a look at the men or the lady, maybe?'

'Mostly the lady,' said the girl. 'She spoke to me.'

Flick leaned forward. 'What did she say to you, Emily?'

Sylvia Langley cleared her throat. 'I think—'

The little girl looked up at Flick and said in a singsong voice, '*Come along, Emily, let me take you back to bed!*'

Emily watched the people downstairs. It was too dark to see their faces, but there was a big man and another man, who stood with his head bowed and his shoulders slumped, as if he was very sad, or very tired, or both. There was a lady, too, who came to the bottom of the stairs.

'Why are you awake, my darling?' Her hand sliding along the smooth bannister, she began to climb the stairs, almost seeming to glide towards Emily in the dim light.

The large man stepped forward. 'What are you doing?'

'Go,' the lady told him. Her face burned pink in the soft glow of the nightlight on the landing, and Emily saw her frightening smile. 'I will follow you out.'

'She's seen us.'

'I said go!'

'Who are you?' asked Emily.

'I am a friend of your mama.' The lady leaned towards her. 'What's your name?'

'Emily. Where's Mummy and Daddy?'

'Come along, Emily, let me take you back to bed.' As the front door closed, Emily took her hand and led her along a strip of fine carpet edged by bleached floorboards.

The lady's hand was slippery, and Emily asked, 'Are you scared?'

'I am just excited, my darling.'

Emily led her into the room she shared with her brother. The lady admired all the furnishings, toys and books; the painted clay figures Emily and George had made with their parents; her favourite stuffed animals; the drawings sticky-taped to the cabinets. A lamp rotated on a side table, spraying a colourful scene, animals in green racing cars and yellow trains and blue yachts, across the walls and ceiling. The vehicles stretched as if picking up speed and then lazily snapped back together. Emily's brother George was asleep in the other bed, lying on his stomach, a fist bunched beneath his chin, one knee folded over the top of the duvet. Emily put a finger to her lips, *ssshhhh*, whispered, 'Do you like my room?'

'It is beautiful.' The colours of the lamp slid across the lady's face, soaking into her features, changing their colour and shape. 'I would have been very happy to have had a room like this.'

'Didn't you have your own bedroom?' asked Emily. 'When you were a little girl?'

'Just for a very short time.'

Emily sat cross-legged in front of a tall doll's house in the corner of the room, which was lit from within so that its four windows seemed to shine with warmth.

'Do you like my house?' Emily patted the floor beside her. The lady hesitated and then sat cross-legged beside her. Emily gave her a slim doll with long, glossy black hair. 'This is for you. Her name is Skye.'

Then she opened the front of the house to reveal two bedrooms above a kitchen and a parlour. Each room was filled with pretty miniature furniture. Emily placed her own blonde-haired doll into a chair in one of the rooms. The doll was far too big for the chair and for the room and sat monstrously hunched beneath the low ceiling.

'This is not Justine's house,' she explained. 'What's the matter? Don't you like Skye?'

'She is very pretty. She looks like my sister.' The lady thoughtfully touched Skye's thick hair. 'I never had a doll when I was young.'

'You never had one?'

'Not a single one.'

'Would you like to take Skye with you?'

That scary smile appeared on the lady's face, and in the wash of the lamplight, it looked like she was about to cry.

'Are you sad?' asked Emily.

'Oh no.' The lady placed Skye on the other seat. The long thin legs of the doll splayed in front of her.

'Skye belongs here, with Justine.' She stood. 'It is late.'

Emily closed the door of the doll's house. 'Will you put me to bed?'

'Of course.'

The lady plumped the pillow around her head when Emily hopped into bed.

'When is my mummy coming to bed?'

The lady looked away. 'I must go.'

'I want to see her.'

Emily tried to move but the lady pressed the duvet tightly around her shoulders. 'People will come soon, Emily, policemen, and you must make a solemn promise that you will not get out of bed until they arrive. You must stay here and look after your brother. He will . . . need all your love.'

'What does solemn mean?'

'It means you place a hand on your heart when you promise. And be very quiet, so as not to disturb anybody.'

She stooped to turn off the lamp, but the girl sat up. 'I want it on!'

'It will stay on,' the lady said, 'if you promise you will not get out of bed.'

The girl placed a hand on her heart. 'I promise.'

'Good night.'

Just before she slipped out the door, the lady smiled, and her teeth were stained red in the colourful wash of the lamp.

Sylvia Langley let out a small moan.

The social worker stepped forward. 'Let's stop there.'

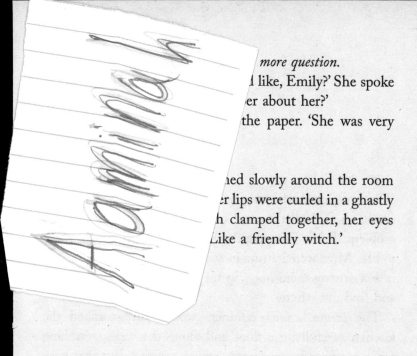

more question.

...d like, Emily?' She spoke

...er about her?'

...the paper. 'She was very

...ed slowly around the room

...er lips were curled in a ghastly

...h clamped together, her eyes

...Like a friendly witch.'

21

'The Langleys had a nice house. Stylish decor, a playroom, a wet room – all the mod cons, basically. But they had a problem.' Eddie Upson opened a laptop and the screen came to life. 'Mice were getting in somewhere in the kitchen, and it was driving them nuts. So they set up a video feed to try and find out where.'

The crime scene examiners would have combed the kitchen carefully, the floor and along the walls, searching for contact evidence: smears, prints, spatters. But they may well have missed the state-of-the-art webcam, its lens smaller than the circumference of a button, hidden high above a clock.

'You could get that lens up your colon.' Eddie swivelled in his chair to face Drake and Flick. 'Should you wish such a thing to happen.'

'Why is it so small?' asked Drake.

'I dunno. The house is spotless, like something from a magazine.' He adjusted the laptop screen so that they could see it. 'With people like that, it's all about the design.' He clicked his fingers, groping for the right word. 'The . . .'

'The *aesthetic*,' suggested Flick.

'That's the one. A big ugly camera would spoil the kitchen.'

Finger twirling round the trackpad, he opened the video timeline. They saw the kitchen from a high angle. A gleaming island unit in the centre, like an aircraft carrier cruising on a sea of tile. White work surfaces and cabinets, a sink on the far side of the room. There was a towering fridge of brushed steel. At the extreme left edge of the image was a glass door to the garden.

They watched Samantha and Bryan with their children on the morning before they were killed. A happy family breakfast. Samantha Langley was trim and pretty in sweat-pants and a T-shirt. She moved gracefully between cabinets and the fridge, taking out bowls and beakers, cereal boxes, a carton of juice. Bryan stood at the island, a pair of glasses wedged in his hair, looping a tie around his neck, a slice of toast clamped in his mouth. Emily and George sat on stools waving their arms about. Samantha said something to her husband, who nodded. He folded the rest of the toast into his mouth and picked up a computer tablet.

'Is there audio?'

'Afraid not. It's the last moments we want to see.' Eddie dragged the marker along the timeline at the bottom of the screen, moving the feed forward. The Langleys exploded into frantic movement, leaving and entering the room at incredible speed. The images jumped in a blur of colour. He pressed the space bar on the keyboard and the video dropped into real time. The empty kitchen was bathed in a lurid green light. The patio window was black and reflected a doorway on the right. Eddie put his finger to it on the screen. 'That leads to the living room.'

'Look at that.' Flick pointed over Eddie's shoulder at movement along the sill behind the sink.

'What is it?' asked Drake.

'It's a mouse.'

They watched it move, barely bigger than a dot, streaking behind a pot plant. Eddie nudged the image forward in jerks, moving closer to the moment they needed.

'There,' said Flick, and Eddie chopped at the space bar. Crawling slowly on his hands and knees into the frame in the bottom right hand of the screen was Bryan Langley. They watched him lumber slowly forward, exhausted, insensible, blood smearing on the tile. Barely able to muster the strength to lift his limbs, some deeply ingrained survival instinct keeping him moving.

Eddie pointed at the timestamp. 'This is around the same time as Alistair Judd was at the front door, and minutes before officers arrived.'

Reflected in the patio door, an indistinct figure appeared in the living-room doorway. Large and imposing, it was about to step into the room when a smaller figure appeared and held out an arm.

Eddie paused the image. The dark reflections of the frozen figures, barely more than outlines, seemed to ever so slightly vibrate.

'A man and a woman,' said Flick.

'Or a tall man and a short man.'

They discussed the detail in the image. The cropped hair and gym-pumped torso of the man and the wide hips of the shorter figure – 'a woman, definitely,' said Flick – and then Drake told Eddie to play the video.

Bryan Langley's body collapsed to the floor. A moment later the figures disappeared from the doorway.

'We're not going to get much from that,' said Flick.

'We've learned one thing.' Drake rotated his finger. 'Run it back.'

Eddie dragged the image into reverse to replay the footage. Reflected in the patio glass, the two figures emerged like ghosts from the darkness.

'Pause it there.' When Eddie was slow to react, Drake reached over to prod the space bar. The blurred movement of the arm was trapped in time. 'She's holding an arm in front of his chest. Stopping him going inside.'

Eddie slurped from a can of coke. 'Because she knows there's a camera there.'

'She's been in that kitchen before,' said Drake. They stared at the frozen image on the screen – two ghosts reflected in the glass window. 'Send this video to my computer.'

'This part?'

'All of it.'

'Are you sure? There's nearly four hours of footage, taken over twenty-four hours, and nothing else of interest.'

'Send it to me, Eddie.' Drake's phone rang. He took it out and answered. 'Ray Drake.'

The way his head snapped back made the others turn to watch. But Flick took the opportunity to lift her own phone from her bag and saw three missed calls from Sam Wylie.

This morning she'd been woken early, the sky still dark, and scrabbled around in a daze, her head thick from all the booze the previous day, and from sitting all day in the sun.

'I have to go,' she'd said, and Wylie jumped out of bed. She heard him banging around in the kitchen, turning the radio from the *Today* programme to noisy music and tune-lessly singing along, and when she had showered and dressed, he presented her with a cup of coffee.

'This'll help,' he said.

It made her wince – it was probably the worst coffee she

had ever tasted – but she didn't care. She'd told him to stay, he could leave in his own time, but he left with her – and promised he'd call later. And she knew he absolutely would – and couldn't wait. On the pavement, when he'd kissed her goodbye, his mouth still tasted furry from sleep.

She'd only been in her car for a moment when he sent her the first text.

LATER xx

'Thanks,' Drake said into the phone now. 'Mail me what you have.' He killed the call, nodded to Flick. 'We've got multiple matches from all the crime scenes, and a few more besides. Prints, DNA, the lot. He's a screamer. We're looking for a serial burglar called Carl Clarke.'

Drake shouldered his way out of the door. Flick dropped the phone in her bag and went after him, feeling his excitement. They had a suspect already. And were much closer, she hoped, to getting this investigation brought to a swift and successful conclusion.

22

'How do space pirates walk the plank? There's no water in space, so you can't drown.'

All these questions, one after the other – she didn't know where they all came from. She usually did her best to encourage Gabriel's insatiable curiosity, but this afternoon she couldn't concentrate.

Poppy had parked her Galaxy at Parliament Hill Lido, looking for a sports car. It wouldn't surprise her at all if Joel arrived in something fancy and expensive. Last night's alcohol was a clammy film on her skin, and the insides of her thighs tightened as she slogged up the slope beneath the pounding sun, pulling Gabriel towards the playground at the edge of the heath. Gabe dropped his dragosaur on the path and she snatched it up, hardly breaking stride. If she was getting tired, then goodness knows how his little legs felt, but she would never forgive herself if she missed Joel.

'Mum!' he asked again. 'How do space pirates walk the plank?'

'Maybe . . .' Arriving at the gate, Poppy scanned the playground. 'They have a swimming pool on board the spaceship.'

'Yes,' agreed Gabriel. 'Because they would need to keep fit.'

She looked down at her son, and considered once again that she didn't deserve him. He didn't whine once on the way up the long incline. 'You're a wonder, do you know that?'

'It makes sense when you think about it.' He shrugged. 'It's not like they can go running.'

Poppy was able to relax now they had arrived. It was a glorious day, with barely a wisp of cloud in the blue sky and the faintest of breezes to take the edge off the heat. The air crackled with the sound of children playing and parents chattering. She wore a mauve athlete vest and compression knee-length jogging pants, a set from Sweaty Betty, and her favourite pair of orange trainers.

'What's the man look like, anyway?'

'He's not a man, he's your Uncle Joel.'

'I don't have an Uncle Joel.'

'But you do.' Poppy retied her ponytail and looked around the play area. 'You just haven't met him.'

It was a sad state of affairs that Gabe had never met her brother, and she hoped he wouldn't ask why, because she didn't want to have to try to explain her tangled family history.

'I'm going to the sandpit.' Gabriel began to run. 'And the climbing frame.'

'Don't leave my sight, okay?'

But Poppy wouldn't let Joel slip away again. He would become a fixture in her son's life. It would be a new start for them both. It was unforgivable that they had lost touch in the first place.

What had torn their family apart had happened a long time ago, and it was time to heal the wounds. Poppy was excited to know what Joel was doing in life and was sure that, whatever it was – something for the benefit of humanity, no doubt – he was a big success. Her brother excelled at whatever he did, just like her own clever son.

A thin man stared at her and then – oh god – walked slowly towards her. The last thing she needed was to get hassle from some creepy guy. But as he approached, shoulders slumped, she realised with shock who it was. She hadn't got a good look on the train, but now she saw how terrible Joel looked. The skin on his gaunt face hung slackly and there were grey hollows gouged into his cheeks. His lank hair was flat against his scalp. The clothes he wore were cheap and dirty. A sports jacket sagged over a beige hoodie; jeans billowed from his frame, the belt cinched tight on his narrow hips; his black trainers were comically large and kept on by curled Velcro straps.

Poppy remembered Joel's athletic build as a young man, and his handsome looks, his boundless energy. There was a spark in his eyes back then, a quick-witted intelligence, but now his gaze was heavy-lidded. She smiled, despite the panic she felt that something was very wrong. He had a terrible disease or some kind of tumour, it was the only explanation.

'Hello, Pops.'

'Oh, Joel,' she said, 'what's happened to you?'

She led him to a bench, hardly daring to touch him in case he fell. He sat, spine curled, hands on his knees. She couldn't take her eyes off him. He smelled the way he looked, like something abandoned.

'It's a shock, I know,' he said. 'I'm just . . . having a bit of trouble sleeping.'

'I'm going to help you.' She didn't have to think twice

about it. He was her *brother*. 'I don't know what's . . . happened, but I'm going to do my best.' She looked to the sandpit and was alarmed when she couldn't see Gabriel. But then she saw him dangling from a climbing frame. 'I tried to contact you, I left messages, but they told me you had moved.'

If he explained how he came to be like that – showed any emotion at all – she would have felt better. But he just sat there, as if he didn't even have the energy to muster a reaction. It was devastating. This person wasn't her brother, this *thing* wasn't Joel.

'That's my son,' she said, trying to get him to talk. 'You'll like Gabriel, he reminds me of you when . . .'

'Are you still with . . . ' He closed his eyes, trying to remember the name.

'With Tim, yes.'

Poppy sat unhappily, trying to absorb everything. A passing mother glanced at them, and Poppy felt embarrassed. They made a strange pairing. Poppy, lithe and healthy, and Joel . . . like a phantom, a wraith forced into daylight.

Poppy saw his head drift to one side, and asked, 'What are you looking at?'

'The cliff,' he said. 'Where Will was.'

'Oh, Joel.' It had been a long time since she'd been forced to think about the terrible thing that had happened to their brother. She felt a knot of fear harden in her stomach. 'What do you see?'

'Just . . . the clifftop,' he said. 'But he's gone.'

'You mustn't . . . ' She shook her head. 'Don't think about what that girl did.' Her hand chopped the air angrily. 'Just don't!'

'I see it all the time.'

Poppy couldn't, *wouldn't*, let those memories back in. What happened on that cliff had been the beginning of the end for them all. For Mum and for Dad, for their family. And it meant Poppy was forced to think about that awful girl, the cause of all their unhappiness.

'Gabe!' Poppy stood when she saw her son clamber to the top of the frame. 'Get down, now!'

'I'm fine,' he yelled.

'Down – right now!'

The boy rolled his eyes, but swung his leg to a lower rung. Gabriel was precious, he was everything, and she would take no chances. She and Tim tried for many years to have a child and feared they would never be blessed. Her parents had exposed their own children to a social experiment without considering their children's safety, and their careless-ness had had tragic consequences.

'A good thing has happened.'

She wondered what he could possibly mean. It didn't look like anything remotely good had happened to Joel for a long time. When she took his hand, the papery touch of his fingers made her nauseous – and ashamed.

'She's back,' he said.

'I don't understand.'

'Sarah's come back to us, Pops.'

She snatched her hand away. It was already a shock seeing him like this, and now he was talking about *her*.

'She wants to see you,' Joel said.

Hell would freeze over before she let that creature back into her life. But when she looked up, a woman was silhou-etted against the sun.

'Oh, Poppy, it is so good to see you.' When Poppy jumped

up and marched to the climbing frame, Tatia fell into step beside her. 'It has been so long.'

'Stay away!' Poppy couldn't bear to look at her. 'Gabe, we're going!'

'We need your help.' Tatia raced to keep up. 'Joel needs your help.'

The boy was tangled in the lower rungs, one leg lifting over his head.

'Gabe, we have to go.' Poppy tried to stay calm among all the children. 'Get down *now*!'

'We just got here!' said her son, hanging upside down.

'I understand how you must feel.' Tatia's fingers plucked at Poppy's arm. 'But please listen to me.'

Poppy snatched her elbow away. 'Keep away!'

'You are so beautiful,' said Tatia. 'Look at you, you have become a gorgeous woman.'

Poppy dragged her son off the frame – 'Ow!' he complained – and pulled him towards the gate, refusing to look back. She stopped in front of Joel.

'Do you remember what happened the last time that woman came into our lives? Do you remember what happened to Will?' She was nearly in tears. The nature of his condition, the state of him, was all too clear to her now. 'My god, Joel, what has she done to you?'

Tatia appeared at her side. 'We would like to—'

Poppy took a good look at Tatia for the first time and wanted to laugh. When she was a girl, everyone had said how pretty Tatia was – it used to infuriate Poppy. But she was no longer the skinny young girl who had bounded into their lives to cause so much unhappiness. Far from it. Now she was a dumpy thing, all lumps and bumps. The badly cut hair didn't help, or the ridiculous knee-length cargo shorts around her thick thighs, the walking boots and long socks edged with red hearts.

But that smile was just the same; she remembered that wretched smile.

'Please be quiet.' Poppy stuck a hand in Tatia's face, and said to Joel, 'I'm sorry for what has happened to you, but I will not – look at me, Joel!' His eyes lifted slowly from the ground to meet hers. 'I will not allow that woman to come anywhere near me or my son. My *son*, Joel.'

'Sarah and I need your help.'

'Don't keep calling her that.' Poppy scowled. 'She's Tatia. Tatia something, Tatia Marmalade.' She laughed bitterly. '*That's* who she is.'

Poppy had painstakingly built something good out of the ruin of her childhood. A time that was meant to be precious, full of innocence and joy. A time of security, of safety, of unconditional love. And it was – until *she* came.

'You have a boy!'

Poppy flinched when she realised Tatia was still following her to the gate.

Her son looked over his shoulder. 'Who's that?'

'Don't look at her!' Poppy pushed him forward.

'He looks like you. Such a handsome boy!'

'Do you like jokes?' Gabriel asked her.

'I love jokes!'

'Stay away from him!'

'I am sorry, it was never my intention to—'

Poppy wheeled to face her. 'Whatever deluded thought you have in your head, you are not, and never will be, part of our family.'

Poppy was almost shouting, and people looked to see what was happening.

'Joel needs your help.' When Poppy lifted Gabriel over the closed gate, Tatia snatched at her wrist. 'Please!'

'Have you told him?' Poppy asked, low. 'About what really happened?'

'Of course not,' said Tatia. 'I would *never* tell him.'

For a split second, Poppy considered whether to give this despicable woman a chance, just hear her out, but the feel of Tatia's rough fingers on her arm made her flesh crawl. There was something *off* about Tatia, always had been. She tried to pull away, but Tatia slipped something into her hand – a piece of paper with a phone number on it.

Yanking her arm away, Poppy screwed up the number and threw it in her bag. She grabbed at a passer-by.

'Is there anything the matter?' The man eyed Tatia. 'Is this person bothering you?'

'I'm scared for my son's safety.' Poppy's voice trembled as she clanged the gate shut behind her. 'Please, if this woman follows me, will you call the police?'

The man pulled his phone out of his pocket. 'Of course.'

Poppy walked quickly down the hill, Gabriel trotting beside her, looking over his shoulder. She was certain she heard Tatia call, 'Goodbye, Poppy!'

She's insane, deranged, thought Poppy. She was almost running towards the car park, trembling with rage – and fear.

Tatia lifted Joel off the bench, avoiding the suspicious looks of all the parents, and led him out of the playground. 'Let's get you back.'

Tatia turned in the opposite direction to Poppy, towards the expanse of Parliament Hill above them, a sea of grass browning in the sun. But when she looked back, Joel – shoulders hunched, spine curved – was watching Poppy and her son stride towards the Lido. Tatia felt a terrible sadness for him.

'We are on our own, my darling,' she told him.

'Yes,' he said, watching Poppy. 'We'll always be on our own.'

23

11 years after Will:

'Dad!' Joel hurled his backpack to the floor and picked up the post inside the door. Bills, circulars, takeaway flyers. 'I've got to go straight out again!'

The living room was dark as usual. His father kept the curtains closed all day and the air was thick with the sour tang of stale booze. The canaries chirped in their cage. But Patrick Bliss wasn't in his usual chair at the fireplace. He could usually be found there, surrounded by a pile of broadsheet newspapers, empty bottles and a tottering selection of political memoirs. Afraid his dad had taken a fall in one of the bedrooms, Joel went upstairs – but couldn't find him.

Which meant he had gone out. On one hand, any kind of exercise Patrick Bliss took had to be a good thing. On the other, if he had been drinking, which was more than likely, he was often delivered home in a police car after getting lost. And it was kind of annoying tonight. Joel was meant to be going out himself. College mates were meeting in a pub, and despite having a ton of coursework to do, he had decided, the hell with it, he was going to let down his hair just this one night.

'Don't worry about me,' Patrick had told his son. 'I can look after myself.'

Which clearly, these days, he couldn't. If Joel wasn't there, sooner or later he would drink himself to death. When he came home, the first thing Joel did was get rid of all the bottles his father kept around the house. When Joel started confiscating them, Patrick became ever more cunning. He'd hide them behind the sofa, in the mattress of his bed, even in the guttering. He prised away skirting to stash them behind the wall.

But Joel still enjoyed the old man's company. He would often sit with his father into the early hours, listening to him put the world to rights. Joel loved to hear about his parents' political crusades when they were young. How they chained themselves to MoD property, and about the time Jill rescued her husband from beneath the legs of a horse at the poll tax riot. It was easy to forget, considering what had happened in the years since Will's death, and the terrible toll it had taken on his parents, that they were once energetic, politically committed people.

Jill and Patrick Bliss gave a damn about society, about the world. There was so much inequality, so much poverty, and Joel wanted to follow in the footsteps of his parents, was already getting involved with a number of charities and campaigns. If he had half his father's former energy he knew he could take on any challenge. But it was a battle to also fit in his studies and the part-time job that brought money into the house. And, of course, he had to look after his dad. But Patrick insisted that Joel finish his business degree. He'd take pills to stay awake and study through the night, and then be exhausted the next day.

Joel came downstairs, despondent. His father may have gone to the pub, but that wasn't his style. Like a lot of alcoholics his drinking was done alone, far from the interference of other people.

'Okay,' Joel said to the empty house. 'You're not here.'

His night off was out of the question now. He couldn't take the chance his dad would be locked out, so Joel ignored the shirt he'd ironed that morning and hung on the back of the kitchen door ready for a quick getaway, and poured himself a glass of water. There was revision he could do instead, and coursework – there was always plenty of that. He had been in the mood to celebrate with a couple of pints, too. His tutor had told him that his coursework was phenomenal, and encouraged him to fulfil his potential at a top university. But the brutal truth was, if he did that, who would look after his dad?

Lifting the glass to his lips, he glanced into the garden.

The body could have been hanging from the tree for hours. Neighbours would probably see the rope attached to the thick branch, but not the noose, or his father's corpse. Patrick's head angled away from the knot on the ligature. One eye was half open, the black tongue swollen between his teeth. His hands were clenched tightly at his sides, making him look angry. Patrick Bliss never had an angry bone in his body, but he looked tense in death, as if he had departed the world with unfinished business.

Joel stared up at his dad's body and felt a terrible sense of relief. Patrick had tried his hardest to drink himself to death but had obviously grown impatient at his lack of progress. When Joel had helped him up to his room the previous night and laid him on the bed, nothing in his behaviour suggested his intention to do anything like this – but then he had been insensible, as usual.

There was no suicide note, no rambling letter of justification. His father had never recovered from losing his wife or his youngest child. Will's death had been the moment everything changed for them all.

One moment Will was there, and the next –

Joel fumbled for his phone. He would call the police, but his first instinct was to tell Poppy. She'd want to come straight here. Standing in the shadow of his father's body, he took out his phone with trembling hands. But when her number finally rang, the tone was unfamiliar.

'Hey, Joely!' The line crackled. In the background waves crashed against a seashore. 'Greetings from the good life!'

Joel turned away from his father's angry grimace. 'Where are you?'

'We're in Cape Town. John and Tanya have rented a house on the beach. You should see this place. The penguins come right up to you!'

She was on holiday. He hadn't realised, couldn't even remember the last time he saw her. Weeks ago, maybe months. Poppy used to visit regularly, but spent most of her time with Tim's family now. When Joel spoke to her about it, she told him that seeing their father so lost was too upsetting.

'Why? Is something wrong?'

For such a young man, Joel had learned to take everything in his stride, but he didn't know how to handle this on his own – not this. Will gone. His mother, gone. Now his father.

His dad's toes pointed down into the earth, shoelaces dangling. Patrick Bliss had taken off his slippers and put on his shoes before he killed himself. 'Can you come home, please?'

Poppy's voice was muffled – he heard her fluttering laugh as she spoke to someone – and then she came back on the line. 'I've got to go. John has organised a volleyball game and everyone's annoyed I'm on the phone. Are you sure you're all right?'

'Not rea—'

'So that's good, then.' Her voice dropped. 'Sorry I've not been around, Joely, but I've been super busy. I'll come see you both as soon as I'm back, I promise! You've never been to Tanya and John's, have you? Will you come and visit? You probably need a break from Dad.'

'Poppy, I need to tell you—'

'We'll make that date as soon as I'm home.' He heard the soft thud of her bare feet on golden sand. 'Speak soon, love you!'

And then the line went dead.

Joel sat on the back step looking up at his old man's clenched fists. Knew that whatever he was going to achieve in this life, it would have to be alone.

24

Now:

They had a prime suspect. Carl Clarke was a habitual offender with a long criminal history – theft, embezzlement, numerous fraud- and drug-related convictions, but mostly burglary. Clarke loved to break into houses and had a string of burglary convictions stretching back nearly two decades to when he was a youth offender.

A CRIS search revealed his prints had turned up in a number of properties, sometimes in unusual circumstances, along with another set of prints, as yet unidentified. Drake's team had begun liaising with a number of borough commands across north London.

But identifying him was one thing, finding him another. Clarke was of no fixed abode, having left his last registered address, a bedsit in Wembley, more than a year ago and had since dropped out of sight. Former friends said he'd kipped at their place, but the arrangement usually came to a sudden end when he disappeared in the middle of the night, taking some of their belongings with him. Nor had Carl been sighted at any of his usual haunts, a low-rent selection of gyms, pubs and clubs.

But even people like Carl Clarke had a mother, and mothers had been the destination of last resort for desperate ne'er-do-wells since before the dawn of civilisation. Jean Clarke lived in a ground-floor flat off Camden Road.

Searching for somewhere to park, Drake drove his Mercedes up and down the street to find a space that wasn't below a tree so that it wouldn't get spattered in bird shit. Recycling bins were pulled onto the pavement ready for collection alongside bags of garden waste. A post trolley was padlocked to a lamp post. Flick had been distracted all the way there, a smile playing across her face as messages dinged on her phone.

'Work?' Drake asked.

'No,' she said, tapping at the screen. 'A friend.'

There was definitely a spring in her step today. He didn't know how or why, but her mood seemed to have turned a corner, and he was grateful for that. He was curious to know who she was texting, but knew she wouldn't thank him for sticking his nose in.

Minutes later, they knocked on Jean Clarke's door. A security chain jerked against the frame when it opened and a slight, bird-like woman stood there, barely as high as Drake's chest.

'Mrs Clarke?' Drake pushed his warrant card into the gap. 'May we speak to you?'

'I can't see that,' she said, 'not with my eyes.'

'Detective Inspector Ray Drake.' He passed it inside so that she could study it. 'And this is Detective Sergeant Flick Crowley. We'd like to speak to you about your son.'

'My son is here,' she said.

Drake tensed. 'Which one, Mrs Clarke?'

'Kevin. My eldest.'

'We want to speak to you about Carl.'

'Carl?' The old woman cocked her head. 'Has anything happened to him?'

'It'd probably be easier if we came inside to explain.'

'Kevin is here,' she said, 'so I warn you, if this is some kind of scam . . .'

She slammed the door on them and it stayed shut long enough for Flick and Drake to contemplate the loss of his warrant card, but then the chain dropped and the door opened. At the end of a narrow hallway was a kitchen where a very large man, the spitting image of Carl, held a chew toy high above a dog. The pit bull jumped at his chest, yelping and growling. When the dog jumped, Kevin Clarke lifted the toy out of its reach, making the animal ever more frustrated.

Kevin Clarke had also done time, for ABH and criminal damage, although his convictions were many years ago. But Drake didn't like the way he was tormenting the dog, which barked and snarled. Kevin kicked the kitchen door shut when he saw them.

Jean Clarke led Drake and Flick into a small sitting room. There was barely enough room for an armchair and sofa, a TV and a gas fire. A low glass coffee table sucked up the remaining space. She looked like she was going to burst into tears any moment. 'Shall I ask Kevin to come in?'

'It may be an idea.'

'Kevin!' She opened the door. 'Come and meet . . . who did you say?'

'DI Drake and DS Crowley.'

'The police are here!' she called down the hall in a quivering voice. 'They want to talk to us, Kevin. Stop messing about with that animal.'

143

Drake hit a shin negotiating his way along the edge of the coffee table to sit on one side of the sofa, and Flick shuffled down beside him. Mrs Clarke perched on the armchair beside the fire, rolling her thumbs in her lap.

'Please tell me nothing's happened to him.'

'When was the last time you saw your son, Mrs Clarke?'

'Please call me Jean,' she told Flick.

'When was the last time you saw your son, Jean?'

'Carl, you mean . . . it's been a number of months. As a salesman, he travels and is often out of contact.'

'What does he sell?' asked Drake.

'All sorts. He's an entrepreneur –' she stumbled on the pronunciation '– and his work takes him up and down the country. Kevin, get in here!'

A moment later her other son appeared. The powerful teeth of the growling dog were still clamped around the toy he held high in his hands, as if pumping weights on a machine. Tail tucked beneath it, the animal's hindquarters jerked and swung.

Drake stood, not liking the look of the dog one bit. 'Kevin, can you put it somewhere else?'

Kevin considered him. Like Carl, his eyes were slightly hooded and there were dark pouches beneath them. He had the same sullen expression Drake had seen in his brother's arrest photos. Arms aloft, he left the room, the dog still thrashing in front of him. Drake sat down.

The old woman was pale. 'Why do you want to know about Carl?'

'Carl is a person of interest in an investigation.'

Jean Clarke chewed her lip. Drake could only imagine the anxiety her sons had caused her. She wanted to believe

144

Carl was a successful man who travelled up and down the M1, buying and selling precious commodities, but he had done considerable time in prison. The possibility that he could go back there must be a recurring nightmare.

'Kevin,' she called. 'Are you coming back in?'

When Kevin Clarke returned – Drake heard the dog yelping and scratching at the kitchen door – he sat on the arm of his mother's chair.

'They say Carl's a person of interest,' she told him, almost in tears. 'What does that even mean?'

'What is it you want?' Kevin asked Drake.

'There've been a series of break-ins,' said Drake. 'And a number of fatalities.'

'Oh no.' Jean Clarke's eyes widened in disbelief. 'He's talking about those murders on the news.' She shook her head. 'Tell him they've got nothing to do with Carl.'

'At this stage, it's important that we talk to Carl in order that we can eliminate him from our inquiries,' said Flick.

'Eliminate him from inquiries, that's what they always say!'

'Mum, calm down.'

'Do you know where we can find him, Kevin?' asked Flick.

'Carl's a good boy. They've got the wrong person. Tell them they've got the wrong person, Kevin.'

'There's forensic evidence that places Carl at a number of crime scenes,' said Drake.

Jean Clarke stood to pace anxiously in the narrow space in front of the fire. Her voice lifted shrilly. 'No, no, no.'

'Mum.' Kevin pressed his fingers into his eyes. 'Why don't you sit down?'

'How can I sit down when these people come into our house and say such terrible things?'

'Mrs Clarke,' said Flick, 'I know what you must be feeling right now.'

'How could you cocksuckers know what I think?'

Drake blinked, wondering if he had heard right.

Kevin's head dropped. 'Mum.'

'That's what you are.' Her upper lip curled over her teeth. 'Cocksuckers. You people disgust me. All you ever do is spread lies about my boy.'

'Mum—'

She spun angrily to face her son. 'And you can shut up. You're jealous of him!'

'Yeah.' Kevin sighed. 'That must be it.'

'Because Carl is a *real* man.' She lunged forward, snarling. 'A masculine man. He's not a henpecked worm, like some.'

Kevin turned his face away. 'That'll be it.'

'Your brother is twice the man you are!'

'Mum.' Kevin folded his arms. 'I'm married to a former Miss Maidstone. I've three lovely kids and a five-bedroomed house, with a company car and annual bonus, private pension and health insurance. I got a Sky subscription – movies, sports, the lot. I'm a member of an expensive golf club and I've got a timeshare in Spain. I'm taking the kids skiing for the second time this year, and on a cruise. Last time I looked, Carl was still stealing and lying, and had jack shit to his name.' He gestured at Drake and Flick. 'And now it turns out he's very possibly killing people. Yeah, Carl's a real fucking role model to me.'

Jean Clarke's face contorted with rage. 'Every time that

146

little bitch throws you out, you come crawling back to your mother. Like a maggot!'

'I stayed here once for three days, and that was twelve years ago. Carl used to turn up every other week and piss off with half your savings.'

His mother turned to Drake and Flick. 'If you want to speak to me then you'll have to drag me kicking and screaming to your shithouse of a station.'

'Remember what the doctor said about your—'

Jean Clarke pointed at her son. 'His own wife stops his kids seeing their grandma and he does nothing.'

Kevin smacked his thighs in exasperation. 'And you wonder why?'

The animal scrabbled at the kitchen door, barking.

'Mrs Clarke,' said Drake. 'I'm going to have to ask you to calm down.'

'You leave my Carl alone,' she said. 'He's a good man, a man's man, and he's worth a hundred thousand of you. I hope wherever he is and whatever he's doing, he's happy. I hope you don't catch him. I hope you get cancer and die.'

Drake looked at Kevin, who nodded towards the door.

'You're scum,' said Jean Clarke. 'Along with the judges and the lawyers and the juries and the social workers and the probation officers who like nothing more than to ruin the lives of innocent people. Go, on, clear off.' She spat on her own carpet. 'And don't come back, or I'll set that dog on you.'

'We'll see ourselves out,' said Drake.

'I'll make sure they go, Mum.'

'Dump 'em in a river like kittens. Line them up against a wall!'

Kevin Clarke led them outside.

147

'Sorry about that. The wife won't let her into our house so I come to see her now and then.' Jean Clarke made an obscene gesture in the window. 'Don't know why I bother. She gets wound up about everything.'

'Wound up?' Flick let out a long breath. 'That's putting it mildly.'

'Is it true what you said?' he asked. 'About those home invasions?'

Drake nodded. 'We have DNA evidence linking Carl to a number of properties, and video footage of someone who looks very like your brother in one of the homes.'

Kevin looked back at the house. 'Carl doesn't give a shit about her, but she thinks the sun shines out of his behind. I've sent her on holidays, filled up her pension pot, she wants for nothing thanks to me. But that big fucking baby of a brother has always been her favourite. Funny old world.'

'Your mother said she hasn't seen Carl – is that true?'

'Not for months. Neither of us have, and I ain't got any interest in seeing him.'

Drake sensed that Kevin wanted to open up. 'We'll take anything.'

'Carl's into his kickboxing.' He walked further along the road so they couldn't be seen from the house. 'There's a pub up by Borehamwood where they put on fights, the Worthington it's called, and Carl was always there, selling whatever he'd nicked. He used to fight, too, but he was as rubbish at that as he is at everything else. He was mates with a promoter called Riz Arda. I bumped into Riz the other week and he told me he'd seen Carl there.'

'When?' asked Flick.

'Two or three weeks ago, maybe a month.'

148

'Where can we find Riz?' asked Flick.

'At the Worthington on fight night.'

'And when do they hold fights?' asked Flick.

'Once a week. Tonight, in actual fact.' He sighed. 'Look, I'd better go in and calm her down.'

'Thanks for your help,' said Drake.

'If he's involved in these murders then Carl deserves everything he gets. You won't believe me but he used to be a sweet kid, except he'd steal your last peppermint if he got the chance. He can't help it, it's a compulsion. Getting into people's homes is the only talent he's ever had, and let's face it, kicking a door down ain't much to shout home about.'

'Does Carl have a girlfriend?' asked Drake.

'Don't know and don't care.'

Flick nodded at the house. 'Are you going to be okay?'

'Mum's bark is usually worse than her bite. A cup of tea and a couple of custard creams and she'll be back in old lady mode.' Kevin shrugged. 'Or she could set the dog on me. It could go either way.'

25

Ray Drake pulled his car off the dual carriageway and onto the rutted gravel surface of the car park, trying to avoid some of the deepest potholes. The Edwardian pub's original features, the colourful tiles and ceramics, had been removed, the etched windows replaced and the masonry painted black. A large plastic banner promising a free cocktail for the ladies every Friday night drooped across the length of the first floor. The only thing that protected the pub from the four lanes of traffic was a hedge that trembled against the force of the lorries trundling past remorselessly. Two bouncers in quilted jackets stood at the entrance, where a scruffy collection of men hunched over cigarettes. When Flick cracked open the window, she heard shouts coming from inside, even over the drone of traffic.

Eddie Upson said, 'This is going to be fun.'

'Stay here.' Drake killed the engine and looked over his shoulder at Flick, who had somehow been relegated to the back when Eddie jumped in front.

'No way.' She was still annoyed Eddie had come with them on account of his once watching a movie that featured martial arts. 'I'm coming in.'

'I was thinking more about my car.' Drake turned to Eddie, but he had already clambered out.

'I'm happy to come back outside,' said Eddie, hunched at the window. 'But I really need a piss.'

As they approached the entrance, the smokers watched them warily. Inside, a bell rang, followed by cheers. One of the doormen, a red-headed fellow with a football club crest tattooed on his neck, told them to pay at a vestibule inside the door. Eager to get inside, Eddie took out his wallet.

'Make sure you claim it back,' said Drake.

The crowded space inside was dimly lit, the walls painted black and studded with pillars. In the middle of the room, starkly bright beneath an array of floodlights hanging from a steel frame, was a boxing ring surrounded by a padded fence webbed with netting. Inside, two barefooted men bobbed and weaved around the canvas, jabbing and kicking, ducking and feinting. They grappled briefly, spinning in each other's arms, before being separated by a referee. One of the fighters landed a punch, sending his opponent bouncing against the padding, and the crowd roared. Flick didn't know much about kickboxing, but the guy getting a kicking looked too old and unhealthy to be in the ring. His gut wobbled as he lumbered about.

Flick, Drake and Eddie loitered at the edge of the crowd of middle-aged men. Pints slopped in their hands as they snarled and shouted at the ring. A pair of customers elbowed each other when they saw the three police. Flick knew they had to be alert in this place, sensing Drake's tension too as he moved from one group to another, asking about Riz Arda.

Eddie pointed at a sign for the toilet at the far end of the room and started pushing through the crowd. 'Won't be long.'

'Wash your hands,' called Flick.

Drake returned. 'He's over there.'

When they headed towards Riz, many of the men made a point of stepping away, as if they were contaminated. Riz was a tall man in a silver puffa jacket, skinny jeans and an elaborate pair of trainers. A razor-thin line around his jaw may or may not have been a beard – it was difficult to tell in the low light.

'People in suits.' He laughed as they approached. 'Don't see that much in here.'

'Riz Arda?' asked Drake.

'I'd love to talk.' Riz nodded at the older fighter, who just about managed to avoid a kick from his opponent. 'But I'm supporting my man Lee right now.'

'Detective Inspector Ray Drake.'

'You look like filth.' Riz turned his attention back to the ring just as the older fighter unexpectedly landed a punch, knocking the younger man sideways. Riz's hands lifted eagerly. 'Get him! Take advantage!'

'Carl Clarke,' said Drake, watching the fight. 'We need to speak to him.'

Lee pranced about the ring, soaking up the excitement, but then nearly toppled under a furious hail of retaliatory punches. The crowd, sensing blood, surged forward.

'Fuck's sake.' Riz turned to Drake. 'Why do you want to speak to him, anyway?'

'Carl is a person of interest in an investigation.'

'Haven't seen Carl for ages.' Riz nudged his mate, a small, round man in a tracksuit who leered at Flick. 'Nev, when was the last time we saw Carl?'

The other man blew out his cheeks. 'Thought he'd joined the merchant navy, it's been that long.'

Riz held up his hands in despair when Lee took a blow to the side of the head and went down. 'Get up and fight!'

'Our understanding is that he was here a couple of weeks ago,' Drake shouted over the roar of the crowd. 'With you.'

'You've been misinformed. Carl used to be one of my fighters, yeah, but not for long. He was enthusiastic, but he couldn't be coached – he just wanted to get in the ring and rip the other fella apart.'

'Where can we find him, Riz?'

The bell rang for the end of the round and Riz shook his head. 'Look, I don't appreciate your coming here to see me at my place of work. In front of my mates, my associates. You'll give me a bad rep.'

'Tell us where and we'll be gone in an instant. Or give us the name of someone who will know.' A man walked past, purposely slopping his pint. Flick had to tug Drake out of the way before it spilled on his shoes. 'Five people have been killed – so far.'

Riz's gaze snapped sharply to Drake. He looked shocked. But when he saw people in the crowd watching him talk to police, his expression hardened. 'Not here,' he said, low. 'This is not a safe place for you.'

The bell rang for the next round and the two fighters stepped forwards. Lee thumped his chest, jutted out his jaw, trying to convince the crowd this bout was in the bag. But he was looking tired. The combatants slammed together in a flurry of kicks and jabs. The screaming crowd edged closer to the ring. Flick smelled the stench of weed somewhere in the pub.

'So let's do it tomorrow,' she heard Drake shout into Riz's ear over the clamour. 'You can tell us about Carl at the station.'

'Fine. We'll do it then, now piss off.'

Drake placed a card into his hand. 'Let's say nine, Riz, or we'll be back.'

Riz yanked his arm away, making a big show of it for the benefit of the people around him.

'Let's go,' Drake said to Flick, just as Lee took a punch to the nose. He fell to the canvas, blood spurting everywhere. 'Where's Eddie?'

'Toilet,' she said.

A man climbed into the ring to attend to Lee's injury. The younger fighter hopped on his toes, sweat flying off him, celebrating as if he'd won a world title in Vegas.

Where the hell was Eddie? Flick's eyes scanned the crowd. She saw Riz talking to a pair of other men, darting anxious glances at Drake. Leaning against a wall, she checked her messages again. She was all over her phone today, like a teenager, checking it every five minutes. She and Wylie had spoken earlier and she'd told him she was coming to this place, and her heart leapt when she saw his message:

Try and stay out of trouble ☺

The cheeky git. Something told her he'd be in his element here, in the thick of it, the life and soul. She imagined him at the bar, one of the lads, buying everybody a drink. The fact was, she couldn't wait to see him again tonight.

Her fingers hovered over the touchscreen as she considered her reply, trying to think of something sarcastic and flirtatious, but which didn't make her sound too keen, and her gaze drifted absently across the crowd.

And she saw him.

Carl Clarke was slipping inside through an emergency exit. Nodding to people, slapping backs, walking about as if he owned the place. She glimpsed Riz press urgently through the crowd towards him.

'Ray.' She pushed herself off the wall. 'Ray!'

Drake tore his eyes from the ring, but Clarke had already been swallowed up in the throng. Instead they saw Riz speak urgently to Nev and another man, who began to move through the crowd, spreading the word.

'Clarke's here,' she told him.

'Let's go.' Drake took her arm to pull her towards the door, but she snatched her elbow back.

'What about Eddie?'

'Get to the car and get a unit here,' he said. 'I'll get Eddie.'

Groups of men began to point. Someone shouted. Drake pressed his keys into her hand. But the crowd had already begun to heave. Clarke was like a heavy stone that had been dropped into a pool of water, churning the surface, sending turbulent waves in every direction. Two burly men came towards Flick and Drake, cutting them off from the exit. One of them smiled, baring his teeth.

'Coppah!' he shouted. 'Coppah!'

The other one pointed. 'Filth!'

They lifted their arms, encouraging others to join in.

Coppah!

Pig!

Within a moment, Flick and Drake were encircled. The atmosphere had turned nasty in a heartbeat. Anger pulsed through the room.

'We have to go,' said Drake. 'Now!'

'But Eddie!'

155

A plastic pint glass of lager arced up in the air and came down in front of them, spraying everywhere. The volume of noise went up. Another plastic glass soared high. Flick glimpsed Riz cupping his mouth to Carl Clarke's ear at the back of the crowd.

The men pressed forward, a pulsing wall of muscle. It would be suicide to even think about trying to get to the entrance. Drake grabbed Flick's hand and led her along the edge of the bar as, emboldened, the men at the front stepped closer.

'Clarke will get away!'

'Move!' said Drake.

A man at the front was pulled from behind by one of the bouncers and he threw a punch. A fight broke out. Flick saw Clarke trying to move towards them, but Riz held him back and pushed something into his hand, something squat and black, and shoved him towards an exit.

A chair smashed behind the bar, shattering bottles and glasses. The crowd's frenzy increased. All it would take was for one of the men to commit to a punch, a kick, and she and Drake would go down in an instant. Faces lunged out of the pack. Shouting, taunting, jaws snapping.

Flick reached for her phone but Drake's was already in his hand.

'Get back!' He held out his ID to the men closest, barked into the receiver. 'We need a response unit right now! We need it now!'

Eddie came out of the toilet at the side of the crowd and saw Clarke slipping out of the back.

'Eddie, wait!' Flick shouted, but there was no way he would hear. He shouldered his way along the wall and raced out of the emergency exit after Clarke. She pressed herself against the bar and followed Drake towards a door behind the counter.

'Carl's got a—'

And then something soared out of the air – a can of lager – and hit Drake in the forehead. It spun away on the floor, spurting liquid. He stumbled and Flick pulled him up, pushed him behind the bar – just as the crowd finally surged. Glasses and bottles exploded around her head and along the bar. Fragments of glass flew in every direction, snagging in her hair. She just about managed to shove Drake through the office door as a group of men ran behind the counter.

Drake dropped to one knee in the small space, still groggy, as Flick slammed shut the door and braced her weight against it. The door thumped angrily and the soles of her feet bounced off the floor.

Climbing to his feet, Drake pulled a desk towards the door. 'Hold them off!'

She wanted to laugh, because she was just one woman against a mob of men. Their combined weight and power would have the door open in a heartbeat. Her shoes slid uselessly on the floor. Palms banged against the safety glass in the door's circular window. Fingers slid through the gap widening against the frame and she knew – terror crackled inside her – that there was no way she would get it closed.

Then Drake bent back the fingers. Flick heard a scream and they disappeared from the gap. He pushed the desk against the door, bracing it beneath the handle. The door juddered angrily against it, but held.

Flick caught her breath and looked around. They were in an office barely bigger than a cell, lit by a single lamp.

There was a small window high in the wall. They weren't going anywhere till backup arrived. Drake leaned into the desk, pressing the heel of his hand into the gash in his temple. Blood poured down his face.

'Where the hell is that response unit?' he said into his phone, and Flick heard an urgent voice on the other end.

'Eddie has gone after Clarke,' she said, but Drake was barking into the phone. She stepped in front of him so he couldn't ignore her. 'Clarke's got a gun, Ray. He's armed!'

26

Lindy was always going on to him about getting to the gym. Getting fit, losing weight. But when you had four kids and worked long hours, the last thing you wanted to do was spend your precious free time running on a treadmill. Eddie didn't have the energy or the inclination. He was fit enough to pass his annual police medical, just about, and that worked for him.

But all those beers and takeaways were taking their toll on Eddie Upson as he tried to keep pace with Carl Clarke along the dirty verge of the road. He felt his breath rattle, his lungs burn, tasted the metallic tang of exhaust from the traffic hurtling past.

The last thing Eddie intended to do was catch Clarke, a man the size of a maisonette, who had possibly killed five people already. But he would follow him to the ends of the earth until help arrived. This whole area would soon be crawling with squad cars, and younger, fitter officers with deadly weapons would take up the chase.

The phone in Eddie's hand rang and rang but he didn't have the breath to run and speak at the same time, so he gripped it in his sweaty hand and concentrated on keeping Clarke, who lumbered along the verge a few hundred yards ahead, in his sights.

Clarke ran into the road. Eddie heard horns blare and

the screech of brakes, and it was his sincerest wish that he would hear a crunch and see Clarke cartwheel in the sky. But then he glimpsed him on the other side of the carriageway, disappearing down the side of the steep verge towards a boarded-up restaurant.

Eddie held his jacket sleeve to his mouth against the filth spewing from exhausts as cars blipped past – three, four, five in the blink of an eye – and tried to find a way across the dense wall of traffic. He could stop the pursuit right now, nobody would blame him for it, but there were trees behind the empty building, and a cycle track. He glimpsed the reflectors of a bike gliding along the trail. Clarke could grab somebody's bike and be gone in a matter of seconds. Eddie needed to know which way he was going or they would lose him for sure.

His phone rang again and he answered it, trying not to slip off the verge into the path of the traffic. He could just about make out Flick's urgent voice on the other end, but not what she was saying. Cars, the flatulent brap of a motorbike, the rumble of a van passing by so close that it made his tie dance in his face, drowned out her words. A space opened in the near lane, a brief miraculous gap in the flow of traffic, and he had to make an instant decision. Eddie rushed towards a narrow island between the two lanes of traffic, glimpsing Clarke disappear into the trees.

'Flick,' he shouted as an articulated lorry blared past his nose, its long load trundling endlessly past, blue tarpaulin flapping in the wind. 'I can't hear you!'

She shouted something. 'Ed – he – as a – un –'

'Wait till I get across!'

He evaluated the distance of the wall of traffic surging

towards him. Calculated he had just enough time to get to the other side. He ran for it but a car came out of nowhere, its horn blared, and Eddie threw himself onto his hands and knees on the far verge, heard a crunch. His mobile had slipped out of his sweaty hand. He saw it shatter into a dozen pieces beneath the wheels of a car, its parts scattering across the road.

'Shit!' Another car crunched over it, but Eddie had no time to watch. He stumbled down the verge and across the empty car park of the restaurant, tentatively negotiating the steep slope of grass to the cycle track. When he got there, the track was empty in both directions.

Eddie groaned. His sopping shirt had chilled against his spine. He walked in a frustrated circle, annoyed that he had let Clarke escape. Eddie climbed back up the hill to the car park, slipping over and smearing mud all over his thigh. *Perfect.* Lindy would kill him for ruining a perfectly good pair of trousers.

And then he felt a searing pain in his neck, as if someone was snapping it in two. His shoulders jerked back and his feet were lifted onto their toes as he was pushed, by an enormous force, towards the metal bins behind the empty building.

His legs picked up momentum on the gravel. A metal bin came towards him at shocking speed. Eddie hit it straight on. The clang as he rebounded off the container was as loud as the crash of a cymbal. He crumpled to the ground.

Head spinning, the world swinging wildly in his vision, he sensed rather than saw a figure leaning over him.

'Leave us alone.'

A hand reached down and the buttons on Eddie's shirt popped as he was pulled up.

'Why can't you just . . .' Eddie was thrown at another canister. He hit it hard and slid down the side, a firestorm of pain wracking his body. 'Leave us alone!' Curled on the ground, he saw Clarke's legs stomp towards him. 'What have we ever done to you?'

Eddie flopped onto his stomach, blindly reaching for the cold wheel of the container to heave himself forward. His brain screamed that he should get away, that he was going to die. Every inch he moved was agony. And then a foot pounded into his ribs and he rolled, his left arm trapped beneath him, the bright blue sky blinding in his eyes.

And when he focused he saw a –

Oh god, a gun.

'You people don't understand.' The cold metal barrel of the weapon was pressed between Eddie's eyes. He felt Carl's tears spatter on his cheek. His attacker's face was a picture of misery. 'We just want to be together.'

And then he saw Carl's finger tighten on the trigger.

Eddie Upson opened his mouth to scream but he had no idea if anything came out.

27

Drake's injury was treated at the scene, but the gouge wasn't deep.

'Where is he?' he asked Millie Steiner, and she nodded across the car park to where Eddie sat on a grass incline going through his pockets. Drake walked to him along the side of the road as traffic roared past in the late evening.

'Lost something?'

'A dry-cleaning ticket.' Eddie ran his hands frantically through all the items he'd thrown on the grass: money, cards, keys, crumpled receipts. 'Lindy's been on at me to pick up her clothes for weeks now, she'll be angry.'

'She's not going to be angry with you, Eddie, she's going to be relieved to have you home.' Drake watched him take off his jacket to search the pockets again. 'And anyway, the dry cleaners will be shut.'

Eddie triumphantly found a small green slip. 'She would have killed me.'

'Let's get you to hospital, Eddie, you could have internal injuries.'

'Yeah.' Eddie picked up all the items. Drake could see his head was all over the place from the shock of confronting, for one terrifying moment, his own death.

It turned out the gun was a fake. When Clarke had tried to squeeze the trigger, it didn't move. A minute later, when a squad car arrived, Clarke was long gone. They'd found the replica in the trees.

Drake looked at the vehicles parked outside the Worthington, blue and yellow lights spinning in the dusk, and the remaining men from the pub being led to vans. Most had disappeared by the time police units arrived at the scene, but there were still drunken stragglers, caught in the frenzy of the moment, who fancied a scrap with the law. Drake saw Flick standing with someone, but he didn't recognise the guy. When Vix Moore came along the verge, he told her to stay with Upson and headed back.

When Drake was out of earshot, Vix told Eddie: 'I'll let you take me out.'

Eddie blinked. 'What?'

'You can take me out for a drink.'

He couldn't get his head round what Vix was saying. She had made her feelings perfectly clear since that snog at the Christmas party, and had given him a wide berth. Eddie, a married man with kids, was disgusted with his behaviour for weeks afterwards. It had been a drunken mistake; he regretted it bitterly every time he clapped eyes on her, and it could never happen again. It was crazy to think he could possibly put his relationship with Lindy at risk. But it didn't stop him thinking about Vix constantly – and working on the same team, in the same office, was a kind of exquisite torture.

The irony was he didn't even like her all that much. She was cold and ambitious. Didn't give you the time of day unless she thought you could be useful to her career, and Eddie definitely fell into the not-useful category. But she stood over him now, as close to him as Clarke was earlier when he'd pointed that gun between Eddie's eyes, and he thought again of how much he desired her, and it made him wince with shame.

'I've got to go to hospital,' he said warily. 'And then get home to Lindy. Another night, maybe.'

'Okay.' She shrugged. 'But I may not want to go out on another night.'

'Help me up.'

Vix held out her hand, which was soft and warm, and he couldn't help but look at the soft blonde hairs on her arm. His ribs clicked in pain when she heaved him up.

'Let's talk about it tomorrow.'

'We'll see,' she said and walked off, leaving Eddie feeling more confused than before.

Drake watched the last of the men from the pub being driven off. A search of the area found no trace of Clarke. Flick was nowhere to be seen but the man she was with earlier was leaning up against the bonnet of a car, legs crossed at the ankles, frowning furiously at his phone.

The guy wore a battered leather jacket and low-slung jeans and a woollen tie over a shirt that strained against his flat stomach. Drake tried to work out how he fitted into what he knew of Flick's solitary life. Then the man's gaze lifted from the phone and he looked at Drake.

Just for a scant moment, a smile played across his face.

Drake walked inside the pub. The floor was sticky and littered with crushed plastic glasses and overturned chairs. Flick was speaking to a pair of officers. He loitered until she was finished.

'You okay?' he asked, crunching over the glass towards

the bar. The mirror behind it was shattered. Broken bottles littered the counter.

'Just about.' She nodded at his forehead. 'And you?'

'It's nothing,' he said. 'Riz was picked up a half mile down the road. He can spend a night in a cell and we'll speak to him first thing.'

'I'm going to go, then.'

'You want a lift?' he asked.

'No,' she said, 'I'm good.'

'Thanks for getting me into that office. If you hadn't picked me up . . .'

She smiled. 'You're welcome.'

He followed her outside, watched her walk to the scruffy man, who fell into step beside her. His hand occasionally touched her back as they walked. Drake knew exactly what would happen next. Sure enough, the guy glanced over his shoulder.

To make sure Drake was watching.

'Who is he?' He nodded at the guy when Millie approached.

'A friend of DS Crowley's,' she said.

'He got a name?'

Millie shrugged, *no idea.*

Drake watched them get into a Mazda, which was caked with a skin of dirt and pollen. The man fell into the driver's seat. Drake made a mental note of the registration. Feeling the hairs on his arms stand on end, that creeping dread return.

What did I tell you? said the voice in his ear. *You're going to need me.*

28

'I'd invite you to my place, but it's not exactly comfortable,' Wylie grinned, 'so maybe we could go to yours again.'

Flick didn't know how everything had happened so fast. She'd only known Wylie for five minutes. They'd spent more time together drunk than sober. She hardly knew anything about him. The old Flick would have run a mile. The sensible thing would have been to take a step back, take it slower. But she liked the guy, felt comfortable around him. The stark truth was, she couldn't think of anyone else to ask to come pick her up. And Wylie didn't think twice; he came straight away.

She was tired of being alone, of picking herself up off the floor. She'd run with whatever this was – it was too early to call it a proper relationship – and see where it took her. If it didn't go anywhere, then fine, no harm done. They may stay friends, or they may not. Maybe, right at this moment, she wasn't thinking straight – tomorrow she may think differently. Getting attacked by a frenzied mob kind of put things into perspective. In Flick's job there may not even be a tomorrow. What did she really have to lose?

But then she realised Wylie wasn't heading to her address at all, and instead they ended up somewhere in Enfield. She reminded herself all over again that she hardly knew a thing about him.

'Wait here,' he said.

'Where are we?'

Kids on the pavement opposite threw fries at each other outside a kebab shop. A thick pillar of glistening meat turned slowly in the window, its pungent smell wafting over the road. All the other units along the row were shuttered.

Wylie whipped the keys from the ignition. 'Won't be long,' he said, climbing out. 'Just need to pick up a couple of things.'

A door opened in a new-build house and she saw a shapely woman, impossibly tall, silhouetted against the light from inside. A baby, no more than a few months old, was planted on her hip. Three small dogs ran around her feet.

'You want to tell me where we are?'

He leaned back in. 'The wife's house.'

'Wait, your wife?' she asked. 'The woman with the baby?'

'Won't be a moment.'

He slammed the door and went inside the house. Bored with throwing food, the kids across the street kicked a waste bin.

Annoyed at being left in the car, Flick jumped out and followed him inside. Balls of fur ran towards her, yapping, jumping at her shins. Coats bulged from a rack. Football boots, trainers and school bags were thrown against the wall. There was a giant bowl of water for the dogs, the carpet was soaked all around it, and a bowl of cat food. Clothes were tossed over the bannister and toys littered the stairs.

In a front room three boys – Flick guessed they were about ten or eleven years old – shouted over the roar of a noisy computer game, where split-screen soldiers lock-and-loaded and the rat-a-tat of explosive gunfire was impossibly loud. Then they rushed out, surrounding Wylie, all three of them speaking at once, trying to get his attention. He held up his hands, barely able to get a word in, told them he'd come and see them in a minute. In an instant, they disappeared back into the front room and the gunfire began again.

As soon as they were gone, the woman out of sight in the kitchen spoke urgently to Wylie. Flick just about heard the words 'unacceptable,' 'selfish,' 'money'. He leaned against the frame of the kitchen door fiddling with his phone.

'Astrid,' he told the woman, 'this is Flick.'

Wylie's wife appeared in the doorway, her long feet planted at an angle on the tiles in a cheap pair of flip-flops so that she could balance the baby on one sharp hip. She was one of the most striking people Flick had ever seen, even without make-up. With her long blonde hair and big blue eyes, the ski-jump nose and her strong, lithe legs, Flick thought she should be striding imperiously down a catwalk rather than standing in the kitchen of a cramped redbrick in Enfield. The baby goggled at Flick.

'Huh.' Astrid gave her the once-over, taking her time about it, and continued her conversation with Wylie, speaking in a thick Nordic accent. 'His dog? Why do you want it?'

Wylie peered at his phone. 'Just let me talk to him.'

'For how long?'

'It'll just be for a night,' he said. 'Don't sweat it.'

'Get off!' screamed one of the boys next door and another rowdy argument started.

'Boys!' Astrid called half-heartedly.

Regretting coming inside, Flick whispered to Wylie, 'I'll wait outside,' but she didn't move.

'Put away your phone while I talk to you and take the child.' Wylie dropped the mobile in his pocket and she heaved the child into his arms. 'And if you want to borrow the dog you must pay him for it.'

'Hold this.' Wylie somehow managed to immediately press the child onto Flick. Its blue eyes, like small planets in its chubby cheeks, stared up at her. It smelled of shampoo and that hot, sweet fragrance common to all babies. Then Wylie disappeared into the front room. Flick heard the kids shout when he went in.

Flick tried to think of something to say. 'You have a nice place.'

'It's a shithole.' Astrid shrugged and took an apple from a bowl and crunched into it. 'But it's all he can afford, or so he says. I don't believe him. What's your name?'

'Flick Crowley.'

She turned the apple in her long fingers. 'You are a brave woman, Flit Crowley.'

'Flick,' she corrected. 'How do you mean, brave?'

Ignoring her, Astrid called to Wylie, who stood in the hallway talking quietly to one of the boys. 'When are you going to move your stuff out?'

'Soon!' called Wylie over his shoulder.

'I'll take it to the tip,' she shouted, but then shook her head at Flick: *no I won't*. 'His things are still all here, it's been months now. I've asked him to take it, but he refuses. It's almost as if he knows he'll move back eventually.' She rotated the apple, looking for somewhere else to bite it. 'Who knows what the future will bring, huh?'

The baby grumbled in Flick's grasp, and Astrid threw the core across the kitchen into the sink and took the child from her. 'And note how he hasn't even acknowledged his youngest. There is a coldness in his heart, Flit Crowley.'

'How long have you been . . . split up?'

'I didn't say we were split up.' Astrid looked annoyed. 'He'll come back eventually, it's what he does. He knows he'll never find anybody who loves him like I do, or who can make such sweet love to him.'

Flick blushed as Wylie came back, holding out his hands like a showman. 'Look at you, my two favourite girls.'

Astrid rolled her eyes. 'What did Edmund say?'

'I can take the dog.'

'When?'

'Soon,' he said, just as a massive explosion came from next door and the kids started shouting again.

Astrid made a dismissive *pfft* sound. 'And what do I get for the trouble?'

Wylie took out another roll of notes and peeled away half of them to give her. Flick couldn't even begin to guess how much money was there. 'Don't spend it all at once. And this is something for the boys.' He peeled off more money, holding it out of her reach. 'The *boys*, Astrid.'

She snatched the money, tucked it in the waist elastic of her leggings. Then she craned her neck forward and kissed him on the lips. Embarrassed, Flick looked away.

'You have your uses, I suppose. Perhaps I will see you again, Flit Crowley. Probably not.' Astrid touched her arm and said grimly, 'Good luck.'

Wylie led her outside. One of the youths across the road called out something and Wylie lifted a middle finger. Moments later, they were accelerating up the street.

He glanced at Flick. 'You're very quiet.'

171

'I'm just trying to figure out what just happened,' she said.

The car picked up speed on the narrow street. If anyone dashed into the road they wouldn't stand a chance.

'I've known you five minutes,' she said, 'and I've just met your crazy supermodel wife.'

'Technically –' he turned to her '– she's not my wife any more, whatever she chooses to believe.'

'You have a baby!'

'What?' Wylie laughed. 'That ain't ours. She babysits for a neighbour.'

'Why would she say something like that?'

'Because she's winding you up. She can't help herself. She's bored and jealous. She's still hurting,' he said. 'You'll get used to it.'

'Will I?' asked Flick, and she braced herself as he tore out of a junction without looking. She shook her head. 'She's very . . . striking.'

'She's a piece of work is what she is. It probably takes a bit of getting used to, I understand that, but it doesn't change how I feel about us.'

'There is no *us*.'

He swung the car over to the side of the road, braking so hard that the seatbelt snapped against her chest.

'There could be.' His jacket brapped against the leather seat when he faced her. 'There could be an us.'

'This is not the kind of thing I'm used to . . . this kind of entanglement.'

'She's just a mate. Whatever she thinks, that's all she is. And the mother of my three brilliant boys.'

'She doesn't seem to think it's over.'

'She's mistaken,' he said quietly. 'So, are we?'

'Are we what?'

'Are we going to your place?'

She sighed. 'You're crazy.'

'You're probably right.' He grinned. 'But the question is, are *you* crazy?'

'You don't make it easy, do you?' Flick let out an exasperated breath and stared out the window. 'All I know is, I don't want to be alone tonight.'

29

'You can't possibly mean it. It's some kind of sick joke.'

But it wasn't a joke, not at all – Tim was leaving her. He sat at the table and calmly announced that their marriage was over. She couldn't understand it. The many years they'd been together meant nothing to him. His child meant *nothing* to him.

Poppy was happy when he'd come home early from work. But more fool her, because Tim wasn't the kind of man who took the afternoon off or indulged in the occasional sickie. It just wasn't in dependable Tim's nature. And it was when he asked her, looking tense and serious, to allow Gabe to watch television, that alarm bells started going off. Because Tim hated Gabriel watching any TV. If it was up to him, they'd ditch the box completely.

And now, a few hours later, after the conversation had gone in circles, she still struggled to comprehend what he was telling her in a gentle, patient voice. Just when she thought this day couldn't get any worse. She had seen Joel this morning, hopeful of a reconciliation, and then encountered that awful woman. It was a shock too far.

'It's not about you.' He had the audacity to roll out that terrible cliché. 'You need to understand that.'

'That's not good enough.' Tim had been forced to make long-time colleagues redundant, lately, and she knew the whole business had left him down. But now Tim was being laid off himself and was using it as an excuse to throw their marriage away. 'You must hate me so much.'

He winced. 'I have never hated you.'

'But you must.' Her nerves shrieked with emotion. 'If you're willing to destroy our marriage. We have a beautiful boy.'

Tim's gaze was full of pity. She imagined it was the kind of compassionate look he gave someone when he made them jobless.

'We've been together for so long that I can't remember a time before you,' he said. 'I need space to discover who I am. I want to travel for a year or two and see the world.'

'You're not some fucking student, Tim, you're a married man, a father!'

'I need time to discover a few things about myself,' he said quietly.

'You're depressed, in shock, it's understandable in the circumstances. But your CV is impeccable and you'll get another job in no time.'

'It's a sign.' There was a look in his eye that she didn't like one bit. 'There are times when I've just felt so trapped on the treadmill, under so much pressure because . . . you want so much.'

'So it's my fault,' she said, aghast.

'There are so many places I've wanted to see, not just from around the pool at a luxury hotel. I don't want to be one of those people who retires and then wonders where all the best years of his life have gone.' He waved at their beautiful kitchen, with its sleek lines and state-of-the-art devices, the kind of kitchen anybody would desire, as if it

175

was a prison cell. 'I don't want this any more. Come with me. We'll sell up and go away. Gabe will wake up to the roar of the ocean and the sand between his toes, he'll sleep under a sky filled with stars.'

She snorted. 'You want us to live in a shack.'

'He will have such a life.'

'His life is here.' She slapped the table in frustration. 'Your life is here.'

Something didn't add up about this whole business. She had never liked bloody camping; the idea of pissing into a hole in the ground repulsed her. This insane plan of his, sending them off god knows where, at the mercy of predators and natural disasters and jihadis – she wondered what was really behind it. He had either lost his mind, or he was a liar. The more Poppy thought about it, the more she sensed there was more to this than he was letting on.

'All Gabriel's friends are here and you want to take him away?'

'He'll make new friends.' He went to the fridge to pour himself a glass of water. That was absolutely typical of him. Most people would reach for the bottle at a time like this, but not Tim. He was always so calm, so understated, so controlled. The more she thought about it, the more she couldn't believe he was going to throw on some friendship bracelets and act like a gap-year teenager.

The malignant thought grew in her head. 'There's someone else.'

'There's no one.'

Oh, he sounded sincere. Tim never wanted to hurt anyone, or cause upset. All this crap about discovering himself was a ruse. He knew Poppy would never join him on such a ridiculous adventure and would use it as an excuse. He'd leave it a few weeks, just for decency's sake, and then up would pop another woman. That's what this was really about. Poppy and Gabriel would be forced to downsize. She would be left counting the pennies, renting somewhere in the sticks where high-speed trains rattled the windows all night, while he moved into a penthouse apartment with a younger model.

'Wow,' she murmured. 'Wow, wow, wow.'

She had been a good wife, a devoted mother. And she was a beauty. Plenty of men would be delighted to be with Poppy. But Tim was happy to blow apart a perfectly good marriage, a good life.

How was she going to explain it to friends, to neighbours? She was on the organising committee of the local literary festival, the annual street party – she couldn't show her face at that now! – and was part of a pressure group campaigning to set up a free school in the area. The humiliation would be total.

'We can discuss it when Gabriel is older.' She was desperate to find some middle ground. 'When he's gone to uni. We'll do whatever you want, if you still feel the same way.'

'I need to go now,' he said quietly.

Her anger boiled over. 'Just get a job like a normal person!'

Tim picked up his jacket, scooped up his car keys.

'Where are you going now?' she asked.

'To work,' he said, 'To finish up a few things.'

'Because work's so important to you, suddenly,' she said with as much sarcasm as she could muster.

But he had already left the room. Poppy heard Tim close the front door softly, so as not to disturb the neighbours. Such a Tim thing to do, so thoughtful and considerate.

30

'In retrospect, my actions were a mistake.' Riz Arda yawned after spending a restless night in a cell. 'But when you think about it, what happened was your fault.'

'How do you reason that?' asked Flick.

'If you hadn't come to the pub and hassled me in front of my mates, putting me in a bad light, throwing into question my good character, I may not have overreacted.'

'Myself and my colleague DI Drake could have been killed.'

'It was just fun and games.' Riz shook his head, emphatic. 'A pantomime, a bit of theatre. Banter, if you like. Nobody was meant to get hurt.'

'And yet here you are facing multiple charges. This is what we're thinking the CPS may go for.' Watching on a monitor in an adjacent room, Drake saw Millie Steiner pass a sheet of paper to Flick, who took her time reading it, before saying: 'Conspiracy to pervert the course of justice, violent disorder, rioting, aiding and abetting an escape, assisting an offender. Stop me when you're getting bored, Riz. Carrying a firearm—'

'The gun wasn't real.'

'Doesn't matter.' Flick put down the paper. 'The law applies to imitation firearms.'

'Thing is . . .' Riz winced. 'In the heat of the moment,

somebody gave it to me and I gave it to Carl, just to get him out of there. He's like a big dog, see. You give him treats as encouragement. It was the only thing I could think of.' Riz lifted his palms. 'Obviously, I regret it now.'

'A good character like yourself, I imagine you do.'

'I was just . . . I was trying to cause a distraction, get Carl out of the way.'

'But it all got out of control.'

'Exactly that.' Riz looked weary, washed out, and he rubbed his chin, which was darkening around his thin line of beard. 'I've a history of very poor decision-making under pressure. Look, are we here to talk about me or shall we talk about Carl? That's what you want to do, right? I can tell you anything you want to know.'

'Okay.' Flick clasped her hands on the table. 'Where do we find him?'

'No idea.' Riz winced again. 'Believe me, nothing would give me greater pleasure at this moment than to tell you ladies, but I can't.'

'That's very disappointing,' said Millie.

Drake watched the monitor, absently running his fingers down the worn fabric of his tie. A faint buzz came from the speaker. Beside him, Vix Moore picked at a nail.

'Millie's got the whole bad cop thing off to a tee,' she said.

'Then tell us something helpful, Riz,' said Flick in the interview room.

'What can I say?' Riz blew out his cheeks. 'Carl has always been a bit of a loner. He's a big kid, really. He tries to get close to people, be their best mate, but he's too clingy, so nobody's much interested.'

'You ever buy any stolen goods off him, Riz?'

'Are you kidding? If Carl handed me a stick of gum, I'd refuse to take it. He's always getting caught, because he's careless.'

'A careless man.' Millie smiled flatly. 'And you gave him a gun.'

'A replica.'

'You managed his career as a kickboxer,' said Flick.

'That was a long time ago. In the ring you need self-control, you need a strategy. Carl had spirit, he loved to fight, but he didn't have much going on up here.' He tapped his temple. 'Other fighters got him riled easily – he's got the emotions of a toddler – and he'd step into a punch or a kick. He was outsmarted every time.'

'We need to find him,' said Flick. 'Very quickly.'

'Let me see, he had a place in . . .' Riz clicked his fingers, making a big show of trying to be helpful. 'Wanstead, off the high street.'

'He left there nearly eighteen months ago, and we know about the place in Holloway. We've no known address for him since.'

'He's got a brother,' said Riz.

'What about a girlfriend?'

Riz peered up at the ceiling, thinking. 'Yeah, he did as it happens.'

Next door, Drake leaned closer to the monitor.

'Tell us about her,' said Flick.

'I met her once in a pub in Earl's Court. She was a nice lady, foreign. Always cheerful, always smiling. She asked lots of questions, she was curious about things.'

'What did she ask?'

180

'Whether you had family, where you lived, all the usual. And she had this disconcerting way of looking at you; she made you feel you were the most fascinating fella ever. You found yourself telling her personal stuff and she listened very carefully to what you had to say. I mean, she was weird, but I liked her.'

'Weird how?'

'She was with Carl for a start, and she definitely wore the trousers, if you get my drift.'

'Foreign, you say,' prompted Flick.

'Eastern European, something like that.' He folded his arms. 'They were an odd couple. God knows why she was with him.'

'Why do you say that?' asked Millie.

'Because it's not like he's good at anything, it's not like he kills it on the stocks and shares, or paints lovely water-colours or renovates classic cars. But he was besotted with her, like a big puppy; it's like she had this hold over him. As I say, he was always searching for a soulmate, someone to love him, to tell him how to behave, and what to do.'

'Don't suppose you have a name?'

'Bliss,' he said, without hesitation. 'Sarah Bliss.'

In the next room, Vix Moore wrote down the name and left.

Flick lifted an eyebrow. 'Impressive recall.'

'It's simple to remember, because that's what she was like – smiley, blissed-out. The name didn't sound very Eastern European to me,' he said, 'but she insisted that's who she was.'

Drake met Flick and Millie Steiner when they came out of the interview room minutes later and they hurried through

181

the labyrinth of corridors in the station, fire doors banging open as Drake surged ahead.

'We'll get him to do an e-fit of this Sarah Bliss, and let's speak to any other friends of Carl's at the pub who may have met her.'

'We don't know for sure it's the same person in the Langley house, do we?' said Millie.

'Alistair Judd said the woman he spoke to had an accent and three witnesses now have mentioned her smile.'

Vix appeared up ahead, and fell into line. 'There's nothing in the Police National Computer, no convictions or outstanding warrants, or any of the other databases – DVLA, social security and so forth – about a Sarah Bliss.'

'What's the likelihood that Bliss is her real name?' asked Flick.

'Keep looking.' Drake arrived at the stairwell. 'And put in a request to Europol.'

'With that name?' asked Millie.

'It's all we've got.'

'Where are you going?' asked Flick.

'I've got some stuff to do in my office,' he said. 'Let's get that facial composite put together and out to the press as soon as possible.'

And then he left them, climbing the stairs to his office.

When he got inside, Drake took off his jacket and hung it behind the door. Sitting at his desk, he pulled the computer keyboard towards him and typed a couple of emails. Then he logged into the DVLA and looked up the registration of the car he'd seen Flick climb into yesterday. The vehicle belonged to a Samuel Wylie. He had a name, and an address in Enfield.

Then he opened a search engine and typed in:

SAM WYLIE
SAMUEL WYLIE

He looked at the search results for both names. Scrolling down, he found nothing that seemed to connect to the man he saw with Flick. Then he stood at the window with his hands in his pockets, rocking on his heels, watching the morning traffic crawl along the busy high road, thinking about that smirk Samuel Wylie had given him yesterday. He felt the anxiety rise in him.

Drake had lived a blameless life for many years. He had been happily married, and raised a daughter. But his wife Laura, his anchor, was dead now, and had left a vacuum inside him.

Forget that, what are you going to do about this guy?

The voice spoke behind him. He sensed, rather than saw, Connor Laird at his shoulder. That feral child, that angry boy, had always been a shadow in his mind. Drake felt him in his nightmares, or glimpsed him in a busy crowd. He sat sometimes in the corner of a room during a meeting, obscured by a pillar. And it was always Connor's voice that caused him to look up from his desk, or turn on the stairs.

Since Elliot had died, since he was . . . murdered, Drake sensed Connor's presence more and more. Heard his whispers, felt his warm breath on his neck.

You need me. If you didn't need me, I wouldn't be here.

Drake's fingers reached once again for the smooth, worn surface of his tie.

The more he felt threatened, the more Connor's chaotic

energy grew stronger inside him. He knew that Connor would take the necessary steps to ensure Ray Drake survived and could one day resume the happy life he had stolen from someone else.

He knew Connor would do whatever was necessary.

There was a rap on the door, and he called, 'Come in.'

Millie Steiner leaned inside and, seeing him alone at the window, asked, 'Shall I come back?'

'It's fine,' he said.

'We've found something,' she said.

He smiled. 'I'll be down.'

Drake turned back to the window, thinking of Sam Wylie.

Thinking: it's not over. It's very much not over.

Knowing he was ready, but afraid he wasn't in control.

Just say the word, Ray.

31

The headline read: OUR SHAME AT THE GIRL WE ABANDONED.

Flick handed Drake a dozen other printed sheets, national newspaper articles from nearly twenty years ago. He scanned those headlines.

LEFTY CANDIDATE SENT 'DAUGHTER' HOME

SHE HAD TO GO – NIGHTMARE GIRL DESTROYED OUR FAMILY, SAYS WANNABE MP

WE WILL NEVER FORGIVE OURSELVES

'Talk to me,' he said.

'Sarah Bliss, real name Tatia Mamaladze, was adopted by a Lewisham couple, Patrick and Jill Bliss, twenty-one years ago. The Blisses were politically motivated people, activists who campaigned for a number of causes on the left. The kind of couple who wake up every day and ask themselves how they're going to save the world.'

Vix Moore shook her head, as if she had the measure of them already.

'They had three children, Joel, Poppy and William, when they took in the girl from a notorious orphanage in the Republic of Georgia,' continued Flick. 'It was one of those places you wouldn't send a dog, let alone a child. Disgusting conditions, brutal staff, a dumping ground for kids with extreme mental and physical disabilities and behavioural problems. Patrick and Jill Bliss took in the girl when international adoptions from former Soviet states were far less regulated. Corners were cut, money may have changed hands. They gave her the name of Sarah. The girl was very intelligent: Patrick and Jill Bliss said she learned English in a matter of weeks. But she stayed with them only temporarily. One of the Bliss children, three-year-old Will, died in a clifftop accident near Beachy Head, and she was returned to the orphanage a couple of months after that.'

Drake shuffled through the papers, failing to find a quick answer to the question he wanted answered. 'Was she responsible?'

'It's unclear. There was clearly some blame attached. Reports at the time suggest he stumbled too close to the edge of the cliff while he was playing.' Flick's phone buzzed on the desk beside her and she peered at it. 'I'm sorry, I'm going to have to take this.'

Drake watched her walk across the incident room, the phone to her ear. 'Where were the parents?'

'They had popped back to the car further up the hill, leaving their eldest, Poppy, in charge.' Eddie picked up the thread. 'The coroner judged it an accident, but Jill and Patrick Bliss were lucky to escape prosecution.'

Vix's eyes bulged with indignation. 'Near a cliff edge!'

'In interviews, the Blisses said their son's death had emotional repercussions for all their children, and Tatia's behaviour in particular, and they had no choice but to send her away.'

'Contact Brighton.' Drake tapped the papers against his palm. 'Let's speak to the investigating officer, if they're still around.'

As Vix reluctantly left the meeting, Drake examined a photo of the parents beneath a sarcastic headline in a tabloid:

A DAUGHTER IS FOR LIFE, NOT JUST FOR CHRISTMAS

'A disastrous social experiment' was how one columnist cheerfully described Patrick and Jill Bliss's brief adoption of the girl. 'Too many do-gooding liberals,' stated the journalist, who was notorious for her provocative views,

> are willing to sacrifice the happiness and well-being of their own children in order to prove their impeccable humanitarian credentials to their lefty chums. Jill and Patrick Bliss are the kind of holier-than-thou couple who will shout about their virtue from the highest mountain, but completely ignore the needs of their own family. They're the kind of people who will never understand the meaning of the phrase held so dearly by the rest of us: charity begins at home!

Underneath the column was an image of the couple holding a framed photo of their dead child, Will. They gazed shamefully into the camera. Drake checked the date on the article. 'These newspaper reports came out long after the incident.'

'The full story of how they took in Tatia only seems to have emerged years later when Patrick Bliss stood for nomination as the Labour candidate in his local constituency.'

Millie removed the plastic lid of a takeaway coffee and waved away the steam. 'A rival candidate indulging in a bit of dirty politics, perhaps. Bliss and his wife tried to respond to the media outcry by doing a number of heart-to-heart newspaper interviews, but if he was trying to cling to the candidacy, he failed. More details emerged about the underhand way he and his wife took in the girl and sent her back. The local party ditched him.'

'Where are they now?'

'They're dead.' Dudley Kendrick's eyes flicked across his monitor. They heard him clicking the mouse. 'There's an online obit for Patrick Bliss in a left-wing mag. He committed suicide years ago and his wife had previously died from cancer.'

Flick came back across the office looking flustered.

'Everything okay?' asked Drake.

'It's Dad.' She dropped the phone in her bag. 'His retirement home have asked me to go in.'

'You want to go now?'

'Do you mind? A friend has agreed to take me, he's on his way.' Drake had a feeling he knew who the friend was. Flick folded her arms, all business. 'So, where are we at?'

'Where are Poppy and Joel Bliss now?' Drake asked Kendrick.

Kendrick tapped at his keyboard. 'Give me a moment.'

He would find them quickly and efficiently, because DS Dudley Kendrick was a machine. One of the old breed of coppers who lived and breathed police life, he knew all the shortcuts. A fine detective, a lover of real ale, a committed family man – and, if rumours were true, one hell of a line dancer – Kendrick was a quiet man who kept his distance from all the personality politics that often divided the office. Drake admired Kendrick's efficiency and liked him, but wasn't sure the feeling was mutual, and would often catch the veteran officer watching him. Drake had the uneasy feeling that Kendrick didn't much like what he saw in Drake's pale eyes.

'Tell me as soon as you've got it.' Drake chopped the sheets against his palm. He had a lot of reading to do. 'Millie, find a channel to Tbilisi. Chances are, Tatia Mamaladze will have a criminal record over there. Eddie, find out if she's come into the country under her own name. Unlikely, but you never know. We'll sit on her name for the moment, until we have more concrete information.' He watched Eddie stand stiffly. 'How are you feeling today?'

'A bit bruised. It hurts when I laugh, but luckily there aren't many laughs to be had around here.'

'That's the spirit,' said Drake. He turned to Flick. 'A word?'

He led her into one of the breakout rooms. She watched him pull down the blinds in the internal window so that nobody in the incident room could see in. 'I'm not going to like this, am I?'

'Sam Wylie,' he said. 'What is he to you?'

She sighed. 'I'm getting tired of having to storm out of rooms, Ray.'

'How did you meet him?'

'I like him.' She looked away. 'Right at this moment, he's a . . . friend.'

'A friend, or more than a friend?'

She blinked. 'Excuse me?'

Drake folded his arms. 'Tell me about him.'

'You know what?' Flick stepped to the door. 'I am going to storm out.'

'Let me guess.' Drake leaned against the sill. 'He turned up at the pub and you got talking, or he popped into your local cafe and you got talking. No, wait, you bumped into each other somewhere. On the street, in a supermarket – it was a total accident – and you just got talking.'

Hand on the door ready to leave, she changed her mind and leaned against the frame. 'Okay, we'll have this conversation one last time.'

'Where did you meet him?'

'We're seeing the same counsellor, or we were. I met him there.'

His fingers drummed against the sill. 'You met him at her office.'

'More or less,' she said.

'Yes or no?'

'Obviously not in her office. But I left the session early and he was already . . .'

'What?'

'He was outside, just arriving.' Her phone buzzed in her bag, and she dug it out, read the message on the screen. 'I'm going to have to go. My lift is here.' She nodded. 'Yes, *him*.'

'Just to be clear, you spoke and –' Drake waved the papers, trying to visualise what happened '– he went inside.'

'No, we went to one bar after the other and got drunk. He came back to mine . . . you want me to give you a written report about the rest, Ray?' Flick dropped her phone back in her bag and swung the door open. 'I've got to go.'

Drake launched himself off the sill. 'I'll see you down.'

'Don't go out of your way on my account.'

They headed towards the lifts, but before they got there, Drake shouldered open the stairwell door. It clanged shut behind them and their steps echoed on the stone steps.

'I bet he's very charming, very funny,' said Drake, following her down. 'The kind of man who gets under your skin very quickly. What does he do?'

'He's in the building trade, does up homes and offices and stuff. We didn't talk very much about it.'

The fire door opened on the floor above them. Drake waited till he heard the click of footsteps fade and the fire door on the landing two floors above boom shut in the echoing space. 'And you believe him?'

'My god, Ray.' Flick couldn't help but laugh. 'You really are paranoid.'

'Has he asked about me?'

'Sorry to disappoint you.' She continued down the stairs. 'But we talked about more interesting things. I could have told the truth about you to the inquiry, but I didn't. You begged me to get on with my life and leave the past behind, and now I'm doing exactly that.' She pushed through the door on the ground floor. 'I suggest you do the same. Meeting Wylie was an accident: just that, a *happy* accident. And I don't have to justify my love life to you or anyone else. I've got one unsatisfactory father, Ray.' Stopping at the exit to the car park, she pulled out her lanyard, lifted it near the pad. 'I don't need another one.'

Drake leaned against the wall. 'Just . . . be careful.'

'Look, he's just a guy who totally rates himself,' she said. 'He's split up with his wife and moved out. But he's fun, and right now I really need to have a good time. It probably won't go anywhere, he's not anyone's idea of a prize catch, but I like him.' She sighed. 'Come and see for yourself.'

Flick pressed her pass against the sensor and the door unlocked. Together they walked through the car park and out of the gate. Drake saw Wylie standing on the other side of the road, hands in his pockets. If he was surprised to see Drake with Flick, he didn't show it.

'Sam Wylie.' He held out his hand and Drake took it. Wylie's grip was firm and he didn't hurry to let go.

'Ray Drake.'

'Good to meet you, Ray. I've heard a lot about you.'

'No, you haven't,' said Flick, annoyed. 'I've never mentioned him.'

Wylie kept hold of Drake's hand. 'You coming, too?'

'Afraid not, I'm busy.'

'Let's go.' Flick tugged at Wylie's arm to lead him back to the car park, and he finally let go of Drake's hand.

'Next time, perhaps,' said Drake.

'See you around, then,' said Wylie cheerily.

And then he followed Flick to her car.

Drake's knuckles tightened around the roll of paper in his hands, twisting it into a tight baton.

32

Everyone shot her a big smile, putting her on edge. The residents grinned like maniacs, the staff offered cheery hellos. The receptionist kept catching her eye and winking. Flick buried her face in a magazine. She heard the melody of a quiz show theme tune in the day room next door. Work was piling up and she could do without having to wait in the hot reception of her father's retirement home.

She had given Wylie strict instructions to stay in the car. Embarrassed by him, she had always kept Harry Crowley well away from the men she was interested in, not that he ever took much of an interest in her relationships. But this time round she had the disconcerting feeling that Harry and Wylie would get on like a house on fire. From her seat in reception, she saw Wylie with his feet up on the dash, playing a game on his phone.

She looked up impatiently. 'Do you have any idea how long I'm going to have to wait?'

'Miss Weaver and Mr Crowley are in her office.' The receptionist smiled again. 'They won't be long.'

'I'm going to have to get back to work soon.' Flick pointed at her cocked wrist, even though there wasn't actually a watch there.

'Won't be long.'

A few minutes later Flick dropped the magazine, determined to leave, when the door behind reception opened and a short, black woman with cropped grey hair came out and offered her hand.

'Minette Weaver.' Her handshake was strong. 'Thanks for waiting.'

The manager's office was bright but stuffy. The last burning rays of the day poured into Flick's eyes when she took a seat beside her father.

Harry Crowley was dressed, as usual, as if he was going hiking in the Alps: in khaki shorts and boots, a Hawaiian shirt. A walking stick rested against a knee. His silver hair was slicked back on his head. Say what you like about her father, and Flick could say plenty, but in his old age he always looked distinguished. Harry was uncharacteristically subdued today, dabbing at the film of sweat on his forehead with a handkerchief.

'I wanted to flag up some, uh, behaviours by Mr Crowley that are giving us cause for concern.' Minette opened a green folder. 'This is not a place where we impose unnecessary rules and regulations, but we have to draw the line somewhere.'

Harry raised his eyes to the ceiling. Flick squinted uncomfortably into the last fierce blast of evening light behind Minette's head and shielded her eyes.

'I can't see a thing. Do you mind?'

The manager tried to drop the old venetian blinds at the window, but when one side of the metal slats slid down with a metallic shiver the other side bunched at the top. Minette moved from one string to another, tugging at them, one half of the blinds shifting up and down, but the other half stubbornly refusing to fall.

'Want me to do it, love?' asked Harry.

'I can manage, thank you, Harry,' said Minette tersely. Finally, both sides of the blind fell with a shudder. It was a blessed relief to Flick; she felt her face cool immediately.

'As I was saying.' Minette took her seat. 'We're not prescriptive here at Valleywell, but this must be a safe place for all our residents.'

'I'm sorry, Miss Weaver,' said Flick. 'Do you mind getting to the point?'

'She's a busy woman,' said Harry.

'I'm afraid your father was found in close physical contact with one of our lady residents,' said Minette.

'It was a clinch.' Harry made a face. 'A quick kiss and a cuddle between consenting adults.'

'I don't understand.' Flick was reluctant to dwell on the physical details. 'Is physical contact, a bit of a cuddle – is that banned?'

'Hugs are healthy. We encourage our residents to form emotional attachments.' Minette clasped her hands. 'Just not with the wives of other residents.'

'What does Ron care?' Harry didn't sound very contrite. 'He don't pay no attention to Sheila, just sits watching television all day. All she wants is a little bit of TLC. And if her husband of sixty years can't give it to her then she's going to find a man who can. She's a handsome woman, still, with needs and desires.'

Flick grimaced. 'Harry, please.'

'But there's another aspect to this situation, isn't there, Harry?' Minette turned over a piece of paper. 'We have reason to believe that your father later received a sum of money from Mrs Beecham.'

'What?' Flick turned to her father, incredulous. 'You're a gigolo now?'

'Sheila offered to lend me the money because she's got a heart of gold.'

'How much?'

'Couple of hundred.' He placed the hankie to his forehead. 'Five hundred or thereabouts.'

'For fuck's sake, Harry,' she muttered.

'That situation has been resolved. Mr Crowley has returned the money, but it has caused upset among all our residents, not least Ron and Sheila Beecham.'

'The whole thing has been blown out of proportion. It was a cuddle and a quick peck.' He buried his finger in his cheek.

'Many of the ladies and gentlemen find it hard to adjust when they come here. So the last thing we want is to create discord. I've spoken to Mr Crowley and he's promised there will not be a repeat of the situation.'

'The old bugger threatened to take me outside and give me a pasting.' Harry laughed. 'Ron can barely stand without his walker!'

'It's not funny, Harry,' said Minette, but Flick had the sense that the manager liked him. People were fond of Harry, it was true; people not related to him by blood.

'Why am I here?' asked Flick.

'Because I wanted to tell you that we're going to go forward on the understanding that a situation like this will not happen again. Harry can't act like some cheap lothario.'

'Chance would be a fine thing!'

The manager raised her voice. 'If it does, we'll have to think seriously about the continuation of his residency.'

'So you said.' Harry shook his head at the injustice of it. 'Can we go now?'

'Your father is a valued and popular member of our community.' Minette placed the file in a tray. 'But my responsibility is to the peace of mind of all our residents.'

'I understand,' said Flick.

Minette made some chitchat as she led them into reception. The old man walked stiffly on his stick, grimacing, making a meal of it. Flick was relieved to find the receptionist wasn't there. In the day room residents played dominoes and read papers, but mostly watched television.

'You can't help yourself, can you?' she said, when they were alone.

Harry rolled his eyes. 'Don't start.'

'What on earth do you need money for?'

'It was a loan. I was going to pay it back.'

Harry was like a fox in a henhouse here, could run rings round these people if he chose to. Using his charm and powers of manipulation to prise money out of a vulnerable old lady – Flick was surprised it hadn't happened earlier.

'Would you rather I begged on the pavement?'

'If you carry on like this, that's exactly what you'll be doing.'

'Go on, admit it.' Harry gave her a sly smile. 'You're a little bit impressed with your dad.'

'Why do you need money, Harry?'

'Call me Dad. I'm your dad.' Harry walked to the window and looked out at the car park where Wylie paced, speaking on the phone. 'Who's that?'

'Who's what?' she said, blushing.

'You've got yourself a man.'

'He's just a friend.'

'Scruffy Herbert, ain't he. Not your usual type.'

'Don't change the subject,' Flick said quickly. 'Why do you need money?'

'I miss Nina.' He looked sombre at the thought of his daughter, Flick's sister, who had gone to live in Australia with her family. 'You don't know what it's like being surrounded by a bunch of people who sit around waiting to die. You expect a mate to come down to breakfast and sometimes they never do.' He caught her eye. 'And it's not like you're ever here. I want to go visit her.'

'She'd pay for you to go over there any time, you know that.'

'She left us, Felicity, the both of us, and took those wonderful kids.' He shook his head. 'What must she think of us to go to the other side of the world?'

What she wanted to tell him was that now he knew how they felt – she and Nina and Daniel, her brother – when he left his family for another woman and they didn't see him for years. But there was something in his eyes that she had never seen before – sadness, vulnerability – that made her bite her tongue.

'You said you were happy here,' she said.

'Nina was the only person who gave a damn, and now she's gone.'

'You're laying it on a bit thick, Harry, don't you think?' She smiled, but he didn't reply. 'Look, I've got to go.'

'Yeah,' he said. 'You better get on.'

'Maybe I'll come next week, just to make sure you're not getting up to mischief.'

His face brightened. 'Only if you've got the time.'

'I want to,' she told him. 'In the meantime, do me a favour and stay away from the ladies. Think you can manage that?'

'It's not like anything's in much of a working order below the neck these days.' When Flick made a face, he said, 'I'd go for a walk to the shops, but times are hard.'

Flick had resented him for so long, for so many reasons, that she hardly remembered what they were any more. The fact was, if Nina hadn't gone away Flick would have nothing to do with Harry Crowley. When he was younger, he was a grasping chancer, one of life's takers. An unreliable husband and father – a bent copper. But what you saw with Harry was what you got.

Back when he was a sergeant in Hackney, Harry had briefly met a boy called Connor Laird, who went on to take the identity of Ray Drake. Harry had described Connor as a wild boy. 'Feral' was the word he had used. As far as the world was concerned, Detective Inspector Ray Drake was a good man, a tragic figure who had lost his wife and was targeted by a homicidal maniac, but Flick knew better. Drake was a man full of secrets. Harry's faults were small potatoes compared to Drake's.

She took a twenty-pound note from her purse, knowing full well he would place the lot on a couple of nags down the bookies.

'Thanks for coming, Felicity.' The money disappeared immediately into Harry's fist. 'Say hello to your new fella for me.'

'See you next week . . . Dad,' she said, and his face lit up.

'That was the old man?' Wylie nodded at the window when she got outside. She had told him all about Harry Crowley on the way there. 'I'd like to meet him one day – he sounds like a total legend.'

She looked back at reception, but Harry had gone.

Yeah, she thought, a total legend. But never much of a father.

33

His mother would put him right.

Tim's parents were devoted to him – and Poppy and their beloved grandson. Tanya would be devastated by his despicable behaviour. His parents were good people, sensible people, and simply wouldn't stand for it. He had a son who needed him, for god's sake. Tanya and John would stage an intervention to ensure this nonsense went no further. Tim would be forced to see the stupidity of his actions. He was having some kind of midlife crisis. The girl, whoever it was, this stupid fling, had preyed on his insecurities.

The night she met Tanya and John had been one of the best of Poppy's life. It was the very night, surrounded by his family and their numerous friends, she had fallen in love with Tim. She remembered walking up the lane towards their big Surrey pile just before sundown, hearing peals of laughter. And when the house swung into view, the sight took her breath away. All its windows glowed softly in the dusk, the long side patio heaved with people. A vast lawn swept towards an enchanted copse where insects danced in the balmy summer heat, around shimmering tea lights hung from the branches of the trees. And as soon as they arrived, everybody made a fuss of them. Tim's mother had been a famous model in the 1960s, his urbane and handsome father a movie actor. Poppy remembered clinging to Tim as she was introduced to people from film, theatre and politics, people she was certain she must have met before, so often had she seen them on television.

Poppy was intoxicated by the company of so many charming and sophisticated people. They were funny and interesting, comfortable in their skin, and happy with the world, unlike her own discontented parents, who only ever saw what was wrong with it. Most of all she enjoyed the laughter and happiness. John kept everybody in stitches with his impressions and anecdotes, and to her astonishment brought Poppy into the jokes. She felt a delicious thrill of validation and belonging. Poppy watched a drunken group crowd into a rowing boat on the lake beyond the trees, and when a man fell in everybody roared. Two famous comedians bet piles of money on a game of snooker. A woman walked up and down the middle of the long trestle table on the patio, a wine glass balanced on her head, and the people eating and drinking below her didn't bat an eyelid.

Poppy wanted so dearly to be like these people. For the first time in her life she felt like she truly belonged.

The party went on long into the night. A famous musician sang songs on a guitar, and she and Tim walked down the lawn – she felt the cooling blades of grass between the toes of her bare feet – to sit on the rickety dock over the lake. Insects hopped across the black, twisting surface of the water.

She listened, fascinated, when Tim told her how, in the 1960s, his mother and father were on the guest list at the most glamorous parties in Cannes and LA. But when he asked her about her own family she nearly died with embarrassment.

The last thing she wanted to tell him about was her miserable life, about what had happened to Will, and about that terrible girl . . .

Instead she lay on the dock and pulled him onto her and gave herself to him, and it was everything she had dreamed the first time would be. It was perfect. And when they walked back up to the house, the first tentative rays of light greying the tops of the trees, the last stragglers were still wrapped in blankets outside. When the time came for her to go, Poppy knew she was going to marry Tim and be a part of this family. This was the life she wanted.

But now when she phoned Tanya and John's number for their help and guidance, it rang and rang. Poppy hung up and dialled again immediately. She would keep calling until someone picked up the phone. To her relief, it was answered the second time.

'Hello?' said Tanya.

'Have you heard? Has he told you?'

She could hear Tanya's fluffy dogs barking. 'How are you, Poppy?'

'Has he told you?'

'Yes,' said Tanya, after a moment. 'He has.'

She couldn't understand it. Tanya sounded reticent, guarded, when Poppy had expected her to be angry about Tim's behaviour.

'I'm scared, Tanya.'

'I know you are. I'm so sorry, Poppy. It's a very . . . difficult business.'

Tanya hadn't condemned Tim yet. She hadn't said he was a bloody fool. Didn't seem furious with him at all, just embarrassed.

'Can you talk to him, please?' Poppy asked. 'Make him see sense?'

'We would rather stay out of it,' Tanya said. 'It's . . . Tim's decision.'

Bereft, Poppy closed her eyes. Tanya's coldness stung. She felt closer to her in-laws than she ever had to her own mother and father. If Tim left her, she wouldn't just lose a husband, she would lose so much more: brothers and sisters-in-law; an extended, loving family. Every year the Mallorys travelled to John and Tanya's luxury villa in Portugal for two weeks. Poppy was never happier than when she was there. Tim might still take Gabriel, but he wouldn't allow Poppy to go, not if he wanted to take his new girlfriend.

It occurred to Poppy that Tanya and John probably didn't know the full story. 'He's seeing someone else.'

'He told you that?'

'He's denied it, of course he has, but I'm sure of it.'

'Whatever has happened between you and Tim, it's best we don't—'

'Nothing's happened where I'm concerned! I've done nothing wrong!'

'Please don't get angry.' Poppy didn't know if the hushing noise Tanya made was for the benefit of the barking dogs or her. 'As I say, it's something that you and Tim must discuss between yourselves.'

'Discuss?'

'The most important thing is that you have a little one. Gabriel should be your main concern.'

'But what about me?' Tears pricked Poppy's eyes. 'Who's thinking of me?'

'I'm going to have to go. I'm happy to talk to you when . . .

things are calmer. But it's important, and John agrees, that we don't take sides.'

'Take sides?' asked Poppy, incredulous.

And then Tanya rang off, leaving Poppy with a dead phone to her ear. She couldn't believe Tanya wasn't prepared to get involved. It felt like a massive betrayal. Tim had acted like a shit. He was walking out on his wife and child. And yet Tanya spoke as if it was Poppy who had done something wrong. But then, the Mallorys had always been a tight-knit bunch. When push came to shove, they looked out for each other. Tim, surely, had crossed a line. And yet it was Poppy who would lose everything.

Her parents: gone.

Joel: gone.

And now Tim and Tanya and John: gone.

Poppy would be left utterly alone. It was catastrophic. It couldn't happen.

It just couldn't be allowed to happen.

34

Tomorrow morning there would be a press conference where Drake's DCI would unveil the e-fit of Tatia Mamaladze. Drake hoped that would get results, but so far they'd found out nothing about her. There wasn't even any proof that she had entered the country.

He thought about the young girl taken in all those years ago by Jill and Patrick Bliss. Rescued from a terrible place and offered a loving home and family in a faraway city. It must have been like a dream come true. And then only a few months later that same dream became a nightmare when she was returned to that cruel home. Tatia was given a tantalising taste of paradise – and then banished.

Drake could only imagine the terror she felt, her bewilderment and confusion, the utter despair, when she was dragged back to the vicious place she believed she'd escaped for ever.

Tatia's tragic story could so easily have been his own. A long time ago Connor Laird had been taken in by Myra and Leonard Drake. Connor was responsible for their son's death, but they offered him their only child's home, his name – his future. If they hadn't given him Ray Drake's life, what would have become of Connor Laird? Where would he have ended up?

Sitting at his desk, Drake jabbed the space bar on his

keyboard to awaken his computer and went through his emails. One from Eddie contained the footage taken by the camera in the Langley kitchen over the period of a day. All they needed to see, perhaps, was that last sickening image of Bryan Langley crawling across the floor. Those ghostly reflections in the glass had been analysed to death by the techs. Carl Clarke was almost certainly one of them – was the other Tatia Mamaladze?

Drake rolled the footage all the way back to the beginning.

The camera switched on at 11.14 p.m. the previous night. Samantha Langley stared up at it from directly below, her face looming in the lens and her body, clothed in slim pyjamas, tapering away below her. She waved at it, laughing silently – a selfie moment. Drinking from a mug, Bryan pecked at a laptop on the kitchen island. He turned the screen to her, revealing the camera image, and together they did little synchronised movements with their hands on their hips. An intensely private moment, never intended to be seen by anybody else. A nostalgic joke, perhaps, an echo of a dance they once shared. Bryan scooped up the laptop and they left the room, switching off the light. The kitchen was plunged into gloom. The camera's night vision snapped on. After a couple of minutes, sensing no movement, the camera turned itself off.

A day later, Bryan and Samantha Langley would be dead.

At 2.33 a.m. the camera switched on, its night light imbuing everything with a green glow, to reveal movement at the edge of the sink in the corner of the room. A speck moved across the draining board. The mouse, moving jerkily over the surface.

7.11 a.m.: Bryan and Samantha and their kids had breakfast. Dressed for work in suit and tie, Bryan stared at a computer tablet and stuffed a slice of toast into his mouth. Sitting at the island, the kids talked animatedly. Samantha filled beakers with orange juice from a jug and threw a grape at her husband. He staggered back as if he had been shot, to the delight of the kids. Samantha opened the fridge to replace the jug. Drake imagined the pucker of the door, the shudder of the coolant, the chill air on her face. Minutes later, the kids climbed off the stools and disappeared, and Bryan and Samantha leaned over the sink, backs to the camera, investigating droppings on the sill.

7.49 a.m.: The cleaner arrived. Samantha swept her hand around the sink, indicating the area where the mouse had been, where it needed to be bleached. Then she pointed vaguely in the direction of the camera, the woman bemusedly following her gaze. When Samantha left the room, the cleaner ran the hot tap and lifted bottles of cleaning products from the cabinet beneath the sink.

11.31 a.m.: Samantha, in T-shirt and sweat pants, leaned into the glowing interior of the fridge – her face was bathed in the bright light – and took out a pot of something, yoghurt maybe. She turned to the granite worktop. Peeling a banana, she cut it into segments with a knife, then chopped oranges and apples, to make a fruit salad.

2.12 p.m.: Samantha sat on a stool, pulling a thumb down her phone. Grace Beer's examination of the device revealed she visited the *Daily Mail*'s so-called sidebar of shame five, six, seven times a day, and numerous entertainment sites. Samantha Langley was a keen user of social media, including an online forum for local mothers. She put down the phone and poured boiling water into a mug. She pressed a teabag against the inside with a teaspoon, releasing its flavour. Then she went to the fridge and took out a litre of milk and tipped a splodge into the tea. A moment later, she looked up at a sound from the hallway – the doorbell – and at the clock beneath the camera.

For a brief moment, it seemed like she was staring right at Drake. Her eyes met his.

She placed the container of milk on the island and left the room, returning several moments later and tucking in the stools at the breakfast bar to allow a window cleaner access to the patio glass at the edge of the frame. The man had been interviewed and ruled out as a suspect. He visited on this same day every month, had done a round on this street for more than four years.

3.56 p.m.: Samantha walked into the kitchen reading a leaflet from a local church, and dropped it in the recycling. The canvassers had also been interviewed. They were going from door to door that day, delivering news of an upcoming fete. The two church workers were well known in the neighbourhood.

6.17 p.m.: Samantha made a tuna pasta supper. Arriving home, Bryan placed his briefcase on a bar stool, folding his suit jacket over it. The children rushed in to give him a hug.

He pulled Emily onto his knee and sat on a stool, the thinning crown of his head directly below the camera. Samantha chatted as she prepared the meal and took from the fridge a bottle of lemonade. Opening it too quickly, the drink spurted from the neck. She ran to the sink and dumped the bottle there, liquid fizzing everywhere.

7.02 p.m.: The Langleys chatted over dinner, and then Samantha stacked the plates. She knelt in front of the dishwasher. There was a method in the way she placed the heavier items at the bottom. Drake could almost hear the thunk of the door as it shut and water flushed into the compartment. Bryan walked into the kitchen, in jeans and a polo shirt. When he finished a call on his phone, Samantha fell into his arms and they held each other, the point of his chin resting on the top of her head.

7.32 p.m.: Samantha left the kitchen, dimming the lights.

9.59 p.m.: The kitchen was bathed in a warm glow as Bryan crouched at the cupboard beneath the sink, a torch between his teeth. He took out the household cleaning products one by one, plastic bottles and sprays, detergents and bleach, dishwasher tablets and scourers, and placed them on the floor. Then he squeezed his torso into the cupboard, looking for any sign of where the mouse could be getting in. Moments later, he heaved himself out to rub his sore knees.

10.21 p.m.: Bryan took a bottle of rosé from the fridge and poured himself a glass, then left the room.

3.47 a.m.: Bryan crawled into the kitchen on his hands and knees, leaving a messy trail of blood on the tiles. He moved slowly, exhausted, moments from death. Drake saw the two figures reflected in the black patio window. Then Bryan collapsed to the floor and the ghosts stepped back into the darkness, as if evaporating into thin air.

Drake stopped the footage and heaved himself stiffly out of the chair, stretching, conscious that the light outside was fading. Leaning over the desk, he moved the cursor absently across the screen. There was something in this video. Something he had seen, something in plain sight. Something significant.

He just didn't know what it was.

Drake clicked the application shut. He opened a search engine and looked up the number of an office in Euston. Then he lifted his jacket from the door, turned out the lights and left the office.

35

Ray Drake pulled his Mercedes into a space outside his house and killed the engine. He took out his phone and rang the number he'd looked up earlier.

When it was answered, he said: 'It's Sam Wylie, Sunita.'

Flick's counsellor hesitated. 'Excuse me?'

'I'm going to have to cancel my next appointment.'

'Uh.' Drake heard her turn the pages of a diary. 'What did you say your name was?'

'Samuel Wylie,' he said. 'My appointment is on Tuesday afternoons?'

'I'm sorry, there must be some mistake,' she said. 'I don't recognise your name. Sam Wylie, you sai—'

Drake cut the call.

Letting himself into the house, he heard raised voices coming from the dining room, and found Myra and Mercy on opposite sides of the dining table, bickering as usual. Drake hesitated in the doorway.

'If I wanted flowers, you silly woman,' said Myra, 'I would have asked you to buy flowers.'

'But they are nice.' Her home help ran her hands up the beautiful blooms – yellows, reds, whites and mauves – in a vase. 'They brighten the place up.'

'My home doesn't need brightening, thank you.' Even in old age and with a stoop, Myra towered over the small

Filipino. When Mercy picked up the vase, Myra rubbed at the table. 'Look, you fool, it's left a wet ring on the surface. At the very least you could have placed a coaster beneath the vase. What on earth were you thinking?'

'You are not a very nice woman,' said Mercy. 'You are unkind and ungrateful. I go to the market to buy you flowers and this is the thanks I get.'

Myra's nostrils flared. 'I don't remember asking for flowers.'

'And look, there's no ring.'

'They're lovely, Mercy.' Drake stepped into the room and flung his keys on a side table. 'And it was kind of you to buy them.'

'I take them away and dump them.' Tearful, Mercy picked up the vase. 'Mrs Drake doesn't like these lovely flowers.'

'Take them home, put them somewhere nice, it'll be a shame to let them go to waste. I'll pay for them.'

'Oh, leave them, then.' Myra let out an exasperated sigh and grabbed the vase, placed it back on the table. 'You make such a terrible fuss about everything. I suppose I can put up with them.'

'One of these days!' said Mercy, and walked out.

Mercy had been coming to the house for nearly thirty years. Washing, cleaning, doing chores three times a week. She and Myra fought like cat and dog. She had been sacked numerous times, had quit twice as many. When that happened, Myra spent hours on the phone convincing her to return, promising to change her behaviour. If that didn't work, she would send gifts to Mercy's home.

'She bought them for you.' Drake dropped onto the sofa and pulled down his tie. 'Would it kill you to be nice?'

Myra adjusted the stems. 'I suppose they are pretty.'

The old woman didn't like change, didn't like a single thing out of place in Drake's home. She lived downstairs in the basement flat but prowled the Islington townhouse like a guard dog, making sure everything was exactly where it should be. But Drake knew she frequently got bored and moved items from one place to another, just to cause an argument with her long-suffering home help.

'I'll add something to her pay this week.'

'Don't lose her.' Drake pulled a cushion out from beneath him and threw it along the sofa. 'She's worth her weight in gold.'

Usually the old woman disliked it when Drake took Mercy's side, and let him know in no uncertain terms. But today she sat and watched him, her crooked, bony fingers twisting in her lap.

'Tell me,' she said, sensing his anxiety.

He pulled a hand down his face. 'It's nothing.'

'Don't play games,' she told him. 'I know you too well.'

Drake gathered his thoughts. 'There's a man. His name is Sam Wylie. He's come out of nowhere. He's engineered a meeting with Flick, and he's got his claws into her. There's something going on, Myra.'

Myra picked a piece of lint from her skirt, rolled it in her fingers. 'I'm worried about you.'

Ignoring her, Drake jumped to his feet. 'The whole situation feels wrong. She's vulnerable, she's not in a good place right now, and this man is all over her like a rash.'

'And you've spoken to her?'

'She won't listen.'

All it would take was for Flick to say one wrong thing to Wylie, the merest hint that they had lied in the internal investigation, and his whole world would come crashing down.

Rubbing the locket around her neck – the locket that contained the only photo of her dead son, the boy whose name and life were taken by the man who paced in front of her – Myra said quietly, 'Did you hear what I said?'

He shook his head. 'I'm fine.'

'The nightmares.' She lifted her chin. 'The ones you have every night. The ones where you wake up screaming *his* name.'

'He's under control,' he murmured.

'What do you mean by that, exactly?' She cocked her head sharply, but he turned away. 'Fine, treat me like an old fool. But if you're not prepared to talk about it, it seems to me that before you go jumping to conclusions about this Wylie person, you must first find out more about the situation. Perhaps I was wrong, but I was under the impression that you are not the kind of person who waits for disaster to strike.'

'I'm going to deal with it.'

'Well, then.' She picked up the keys and threw them. Drake snatched them out of the air before they hit him in the face. 'No time like the present.'

36

'I'm really sorry,' Drake told Flick. 'I know it's been a long day.'

'It's no problem,' she told him, but her voice was guarded.

'I'd do it myself but, long story, I'm out of London on personal business.'

Careful to stay out of sight if her curtains opened, Drake walked along the pavement beneath Flick's flat to where Wylie's dirty Mazda was parked. He took out the compact box bought from a specialist electronics shop on Old Street. On the end of the phone, he heard Flick turn away briefly to murmur something, presumably to Wylie, then say, 'What did you say you left out?'

'There are transcripts on my desk which really should be locked away.' Silence on the other end of the phone. She was going to make him say it again. 'Do you mind popping back to the station and locking them in my drawer?'

'I'll be in early, in any case, so I can—'

'We have to be super careful right now,' he said. 'There's a lot of pressure on us in this investigation. The last thing we need is for evidence to get mislaid.'

Pressing the phone between his shoulder and ear, he knelt on the pavement so that he looked as if he was tying a shoelace, and reached beneath Wylie's car to place the tracker on the underside. The powerful magnets on the bottom of the device clamped greedily against the metal. Then he walked quickly back to his own car at the end of the road.

'Sure,' said Flick, finally. 'I'll go in.'

'Thank you,' he said. 'I really appreciate it.'

He cut the call and angled the side mirror so that he could see the front of her apartment building from the driver's seat. Ten minutes later, when she and Wylie came out of the building, he readjusted the view. They stood on the pavement and kissed, then reluctantly parted. Flick crossed the road to her car, and Wylie went to his. Flick had said Wylie had moved out of his address in Enfield. Drake wanted to know where to.

He checked that the GPS signal on the tracker worked on his phone. The red circle on a street map on the screen pulsed as Wylie's Mazda disappeared around a corner. There was something mesmerising about the way the circle remained in the middle of the screen, and streets and junctions twisted about, as if Wylie's car remained at a fixed point in time and space while the world moved around it.

Placing his phone on the passenger seat where he could see it, Drake waited for a couple of minutes and then started the engine. He followed Wylie's route south, shadowing the Northern Line tube stations, dropping through Archway, Kentish Town and Camden, onto the inner ring road at Euston. The city's lights soared ever higher as he skirted the top edge of the West End. He tried to keep the red spot at a steady distance, although it sometimes raced away while Drake was stuck at traffic lights, but Wylie wasn't in any hurry, and it was easy to stay close. After nearly an hour's driving in congested traffic the red spot approached Paddington and stopped several blocks from the train station.

Barely a minute or so behind the red circle, Drake pulled into a space at the top of the road and killed the lights, just in time to see Wylie climb the exterior stairwell of a block of flats. Drake jumped out and, staying out of sight, crossed to the pavement opposite to watch Wylie walk along a first-floor balcony and let himself into a flat. A moment later, a light went on behind the frosted glass in the door.

It was late, and Drake couldn't stand outside all night, so he went to an apartment building opposite the block of flats and pressed random buttons on the intercom until someone finally buzzed him into the building. He leaned against the wall in the foyer, catching up on a bit of work on his phone, trying to look as though there was a perfectly good reason for him to be standing there when people walked in or out.

Outside, mopeds roared up and down the road delivering takeaways, and men and women lugged shopping bags home from the supermarket around the corner. A jogger in a fluorescent top ran past.

An hour later, Wylie came out of the flat and trotted downstairs. Drake waited for him to climb into his car and drive away. He used the time to finish a mail about postponing a health and safety course he was obliged to attend. Then, pocketing his phone, he let himself out of the building and crossed the road, then climbed the stairwell of Wylie's block.

The first-floor flat Wylie had gone inside faced directly onto the street, but the door was mostly obscured by the concrete balcony. It was the only way in. Drake listened for the sound of footsteps on the stairwell, but could only hear the street traffic and the hornet buzz of Formula One coming from the TV in a neighbouring flat.

He slipped overshoes onto his feet, nitrile gloves onto his hands. Lifting the flap of the letterbox, he saw the flat was dark. Then he stepped back against the balustrade and slammed his foot hard against the door. It flew open and Drake stepped quickly inside, catching the door before it banged against the frame, and wedged it ajar with the folded edge of a welcome mat. The roar of the race on next door's TV blared through the thin walls. Doors led off the narrow hallway on either side. On the left was a bedroom. There was a thin mattress on a cheap wooden frame with a single crumpled sheet, and beside it on the floor was an anglepoise lamp, with a broken spring that made it bow forlornly. Drake pulled the curtains closed and toed the switch on the lamp, throwing an elongated circle of light across the carpet. Clothes – shirts, tops, underwear – were dumped on a fold-out table, a toilet bag placed on top. Strings of dust trembled along the skirting.

Opposite was a kitchen. There was a stained Formica counter and a growling fridge, a microwave, but nothing in the cupboards except chipped bowls and plates. A white plastic kettle and a pair of cups were lined up on the counter. The bin was full of takeaway cartons and empty lager cans.

At the end of the hallway, beyond a bathroom and a box room, was a lounge. Drake jabbed at the light switch. A long-life bulb warmed slowly beneath a paper shade. He saw a table, an old sofa, a circular glass table and a single square window high in the wall that would barely let in any light during the day.

He moved about the room, his instincts prickling. The

space had a functional, unloved feeling to it. Wylie may be staying here, but not for long. This was nobody's home.

The silence was broken by that familiar voice.

You know what this is. You've been to places like this before.

'We don't know that,' said Drake.

Come on, Ray. Get real.

Drake turned to leave, he'd seen enough, but then saw the corner of a plastic envelope poking out beneath the sofa. He knelt and reached for it. The police evidence bag, with its anti-tamper seal, bar code and numerous boxes for exhibit and officer details, emerged from the dark. There was a slip of paper inside.

This is a safe house, Ray, said Connor. *And you're in big trouble.*

Drake's phone began to ring – a FaceTime call – and he ignored it. Instead he ripped open the bag and took out the slip of paper. On it was written:

ANSWER THE PHONE, RAY.

Drake thumbed the screen. His phone connected to a video call. He saw a starkly lit room with cheap furniture and plastic fittings. A figure knelt beside a sofa, an evidence bag in his hand. When Drake stood, the man on the video did the same – with just the tiniest of delays on the feed.

He watched himself turn in the small flat as he tried to work out where the camera was. Found it on the edge of the window above the sofa, set up so that it had a clear view of the front door. It had filmed him breaking in and slipping from room to room. Drake stared up the camera, then down at the phone, and saw the tension in his own face on the screen, shadows gathering in the steep plummet of his cheeks. He cut the call.

37

The sun poured through the large south-facing window onto all the colourful ceramic teapots, across the vibrant screen prints on the white walls, and along the counter where glistening pastries and cakes dusted in icing sugar were laid out on trays.

Poppy's friends met in this cafe every half-term morning to chat and gossip while the kids ran between the tables. She came most days, usually loved to meet up for a chinwag, but today she was exhausted with worry. Bea asked more than once if she was ill, and looked genuinely concerned for her, but also didn't want her four-year-old Mathilde, who was inclined to pick up every bug going, to catch anything. Poppy tried her best to listen to the conversations up and down the table, but all she could think about was the imminent end of her marriage and the repercussions for her and Gabriel. Her son was at a nearby table looking at something on YouTube over the shoulder of another boy.

Cath told Bea her husband had gone out and bought a sailing boat on a whim, a fiftieth birthday present to himself, but didn't have the faintest idea about where to berth it. Penny had just had to sack her *fifth* au pair when she came home to find the girl smoking weed behind the gazebo. Malin was planning a surprise trip to California for her son.

'It's scary,' said Issy, talking about the murders on the news. 'Those people killed in their own homes.'

Penny shuddered. 'I read they were tortured.'

'Any one of us could be next.'

Poppy had sickening news of her own, which would make her friends gasp in horror. In particular, Issy and Bea – who knew Tim well – would take it very badly. There would be tears. They would all be heartbroken and kind and offer all their support. But it wouldn't take long for the whispers to start and for Poppy to become an object of pity. Telling her friends would be like firing the starting gun on the rest of her miserable life. Nobody knew yet what was happening and that's the way she wanted it to remain until she had decided what to do.

'She hasn't seen her ex in years.' Bea was talking about a friend who had been forced to return to live with her elderly parents in Croydon when her marriage disintegrated. 'And she hasn't got a penny out of him.'

Malin made a face over the top of her decaf. 'Let's be honest, those two were never a good fit.'

That's how they would talk about Poppy soon enough. She could try to get Tim to see the error of his ways, but she knew she would never change his mind. He considered his options carefully and wasn't the kind of man to be need-lessly unkind unless he was certain he had made the right decision. She knew she would lose him, and Tanya and John and everything she had. Her home, her lifestyle. Life would be a struggle.

The roar of the kids, the hiss of the coffee machine and clatter of cutlery, the heat of the midday sun pouring through the window, became too much. Poppy felt lightheaded.

There was a very real possibility she would faint or burst into tears.

'Got to go,' she whispered to Issy, and squeezed past the cluster of buggies and prams to queue at the counter to pay. A little girl ran past shrieking, making her nerves jangle.

'Gabe,' she called. 'We're going.'

The boy barely looked up from the screen. 'I want to stay!'

'Say goodbye to your friend,' she said.

The queue moved. Poppy shuffled past an empty table with an iPad on it, the screen opened at a news page. A report about those murders. It was all you could read about these days. Not that Poppy had been paying much attention to events. Police had released a photofit of a woman they wanted to talk to. The image was small, but something about it made her look again. Poppy placed two fingers on the screen and pulled them apart to increase the size of the photo, and there was no mistaking what she saw.

Who she saw.

She moved the article across the screen in small, jerking movements, emphasising different parts of the story. Increasing the size of the print made certain words pop in her vision:

Murdered . . . tortured . . . corpses . . . dangerous . . . suspects.

Senseless home invasions. Couples attacked in the dead of night. Children made orphans. By a man, the police said, possibly two – and a woman. Maybe this woman in the photo.

The face was thinner and the hair too long and straight, but that was *her*.

It was Tatia.

'Excuse me,' said a voice, and Poppy jumped. A man took the tablet. 'This is my table.'

'I'm sorry.' She fled to the back of the cafe. Someone called her name, another mum wanting to say hello, but she stumbled into the toilet and locked it. Fell to her knees in the cool, dark space. Hunched forward, her hair splayed on the dirty tiles, she gasped. Her lungs felt as if they were packed with cement.

All these thoughts. She didn't know what she had done to deserve any of this. All these terrible things happening.

Divorce. Murder. Joel. Kill. Marriage. Love. Tatia.

The walls of the cramped space seemed to fold around her like a clammy skin.

Murder. Divorce. Tim.

Tatia was involved, which meant somehow Joel was, too. One man, the report said, possibly two. She had forced him to do terrible things, it was the only explanation, and now he was a broken shell of a man. You only had to look at the pathetic state of him to see something had gone very wrong in his life.

Poppy groaned, dropping her forehead to the cool tiles, scraping her nails into the grouting.

'Oh my god.' Saying it again and again, her breath bouncing off the floor back into her face. Her bare knees, exposed by the fashionable rips in her jeans, hurt on the hard floor. 'Ohmygodohmygodohmygod.'

That was Tatia in the photofit. Those killings. Those people murdered in their homes. Someone banged on the door.

'Poppy,' called Issy. 'Are you in there?'

'Won't be a moment!'

225

Divorce. Murder. Joel. Marriage. Love. Tatia. Kill.

'Are you okay?'

'Out in a minute!'

Joel. Murder. Tatia.

She squeezed her arms over her head, trying to rid her mind of the worst thoughts. But one took hold. It was bad, it was wrong. And it was enough to bring her whole world crashing down.

Murder.

Poppy moaned softly into the tiles because she knew she couldn't get rid of it. A terrible idea grew in her head like a tumour.

Tatia.

Poppy had no idea how long she had been beneath the fold-down baby-changing table.

Tim.

Another rap on the door. 'Poppy, we're worried about you!'

Sick with fear and disgust, her voice came out as a croak. 'Coming now!'

Poppy reached for her bag, rifled through it, but couldn't find what she was looking for. She tipped all her things onto the floor. Her phone, her purse, her mints and keys and tampons and tube of hand cream and wipes and make-up, and her diary and pen. Panicking, she scrabbled through it, spreading it over the floor, a lipstick rolling away behind the toilet, until she found what she was looking for. A screwed-up ball of paper.

The number that Tatia had pressed into her hand at the park.

Dragging herself to her feet, Poppy held onto the edge of the sink and stared into the mirror. She didn't recognise the woman who stared back. She was someone whose life was spiralling out of control.

A knock on the door. 'Poppy?'

'I'm coming now!'

Poppy sucked down a breath, rubbed the tears from her cheeks and tied her hair into a ponytail high on the back of her head, ready for the world.

38

Ray Drake climbed the stairs to the HR office. He had access to the personnel records of the people who ranked lower in his team, but couldn't see general files. The Met's entire HR department had been moved to Victoria and all the old paper files, containing service records and personal details of Met employees, were in storage somewhere up north. He had no idea whether Marion Cresswell still used her old room on the fourth floor when she came to the station, or whether she hot-desked, or even if there was a computer there any more, but going there was the only thing he could think to do.

The corridor was empty, but when he swiped his pass against the pad and yanked on the handle, the door didn't open. Drake swore, at a loss about what to do next, when it swung open. Marion stood there with a sandwich in her hand.

'DI Drake. What a lovely surprise.'

'Marion,' he said. 'You're here.'

'For my sins!' She rolled her eyes. 'It's appraisal time, so you're going to see me around a lot. What can I do for you?'

'Your car,' he said. 'Remind me of the make.'

She hesitated. 'It's a blue Mondeo.'

'I thought that was what it was.' He frowned. 'Where did you park it?'

'In one of the bays down the road.'

'I thought I recognised it.' He shook his head. 'I'm sorry, Marion, I think someone's keyed it.'

'Little fuckers!' Marion hurried to the desk in the corner of the small, anonymous room and dropped the sandwich in a bin. She pulled her lanyard over her head, snatched up her keys. 'It's incomprehensible to me why somebody would do that.'

He made a sympathetic face as he held the door open. 'Make sure you report it at the front desk.'

'I will,' she said, and rushed out. 'And thank you.'

Drake pretended to look at his phone in the corridor, keeping the door ajar with the toe of his shoe, until he was sure Marion was gone. Then he went inside, closed the door and sat at her computer. Minimising the document she'd been working on, he opened the HR database. Marion's Met employee number appeared already in the login box.

But to get into the system he needed a password, and hadn't the faintest idea what it was. He guessed it would be something to do with her son. Marion doted on the boy. But despite her talking about him whenever they met, Drake couldn't remember the teenager's name.

He opened the top drawer of the desk – the paperclips shivered in the plastic tray – and went through everything. There were magazines, ring binders, notebooks; a hairbrush and a bag of make-up. A packet of crisps, a KitKat. Pins, rubber bands and loose bent staples.

Drake lifted out a fat Filofax, plump with folded pieces of paper, business cards and post-its, and clicked open the stud. The diary pages were full of appointments and meetings, work deadlines and holiday bookings, cinema times, the date of a college reunion, a restaurant opening and a school parents' evening, a dentist appointment, friends' birthdays and wedding anniversaries. He found Marion's fifty-third birthday highlighted – she had drawn a tiny cake on 18 December – and he typed in the date numerically in the password box. It was rejected.

Drake turned to the empty pages at the back, where important information was often jotted down. He saw lots of names and random information – the address of a hairdresser, a delicatessen, a cookery school and a delivery reference number, but nothing that looked like a password. He put the organiser back and opened the lower drawer. Here were more files, a laminated list of phone extensions, receipts, an instruction manual for a steam cleaner, supermarket coupons, a ball of rubber bands and a Mother's Day card. When Drake opened the card, a photo fell out. It was of her son at his birthday party. A banner trailed across a wall behind him. It said: *Happy Birthday Justin!!!*

Drake's fingers clicked noisily across the keyboard as he typed the name into the box. JUSTIN. He hit ENTER. Too short, the password had to be at least ten letters long, so he typed,

JUSTINCRESSWELL

Hit ENTER. No luck. He tried:

JUSTINCRESSWELL1
JUSTINCRESSWELL10
JUSTINCRESSWELL100

and was rejected each time. Drake remembered the boy's age, and typed

JUSTINCRESSWELL15

The system wouldn't let him in.

A fire door boomed shut at the end of the corridor. Drake glanced up uneasily, his hands lifting from the keyboard, as footsteps came down the corridor – *clop, clop, clop* – and stopped outside the door. The handle rattled as someone tried to come into the room. Then they knocked.

'Marion?' called a voice. 'I'm here for my appointment.' The handle jerked again. 'Are you in there?'

Drake waited till he heard the footsteps recede, and turned back to the keyboard. He glanced at the clock. He had been here for nearly ten minutes and was running out of time. As soon as Marion saw there was no damage to her car, she'd come straight back.

He checked every scrap of paper in the drawer – and came up with nothing. Then he put everything back, replacing a thin paper packet back on top where he'd found it. Worming tablets for a dog. He recalled their last conversation and put his fingers to the keyboard, typed

BERNIEBATTENBERG

He hit ENTER, and the screen changed. He was in, free to roam around the Metropolitan Police's HR database. He typed in Samuel Wylie's name.

And found the thing he feared most of all. A thick personnel file. All the details of Sam Wylie's history as an undercover officer in the Metropolitan Police and the National Crime Agency.

Just say the word, Ray, said Connor softly. *And I'll make this all go away.*

39

Millie put the phone down and called to Drake, who was examining ANPR data on the other side of the office. 'Sir.'

When he walked over she was scribbling furiously on a notepad. 'That was the police in Tbilisi.' She underlined something twice and dropped the pen. 'Tatia Mamaladze has been missing, presumed dead, for more than two years now.'

Behind her, Eddie Upson slammed a paper cartridge into a photocopier. The sound was as loud as a gunshot. Drake clapped his hands together and everyone came over, crowding around Millie's desk.

'She was known to the authorities for years,' she said.

'Wait.' Drake spun a finger. 'Go back. Are we sure she was at the orphanage?'

'Tatia's circumstances, of her being sent back there, were well known. It's her. As an adult, she was a familiar visitor to various police stations in the city. Whenever one of the former kids from the home got arrested she'd be there to support them. Many of these people were vulnerable, damaged, and fell prey to hardcore criminals. They dropped into crime, addiction, prostitution. They had no education, no future,' said Millie, 'and organised crime gangs were ready to recruit them and put them to work. Tatia would turn up at the cells to ensure they were treated well and organise legal representation or childcare. The officer I spoke to described her as quiet, polite, optimistic and intelligent. He said she had a nice smile.'

'Quite the guardian angel,' said Flick.

'And brave.' Dudley Kendrick clasped his hands behind his head as he leaned back in his chair. 'I imagine you mess with the Georgian police at your peril.'

'But this is where it gets interesting.' Millie turned the pages of her notebook. 'Because Tatia moved in very unsavoury circles. She was closely associated with a criminal organisation run by a man called Darejan . . . give me a moment, my handwriting isn't . . .' Her finger hovered over a word in the notebook. 'Dolidze. He was one of the biggest gangsters in Georgia. He was a flamboyant character who kept a live bear at his mansion and crocodiles in his moat.'

Eddie nodded, impressed. 'Can't have an empty moat.'

'Basically, nothing happened in the Georgian underworld without Dolidze's permission. Drugs, gunrunning, prostitution, etcetera, and his influence reached into the upper reaches of the state. He had politicians in his pocket, and government officials. And whenever one of his men got arrested, guess who was there sorting out lawyers, making sure they were treated well until Darejan Dolidze was able to pull some strings?'

'Tatia,' said Vix Moore, tugging absently at a strand of hair. 'She worked for him in some way.'

'His mistress?' asked Eddie.

'There's no evidence of that,' said Millie. 'She was more like an advisor. Someone whose opinion he trusted.'

'Why?' asked Eddie.

'Because she was bright,' said Millie, 'and people liked

234

her. Darejan was a psychopathic thug, notorious for his cruelty and ruthlessness, a proper old-school post-Soviet crim, but he was clever enough to know to surround himself with people who could get things done.'

'You keep referring to him in the past tense.'

'A couple of years back, Darejan and three of his men were shot dead in a police raid following an armed robbery in the city centre. Witnesses suggested he pulled a pistol on police officers and died in a hail of gunfire.'

'Who were the witnesses?' asked Drake.

'That would be other police officers,' said Millie, raising an eyebrow. 'The cops were acting on an anonymous tip-off. By a woman. Days later, Tatia went missing. The rumour was that she was the informant and Darejan's associates killed her in revenge. No great surprise to anyone – people go missing in the Georgian underworld all the time.'

'But instead she slipped out of the country.'

'The cops in Tbilisi are as surprised as anyone that she may have resurfaced over here.'

They'd had no success finding out if Tatia Mamaladze had come into the country. It took a lot of money to get a fake passport, and it was risky. Even better was a *real* passport – a new name and a whole new identity courtesy of the state – but that took a lot of influence at the highest level.

'She got close to this Dolidze,' said Drake. 'She was using him in the same way she's been using Carl.'

'What could she possibly want?' asked Eddie.

'A passport that identifies her as a European national, that gives her dual nationality perhaps, and enabled her to get a work permit before Brexit restrictions begin to bite.

If Dolidze had connections within government, he could get her one of those.'

'If anyone can, Darejan can,' said Eddie, fishing for a laugh.

'But then why arrange for him to be arrested, or maybe even killed?'

'To cover her tracks,' said Drake. 'Or maybe it wasn't her who made that call, and she used the chaos of the moment to slip away.' He turned to Millie. 'Can we get Tatia's DNA profile over there so we can confirm we're talking about the same person?'

She made a note.

'Our Tatia is certainly a woman of contradictions,' said Flick.

'Aren't they all?' said Eddie, glancing at Vix.

But Dolidze's death and Tatia's immediate disappearance was an unlikely coincidence. Drake knew all too well how far some people would go to protect themselves. He sensed Tatia's genuine concern for the other children from that orphanage, but also her ruthless ambition to get away. First and foremost, Tatia was a survivor, negotiating the shifting allegiances and loyalties in the snake pit of Tbilisi's dangerous criminal underworld. She had built a relationship with perhaps the only man who could get her what she needed, gaining his trust in order to climb out of a terrifying world of violence and bringing to an end a life lived in the shadow of constant danger. Getting a new identity, a chance to escape . . .

To go home.

Sometimes people did bad things for all the right reasons – but it was a slippery slope. Once you crossed a line, it was impossible to go back.

236

Nobody knew that better than Ray Drake.

'I don't get it,' said Eddie. 'Tatia's fallen in with bad men in Georgia so she can get here, and then she hooks up with a low-rent burglar like Carl. What does she want from him?'

'Access,' said Drake. 'To those homes.'

'There are a lot of Eastern European criminal gangs knocking around London,' said Vix Moore. 'Maybe she's stealing to order.'

'Carl doesn't strike me as someone who has the brains to play with the big boys. And nothing of notable value has been taken from any of those homes. A bit of jewellery, some electronic gear. Stuff that can be flogged quickly. This is something more desperate.'

'She steps into someone else's life for a few hours,' suggested Flick.

'She's living a fantasy,' agreed Drake. 'She sees all these normal lives around her, people with beautiful homes, and she can't help but taste what they have, just for a little while. She goes into their homes and eats their food and relaxes in their armchairs, luxuriates in their baths. She uses their coffee maker, lights their scented candles and wears their clothes. Tatia was given the chance of a new beginning when she was a child – a normal life with a good family – and it was all ripped from her. She's snatching moments of comfort in the dead of night.'

'But now . . .' prompted Flick.

'It's all gone wrong. After months of breaking and entering into empty properties, places where the owners are absent or non-domiciled, Gareth Walker changes his weekend plans. He's home when they arrive. There's a confrontation and he's killed.'

'And soon after that,' said Flick, 'it happens again and then again.'

Drake's team thought about the consequences of that statement. A few months ago, Carl and Tatia broke into empty homes. Now they clearly didn't care if the homes were empty or not. They were prepared to kill.

Maybe Tatia and Carl needed it now. Maybe it was all part of the fun.

While his team discussed Tatia, Drake picked up the newspaper printouts about the Bliss family and read them again. Years ago, a couple took in a girl called Tatia Mamaladze, and following the death of their youngest child, sent her back to the same Georgian orphanage from which she was rescued. A hell on earth, by all contemporary accounts.

As she lay awake at night in that orphanage, listening to the screams and nightmares of the kids in the dark, she must have dreamed of what was given to her – a life of love and stability – and then taken away. In all likelihood, Tatia had been trying to find a way back ever since. Clawing her way up from poverty by working for a gangster. Earning money, increasing her status in order to obtain a precious freedom. A passport, a way home.

Tatia wanted to believe in a future that had been lost to her many years ago. But it had all gone sour – like everything else in her life, it had all gone horribly wrong.

People were dying. Maybe Will Bliss's death all those years ago had been a foretaste of things to come, and the Blisses knew full well the kind of unhinged character she was when they sent her far away. Maybe Tatia couldn't wait to kill again.

Drake felt his phone buzz in his pocket. He took it out and checked the text message on the screen from a number he didn't recognise.

THE RED LION, DALSTON.
TONIGHT, 8 P.M.

Drake replaced the phone in his jacket.
'What's the plan?' asked Eddie.
Drake dropped the sheets back on the desk and nodded at Flick. 'Let's go and see Poppy Bliss.'

40

Tatia couldn't remember being this nervous in her entire life. She had been scared many times, but this was worse – because she had a feeling of hope. She was afraid that it was all a sick joke, and scanned the park for police, half expecting at any moment to see officers jump out of the bushes.

The phone call had come completely out of the blue. Poppy had asked to meet. Tatia listened, dumbstruck, when she suggested a time and place.

Waiting on the bench, she had a jolting memory of being forced as a punishment to sit on her hands outside the orphanage during a snowstorm, her body shaking with unbearable cold, her fingers so numb beneath her that she thought they had already fallen off.

She could hardly believe she was here, in this park, on this lovely day. A single puffy cloud drifted slowly across the blue sky; a dog chased a ball; a baby thrashed its arms on a picnic rug. Tatia carefully watched a drone buzz over the treetops, afraid that it was spying on her, and was relieved when it landed at the feet of a teenager. Unable to contain her anxiety, she looked to the entrance of the park for the millionth time.

'What do you think it is she wants?' she asked Joel, who was staring at a patch of grass. Tatia knew that he was back in that moment on the cliff, reliving it again.

One moment Will was there, and the next—

If only she could set him free from that terrible sequence of events, what a gift that would be.

'I wonder if she will bring her little boy?'

And she had no sooner spoken than she saw Poppy approaching. Once again Tatia was struck by how beautiful she was, how sleek and graceful, her tanned legs long and lithe in a simple denim skirt and sandals, those arching collarbones delicately accentuating her long neck. Tatia felt so proud – and so full of regret. Poppy would have been the perfect sister if events hadn't turned out so badly.

Poppy sat, placing her purse and keys and phone on the bench. Her eyes were hidden behind an oversized pair of sunglasses. 'Thank you for coming.'

'You are most welcome.'

'This is difficult for me to say.' She kept clearing her throat, as if she had something stuck in there, and Tatia wished she had a pastel to offer, or a bottle of water. 'I owe you an apology.'

'No,' whispered Tatia.

'Please.' Poppy took off the glasses and folded them in her fingers, revealing those lovely brown eyes. 'I've treated you badly, I have been judgemental and I realise now . . . unkind. I hope that we can start again.'

'It is all I have ever wanted. I have always hoped and prayed that we would be reunited again, the three of us. I always believed, despite everything, that it would one day happen.'

Tatia clambered off the bench to throw her arms around her sister. She smelled her perfume, the moisturiser on her skin. The glasses still clamped in her hand, Poppy's body was rigid. But she was not a demonstrative person, Tatia understood that, and let her go.

'I have always been proud to call you my sister.' Tatia felt a joy so powerful that it made her giddy. Her head filled with happy possibilities. Maybe Poppy would even call her Sarah. 'It has been . . . difficult for us.'

'I understand.' Poppy glanced at Joel, who stared blankly.

'But everything has been worth it. Everything!'

Poppy didn't look inclined to ask what those difficult things were, but if she did, Tatia couldn't tell her yet about Carl and the complicated situation in which she and Joel found themselves. She didn't want to spoil this emotional moment.

But then Poppy said, 'You must visit.'

'Really?'

'To meet Gabriel and . . . my husband. They'll be so excited to meet you.'

'Do they know about me?' asked Tatia.

'No,' admitted Poppy, 'but I'll tell them.'

'Because we are a family now.'

'Yes.' Poppy slipped her sunglasses back on. She was about to cry tears of gladness, Tatia thought, and didn't want anybody to be embarrassed.

Tatia wanted to touch her sister again. She was so perfect – there wasn't a single blemish on her broad, brown shoulders. She grabbed her hands, but Poppy yelped.

'I am sorry.' Tatia pulled away, mortified. 'I did not mean to hurt you!'

'It's just my ring.' Poppy held up her hand to show Tatia a gorgeous jade stone on her third finger. 'It dug into me.'

Tatia admired the ring, and Poppy's manicured nails. 'It is the most beautiful thing.'

'So.' Poppy removed her hand. 'I hope we can be friends now.'

'Better, we are brothers and sisters, and I can be Sarah again!' When Poppy didn't reply, Tatia asked, 'What is his name?'

'Whose name?'

'Your husband. I imagine he is a handsome prince!'

Poppy smiled. 'His name is Tim.'

What had happened on that cliff had been a tragic accident, and had terrible consequences for them all, but Poppy didn't have to be afraid any more. It had taken extraordinary strength of character for her to admit that she had behaved badly, out of an unreasonable fear. She was clearly a good person, who had found the compassion to invite Tatia and Joel into the bosom of her family.

'Joel,' Poppy said. 'I want to speak to Tatia alone for a moment. Why don't you go and get yourself an ice cream or something?'

'He is not the strongest,' said Tatia. 'Perhaps we should walk.'

'Of course.' Poppy snatched up her phone, purse and keys. 'We won't be a moment.'

When Tatia joined her on the path, she caught her sister dabbing a finger beneath her glasses.

'Poppy?'

'I'm sorry.' She composed herself. 'It's just a shock to see him like that.'

Tatia was worried that Poppy would blame her for his condition. Tatia could be accused of many bad things but she had been there for Joel when all his so-called friends had turned their backs. Together, she and Poppy would make him well.

'What is it, some kind of psychological condition?'

'He cannot sleep,' said Tatia. 'Or will not.'

'I should have been there for him.'

'It is not too late. May I ask why . . . you and Joel lost touch?'

'We drifted apart. The truth is, I treated Joel very badly. Mum and Dad, too, when they were alive. I was ashamed of them, and of what happened, and ashamed of myself.' Maybe she glanced at Tatia – her eyes were hidden by the sunglasses and it was difficult to tell. 'I treated you all very badly.'

Tatia smiled sadly. 'Your parents never forgave me for what happened.'

'I should have tried to help you more . . . but I didn't.' Poppy watched Joel slumped on the bench. 'But I need to know, I need to be sure, that you have never told him what really happened.'

'Never!'

'I need to *know*.'

'It has never occurred to me to tell him. Why would I, Poppy? My dreams have come true. We are back together, the three of us, and we can begin again.'

Poppy's smile was pained. 'You are a good person.'

'Thank you,' said Tatia, with emotion.

'I had better go pick up Gabriel.'

'Of course.'

Tatia couldn't stop smiling, but knew she was making her sister uncomfortable – Poppy, who was so sensitive to other people's needs, so full of grace. Tatia cursed herself for always doing the wrong thing, for saying the wrong thing. It had been the same when they were children. She would do anything to please Poppy. But her sister had exacting standards, and Tatia was too crass, too oafish, ever to be a lady like her.

There was a time, she remembered, when they had gone to a birthday party where a clown performed. Tatia had never seen anything so funny as his tricks and jokes and pratfalls. All the children giggled and Tatia, cross-legged in the middle of the group, couldn't believe she was surrounded by so many happy kids. It was a revelation to her that there could be such joy in the world – and that she could be a part of it. She laughed so much and so loudly that her sides ached. Within moments she was hysterical. Fat tears of happiness poured down her cheeks. And after a few minutes, she realised the children were all staring at her. Embarrassed by her behaviour, Poppy pulled her from the room in a fury and then spent the rest of the afternoon sulking. Tatia burned with shame that she had made her sister so unhappy.

But! They were happy now. Poppy's heartfelt apology was a gift from heaven. She was truly a loving person. And when Poppy left, Tatia lifted her face to the sky. Her life had been lived in darkness for so long that she couldn't remember the last time she had enjoyed the simple pleasure of the warm sun on her skin.

But then a chill dropped down Tatia's spine, like a dark cloud obliterating the sunshine. She felt sad and afraid, because she knew they could never be happy, they could never be a family, her and Joel and Poppy.

There was someone who would simply not allow her to share her love with anyone else.

Carl.

41

'He's police,' said Drake, racing an amber light. 'Sam Wylie is a level one undercover officer.'

'Don't be ridiculous.'

He swung the car past a cyclist on Tottenham Lane, driving towards the well-to-do suburb of Crouch End.

'He's a detective sergeant. But he's been signed off for two years with PTSD. He worked with the National Crime Agency's Serious and Organised Crime Squad, with the Matrix unit in Merseyside, on Operation Trident.' He met her eyes. 'And the Ghost Squad.'

He saw her redden before she turned away, shoulders stiffening, to watch the streets rush past. People sat outside cafes, drinking coffee, oblivious to the traffic crawling past.

'It's disbanded,' she said.

'So they say.' SO10 – the Ghost Squad – was a notorious Metropolitan Police undercover department, an ultra-secret unit that covertly investigated other cops for corruption and serious misdemeanours. 'What if it's not been disbanded? What if it's still in operation in some shape or form, hidden deep within the Met structure? And this guy is good, Flick, he's got a hell of a service record.'

They approached the junction of Crouch End Broadway, the busy traffic thickening around them. In the middle of the road, isolated on a traffic island, was a tall clock tower which had stood there for over a hundred years.

'He lied to you. He's been a police officer for ten years and he didn't tell you. Why would he do that?'

'If he's signed off with stress,' she said indignantly, 'the last thing he'll want to do is talk about it. There's probably a good explanation. You're being paranoid.'

'Did you speak to him about me?'

'No.'

'Did he ask you anything at all about us?'

She kept shaking her head. 'No.'

'Did you talk about what happened?'

'I don't—' she opened the window a crack and he saw her fringe lift in the breeze. 'Not directly.'

'Not directly?' he asked.

'No,' she snapped. 'Nothing.'

'Then talk to him.' He pulled up at a zebra crossing to allow a family to cross the road and then pulled off the high street, the car climbing to the crest of the hill. 'Ask him why he lied.'

'Ray,' she said shortly. 'Your whole life is one gigantic lie.'

The car surged over the hill. Drake didn't say anything else, just let what he told her sink in. He took a turning, then another, and pulled his Mercedes to the kerb outside Poppy Bliss's address, cutting the ignition. For a moment, they sat in silence in the quiet street. He heard the screech of a window being lifted in one of the tall homes. Turrets and first-floor balconies and intricate decorative plasterwork set each house apart from the ones on either side.

'How do you know he's police?'

He could tell her about how he'd fitted a tracker beneath Wylie's car and followed him to a police safe house, how he was filmed breaking into the flat by Wylie, or his unauthorised accessing of the Met's HR files; he could tell her about the text from Wylie. But that wasn't going to simplify matters. He just wanted her away from the guy.

'I asked around,' he said. 'It wasn't so difficult.'

Grim-faced, Flick swung open the door and walked up a patterned tiled pathway edged with beds of white pebbles to the door of Poppy's double-fronted Victorian house. Her phone rang just as Drake joined her.

'Excuse me?' she said when she answered it. 'No, I'm not coming to see you.'

Then, to Drake's surprise, she passed him the phone. 'You speak to her.'

He heard her voice before he even pressed the phone to his ear. 'Myra.'

'Who is this?' said the old woman sharply.

'It's Ray,' he said. 'What do you want?'

'Raymond. I thought I had phoned the girl. Put her on.'

'Stay out of it, Myra. I'm handling it.'

Myra was insistent. 'I want to speak to her.'

At that moment, a people carrier pulled into the drive. A woman in sunglasses peered at them from behind the wheel. Drake turned away. 'It's all under control.'

'Tell her I'm expecting her,' said Myra. 'And I won't take no for an answer.'

Drake killed the call and returned the phone to Flick.

'I'm not going,' she said, as the woman helped a young boy out of the car, locking the vehicle with her fob. 'So you can call off your attack dog.'

'She's not great with boundaries.'

'I've been summoned.' Flick spoke in an angry murmur. 'Like a commoner ordered to court.'

'I'm sorry,' he said, as the boy bounced up the path. 'I'll speak to her about it later.'

It was typical of Myra to stick her nose in. Whatever this was about, whatever Wylie's intentions were, Drake would handle it himself.

'Poppy Bliss?' Drake asked. The woman came to the door, her bulky purse and slim phone pressed together in one hand. A set of keys dangled from her fingers.

'Yes.' She looked from Drake to Flick. 'But it's Poppy Mallory these days.'

'I'm Detective Inspector Ray Drake and this is Detective Sergeant Flick Crowley.' He flashed his warrant card. 'May we come in?'

42

Flick stepped aside to allow Poppy to unlock the door. 'What's it about?'

'We'd like to talk to you about Tatia Mamaladze.'

Poppy nodded urgently at her son. 'Not yet.'

'Who are they?' the boy asked.

'The man and lady have come to talk to Mummy, Gabe.' Inside the spacious hallway, Poppy touched his shoulder. 'Why don't you go and play in your bedroom?'

'Can I tell them a joke?' asked Gabriel. 'I've got plenty of jokes.'

'I bet you have,' said Flick. 'I love jokes. I look forward to hearing one.'

His mother gently turned him towards the stairs and he clattered up. 'We'll play a game later.'

Then she kicked off her sandals and, barefoot, took them into a vast bright kitchen. One whole wall was covered with blackboard paint and filled with vibrant chalk drawings. A long table was spattered with angular offcuts of pastry, plastic moulds and wads of soggy tissue. The far end of the room widened into a conservatory bursting with plants.

'Sorry about the mess,' said Poppy. 'We were baking but I had to pop out. Would you like something to drink? Tea, some juice?'

'We're fine.' Drake tried to find a chair at the table that wasn't covered with a fine layer of flour. 'Thank you.'

'Got to keep up with my five a day.' Poppy held a glass against a lever set into the door of the fridge – ice clinked noisily into the bottom – and then slopped into it some kind of dark vegetable juice from a carton.

'Your home is beautiful,' said Flick. 'This room is bigger than my flat.'

'Thank you.' Poppy started tidying. She picked up a cake tin, moved bowls to the sink. 'I'm a little confused about why you're here – it was a very long time ago that I knew Tatia.'

'How well do you remember her?'

Drake moved out of the way to allow Poppy to wipe a chair with a cloth. She motioned for him to sit. 'It was decades ago and only for a short while. What's this about?'

'We believe Tatia may be back in the city,' he said. 'Have you seen her?'

'God, no, why would I?'

'Miss Mamaladze may be using the surname Bliss,' said Flick.

Poppy threw the cloth to the floor and covered her eyes for a moment. 'I'm sorry, this is a shock. Hearing her name again, after all these years.'

'Why do you think she would use the name Bliss after all these years?' asked Flick.

'She hates my family and it's exactly the kind of contempt-ible thing she would do.'

'She may have been in London for some time,' said Flick. 'Maybe a couple of years or more. If she hasn't already, there's no reason to suggest that she'll try to contact you.'

'We know a little about what happened.' Drake picked up the cloth and handed it to Poppy. 'What was in the papers.'

Placing it on a counter, she said, 'And what was that?'

'That she was taken in by your parents and was then—'

'Sent away, after what happened to Will.' Poppy closed the kitchen door. 'Sent back to rot in that place. That's what you read.'

'What were the circumstances of Tatia's being taken in by your family?'

'My parents were good people, Detective Crowley, who were very conscious that they lived in a world where they had everything they could possibly want while others had nothing. The refugee crisis we have now would have upset them both greatly. They had a big house and a nice life and they felt guilty about that – my parents were big on guilt – and it was their intention to save the children.' She smiled grimly. 'All the little children.'

Poppy came to the table, clamping beakers and glasses between her fingers to take them to the sink. 'And Tatia was meant to be the first. I remember those hateful articles. They suggested my parents were bad people who gave a poor little girl hope, who took her out of a life of poverty, abuse and neglect, gave her a home and a family – then just threw her away.' She placed a hand on her hip. 'But neither of my parents had a bad bone in their bodies. Following the collapse of the Soviet Union, they took advantage of the political uncertainty to bring Tatia here. I've never known the full story of how they took her from that place. It was all very murky. But they meant well. Trouble was, Tatia was a bad seed. Always was, always will be.'

'Tell us what happened to your brother.'

Poppy's hand lifted to her mouth. 'Sorry, it upsets me to think about it.'

'Take your time,' said Drake.

'It never came out at the time, my parents wouldn't allow anyone to know, because they couldn't, just wouldn't, contemplate that Tatia could do such a thing. But the fact is . . .' She let out a long breath. 'I saw her . . . shove him off that cliff. There, I've said it.'

'The inquest suggested it was an accident.'

'My parents went to their graves convinced it was an accident. But I saw Tatia do it. I saw the look on her face as Will fell to his death.' There were tears in her eyes. 'You never forget something like that.'

'You told them what you saw.'

'Yes. But they believed, they had to believe, I was mistaken, that I was just a child who had gotten everything jumbled in my head in the heat of the moment, and they asked me not to tell anyone.'

'And you agreed?'

'Of course,' said Poppy. 'They were my parents. They were aware that Tatia was disturbed, anyone could see that, but they always looked for the good in everybody.'

'How old was she?'

'Tatia was a couple of years younger than me and I was, what, twelve. Certainly old enough to know what she was doing when she pushed my brother to his death. My parents tried to carry on as if it was an accident, but it wasn't an isolated incident. Tatia had physically assaulted me before, and my brother Joel. And when my parents finally came to their senses and realised that Joel and I would be put at further risk, I think they were panicked by the possibility that we could even be taken away, and so with great reluctance they sent Tatia back.'

Poppy pulled out another chair from the table and slid down into it, scraped a hand through her hair. 'They never recovered from what happened to Will. In the years that followed, my mother fell ill and my father killed himself.'

'The papers picked up on the story years later.'

'Yes, my parents were pilloried, portrayed as lefty zealots who didn't give a thought to the needs of their own children. More details emerged about how they took in Tatia and then discarded her. My parents were good people, but maybe . . .' She sighed. 'The newspapers had a point on that score.'

'What about your brother, Joel?'

'What about him?'

'How did he take it?'

'Not very well. He is . . . was fond of Tatia. He was like my parents, and liked to see the good in people.'

'We've been unable to locate him. He's not been at his last known address for several months now.'

'I won't be able to help you.' Poppy jumped up to stack dirty plates and cutlery into a dishwasher, crashing glass and china together. 'We lost contact. Quite a long time ago, actually. Another consequence of what happened. Joel was destined for great things, I think – he was a clever young man. But things became strained between us.' She looked up at a wall clock. 'I'm sorry, I'm going to have to fix Gabriel something to eat.'

'Of course.' Drake stood. 'Tatia is implicated in a number of intrusions into homes in which people have been killed.'

Poppy reddened. '*Those* murders.'

'Maybe it would be an idea to place an officer outside your house to ensure you and your family are safe,' he said. 'Just as a precaution.'

'Tatia would be mad to come near me after all these years.' Poppy shivered. 'Just saying her name out loud makes my flesh crawl.'

'It could be something to consider if you have a young—'

'I will not scare my family, DI Drake, and I don't relish the idea of neighbours asking awkward questions about why there are police here. The truth is, there are details of my childhood that I haven't yet discussed with my husband. I'll be sure to now, of course.'

'We can provide an alarm system, or a camera.'

'We have a perfectly good alarm system.'

'It's your choice, but I'll have to send you a formal letter which states you declined an offer of protection,' said Drake. 'You just have to sign it.'

'Whatever you need.'

'Do you have any photographs of Tatia?' asked Flick.

'The girl was responsible for the death of my brother. If I found any photos of her, I can assure you I would have destroyed them years ago.'

When they walked into the hallway Gabriel thundered down the stairs.

'Knock knock,' he said to Drake.

'Say "who's there?", DI Drake,' prompted Flick.

'Who's there?' asked Drake.

'Mikey!'

'Mikey who?'

'My key doesn't fit in the keyhole!'

'Very good. I could listen to knock knock jokes all day . . .'

'I've got loads more!'

Drake walked to the door. 'But we've got to get back to work.'

'If she attempts to come anywhere near,' said Poppy. 'I can assure you I'll give you a call.'

'And your husband,' said Drake, stepping outside with Flick.

'I'll speak to him. Thank you for coming,' she said, and closed the door.

Drake pointed his fob at his car as he approached it and the doors unlocked. He looked back up at the house, thoughtfully. 'She didn't ask.'

'Didn't ask what?'

'She never asked why Tatia was under investigation,' he said. 'I had to offer the information.'

'Take me home,' said Flick, climbing inside.

'We have work to do,' said Drake.

'To your house, Ray.' Flick whipped the seatbelt across her chest and clicked it into place. 'If Myra has something to say to me, she can tell me now.'

43

8 years after Will:

'Thank you all for coming,' Patrick Bliss told the audience. 'It's good to see so many of you here.'

The church hall erupted in appreciative applause, and Joel felt a thrill that all these people were here to support his father. He had never felt so proud. But Poppy's constant fidgeting beside him was annoying.

He nudged her with his elbow. 'Are you listening?'

His mother sat in the front row and when his father spoke from the stage, Joel noticed, his gaze dropped regularly to hers. Jill Bliss gave her husband energy, gave him purpose, always had done.

'I promise that if I'm elected as your Labour candidate I'm going to give it my all.' Patrick Bliss stood in front of his rivals for the nomination. Joel thought they all looked tense and miserable. His father had never been a demonstrative man, and he wasn't as well groomed as the other candidates, but his inherent goodness shone through. The audience hung on his every word. They knew his concerns were their concerns, and that he would work tirelessly to represent them. 'For too long the ears of people in power have been closed to your concerns, but I'm going to change that.' Someone cheered at the back. Joel twisted

257

in his seat to look. 'We're a community and we stand or fall together!'

The speech finished, everyone clapped. The people in front of Joel actually stood. His father modestly accepted the applause. He caught Joel's eye and smiled, sensing he had the nomination in the bag. Full of pride, Joel turned to his sister, but Poppy sat with her head bowed, picking the polish off the nail of one finger. Patrick Bliss asked the audience if they had any questions. He pointed to a man in the third row.

'What makes you want to run as an MP?'

'Good question.' Patrick steepled his fingers to consider how to answer. 'We all have a responsibility, don't we? We can't just let other people make all the important decisions. I think it's time we made our voices heard.'

'And what about the girl you abandoned?' called someone. Joel craned his neck to see who it was. A man with a notebook and pen stood in the middle of the hall. 'Does she have a voice?'

Patrick Bliss cleared his throat. 'I don't know what you—'

'Isn't it true that you took in a child from a notorious orphanage in Eastern Europe and then sent her back home a few months later, following an incident in which your youngest child died?'

Someone in the hall shouted, 'Sit down!'

'You gave her hope and then discarded her, riding roughshod over adoption procedures in the process.' The man cocked his head. 'Forgive me, but how is that showing personal responsibility?'

The audience became agitated. People tried to get a better look at the man, who wore press accreditation around his neck.

'I'm not going to talk about my family's personal business – it has no bearing on the policies we're discussing now.'

'Voters may think otherwise,' said the journalist. 'They may decide that someone who is capable of sending a vulnerable young girl back to a place like that isn't the kind of man fit to represent them. They may conclude that there are important questions to be answered about this extraordinary train of events.'

'The circumstances were complex.'

'And very possibly illegal.'

Patrick's voice rose above the clamour. 'This is not the time or the place to discuss it.'

'But it's exactly the time and place.' The man gestured at the audience. 'You're running on a platform of personal responsibility. I've done my research on that orphanage. It was a squalid, chaotic place. Degrading and brutal by any civilised standards. The children there were treated no better than animals. And yet you –' he jabbed his pen '– sent her back.'

Someone shouted for the journalist to shut up but another member of the audience demanded he be heard. Heated arguments broke out all around the hall as he slipped away.

Caught up in the angry exchanges, it was a few minutes later when Joel realised Poppy had left and he went to find her. She wasn't in the corridor. He checked the toilet and other rooms, then walked around a corner to see her pressed up against the wall. The journalist's hand was planted above her shoulder as he spoke quietly.

'Get away from her.' Joel marched towards them, his blood boiling. This man had already done enough damage. 'Or I'll call the police.'

'Joel,' Poppy said, 'let me handle this.'

'It's disgusting that he's bothering you.'

'You're the brother.' The journalist smiled. 'Do you have any information you want to give me?'

Joel looked at each of them in turn. At Poppy's crimson face, lowered shamefully, and then at the smirking journalist. 'I'll wait outside.'

Ignoring the noise coming from inside the hall, Joel walked into the graveyard. He saw Poppy dart down the slippery path towards the street and caught up with her.

'You told that journalist about Sarah.'

'Go back inside, Joel,' she said, refusing to look at him.

'Why? What possible reason would you have?'

She walked through the gate. 'Go look after Mum and Dad.'

He grabbed her arm. 'Why would you do that?'

'They brought this on themselves by bringing that creature into our house. They ruined everything. Not me!' Her angry words stunned him. Poppy never talked about what happened to Will; it was one of those things he knew never to bring up, knew how much it upset her. 'Everything was fine until she came. We were happy till *she* came.'

'You're being ridiculous.'

'They've ruined my life!'

'All he ever wanted was to make a difference to people's lives, but now you've destroyed any chance Dad has of being chosen as a candidate.'

'I couldn't bear it if every time he stood up to make a speech, every time he tried to do his do-gooding, someone would say, *that's the man who got his son killed because he brought a monster into his house.* They would judge him, they would judge us. It's better that people know now.' She looked up and down the road. 'Tim and his parents are coming to pick me up.'

Her new boyfriend. His parents were in show business or something. Poppy already spent a lot of time at their house, far more than she ever spent now with her own family.

'Please stay.'

'I can't.' There was a choke in her voice. 'Not after what I've done.'

He thought of that disgusting reporter, and the truth hit him like a hammer blow. 'You're embarrassed by us.'

'And is it any wonder? Our family is a joke.'

Members of the audience started to come outside, still debating the turn of events. His dad was hardly likely to get the nomination now. It was his lifelong dream to be elected to parliament, but that dream was in tatters.

'I love Tim and he loves me,' she said. 'But his parents, they're not political people and if they see Dad on the television every week, knowing what they know . . . I couldn't bear it if they didn't like me.' A car approached, something long and silver and classic. 'They're coming, go inside.'

'I don't know who you are any more.'

'It's not me who caused all this, Joel. *She* did.'

'Sarah's long gone,' he said. 'Because of you.'

'There's more to what happened than you will ever know.'

'I wish I remembered any of it, but I can't.'

'Believe me,' Poppy gave his hand a quick squeeze, 'it's best forgotten. Look after Mum and Dad.'

'I'll tell them what you did,' he called as she walked off.

'Do what you have to,' she said, and ran down the road to climb into the car.

Patrick and Jill were sitting holding hands on the edge of the stage when Joel walked back between broken rows of chairs.

'Where's your sister?' His dad started stacking chairs. The clashing metal struts slammed loudly in the empty hall.

'She had to leave.'

Joel was determined to tell them what Poppy had done. She was cruel to destroy her father's dream like that – because she was embarrassed.

'She doesn't handle upset very well.'

Joel was getting sick of the way his parents excused her behaviour. They surely wouldn't when he told them Poppy had spoken to that journalist. But before he could say anything, his mum jumped off the stage.

'Now don't get upset.' She placed her hands on his shoulders. 'But your dad is probably going to withdraw from the nomination process.'

'You can't let these people dictate what you do.'

'This won't be the end of it.' Patrick slapped dust from his palms. 'I can't stand before the electorate knowing that the press will crucify me.'

'You're giving in!' said Joel angrily.

'The way we took in Tatia—'

'Sarah,' insisted Joel.

'The way we took her in wasn't exactly . . . legal. We went about it the wrong way. Money changed hands. We did it for the best of reasons, but Tatia was . . . damaged. We'll never forgive ourselves for what happened to your brother.'

262

Giddy, Joel shut his eyes and saw that clifftop, the clumps of grass swaying in the wind.

One moment he was there, and then –

'There are other things we can do,' said Jill Bliss. 'We have plenty of plans, Joel, that won't rebound on you and Poppy.'

'She doesn't deserve your sympathy.'

Jill darted a look at her husband that was full of meaning. 'Maybe it's a blessing in disguise.'

There was something they were keeping from him. 'What are you talking about?'

'Tell him,' said Patrick.

'They're doing tests.' Jill Bliss faltered, and her husband slipped his hand into hers. 'We don't know the extent of it yet, of how far it's . . . spread.' The sad look she gave him made his insides twist into a hard, tight knot. 'Joel, I'm not very well.'

44

Now:

Joel had never seen Tatia so happy. Despite her attempts to contain her excitement, the smile kept flashing on her face, her eyes bulged with joy. She couldn't stop touching him. Licked a finger to rub away imaginary blemishes on his face, ruffled his hair.

'Oh, little bear!' She took his hands in hers and rubbed them so hard that he heard the joints in his fingers click. 'Can it be true? We have the chance to begin again, you and I, and we must be sure to take it.'

Her lips trembled with emotion. 'She has reached out to us, Joel. Our sister has found it in her heart to forgive. I always knew, despite everything that has happened, I have always sensed that deep down she was a good person, a forgiving person. Poppy looks like an angel, Joel, and she has the heart of an angel. You don't know how I have lived all these years –' she spoke in a fervent whisper '– in that place, and then afterwards. Chaos, struggle, violence, despair – these are the things that have plagued me all my life.'

There was a noise from the bed, a deep rumble, and she froze. Carl's bulk heaved over in the dark like a beast breaking the surface of a black ocean. Only when she was absolutely certain he was asleep did Tatia continue.

'But now . . .' She moaned softly and pressed Joel's bony hand to her lips. 'Oh, now . . . we can be together again, you, me and Poppy.'

A scooter buzzed past on the empty market road below, scattering light across the wall. For a brief moment Tatia's joyful face, her garish smile, were illuminated. He wished he could share her elation, but every day he felt as if another part of his personality had left him. Happiness, sadness – it was difficult for him to dredge up any emotion at all. It was as if small fragments of his soul fell with Will from that cliff every time he saw it in his mind's eye. There were so many things he still didn't understand about what had happened to him on that day so long ago.

One moment he was there, and the next –

'How did Will fall?' he asked.

He felt her tense beside him. 'Why do you ask?'

'I don't . . . I have never remembered. Why did you kill him?'

'I did not mean to – it was an accident, Joel, you know that.' She nervously scratched the web of silver scars on her shoulder, which threaded down her back, a physical reminder of her years at the orphanage. 'A terrible accident.'

'Then why has Poppy always hated you so much?'

'When bad things happen, the people involved sometimes find it difficult to come to terms with it. Poppy . . . she was hurt and she never . . . the truth is, she did not like me, little bear. She never did. I wish it were not the case, and that has been my burden. But it is different now. She has forgiven me.' He felt her lips on his forehead. 'We have a happy future ahead of us, you and I.'

The bedside lamp went on and Joel saw Carl propped

265

on his elbows, his eyes bleary slits against the naked bulb.

'What time is it?' He got out of bed. 'What are you doing up?'

Tatia jumped up and went to him. 'We are just talking!'

'Talking about what?'

'You are going to like what we talked about, Carl. Because we have decided, Joel and I, that we want to go out again. We want to visit another home.' She picked up the notebook with the addresses in it. 'One from the list.'

Carl beamed with pleasure. 'When?'

She hoped she looked excited. 'Soon.'

'Tomorrow, then.' Carl nodded, eager. 'We'll go out tomorrow night.'

'Yes.' She smiled. 'Perfect.'

'I'll choose.' He tried to snatch the notebook, but she held it behind her, out of his reach.

'No. But I will choose well, Carl. Empty homes bore me now. I like it when people are there, and we can . . . have fun.'

'Yes.' Carl's tongue raked his dry lips, and his breath was heavy, excited. 'Come to bed.'

'Soon,' she told him. 'I want to stay with Joel for a little bit longer.'

Tatia sat back down beside Joel and they waited in silence for long minutes until Carl's breath flattened and slowed, and his soft snores filled the room.

She slipped her hand into his. 'I will choose the right address, somewhere empty. And we will tell him there. Where we are all certain to be alone. Where we can talk. Carl will understand.' She sounded uncertain, hesitant. 'If he truly loves me, little bear, he will want me to be happy.

Because that is how love works. He will be happy to let us go.'

'And if he doesn't?' asked Joel.

Her eyes turned towards his, two pinpricks of light in the dark, and she lifted her arms above her head.

'Ring-a-ring o' roses, a pocket full of posies, a-tishoo, a-tishoo . . .'

He said, 'We all fall down.'

They sat in the dark listening to Carl's snores, and eventually Tatia said, 'He must, little bear. He has to.'

45

'Thank you for coming.' Myra stepped aside but Flick was reluctant to go into the house where, only a few months before, they had nearly been killed. 'Well, come in.'

Flick finally went into the large, gloomy hallway. After everything that had happened, it beggared belief that Myra and Ray could still live in this house. But then, the old woman was stubborn and perverse, and nothing about Ray Drake surprised her any more. Myra led her into the front room where the heavy tick of a grandfather clock slowed time.

Colourful blooms sat in a vase on a table in the next room. 'I like your flowers.'

'Thank you. Raymond bought them. He knows how much I love flowers.'

Flick didn't want to stay for longer than was absolutely necessary. 'He's waiting outside. We've got to get back to work soon.'

'He told me about those people killed in their own homes. It's disgusting. I wonder how you and Raymond get through the day, sometimes. But I rather suspect you both enjoy what you do.'

'What do you want, Myra?'

'It has come to my attention that you are . . . courting.'

Flick almost laughed. 'Courting?'

'Raymond is concerned.' Myra perched on the edge of a chair. 'We both are.'

'Thank you both for your interest in my love life. But I'll tell you the same thing as I told Ray. It's none of your concern.'

'This man sounds very unsuitable. In the circumstances.'

'What circumstances are those, Myra?' Once upon a time this old woman, with her withering stare and aristocratic bearing, and the gnarled fingers which twisted in her lap like adders, would have frightened Flick, but she wasn't going to be intimidated any more.

'Raymond tells me he may be an undercover policeman.'

'What's your point?'

'My point is obvious. If you tell him the wrong thing . . .'

'I've lied for Ray, Myra,' said Flick. 'I've put my job and career and reputation on the line for him. I wished, in retrospect, that I hadn't. I wished that I had told the truth about him, but it's too late now. I'm moving on, which, by the way is what Ray has spent months asking me to do. And if I choose for Sam Wylie to be part of my life going forward, then it's my decision, and nobody else's. Not Ray's –' she pointed at the old woman '– and certainly not yours.'

'Despite what you think of him,' said Myra quickly, 'Raymond's heart is in the right place. He has your best interests in mind.'

'Understood.' Flick walked to the door. 'Nice to see you again, Myra.'

'Would it be too much to ask you something else, then?' said Myra, and a tension in her voice, a flutter, made Flick hesitate at the door. 'It's the real reason I asked you here, actually.'

Myra lifted herself stiffly from the chair and walked to the window. Ray Drake sat in his car somewhere on the other side of the Islington square, hidden by the lush green space beyond the ornate railings. The old woman seemed to stare so intently across the road that Flick didn't rule out her having x-ray vision.

'Raymond has, for the most part, lived a blameless life. But recent events have unsettled him. He would never tell me, but I'm as close to him as anyone will ever be, and I know he feels enormous guilt for what happened to us both.'

'Myra—'

'Let me finish.' There was hesitation in her voice. 'All I ask is that you be as strong and loyal a friend to him as he is to you. I'm not going to be around for ever and it would make me happy to know that there is someone out there who will help him when times are tough, who will . . . give him boundaries.'

Flick frowned. 'I'm not sure what you mean.'

'Oh, Raymond thinks he has changed since he was a boy. That unpredictable energy of his, he thinks he's in control of it, but he's not. Since that wife . . . since Laura died, and the problems that befell us all, I have watched him carefully and he's –' she said the final word so quietly that Flick almost missed it '– struggling.'

'I've not noticed any difference.'

'You wouldn't. I'm worried about him,' Myra said. 'I think he is . . .' Flick waited while the old woman grasped for the right word. Her eyes, when they lifted, were like mirrors that reflected the world, leaving her in a state of cold isolation behind them. 'He is *disturbed*. I'm asking you, please, to look after him. Because one of these days I'm very much afraid he's going to do something he'll regret – and god help us all when that happens.'

There was something that Flick didn't understand. 'Your own son died many years ago, and you gave another boy his name – and his life. How can you look at him every day, how can you treat him as your own?'

Myra blinked, surprised by the question. 'I've tried to make the best of a bad situation for everyone. Perhaps I'm not quite the nasty old so-and-so you believe. I have done my best, following the death of my only son and my husband, to keep this show on the road. And I will do so until my dying breath.'

'I'm not his responsibility or yours,' said Flick, 'and he's not mine.'

'Oh, but you are,' said Myra quietly. 'The pair of you are bound together now, whether you like it or not. A woman of your age should be able to organise your life to your own satisfaction. But never forget that he saved your life, the life that you seem so intent on making a mess of.'

Flick opened the door. 'Goodbye, Myra.'

'He's very fond of you, as I suppose I am, too, in a way.' Myra's smile was edged with sadness. 'Raymond will always be a good friend to you, and he needs your friendship.'

'And what about Connor Laird?' asked Flick sarcastically about the child Myra had taken in all those years ago. The angry, dangerous boy who became Ray Drake. 'Does he need a friend, too?'

'Oh yes,' Myra said quietly. 'More than ever.'

Flick let herself out of the house and walked across the square, conscious of Myra Drake's eyes following her from the window.

46

In the dead of night, in a dark, empty house in West London, Carl's footsteps thundered on the floorboards above. Joel listened to him crashing from room to room above his head.

'What's he doing?' he asked Tatia, who stood beside him in the dark, her face lifted to the ceiling.

'Looking for someone to kill,' she said. 'But there has been nobody here for months, I made sure of that.'

Inside, it was difficult to see much in the gloom behind the shutters, but the rooms were sparsely decorated. There was a thick layer of dust everywhere, a smell of damp. Post and flyers littered the mat inside the front door. Magazines stacked sloppily in a corner were written in an Asian language. The lights didn't even work when she tried to turn them on. Whoever owned this property didn't live here. It was a space to stay when they came to the city, perhaps, or maybe an investment.

'There must have been people living here when I visited it, but I cannot remember. I have been to so many homes, little bear, so many.'

A door crashed open above their heads and they heard Carl's footsteps thud on the stairs. Tatia took Joel's hand in hers. She swung his hand brightly, like she used to do when they were children, but her smile, usually so fierce, flickered uncertainly on her face.

'It will be fine. He will understand that we have to leave. In order that we can be happy, we can become a family again.'

And then Carl was silhouetted in the doorway, his hand gripping the frame. Joel heard his heavy, panting breath. 'There's no one here,' he said.

'No', said Tatia, swinging Joel behind her. 'Do you love me, Carl?'

He stepped forward. 'You know I do.'

'And you would do anything for me?'

'Anything.' Carl came closer, and Tatia edged backwards. 'What's this about?'

'It is over, Carl.' Tatia swallowed. 'We are leaving.'

'Where are we going?'

'Not us, Carl. Joel and I.' She turned to Joel and pushed him. 'Go outside, my darling.'

'I don't understand.' Carl grimaced. 'I don't understand what you're telling me.'

'If you truly love me, as you say you do, you will let us go.'

Joel started to move to the door, but Carl pointed – 'Stay!' – and he stopped dead. Something stirred in his chest; he felt it flutter. An emotion – fear.

'We're good together, me and you,' Carl said to Tatia. 'We love each other.'

'How can I love you?' hissed Tatia, making Carl flinch. 'After everything that has happened. *How?* After what happened to those people, Carl. Those poor people.'

He took another step towards her in the dark, and Joel saw tears gleam in his eyes. 'Don't leave me. I love you.'

'It is over, Carl,' she said. 'I am sorry.'

Carl's shoulders heaved; he began to weep.

'*Go*,' whispered Tatia to Joel.

But Carl pointed suddenly at him. 'She killed your brother!' he said, and his voice was full of resentment. 'She dropped him off a cliff, and she'll do the same to you.'

'It was an accident,' Tatia said calmly. 'Joel knows that.'

'Was it, though?' Carl stepped forward. 'Because you and me, we've killed people together.'

'You did it.' Tatia kept her voice low. 'You killed them.'

'We did it together. We deserve each other.'

'No. It was you who killed those people, not me.' Tatia shot an urgent look at Joel. *Go*. 'You have put us in a very difficult position, Carl – very difficult!'

'I did it for you.' Carl's voice was a whine. 'I only wanted to make you happy.'

'Do not blame it on me. Do not! You killed them, Carl. *You*. How can I love a man who would do such a thing? We are not good for each other.'

He came nearer. 'We love each other. You love me. You said you did.'

'I take it back. I am unhappy, Carl. I do not love you. How could I?'

'I couldn't have done it without you,' he cried.

'Do not blame me. You did it because you cannot help yourself,' she said, and Joel heard the revulsion in her voice. 'There is something wrong with you.'

When he took another step towards her, she held up a warning finger. 'Stand back!'

Carl's teary eyes glimmered in the dark. 'You let me do it. You didn't stop me.'

'I could not stop you – how I wish I could – and I will

go to hell for it.' Her voice rose in panic when he stepped forward again. 'Stay away!'

'I love you.' His voice rattled with misery. 'Don't leave me. I promise I'll be good. I'll be a better person, I'll do anything, just tell me you won't leave.'

'Carl,' she pleaded. 'You must let us go.'

'He's to blame.' Carl stabbed a finger at Joel. 'We'd be happy if he wasn't around.'

Smearing a sleeve across his wet eyes, he charged at Joel, shoving him into a wall. Glittering stars and shapes zigzagged in Joel's eyes. Carl's outline became a starburst of pulsing shadow and light. And when his vision cleared, he saw Carl's upper lip was curled, his teeth bared – and his clenched fist pulled back behind his head.

'It's all your fault!'

And then, with a cry, Tatia jumped on Carl's back.

'Get off!' cried Carl as he spun around the room with Tatia clinging to his back. 'We're in love!'

'Get out!' she screamed at Joel, wrapping her legs around Carl's waist, scratching at his neck and face. 'You must!'

Blood pounded in Joel's ears as he watched Carl and Tatia fly around the room. Chairs went flying as Carl blundered about, turning, spinning, trying to shake her off. Stumbling past Joel, he flung his shoulders forward and staggered left and right, turning in circles. Clamping an arm round his neck, Tatia desperately held on. Carl plucked ineffectually at her fingers digging into his cheek.

'I love you! I love you!'

'Go!' she screamed at Joel.

Carl careened backwards and Tatia's back smashed into a wall. Joel saw her grip loosen, but she held on for dear

275

life as Carl stepped forward – and heaved backwards again. And this time her spine hit the wall and she screamed in agony. Carl fell forward on his knees and she tumbled over his shoulders. Her forehead banged into the back of his skull as she rolled over him and onto her back.

Scrambling onto her front, she crawled forwards. 'Get away!'

Carl, his eyes filled with tears, planted his palms on the floor behind her and roared.

Joel had seen how he had killed those people in an angry frenzy.

Carl swinging the heavy ornament high – and then dashing it down.

He knew he should slip away into the night, because the same thing would happen to him.

His eyes full of angry tears.

But he couldn't leave her, he couldn't let Tatia die alone – she had killed his brother, but she had come back for him, she had cared for him, and she was the only one.

Beating, pounding, pummelling.

'Get out,' Tatia screeched over her shoulder. She scrambled towards the kitchen on her hands and knees as Carl climbed to his feet.

The man, the woman, slumping beneath him.

'Love me!' Carl wailed, in a frenzy now. 'Don't go!'

He grabbed at her foot. She kicked out but he held on, and then slipped from the shoe and kept going. Tatia reached up to grab a book on a side cabinet and threw it over her shoulder. It glanced off Carl's head, but he followed her into the kitchen.

Joel was so weak, so frail, and knew the heart feebly

pumping blood around his body could give up at any moment – but he had to do something. He stumbled after them into the kitchen, squinting against the powerful wash of the moon in the window.

Tatia pulled herself to her feet, but Carl grabbed her. Slammed her face first into the cold terracotta surface of a wall.

Above them was a framed photograph, and her hand found it and she pulled it down behind her head. The glass shattered on the crown of his head.

Carl stumbled into the blue pool of moonlight.

Tatia pulled open cabinet doors to throw pots and pans and plates. Most of them missed, clattering to the floor, smashing against the wall, and sometimes they hit him low in the thigh or hip or stomach, making him pause.

But then he came again.

'Joel!' she shouted again. 'Get out!'

Then Carl was upon her, weeping as he slapped and punched her. His splayed fingers reached out to smother her face. He pressed her hard against the wall.

'I love you,' he wailed. 'If I can't have you, nobody will!'

Joel watched, not knowing what to do, and then went to a drawer beneath a counter. Cutlery shivered in its compartments when he wrenched it open. He saw forks, spoons, knives, all kinds of utensils. He took out the longest knife – it was a blunt, miserable thing, but the best he could find – and stood behind Carl, holding it out in front of him.

'Stop.' His voice was a whisper. The knife shook in his hand. He was so weak, and knew he wouldn't be able to do much damage, but maybe he could injure Carl, stop him long enough to give them a chance to flee. Maybe he could –

And then he watched the knife fly away into the darkness as Carl swiped it out of his hand.

Tatia reached blindly across the surface of a counter and her thumb dropped into a cold metal slot. Gritty crumbs stuck to it. She mustered all her remaining strength to yank at the toaster – but it moved a few inches and jerked to a stop, fell from her grasp.

Carl pulled her head towards him and then smashed it back against the wall. Joel saw her head begin to loll. The moonlight flooding in through the window was like a powerful camera flash obliterating Carl, filling the room with silver light.

Tatia's hand fumbled across the toaster's brushed metal surface to the plug attaching it to the wall, ineffectually plucking at it, strength ebbing from her fingers. The only thing keeping her upright was Carl's hand on her face. If he rammed her head into the wall again she would fall unconscious. And she would never wake up.

Her voice was becoming a tired croak. 'Go . . . go . . .'

Carl pressed his body against hers to stop her toppling forward. He yanked her head upright, his fingers gouging into her jaw and cheeks.

'I'm sorry.' He cried hot, wet tears on her face. 'I'm so sorry. I love you!'

There was only one thing Joel could think to do. He pulled at the plug of the toaster in the wall and it fell from the socket. He stepped back as Tatia's fingers fumbled back to the slot of the toaster.

And she swung it as hard as she could into the side of

Carl's head. He flew across the kitchen and fell to the tiled floor. Tatia staggered forwards, gasping for breath.

Carl moaned. He lifted himself to his elbows, but a pancake of vomit spattered the linoleum below him.

In the corner of the room was a dead plant in a giant pot. Tatia staggered towards it and, bracing her legs on either side, heaved it off its stone podium. To Joel, the pot looked as heavy as a boulder.

Straining with the enormous effort, Tatia tottered to Carl, bracing her feet on either side of his head – held the pot above it. 'Now we are free,' she said.

Carl looked up, afraid. 'No.'

And she dropped the pot. It cracked loudly, spilling soil over his head, his shoulders, the floor. Carl's body twitched. And went still.

Somewhere outside a dog barked furiously. A jet was a distant drone as it crossed the night sky.

'Your face,' Joel said.

She smiled, conscious of the blood pouring down her head. 'It is nothing.'

'I'm sorry,' he said and felt his legs almost give way. Tatia took him in her arms and held him upright. She had almost been killed; she had fought to save his life – and he was useless.

'Do you know what this means? Oh, Joel, we are alive, and we are free!'

She laughed. It was a high, fluttering thing. It had been many years since he had heard her laugh. Her face was cut and bruised, and she was almost bent double with exhaustion – but he didn't think she would stop.

Finally, wiping the tears of happiness from her eyes, she

went next door and came back with her shoe, wriggling her foot back inside it.

'Ring-a-ring o' roses.' She lifted her hands above her head. 'A pocket full of posies, a-tishoo, a-tishoo . . .'

'We all fall down,' he replied faintly.

Tatia took his hand in hers. 'And now a new life awaits us.'

47

Wylie sat against a wall of distressed brick in a pub that was a former dairy, swiping back and forth across the screen of his phone with his thumbs. Irritating electronic music and sound effects spewed loudly from the device, to the annoyance of other customers. A pint sat on the round table in front of him.

'Sit yourself down.' Wylie didn't even look up when Drake approached. 'I'm on level seven of this thing and can't get past it. It's doing my head in.'

Drake pulled out a stool to watch the way Wylie's lips puckered and pouted in concentration. After a couple of minutes, the phone made a flatulent noise and Wylie slapped it on the table.

'This close.' He held his thumb and forefinger together. 'I was *this* close. Don't know why I waste my time.' He sipped from his pint. 'But then I've got to do something while I wait for you to break into my flat.'

'It's not your flat,' said Drake.

'True.' Wylie wiped the foam from his lips with the back of a hand. 'It's a Met safe house, but it's not in use all the time, and I needed somewhere to lay my hat for a couple of days.' He whispered, 'I've still got a key.'

Drake glanced around the pub, at the kids playing pool

in the corner and the pair of old men reading papers at the bar. 'What is it you want?'

'Let me get you a drink. No, wait, I hear you don't drink. And you don't attend any twelve-step meetings. Which means either that you don't have a problem in that area, or that – and this is my personal belief, Ray – you are a man of immense self-control.'

'Am I under investigation?'

'That's what I like about you, Ray – you come straight out with it, there's no messing about. You're a man of action, which is a very admirable quality in a person.' Wylie opened the video footage on his phone of Drake prowling around the flat. 'See, that's not normal behaviour for a policeman. A guy starts dating one of your colleagues and suddenly you're following him about, poking your nose into his business.' Drake saw himself move towards the camera on the screen, his face partially hidden in the dark of the room. 'Breaking into Met property will get you into all kinds of trouble. Anybody would look at behaviour like that and come to certain negative conclusions.' He grinned. 'And there are so many interesting questions swirling about you already, DI Drake.'

'What do you want?'

Wylie held up his arms in appeal, *what can you do?* 'I want to go home and get some sleep, but somebody's gone and bashed my door in.'

'Am I under investigation?' repeated Drake.

Wylie gazed around the pub. 'You play pool, Ray? I bet you don't. I bet you've never played a game in your life, or a quiz machine, or a round of darts, or ever put money in a jukebox. I'm guessing you and your lady wife –' Wylie held up a hand in apology when a muscle ticked in Drake's jaw '– never had a special song. Because you're not a frivolous man. In the same way a shark isn't frivolous, or a barracuda. You've an exemplary police record, you come from a privileged background. But a number of months ago it all went wrong. You and your family were targeted by a maniac. People got killed, but you came out of the whole thing smelling of roses.'

'Professional Standards looked into—'

'Yeah, course they did. But you keep overreacting, Ray.' Wylie sat back and laughed. 'You're a man after my own heart.'

'I'm very touched. What is it you want from me?'

'Here's the thing.' For the first time an uneasiness passed across Wylie's face. 'I'm in a bit of a fix. I need a good man at my side, and I think that man is you.'

'Is this official police business?'

Wylie ignored the question, and said, 'Somebody has something. Don't worry, we're not talking drugs, guns, bullion or anything like that. It's something personal. Something I should never have given to them, and which I need to get back.'

'What is it?'

'I was farmed out across the country, I'd do undercover jobs for other forces in faraway places where I wasn't going to be recognised, you know how it works. But this job, getting to know a big criminal guy – he's into all kinds of bad things, guns and drugs and so on – was closer, in Kent. I gave him this thing, it was a personal item, and it was a mistake to give it, and it's very important that I get it back.'

'But he doesn't want to give it back.'

'Several of his associates went to jail as a result of my undercover work, so no, it would be a big mistake to ring on his doorbell like a kid asking for his ball back. Help me get it and I'll leave you alone, I'll leave Flick alone. Neither of you will see me for dust.'

Are you taken in by any of this? Drake was jolted by Connor's voice in his ear. *Because I'm not.*

He took a breath to clear his head. 'You're setting me up.'

'I've already set you up, Ray.' Wylie tapped the phone. 'I've footage of you breaking into Met property. I'm offering you a way out. I need someone who can watch my back, and instinct tells me you're the man for the job.' He shrugged. 'I'm trying to take the edge off the threats with some healthy flattery. Carrot and stick kind of thing.'

Drake thought about it. 'When?'

'The man I spoke about will not be at his house tomorrow night, so let's get it over and done with.'

'And then you disappear,' said Drake. 'This situation, whatever it is, comes to an end.'

He could be telling the truth, but I don't think so, and neither do you, said Connor quietly. *When push comes to shove, you're going to have to protect yourself.*

'I'm gone and the footage is gone, too.' Wylie drained his pint and slammed it down. 'What do you say?'

You may not be able to protect yourself, but I can.

'Are you okay, Ray? You don't look well.'

'I'm good, thank you.'

Wylie clapped his hands on the table. 'I'm going to have to go soon. I'm taking my sons to the cinema, some superhero thing. I love those movies. Being a parent is the best thing ever.'

284

I'll protect you, Connor insisted.

'Then I'm meeting Flick. I'm thinking dinner at a fancy restaurant, candlelight, a guy playing a violin during dessert, that kind of vibe.'

What do you say, Ray?

Drake nodded. 'Let's do it.'

'Grand.' Wylie pushed the empty glass across the table and smiled. 'Don't look so down, Ray. We're going to have such fun.'

Such fun.

48

The cafe was a noisy, colourful place full of sunshine and laughter – and soon, Tatia hardly dared to believe, it would be somewhere she would spend many happy hours!

The conversation of the mothers and the delighted screams of the children was like the roar of a jet engine; jolly music pumped from speakers; the coffee machine blasted steam across a blackboard menu which promised cakes and salads and rolls and delicious organic produce.

Hidden behind a coat stand, Tatia watched Gabriel play. He was full of energy and confidence, and the centre of a group of friends. She loved his serious expression as he assigned everyone different roles to play. It was clear to Tatia that he would be loved and respected in his life.

Tatia hadn't had many friends when she was his age, not in that place.

There was a girl called Lizi who had taken Tatia under her wing in those dark days when she was returned there. Lizi offered companionship and protection. Late at night they would lie in bed and imagine the perfect lives they would have when they grew up: their beautiful homes; the handsome, aristocratic husbands who would give them everything they desired. But when she left the orphanage, Lizi's life spiralled out of control and she became a ghost of the pretty girl she had once been – a prostitute addicted to

Krokodil. The last Tatia heard, she had been beaten to death by a customer. Tatia thought about Lizi sometimes, and the other children she had known. But not, if she was honest, very often. There was so much about her past she longed to forget.

She tried to imagine the kind of homes all these ladies and gentlemen lived in, and imagined them to be vibrant places, filled day and night with music, conversation, laughter – the sound of happy children.

That was all she had ever wanted – to taste that life, if only for a short time.

They went into those empty houses at night, she and Carl, and she was able to wander from room to room wearing someone else's slippers, their clothes; pour tea from a pot shaped like a cottage; linger beneath a powerful jet of water in a shower room tiled with dark slate; lie beneath crisp, clean bed sheets; she could enjoy the simple pleasure of sitting in a comfortable armchair beneath a splash of soft lamplight. She could imagine, she could *believe*, just for a short while, what it must be like to live an exquisite life.

But then, as always seemed to happen in her life, things started to go very wrong.

The man in East Finchley should not have been at home – if they had known he was there they would never have chosen to go inside – and when he rushed to his phone, Carl knocked it from his hand and, in a fury, chased him upstairs. Tatia stood at the bottom of the steps, calling for Carl to stop, pleading for them to go. But he didn't listen. She heard the shouts and screams – and was sickened.

Minutes later, as the man groaned upstairs, Carl rushed down, breathless, blood spattered on his top, sweat soaking his face. And there was something in his eyes – a wildness, a sickening triumph – she'd never seen before.

He disappeared into the living room to tip everything to the floor in a frantic search. Then flung open a door beneath the stairs, took out a golf club he found and felt the weight of it in his hands before he flew back upstairs.

Tatia listened to Carl's grunts of exertion, the soft thud of the club, heard it clatter to the floor. Carl came downstairs sobbing, his face twisted in despair at the knowledge of what he'd done, and she led him out. But first she closed the shutters, switched on the heating to allow nature to take its course. She took the man's phone, fully intending to tell the authorities where they could find him.

After that, everything changed.

When the Harrows came home, Carl killed again. Didn't think twice about it. She sensed his excitement when they appeared unexpectedly at the door. She watched him grapple with the man in the hallway. Clenched together, they spun against the wall in a violent dance, but it was never going to be a fair fight. Carl was young, strong and vicious, and when Mr Harrow fell groaning to the floor, he went to the fireplace, stepping over the cowering Mrs Harrow, and picked up a poker. Tatia commanded him to stop, but he was consumed by that same frenzied anger as he stood over the woman and brought the steel rod down.

And the next time they went out, Carl only had one intention: to kill.

He knew the Langleys would be at home. It was never his intention to break into an empty house. He set upon them quickly, while Tatia and Joel could only watch in horror. The man and woman cowered as Carl stomped around, lifting his elbows, rolling his shoulders, kicking and punching and swiping with an ornament he had picked up.

We did this, he always told her afterwards, his face sopping with tears – because the remorse came the moment it was over. *Me and you.* As if he didn't understand how it could have happened. As if she had forced him to kill those people. He blamed Tatia, just as he begged her to take charge. But no amount of remorse could ever make up for his crimes.

Carl was addicted to slaughter. Something inside his head had whipped loose like an electric cable. She felt sick at what she had done, leaving his body to rot in an empty house, but the truth was, his insanity would sooner or later have consumed them all.

But she had encouraged him to take her into those homes, because he was the kind of man who knew how to get past security systems, or so he said. Those people would be alive if it weren't for Tatia.

She was guilty. She was responsible.

'No,' she admonished herself sharply, pinching herself on the arm. Here in this happy environment it wasn't appropriate to think about such awful things. Look forward, not back. She was barely able to believe it, but in a short while she would be part of a family again.

And there was Poppy, sitting with a group of women! Tatia watched her, admiring the way her hands fluttered delicately in front of her face when she spoke, that glittering ring a point of green light in the sunshine. Tatia would love to have something like that one day, a single precious item she could call her own.

She felt a tug at the hem of her shorts and looked down

to see a small boy. Black hair, pastry flakes clinging to his cheeks, a toy truck in his hand.

'Good morning, my darling!' said Tatia.

The child burst into tears and his mother scooped him up in her arms, flashing a brittle smile of distrust at Tatia. A moment later, someone pulled her from behind the coat stand. Poppy pushed Tatia quickly to the rear of the cafe, past the toilets – and outside, into a small paved area at the rear.

Flustered, Poppy slammed the door behind her. 'What are you doing here?'

Tatia looked around the cramped concrete space. Plastic toys were scattered everywhere, their bright colours faded by sun and rain.

Poppy's voice was shrill. 'You can't come here.'

'I am sorry,' Tatia gushed. 'But I could not help myself. I am so excited, you see, and we have not . . . heard from you.'

'I haven't had time.'

'This is such a lovely place. It must make you happy to come here with your friends.'

'You have to go,' said Poppy.

Tatia's smile faltered. 'It was never my intention to embarrass you.'

'I know that.' Poppy slumped against the door. 'But I haven't told Tim yet.'

'He does not know about us?'

'Not yet,' said Poppy. 'It's . . . complicated.'

Tatia was momentarily disappointed that Poppy hadn't told her husband about her and Joel. But so much had changed in such a short period of time. Tatia realised she was being unreasonable and had to be patient. She and Joel were free now. Carl was gone. But Poppy had her own cares to consider, which were just as important – if not more so.

'I understand.'

'Does anybody else know you're here?'

'No.'

'Thank god,' muttered Poppy, and pressed a hand to her face. 'You have to go, Tatia.'

'When will we be able to see you?'

Poppy stared at her cuts and bruises. For one terrifying second Tatia had a sickening sense that she had changed her mind about their being a family again.

But to her astonishment, Poppy said, 'Tomorrow night.'

Tatia was speechless. So soon!

'Why don't you and Joel—' Poppy tipped forward suddenly when somebody pushed the door from inside, and she placed her head quickly into the tiny gap so that whoever it was couldn't come out. 'I'm sorry,' she told the person, 'can you give me just one minute. Thank you so much!'

Poppy braced her feet against the door so that it wouldn't open. 'Why don't you and Joel come to dinner tomorrow night? To meet Tim and Gabriel.'

'And then we will be a family,' said Tatia.

'Yes.' Poppy swallowed. 'Exactly that.'

Tatia placed her hands together in a silent prayer of gratitude. 'I will go.'

'Actually.' Poppy stiffened against the door. 'It's probably better if you leave the back way.'

Walking along the dank alley behind the cafe, Tatia barely felt the injuries from her struggle with Carl. She had never been so happy. Because tomorrow, finally, everything would change.

Very soon they would be together, the three of them. Tatia, Poppy and Joel. She would have a family again. She sensed very clearly that she was nearing the end of a long, hard journey, and about to embark on a glorious new stage in her life. Sometimes, just sometimes, happy endings did happen.

But as she walked out of the shadows and onto the sunny street, another problem presented itself. The police would never stop trying to find her unless they understood that there was no reason for anyone to be afraid any more, and that the nightmare was over.

49

Vix Moore was having trouble accessing the Crime Reporting Information System and Ray Drake was sitting at her desk trying to work out what the problem was, when the call came on his mobile. Usually, if it was from an unknown number he ignored it, tired of the automated voices warning him of PPI deadlines, but this time some instinct made him pick it up.

'Yes,' he said, on his guard.

'I would like to speak to Detective Inspector Ray Drake, please.'

The voice was female, pleasant, with a hint of an accent. Drake stood quickly, as if struck by a bolt of electricity. 'Who's speaking?'

At her desk, Millie Steiner saw his reaction and hastened her own phone call to an end. 'Something's come up,' she told the caller. 'I'll get back to you.'

'Tatia?' said Drake. 'Is that you?'

She gasped when he said her name. 'Yes, it is Tatia.'

There were conversations going on all about the office, but Drake mouthed Tatia's name at Millie and she moved urgently from desk to desk, spreading the word: *quiet, we need to hear this*.

'Thanks for calling,' he said. 'I very much appreciate it.'

He heard plenty of indistinct background noise, and his mind went to work.

Dudley Kendrick came to stand in front of him, hands on his hips, ready to provide whatever assistance Drake required. Millie lifted her phone: she could try to arrange a ping from a cell site if Drake gave her a number. But the truth was, even if he had it, a trace at this short notice wouldn't be viable.

'How did you reach me?' Drake turned away from Kendrick, needing space to think. He was genuinely bewildered, couldn't understand how she had obtained his personal mobile number.

'That does not matter.' He heard her footsteps, the swish of her clothes. The ambient atmosphere suggested a large indoor space, a *vast* space. Wherever she was, she was moving fast. 'He is gone now. I promise you it is all over and I beg you to leave us alone.'

'Who's gone, Tatia?'

'Carl is gone, and we will be no more trouble. We just want to get on with our lives. Please do not attempt to find us, because you have my word – my word, sir, I make a solemn vow – that we did not kill those poor people. Carl did it, Carl killed them, and now he is gone.'

'Where's Carl, Tatia?'

'He is gone,' she repeated. 'Just gone.'

He tried to get a sense of where she was. The echoing space; fragments of conversation as people passed close; the occasional thump of pop music. And then he heard it: the blare of a tannoy. A service announcement.

He spun towards a desk, gesturing. His team circled around him. Listening, waiting. Kendrick stepped forward with a pad and pen. Drake snatched the pen, clicking the top, but the point didn't drop and it pressed a line, like a fading scar, into the paper. He dropped it, and another was pressed immediately into his hand.

He wrote: SHOPS??

'It's loud where you are, Tatia,' said Drake. 'I can hear people. Where are you?'

'No, please, sir!' The words tumbled from her. 'Please do not ask questions. Stop trying to find me. I am going away. I am leaving the country, we are both going far away. You will never find us. I promise we will never come back.'

'Are you with someone else, Tatia?'

The frustration rose in her voice. 'Please, sir.'

Drake heard a heavy grille smash into a floor, the warning beep of a motorised cleaner cart.

SHOPPING CENTRE? he wrote.

'Please, sir, do not—'

And then he heard it, the sound obliterating her final words. The tannoy announcing car park closing times for that evening at Stratford City.

He scrawled: WESTFIELD, E20!!!

'I'm sorry, Tatia.' Drake strode across the room to Millie Steiner's desk, detectives scattering in front of him as if he were holding something precious to his ear, something perishable. 'Would you repeat that for me?'

'Please leave us alone.'

'Tell me who you're with,' he said. 'Who are you talking about? You said Carl is gone, so who else you are with?'

She let out a little cry. 'There is nobody, sir, you are mistaken, I am not thinking straight. You have made me confused because you are so clever.'

'Come in and talk, Tatia. Let's get this misunderstanding cleared up.'

'No,' she said quickly. 'I do not think so. Please, no.'

'Wait a moment, Tatia,' said Drake.

'I am going to hang up now, I—'

'Please.' He took a breath. 'Will you wait, Tatia, just for one moment?'

'Yes,' she said, finally.

Drake pressed the phone to his shoulder.

'Flick and Eddie are on their way back from interviewing in Leyton.' Kendrick spoke fast as Millie prodded numbers into her desk phone with a pencil. 'They're about five minutes from the Westfield in Stratford.'

'Get as many units there as you can.' Drake lifted the phone to his ear. 'Tatia, are you still there?'

'Yes, sir.'

'The most important thing is that you and I meet face to face. You can tell me exactly what's happened. If Carl is responsible—'

Her voice cracked with emotion. 'He is!'

'Then let's meet as soon as possible. But, listen to me, Tatia. Running away is not going to help. Wherever you go, wherever in the world you run to, we will find you and bring you back.'

'No.' Tatia sounded panicked. 'You will not find me.'

Drake looked over at Millie, who was on the phone to Flick.

'We're on our way,' said Flick.

Turning in her seat, trying to get her bearings as the car dropped down the Leyton Road and flew across the bridge beside the tube station, she glimpsed the Westfield building, with the Olympic Park beyond. The blue light flashed on

296

the car's roof and the siren wailed. They would keep it on for as long as they could to punch through the gridlock as they approached Stratford International station, below the massive shopping complex. Flick braced a hand against the dash, pressed her feet against the floor, as Eddie, the wheel spinning beneath his fingers, flung the car down Temple Mills Road, swerving through the traffic beneath the tall tower blocks on either side.

Stratford station was straight ahead now. Eddie accelerated, cars pulling in to the kerb to let them pass. Flick saw blue lights approach from other directions. She had no idea how long Drake could keep Tatia on the phone. The woman was jumpy, Millie said, they could lose her at any moment.

A van crossing the junction ahead stalled and Eddie braked hard. The wheels screeched. The seatbelt snapped against Flick's shoulder. She smelled burning rubber. Eddie hung out of the window to shout at the driver. When he wrenched the gear into reverse, Flick slapped the dash.

'Let me out!'

'We're nearly there,' he shouted over the siren.

But she had already released the belt, flung open the door to run down the middle of the road. Slipping through the clogged traffic, she swerved around bonnets as horns went off all around her. Stratford station loomed near – and behind it the Westfield building.

Eddie had accelerated past her already, but he'd have to find somewhere to pull in and by then she'd be inside. She sensed police cars swinging in to her left and right. The phone was slipping in her fingers, the call still connected to Millie, as she ran towards the building.

* * *

'Where's Carl, Tatia? You said he's gone – did you kill him?'

'He was violent, sir, and unkind,' said Tatia. 'He did those things, those terrible things, to those poor people.'

'Where is he, Tatia?'

'He did not mean to do it, but he was unwell and I am very sorry, truly I am. But nobody will ever be hurt again, you have my word, sir.'

'I understand, but it's very important that we find Carl, Tatia.' Drake looked up and Millie twirled her finger, *keep her talking*, and he mouthed back, *where's Flick?*

'DS Crowley,' said Millie Steiner into her phone. 'Where are you?'

'I'm inside.' Her arm ached as she pressed the phone tightly to her ear.

The ambience changed immediately inside the shopping centre – the cavernous building soared to a vast height – and noise swam in the space. She heard the moan of a cleaning machine, music pumping from shops and restaurants, the back-and-forth of the shoppers, the cartoon squeak of a character on an animated billboard. The centre was mostly empty, but there were still too many people, walking in every direction, moving up and down between the three floors. Flick trotted into the centre of the space, past the concession stands – the cart selling sweets, the counter selling watches – spinning in a circle, frantically searching. The long ground-floor plaza curved away in front of her, and it was impossible to see over the two balconies on the floors above.

'I can't see her,' she said, frustrated. Turning, turning. Heading to the escalators. Climbing towards the first floor where she would have a better vantage point. Spotting Eddie Upson coming inside with other officers.

Millie shook her head. *She can't find her.*

'Tell me about the phone in the home of Mr and Mrs Harrow,' said Drake.

'Oh.' He sensed Tatia trying to gather her thoughts. 'I felt sorry for that man, the first one Carl killed.'

'Walker. His name was Gareth Walker.' He dropped the phone to his shoulder for a moment, and said, 'She's still inside.'

'He was laying there alone,' continued Tatia. 'I was scared that he would never be found, which would be a terrible thing, sir, so I took his phone. I wanted someone to find him, but when I switched it on I could not get it to work.'

'She's definitely there,' Millie told Flick.

'Mr Walker, Mr and Mrs Harrow, the Langleys . . .' said Drake.

'Yes,' whispered Tatia. 'Those poor children.'

'Are there any more, Tatia? Any victims we're missing?'

'No!' she said. 'It is over. You have my word.'

'Why?' asked Drake. 'Why did you do it?'

'All I wanted was to have what they had! If other people can have nice lives, why could I not? Why not?' she said. 'It was wrong to go into those houses, but I meant no harm, sir, you must believe me.'

Drake imagined her drifting through those homes at night, her fingers touching the tops of photos and trinkets and rows of clothes hanging from wooden hangers. Flipping through the photograph albums of strangers; lighting a fragrant candle; soaking beneath a steaming jet of water in a shower. It could be in any home in the city. Slipping inside in the dead of night, while neighbours slept next door, and out before daybreak.

'Carl said he could get me inside, he knew how to do these things. But then . . . Oh, sir, my heart is broken for those people.'

Drake glanced at Millie, forehead rested on the heel of her hand, waiting for Flick to say that she had seen her – that she was closing in on Tatia.

'Tell me what happened, Tatia?' said Drake.

'Carl and Mr Walker started fighting and Carl killed him – and then everything was spoiled. And then that couple came home and . . . I never meant any harm. I begged him to stop, I did everything in my power, you must believe me. But he would not listen.'

'Why those homes, Tatia?'

'It does not matter any more.' She was out of breath. 'None of it matters.'

'You know those houses,' he said. 'You've been inside them.'

'Yes,' she said. 'No – a little bit! Please, sir, I am becoming muddled.'

Everyone in the office crowded around Drake, hanging on his every word. 'I understand how you feel, Tatia.'

'Do you, sir?' she asked, upset. 'Do you really?'

'Yes,' he said. 'You were sent away by the Bliss family. They did you a terrible wrong—'

'No, I am guilty.' He heard her stop dead. Her heavy breaths exploded in his ear. He felt her desolation, her loneliness, amid the crowds of happy shoppers. He was losing her. Tatia was slipping away. 'I have always been guilty.'

'Let's meet,' said Drake softly.

'I must not talk to you any more. I am sorry, I have to go. Leave me alone, please let us be.'

'Then tell us where we can find Carl. Where can we find his body, Tatia?'

But she'd hung up.

'She's gone,' he barked at Millie and rang the number again.

'The DI's ringing,' Flick heard Millie say. 'Can you hear the phone?'

She stood on the first floor of the shopping centre, straining to listen, while Eddie puffed up the escalator, but the centre disappeared off in too many directions. Noise bounced everywhere around the cavernous space.

Turning slowly, she tried to focus all her senses before the ring was switched off. And she heard it, very faintly, somewhere not too far away – the insistent ring of a phone. Coming from nowhere and everywhere at once, the poor acoustics frustrating her attempts to locate it. Beckoning to the officers below, Eddie moved along the balcony in one direction and Flick headed in the other. The ring was definitely getting louder.

'Guv,' called Eddie, gesturing at a ringing phone lying on the floor ahead of him. Its blue screen flashed.

Glancing up, she glimpsed someone moving fast on the second-floor balcony – and rushed to the nearest escalator, pushing roughly past shoppers to run onto the trundling metal stairs, taking two, three steps at a time. Eddie followed her.

At the top, Flick saw a woman moving swiftly ahead.

'We're on it,' she blurted into the phone. 'We've got her!'

She rushed towards the figure, nearly slipping on the glassy floor.

'Stop!' she shouted. 'I said stop!'

But the woman hurried along the balcony.

'What's happening?' Millie said into the phone. 'Flick, tell me what's happening.'

'Put it on speaker,' Drake told her. Millie touched a button and they heard Flick's clattering footsteps, heard her breathy gasps. Everyone in the team pressed into a tight circle around the desk.

'Quiet!' barked Drake when someone spoke.

'I'm almost on her,' blurted Flick. 'We're almost there – she's trapped!'

And then they heard Eddie shout in the background, and Flick say, 'Excuse me, madam. Stay there, please!' There were tearing noises, the phone rubbing against fabric, the sound swooping and distorting.

'Stop!' they heard Flick shout. 'Stay still – *now!*'

'Is it her?' asked Drake into the phone.

Urgent noises came from Eddie and Flick, and another voice was talking quickly – too quickly to understand.

'Talk to me, Flick!' said Drake, leaning over the phone.

And then Flick came back on, trying to get her breath, hardly able to speak. 'It's not her,' she said. 'It's not Tatia.'

Drake wheeled away from the desk, letting out a cry of frustration.

50

There were so many things to do, so many problems and responsibilities pushing him in different directions, and that was even without worrying about what Wylie had in store for him. He needed to write down his conversation with Tatia as soon as possible.

But the first thing Drake did when he got back to his office was open up the video footage on his computer. He would watch it all again while Tatia's voice was still clear in his head. Shrugging off his jacket, he clicked on the play icon.

He saw Bryan Langley crawl across the floor and Tatia's reflection fling an arm across Carl's chest to stop him walking into the room – and into the eye of the camera lens.

'You know those houses,' Drake said out loud. 'You've been inside them, you told me so.'

Something about this footage wouldn't let him go. He was drawn back to it, convinced there was something in it that would explain everything if he only he looked hard enough.

'Tell me how you've been here, Tatia.'

He pulled the timeline back to the beginning.

It was fiddly work moving backwards and forwards quickly through the footage. The cursor sometimes spun off to hide at the fringes of the screen. But he punched through the different sequences. Pushing hours and minutes forward in a blur, pulling them back in slow motion. Manipulating time on the last day in the lives of Bryan and Samantha Langley.

The camera switched on at 11.14 p.m. Samantha Langley stared up at it. Waved, laughing. Bryan tapped at a laptop. He turned the screen and they danced, hands on hips. Bryan closed the laptop. Scooped it up. Left the room. Snapped off the light. The room was plunged into gloom. The camera's night vision switched on. Then the camera turned itself off.

2.33 a.m.: That mouse edging behind the sink, barely a dot in the green gloom.

7.11 a.m.: The family breakfast. Dressed for work, Bryan stuffed toast into his mouth. Samantha filled beakers of juice from a jug, threw a grape at her husband. He staggered back. She moved between the island and the fridge. The pucker of the fridge door, the shudder of the coolant, chill air on her face. The kids left. Bryan and Samantha leaned over the sink, backs to the camera, investigating droppings.

Drake slapped the space bar to stop the surging waves of images for a moment, thinking about what he had seen, then continued, tugging the cursor along the timeline, making static consume the screen. He resumed watching at 7.49 a.m. The cleaner arrived. Samantha swept her hand around the sink. Pointed at the camera. Samantha left the room. The cleaner ran the tap. Lifted bottles of cleaning products from the cabinet.

11.31 a.m.: Samantha leaned into the glowing interior of the fridge, her face bathed in bright light. Took out a pot of yoghurt. Slammed the door. Took a banana from a bowl. A knife from a drawer. Cut the fruit into segments, placed it in a bowl. Oranges and apples.

2.12 p.m.: Samantha on a stool, phone in hand. She pressed the teabag against the mug. Took milk from the fridge. A sound from the hallway – the doorbell. She looked up at the clock. Stared right at Drake, as if to say, *Help us.*

She left the room and returned, tucking in stools to allow a window cleaner access to the patio window. Not him, not the cleaner.

3.56 p.m.: She walked into the kitchen reading a leaflet. Not this.

At 6.17 p.m. Samantha made dinner. Bryan placed his briefcase down, his suit jacket. The two children rushed in. He pulled Emily onto his knee. Samantha took a bottle of lemonade from the fridge. When it spurted, she ran to the sink and dumped it. None of this.

Drake ran the feed forward, frustrated. He couldn't find it. Whatever it was he was looking for, that elusive clue, was screaming for his attention, but he couldn't see it.

7.02 p.m.: The Langleys at dinner. Samantha stacked the plates. Knelt in front of the dishwasher. Bryan walked in and put down his mobile. Samantha fell into his arms and they held each other. If not this, then what?

7.32 p.m.: Samantha left the kitchen.

9.59 p.m.: Bryan crouched at the cupboard beneath the sink, a torch between his teeth. He took out the cleaning products. Bottles and sprays, detergents, bleach, scourers and dishwasher tablets. Squeezed his torso into the cupboard. Heaved himself out and rubbed his sore knees.

At 10.21 p.m. Bryan poured a glass of wine.

3.47 a.m.: Bryan crawled into the kitchen on his hands and knees, leaving a messy trail of blood. Exhausted, moments from death. Figures reflected in the window. Ghosts in the darkness. Carl, Tatia. Bryan's fingers scrabbled at the floor – and then he collapsed, and the ghosts retreated. Not this.

Drake had watched this footage so many times – but he couldn't find the answer. It was there, something significant. He whipped backwards and forwards along the timeline . . .

She threw a grape and he staggered back . . .
 A leaflet from a local church . . .
  The mouse scurrying across the sill . . .
   A bottle of wine . . .
    Two ghosts reflected . . .
     His torso squeezed beneath the sink . . .
      The window cleaner walking in with the ladder . . .

Drake moved the cursor back and forth over the timeline, uncertain what to look at again – one last time. Instinctively he went to 2.12 p.m., the time frame he returned to more than the others. He clicked it open to watch it again.

The door to his office swung open to reveal Vix Moore. 'DS Crowley and DC Upson are back, sir, if you want to talk to them?'

'Thanks, Vix.'

He watched Samantha on the stool, pulling a thumb down the screen of her phone while the kettle boiled. She went to the fridge and took out the milk, placed it on the island unit, then pressed a teabag against the side of the mug, releasing the flavour. She looked up at a sound from the hallway – the doorbell – and at the clock, staring right at Drake.

Then she left the room.

Vix Moore loitered at the door. He hit pause. 'Be down in a moment, Vix.'

And when she had gone, he looked down at the frozen image – and saw it immediately.

He *saw* it.

Sat on the island in the empty room, its label turned towards the camera, just about legible. Drake stared at it, his knee juddering in excitement, then reached for his desk phone and called Eddie Upson's number. It rang three, four times. When Eddie answered, Drake said, 'What was the name of Gareth Walker's mother?'

'His mother?' asked Eddie. 'You mean Valerie Walker?'

'Call her. I want to know whether her son had his shopping delivered, and if so, by which supermarket.'

Eddie hesitated, as if he didn't understand, but knew better than to argue when Drake was in this kind of mood. 'Will do.'

Drake was already dialling a number on his mobile with his other hand. 'Come and see me as soon as you know.'

He killed the call to Eddie and waited for his own home phone to answer. Expecting Eddie to answer was one thing, waiting for Myra to pick up the phone was another matter entirely.

'Come on,' he said under his breath, as Flick and Dudley Kendrick and Millie Steiner walked in, picking up on Eddie's excitement in the incident room. They came around the side of the desk to see what he was staring at.

Keeping the phone to his ear, listening to the ringing tone, he pointed at the litre of milk left on the island unit.

'What does it mean?' asked Millie.

'It might mean nothing, but—' Before he could say anything else, the old woman answered, saying their home telephone number slowly and precisely.

'It's me,' said Drake quickly.

'Yes, Raymond.'

'Remind me who does our supermarket deliveries?'

'Mercy organises that,' said Myra. 'If the shopping isn't satisfactory then you need to speak to her yourself. I can't seem to say anything to her these days without her getting all high and mighty.'

'Just tell me, Myra.' He tried to keep his temper in check, knowing that if he got angry she would hang up on him. Tatia had his personal mobile number. It hadn't been released to the media, it never would be – but she had it. 'You must have seen the van outside, Myra. Who does the deliveries?'

'Please hold, caller.' He heard her put down the phone and call to Mercy.

'I don't understand what we're looking at,' said Millie, but Flick was nodding.

'The milk,' she said. 'The label.'

He heard Myra speaking loudly to Mercy, heard the cleaner's sharp response in the background. Their conversation, curt and antagonistic, and conducted across different rooms, seemed to last for ever. Drake needed to know one simple thing – why did Myra have to complicate absolutely everything?

'Yes, Raymond,' she said, finally returning to the phone.

'The supermarket, Myra.'

'She says it's Quartley's.'

'Thanks,' he said, and cut the call. He tapped the screen. 'It's got a Quartley's label on it. When we were at the Harrow house, the food in the fridge was mostly Quartley's own brand.' Running the timeline up and down he saw, very indistinctly, the Quartley's logo on the yoghurt and on the cleaning products Bryan Langley took from beneath the sink.

Eddie came into the office. 'She says they got all their shopping delivered every week from—'

They both said, 'Quartley's.'

'That's the connection.' Drake stood. 'Those homes weren't chosen randomly at all. Tatia has been inside them because she delivered shopping there.'

309

51

Quartley's regional HQ was based on the M11 corridor. It was a 20,000-square-foot warehouse of steel and concrete, a vast grey metal rectangle hunkered in rolling countryside. Inside was enough produce to feed a city till Armageddon.

Workers toiled through the night collecting household goods from giant pallets along its massive aisles. Lorries rolled in and out round the clock, seven days a week. It was from here that the supermarket's distinctive fleet of blue and yellow vans and lorries delivered shopping to homes across London and the South East, and to its chain of high street and out-of-town stores which catered to the expensive end of the retail grocery market. Attached to the warehouse was an administrative office block of mirrored glass and steel, which was just as functional and anonymous. The Quartley's logo and its famous tagline, *Saving You Money One Day At A Time*, was emblazoned above the entrance.

At the gate, Flick and Eddie identified themselves to a security guard who pointed them to a car park behind the office building. A nervous woman in a grey trouser suit was waiting in reception. After a brisk handshake, she signed them in and gave them both visitor lanyards.

'I'm Cathy Tautopolos, the Service Delivery Manager,' she said, 'and this is Dennis Whooley from our corporate press office.'

Whooley was a tense-looking man whose over-sincere handshake nearly fractured the bones in Flick's hand. Any more pressure and she could have had him for assault.

'Shall we?' Cathy slapped her pass to a pad on an electronic gate and led them briskly into the depths of the building, turning left and right and left again along a maze of corridors decorated with ceiling-high photos of salads and roasts and cheeses, and cakes smothered in cream. Flick completely lost her sense of direction in the windowless space. They turned left past an enormous image of a bottle of tawny port and into the noisy warehouse space, where staff loaded trolleys and forklift trucks with spinning yellow warning lights moved pallets of stretched-wrap goods – sugar and flour and cereals, detergents and kitchen roll – past towering shelves. Pop music played on a radio somewhere.

'Deliveries are a massive part of our business now,' Cathy said. 'I'll be surprised if we have any shops on the high street at all in a few years. People just don't have the time or the inclination to do a weekly shop any more.'

'We'll always need the human element,' corrected Dennis, as if worried she was revealing too much of the company's strategic plan. 'Support and retail staff.'

'Maybe one day all your produce will be delivered by drones and packed away by robots,' suggested Eddie, 'and we can all put our feet up.'

The press officer had a habit of cutting in front of Flick, forcing her to check her pace. She felt like she had been walking for ever through this gigantic space. 'Are we there yet?'

'You sound like my kids in the car,' said Eddie.

'I just want to make clear –' Dennis veered close again

'– that Quartley's is cooperating fully. We're being as transparent as possible.'

Flick dropped back as a beeping forklift passed in front of them. 'And we appreciate that.'

'But we would ask that you keep the company's name out of the press for the time being.'

'What do you mean?' she asked.

'Dennis!' said Cathy in a nervous singsong, 'let's just help the officers.'

'It comes at a bad time for our brand,' he continued. 'With the profit warning and everything. The retail sector isn't in good shape.'

'That's way above my pay grade, I'm afraid,' said Flick. 'I just work on the investigation side of things.'

'Here we are!' said Cathy, gesturing to a door at the edge of the warehouse.

Dennis hopped ahead to stand in front of it. 'It's important you understand that we're cooperating fully with your inquiry.'

'Not yet you're not,' said Flick.

'And in that spirit of cooperation I need a promise that the Quartley's name will not be released until you're sure, absolutely sure, that there's a definite connection with this . . . person.'

'You need to speak to . . .' Flick clicked her fingers at Eddie, who knew even less about the public relations side of things than she did. 'That woman in the press office. Red hair.'

'Charlotte something,' said Eddie.

'I really have to insist.'

'I tell you what, Dennis.' Flick stepped forward. 'Here's

what we'll do. We'll drive back to the station and cry our eyes out to our notoriously short-tempered senior investigating officer. Sorry, sir, Dennis the PR guy wouldn't give us the name of a woman implicated in a series of brutal murders.'

'A homicidal maniac, possibly,' said Eddie, helpfully.

'The maniac who's been invading the homes of Quartley's customers.'

'And battering them to death.' Eddie's eyes dropped to the tagline on Dennis's ID. 'One day at a time.'

'Let's just see how that helps your profit warning,' Flick said.

Dennis nodded grimly, and stepped aside.

They followed Cathy into a small office where a round man in a short-sleeved shirt pecked on a keyboard at a computer terminal.

'This is Craig,' said Cathy as Dennis stood at the door, urgently firing off an email. 'We keep a record of all our deliveries and who they were made by, going back years. He's been cross-checking drivers with the deliveries to the addresses you gave us.'

The team had earlier sent over the list of properties of the five victims, plus the address of Douglas and Bailey, and other homes where Carl Clarke's prints, and the unknown set, had been found. Craig took papers off the printer and handed them to Cathy, who passed them to Eddie as if they were on fire, and he gave them to Flick.

She looked at the delivery sheets. 'And the driver's name is where?'

Craig jumped up to point at the top right-hand corner of the pages. 'Basically, the same driver has delivered to all the addresses you provided at least once in the last eighteen months, and of course more besides. In north London, and other parts of the city too.'

'Sandrine Ellinger,' read Flick. On every sheet was that same name: Sandrine Ellinger, Sandrine Ellinger, Sandrine Ellinger. 'She's worked as a driver for how long?'

'Nearly two years now.'

'So how many—'

'In that time?' Craig thought about it. 'She's probably made something in the region of three thousand deliveries.'

Dennis let out a little groan at the door.

'Is she working today?'

'She's on her shift.' Cathy's eyes glanced up at a clock on the wall. 'And due to return at six.'

Moving Dennis out of the way, Eddie went outside to call the office.

'What's this number?' asked Flick, pointing at a mobile number on each sheet.

'It's her phone number,' said Cathy tensely.

'Here's what we're going to do, Cathy,' said Flick. 'We're going to get more officers here, and then you're going to bring her back. In the meantime, we'll need a home address.'

52

Tatia never remembered the words to songs but this afternoon she turned up the radio in the van and sang along with the happy tunes as best she could. It was a glorious day. The sun was beating down, but there was a cool breeze that kept the heat from getting sticky.

Circumstances changed so quickly! Just days ago she and Joel were trapped in an impossible situation, virtual prisoners of a disturbed man who killed for pleasure.

But now. Oh, now.

Carl was gone and all the terror and anxiety had lifted from her shoulders. Tatia's life had been a struggle, full of violence and horror. She had been forced to fall in with some very bad people in order to put into place the building blocks of a happy future. But the scars she had borne, both mental and physical, had all been worth it – because now she was home and free.

She and Joel were reunited with Poppy. The three of them would be a family again. Tatia would be a sister, a sister-in-law – an aunt! Together she and Poppy would make Joel well again, and they would all live out their lives into peaceful old age.

Tatia dragged the last of the crates from the van and checked the contents against the items on the delivery order. As she did, Tatia imagined the inside of Poppy's house.

There was no doubt in her mind that it would be very stylish and full of fine things. But above all else it would be a loving home. She looked forward to living close to Poppy and Gabriel and Tim, maybe not on the same street or even neighbourhood, but near enough so that she could babysit. She and Gabriel would play chess and watch PG-certificate films and eat ice cream. They would go to museums and galleries and adventure playgrounds. One day, maybe, Tatia would find a respectable husband of her own, and have children. She had never before dared imagine such a thing could happen. But now anything was possible.

Hefting the crates on the trolley, she felt the temperature drop. It had begun to blow. A fresh wind, blowing away old horrors. She checked the bags one last time at the door. There were order changes for the customer to accept. Cauliflower pieces replaced by a packet of kale, Quartley's own-brand hot wings instead of piri piri chicken. She rang the bell.

Tatia was free, but she would never forget that she had witnessed terrible things – and done terrible things. Certain actions gnawed at the back of her mind. She had killed Carl in self-defence – she would have to live with that burden – and she felt a nagging responsibility for the people she had witnessed dying at his hands. After all, she had encouraged him to take her into those homes.

And she thought of what had happened to Darejan Dolidze. For all his many faults, she had liked him – in the beginning he had been very kind to her – but he had left her no option but to inform the police about that robbery. She knew all too well what would happen – he would be gunned down like a dog, having made too many enemies within the local police department. He had promised that she could leave the country and then changed his mind when he decided she was too valuable, had even withheld the passport he had obtained for her. Darejan had broken a solemn promise. If she hadn't acted, she would be stuck there still, working for him, with no hope of escaping his brutal orbit.

The polythene grocery bags were attached to the edge of the crates by plastic teeth, and easy to pick up. There was a lot of shopping here. Expensive stuff. Prime cuts of meat and luxury ready meals, organic vegetables, exotic fruits. Sparkling water, bottles of fine wine.

From now on, Tatia would live a blameless life so that the police would never be able to catch her. They had her DNA, yes, but unless she was ever tested – and she would ensure she never got into trouble – they would not be able to match her to the prints in those homes.

When the door opened, she smiled. 'Good afternoon, madam!'

The customer, phone clamped to her ear, jerked her head along the hallway: *through there.* 'He's talking about a mini break!' she said, walking away.

Tatia had a vague recollection of delivering on this street before. She had delivered to thousands of homes and they all became a bit of a blur in her head.

The woman – the delivery form identified her as Julia Henry – was short, and down her back flowed the long blonde hair of a younger woman. She was dressed in leggings, shiny ballet pumps, a backless top that revealed the tattoo of a writhing snake. She made no effort to help Tatia bring in the shopping. Sometimes customers helped her carry in the bags and sometimes they didn't.

Tatia hefted two bags in each hand – the skin had hardened where the thin plastic handles snagged in the joints of her fingers – and walked down the corridor. The bag strap caught on the handlebar of a mountain bike leaning against the wall, nearly pulling it over. Tatia tugged at the bag and the bottles clinked.

'Watch the walls!' The woman's attention snapped up from her phone, then returned to her call. 'He thinks he can buy an apology just like that. But I assure you, it's going to take a bit more than a weekend in bloody Bath.'

A chat show played silently on a television built into a wall in the kitchen. Tatia placed the bags on a table, but the woman jabbed a finger. 'Not there – on the floor.'

Mrs Henry disappeared down the corridor while Tatia moved between the crates and the kitchen with the heavy bags, lifting them high to avoid the bike.

'I mean it, Mum,' she heard the customer say somewhere in the house, 'he's got to eat a lot of humble fucking pie.'

When Tatia had delivered the last bags all she needed to do was hand Mrs Henry the delivery sheet and inform her of the substitutions. But she didn't know where she was.

Walking past the living room, Tatia peeked inside, and saw a room that took her breath away. There were plump chairs upholstered in velvet. Cushions were piled high on a long L-shaped sofa. A table at the back of the room was adorned with tall candlesticks in ornate holders. Logs were stacked neatly in an alcove beside the gaping fireplace. The mirror above the mantelpiece unfurled in an elegant spiral. Curious egg-shaped sculptures sat on walnut floating shelves. The biggest television she had ever seen – the screen was curved! – dominated an entire wall.

It was the kind of room that Tatia had always dreamed would one day be hers. She dropped to the sofa, just to see how comfortable it was, felt her weight sink into the soft cushions. She was weary after a long day lugging those crates. She'd sit just for a moment. Tatia stretched out her arms and felt the feathery undulations of the pattern on the botanical wallpaper behind her.

She picked up a lifestyle magazine from the coffee table and leafed through the glossy pages, which was full of even more wonderful homes. Astonishing houses perched on stilts; clinging to the side of cliffs or sun-drenched hillsides, or on a beach; penthouses atop skyscrapers. Ceiling-high doors opened onto verandas full of furniture; staircases spiralled in huge atriums; aquamarine infinity pools disappeared over the edge of the world. Each exquisitely furnished home must cost millions.

But every one of them, she noticed, was beautiful but empty – and Tatia had something much better than an empty room to look forward to. A life, a family. Maybe, just maybe, everything had been worth it. She pressed her fingers to her chest, which was heavy with emotion.

'What the hell are you doing in here?'

The voice made Tatia jump up. The magazine fell to the table.

She thrust the delivery sheet at the woman, who had come in behind her. 'You have kale.'

'Get out of my house.'

When the door slammed behind her, Tatia's good mood was dented just a little, but she cheered herself up by reminding herself that tonight she would be going to Poppy's house – where her new life would begin. This rude customer would soon be forgotten. Checking her itinerary on the clipboard, she looked to see where she was delivering next – an address in Watford – and was stacking the crates on the trolley when her mobile rang. The office number. She connected to her earpiece.

'Yes,' she said, 'Sandrine here.'

'Sandrine,' said a voice on the other end. 'It's Cathy. How are you?'

'I am very well, Cathy, thank you.' Tatia hesitated to ask. 'What can I do for you?'

A moment, and then, 'There's a problem.'

'Problem?'

'We're going to have to ask you to come back. It's not your fault, but it needs to be sorted out.'

'Come back?'

'It's a computer thing. I don't quite understand it myself, really.'

Tatia heard the anxiety in Cathy's voice, and an odd atmosphere to the call, a slight echo, as if she were on a speakerphone. But that wasn't what troubled her. Cathy had never before shown the slightest interest in Tatia's health, not once. She was a brusque lady and not prone to small talk.

'I think that, uh, there's a problem with the delivery manifests. The dates are all wrong.'

Tatia climbed in the cab, picked up her clipboard and thumbed through all her forms. 'Which dates, Cathy? Nobody has complained so far. Tell me which ones and I will double-check.'

'Please.' Cathy was stern. 'This has . . . come from above. Return to the office right now, please.'

'Of course, Cathy. It will be my pleasure.'

Switching off her earpiece, Tatia climbed out to stack all the remaining crates into the van. She sat in the cab, fingers on the ignition. A terrible dread washed over her. She sensed danger – and Tatia hadn't got this far in life by ignoring her instincts.

But nothing was going to spoil her day.

Nothing.

53

She dumped the van a couple of streets from the bedsit and walked the rest of the way, jumping at the sound of every siren and horn blasting across the city, every sudden movement. Tatia expected police cars to swerve towards her any moment, cutting off her escape in every direction.

This was no way to behave – she was working herself into a frenzy over what? A hunch, an instinct. That instinct, the hair-trigger alarm inside her, had served her well in the past, but she had been wrong before. She stopped in the middle of the pavement – she was hot and itchy in her Quartley's tabard so she took it off and shoved it in a bin – and considered the possibilities.

Tatia could have got everything wrong. Her silly paranoia could be playing tricks on her . . . but she didn't think so. If the police had discovered her identity as Sandrine Ellinger then it would make things very difficult for her. Tatia didn't want to believe it. Happiness was within her grasp. She hadn't come this far for it all to be ripped away. She was so close to putting her family back together, so near to making an impossible dream come true. A new beginning beckoned, a wonderful future.

She started walking again, past the charity shops and nail parlours and fried chicken takeaways. If the police knew where she worked, then they would have her address – and would find the notebook. That didn't matter any more, but Joel would be in the room, and she had to get him out.

At the corner of her street Tatia stopped to watch the market traders, all the grocers and fishmongers and the stallholders who sold cheap dishrags and cleaning products, football shirts and phone covers. The curtain of her bedsit above the Poundshop was closed, as usual. She carefully searched the faces of the customers who went in and out of the shop for any indication they were police. The road was so packed with stalls and shoppers it would be impossible for squad cars to get close, at least.

But the police wouldn't announce their arrival like they do in the movies, flying in from every direction, sirens screaming. They would do it quietly, calmly, with a minimum of fuss. Which is what Tatia had to do.

So she walked across the road, ignoring the shouts of the hawkers and the smell of sizzling meat at the burger van, stepping carefully over the generator cables, trying not to look anyone in the eye. At the door, her key tapped against the lock surround because she was too busy darting glances up and down the road, searching for cars, for vans, the flash of a uniform.

Then she was thumping up the stairs as fast as possible. Unlocking the room, rushing in. 'Joel! Joel!'

Inside, it was stifling and gloomy. The closed curtain stopped the sunlight pouring in and hurting Joel's eyes, but it also trapped the heat of the day. The room was empty. Tatia was astonished. He had promised to stay here before they went to Poppy's.

But then she heard the rattle of the extractor fan in the tiny cubicle of the bathroom and she found him standing in the dirty shower beneath a dribble of water. His emaciated body, with ribs jutting sharply from his chest and tendons sliding like eels beneath his slack skin, was almost translucent beneath the harsh wink of the fluorescent light. It was Tatia's own fault; she had begged him to try to clean himself before they left.

She pulled him from the shower, and his wet body stumbled against hers.

'Get dressed, little bear. We have to go.'

His eyes focused slowly on hers. 'Where?'

'To Poppy, of course,' she said, trying to keep her voice light. 'We are going to start again, you and I. Tonight is the beginning of the rest of our lives.' She picked up his wet socks from the damp floor. 'Lift your leg.' But he just stared at her. 'Come along, darling, your left leg.'

He slumped against the wall so she could lift one bony leg after the other and push socks onto his feet. 'I don't want to go.'

'Nonsense.' She pulled his underpants up over his sunken groin. 'She is your sister and she loves you.'

'I don't like her. She's not nice.'

'We will have such a life, Joel.'

'I don't see you.' He stared over the top of her head. 'I see Will, but you're not there, when I see the cliff.'

'Please, darling.' She pushed the rest of his clothes into his arms. 'We have to go now.'

'Why aren't you there?' he asked, but Tatia rushed next door.

The notebook with all the addresses was on the bed, but she didn't bother picking it up. Instead she stuffed clothes into a rustling Quartley's polythene bag, then went to the window, pushing aside the curtain to look down. She saw the shoppers moving below, the tops of the market stall awnings, but couldn't see any police. There were no helicopters in the sky, no flashing lights or uniforms. Tatia hoped her instincts had been wrong. When she returned to the bathroom Joel's arms were hopelessly tangled in his jumper.

'Oh, Joel.' When she helped pull the jumper over his head, his lank hair crackled with static.

'I don't see you,' he said.

'You must let it go, Joel,' she told him gently as she helped thread his arms through the holes. 'I was there, and I killed Will, it is true, and I will never, ever forgive myself for what happened. I am guilty, I have always been guilty.' Pulling the jumper down his pigeon chest, Tatia placed her hands on his shoulders, feeling such pity for this shell of a man. 'We must go – now.'

She led him downstairs, making him hold the bannister so that he didn't fall, and into the noise and energy of the street – all the shouts and conversations, the throng of people surging past in every direction, the thumping bass from the second-hand record shop – tensely expecting at any moment to be wrestled to the ground. But the more she looked, the more she decided that nobody was coming for them. There were no police. She would get Joel something sugary to give him energy and take him to a park bench where they could sit in the sun, then bring him back in an hour or two. If there were no police here, she would take the van back to work, telling Cathy it had broken down. Tatia pushed Joel into the Poundshop.

'What would you like, my darling?' She gestured at the chocolate bars at the till. 'Anything you want!'

But Joel didn't respond. His health had gone downhill fast since the terrible scene he had witnessed at the Langley house, and she was afraid that very soon his heart would simply stop.

It was more imperative than ever that they get to Poppy's house, where they could decide how best to help him. Tatia grabbed chocolate and a fizzy drink and dropped them in front of the cashier.

Glancing outside, she saw black figures move past the shop. Police converging on their door to the left.

'My brother needs the toilet,' she said. 'I am so sorry, but he has a condition.'

The girl stared at Joel, at his damp jumper and trousers, and pointed to the back of the shop.

'Thank you,' said Tatia, and she took Joel's arm, trying not to look back at the officers pouring between the market stalls or listen to the thump of their boots on the stairs next door.

At the rear of the shop, she pushed him past the toilet and into the storeroom, ignoring all the demands from the people there to leave, and out of the emergency exit into the alley beyond.

Whatever happened, she would stay with Joel. Tatia would never leave him again.

54

Joel thrashed his legs as much as he could, screaming with delight.

He loved the way his stomach fluttered and tickled when he soared high above the grass, as if it was as giddy with excitement as he was. Flying ever higher, the whole garden threatening to turn completely upside down. He saw the blue sky, then the green lawn, then the blue sky. Sarah, clapping and laughing, was a blur beneath him.

'So high, Joel!' she shouted. 'So high!'

'Are you ready?' he asked.

He loved this bit. Together they sang the nursery rhyme. 'Ring-a-ring o' roses, a pocket full of posies! A-tishoo! A-tishoo! We all . . .'

Sarah raised her hands above her head. 'Fall down!'

And then Joel launched himself into the air, trying to take flight – the seat twisted as he left it, its chains clashing – and he would hit the grass and roll, confident that this was his biggest, mightiest jump ever.

Sarah cheered and Joel ran back to the swing to clamber back on. All his previous leaps had just been practice attempts, and this very next one would be the longest – he felt it in his bones! But as he stiffened his whole body to

327

gain momentum, trying to pick up speed, his mother called from the garden door.

'Tatia,' she called. 'Can you come inside?'

She was spoiling his big moment, his monster jump. When Sarah swung into view, he saw her looking anxiously up the garden – she wasn't even taking any notice of him!

'Tatia!' repeated his mother.

'Look at me!' He swung up, that familiar giddy lurch in his guts.

'I am sorry, little bear.' Sarah didn't know which way to look. 'I have to—'

'No!' He glimpsed his mother pull a cardigan tight around her; she was ruining everything. 'Go away!'

'Tatia, can you come inside?'

The frame of the swing shuddered as if it sensed Joel's annoyance; the chains lurched. For one terrible moment he thought they would tangle and his attempt would be spoiled.

'Watch how high I can go,' he begged Sarah. 'Watch how far!'

The girl kept glancing over her shoulder. 'Very high, Joel! You are almost flying.'

'Tatia!' called their mother.

With every soaring swing, he glimpsed his mum at the door, her arms folded tightly, and Sarah looking at her, then at him, back at the door. She started to intone, 'Ring-a-ring o' roses, a pocket full of . . .'

'Posies!'

'Tatia!' called his mother.

'A-tishoo, a-tishoo! We all . . .'

'Fall down!' Joel propelled himself forward, to land feet first on the grass.

'That was a good jump, Joel!' Sarah clapped wildly. 'Your best yet!'

'Was it?' He searched for the imprint of his feet on the flattened grass.

'Tatia,' called their mother.

'Stop calling her that!' said Joel, who wanted the fun to continue.

'I must go,' said Sarah. 'They want to – talk to me.'

'No!' Joel whined, running back to the swing, wanting her to push him high into the sky again. It was still early. The sun was only just beginning to drop. He didn't understand why his mum and dad wanted to speak to her yet again. Lots of ladies and gentlemen had come to the house to discuss what had happened to Will. Joel saw people inside the house now, indistinct shapes moving about.

His mother waited tensely. Sarah's smile was edged with something he didn't understand. 'I will come back. And when I do, I will show you how to jump. Because I am the best jumper in the world!'

'No, you're not!' Clambering back on the seat, Joel pushed his feet against the hard mud path beneath the swing. 'Hurry back!'

She hesitated, as he began singing softly to himself: 'Ring-a-ring o' roses . . .'

Then she gave him a little wave, but he couldn't wave back because his hands were on the chains, and she walked away.

'Wait,' he said, an odd feeling of panic coming over him.

He saw his mother step away from Sarah as she went inside. Since the accident, she didn't touch her any more, didn't even call her Sarah. Then the back door closed and he was alone in the garden. Almost immediately Joel didn't want to be on the swing. He scuffed his heels in the mud to bring it to a stop and watched the shadows move about inside the house. He recognised his mum and dad, but not the other grown-ups walking back and forth.

He gazed at his feet bumping on the soft mud and must have lost track of time, because when he looked up again the room was empty. Joel walked to the window to get a better look. There was nobody there, or so he thought – because when he went inside his mother was sitting in the armchair facing away from him. When he got closer, he saw tears falling down her face.

'Mummy?' he asked. 'Mum?'

A cold breeze came from the open front door. He heard the sound of a car engine. His stomach, which had fluttered with joy on the swing, now clenched with fear.

Joel raced to the door, but Poppy was coming inside and she tried to grab him. 'No, Joely!'

He ducked beneath her arms and rushed outside – just in time to see a car accelerate from the kerb, his dad watching it go.

He screamed: 'No!'

And Joel ran as fast as he could, swerving out of reach of his father's outstretched arms, heart pumping in his chest, to chase the car. But it was already roaring up the road. The only thing that kept him going was the sight of Sarah in the back seat, squeezed between two people. Her hands were pressed up against the rear window, and she smiled.

'Sarah!' He ran as fast as he could, but it was no good, he couldn't keep up. 'Sarah! Sarah!'

Joel screamed her name again and again, even after the

car had disappeared around the corner and he had fallen to his knees, and his dad had wrapped his arms around him, and all that was left of her was the faint ghost of a sad smile.

55

Now:

Ray Drake waited until the cramped bedsit had emptied of officers before he climbed the stairs and went inside.

The net curtain at the single window was thick with decades of grime, and the glass filthy. The smells of Walthamstow market – the burgers, the fresh fish and the citrus tang of cheap air-freshener – drifted up from below to mingle with the musty scent of body odour and damp in the room. Drake heard angry voices. The stallholders closest to the street door who had been forced to shut for the rest of the day were engaged in a bad-tempered argument with officers. A double bed took up one whole side of the room and a jumble of furniture was packed into the other. Clothes were strewn about the floor.

Drake followed the sound of an extractor fan, like a rattling cough, into a tiny room with a stained toilet and sink, and a decrepit-looking shower. Water pattered from the mouldy showerhead onto the sunken plastic base where white maggots of silicon curled at the edges. A towel lay crumpled on the wet linoleum floor.

'Sir.' Back in the bedroom, Millie Steiner held a small red cash book, the kind that could be bought in any newsagent. Drake took the book. Turning the pages, he saw line after line of addresses written in small, neat handwriting. House numbers, street names and postcodes, stretching across north London and south of the river.

'The Langleys' address is in there.' Millie leaned across him to turn to the page in question, 'and Gareth Walker's address, and the Harrows. You'll see a cross has been made against those, and some of the others. Homes all over the city, in fact.'

'They're in no particular order.' Drake flicked backwards and forwards through the book, astonished by the sheer number of addresses written down. 'How many do you think are in here?'

'Several dozen, at least,' guessed Millie.

Notes had been made in the margin beside various addresses. Drake read 'burglar alarm', 'side entrance', 'empty at weekends', 'key inside door', 'window open' and other descriptions in a precise hand.

'The addresses that have crosses beside them could be the properties they've already been inside. The others, for whatever reason, weren't chosen, or were yet to be visited.'

'We'll be able to compare this lot against recorded break-ins.' Drake used a single gloved finger to lightly turn the pages of the book, which was laid flat in the palm of his hand so that he didn't smudge any prints on the cover. 'Where's Flick?'

'She's on her way.'

Flick and other officers had waited at Quartley's head office for Tatia Mamaladze to return. But a couple of hours later she still hadn't arrived back or responded to attempts to make contact, and her delivery van was found abandoned a few streets away. For whatever reason she had been spooked by the instruction to return to the depot. If she had come back to this dark, dismal room, it had been a flying visit. There were so many clothes strewn across the floor and so much clutter – scattered items such as a brooch, a figurine, an art deco cigarette lighter, that looked so out of place in this chaotic setting that Drake suspected they'd been taken from homes as keepsakes – it was difficult to know what, if anything, she had taken with her. Maybe Tatia was already attempting to flee the country – by ferry, by plane, or some other way.

His phone rang.

Turning to the back page of the book, Drake saw an address in Crouch End that made him uneasy. 'Get Kendrick to send a couple of officers to the home of Poppy Mallory.'

'I thought she turned down the offer of protection?'

'She did, but let's get a couple of plain clothes there right away. Tell them to keep it discreet.'

At least now, with this notebook, they could begin to piece together just how many homes Tatia and Carl had broken into. The crosses against certain addresses would provide a guide. And Drake hoped the book would clear up another mystery.

The phone continued to ring in his pocket, he felt it thrum patiently against his chest, and he took it out, connected the call. 'Give me a moment.'

'Sure thing, Ray,' said Sam Wylie on the other end.

Drake pressed the phone to his shoulder as Millie dropped the notebook into an evidence bag. 'Get it back to the office and copied. I want officers to visit every address in there, start with the ones that have crosses beside them, and check them against outstanding burglary reports. Chances are, Tatia and Carl will have been there.'

'All of them?' asked Millie.

'Every single one,' he said. 'And let's get it done as quick as we can. I've a feeling we'll find Carl Clarke's body at one of those homes.'

He followed her down the narrow stairs, nodding to the forensic examiners who waited patiently on the street. 'It's all yours,' he said.

Drake squinted as he walked into the bright late-afternoon sunlight. The noise and bustle of the market made it difficult for him to hear Wylie properly.

'It's Date Night, Ray,' said Wylie.

'Not tonight,' said Drake, ducking under the police tape. 'I'm too busy.'

'Come on, Ray. You promised me. We've a single window of opportunity to get this thing done, and it's tonight.'

Drake looked at his watch. 'There've been developments in a case I'm working on. I can't just drop everything.'

'What's the point in running a Murder Investigation Team if you can't take time out of the office?'

Drake walked up and down in front of the Poundshop window, scanning the busy market, half expecting to glimpse Tatia lurking behind a stall, slipping through the crowds, but the street was crawling with officers and he knew it was hardly likely she was still here. If she was clever, she would already be planning her escape, perhaps back to Tbilisi. Alerts at airports and ports would be put in place. But Tatia had spent so long trying to get back to London that it was inconceivable to Drake that she would leave just like that. It would be the last thing she wanted to do.

'Ray, are you there?'

He slipped into the middle of the stream of shoppers on

the other side of the road. Men and women pushed past, jostling and shoving, but Drake felt oddly at ease in the middle of the crowd. 'I'm here.'

'Tonight's the night, Ray. I'll come and pick you up. Just give me a time and I'll be there.'

Give him a time, said that familiar voice. *And let's get this finished.*

'Okay, then.'

'Good man,' said Wylie.

Ray Drake knew that something was building to a climax – and that, one way or the other, he was damned.

56

Tim dropped his briefcase inside the door, hung up his jacket and listened.

The house was quiet. Poppy must be out somewhere with Gabriel, which was a surprise. His wife was a creature of habit, and always made sure to give Gabe his supper at the same time every day.

'Poppy?' He walked into the kitchen they had renovated, along with the rest of the house, before they had moved in. It had been an insanely costly and protracted project. In Tim's opinion, it would have been cheaper and quicker to demolish the whole house and build another one from scratch. Poppy had been the driving force behind that, of course. She had driven the builders to breaking point with her determination – some may have called it stubbornness – to ensure everything was done exactly the way she pictured it in her mind's eye. Tim poured himself a juice. Her bag, he saw, was on a chair. Her keys were in it, and her mobile – Poppy didn't go anywhere without her phone.

The sun burned through the glass in the conservatory. Tim loved standing among all the plants, breathing in the scent of the flowers and shrubs and climbers. He picked up the small can with the long neck to water the bougainvilleas. Calling her name again, this time he got a faint reply. He put down the can. The door to the basement was ajar and the light was on below. At the top of the stairs he called her name again and this time heard her clearly.

'Down here.'

He was about to head down when his eye caught the faulty latch on the door. It had been like that for a while now: you thought you'd locked it, but it clicked open anyway. He'd been meaning to get it fixed for months but hadn't got round to it. Maybe now he would finally do it.

Then he stepped down. Tim was struck once again by how large the basement was. This floor was the last piece of the jigsaw in the renovation. The aim had been to convert it into another living area, but neither of them could agree what kind of space they wanted it to be. Poppy had got it into her head to dig deep underground and add another two floors below this one – a playroom, a gym, even a swimming pool – as if she were some kind of Russian oligarch. But Tim had always resisted. There were only three of them – how much room did three people really need? He was happy for it to remain a utility space. The washing machine was down here, and it was where they kept the iron and ironing board, and his tools. Gabriel's baby toys were boxed up in the corner waiting to be thrown out, and there were some bags of hardened cement.

He saw her, a smudge behind one of the many sheets of plastic. Poppy had hung them from the exposed beams to give Tim a sense of the size of the rooms she had envisioned, confident that she would get him to change his mind eventually. The plastic sheeting crackled in his hand when he moved it and found her sitting on a box, hands pressed against her exposed knees in her ripped jeans.

'What are you doing down here? Where's Gabriel?'

She stared at him for a moment, and he blanched at the hurt and resentment in her eyes. 'He's at Issy's for a play date. I came down to get something and then my necklace broke. Will you help me look for it?'

'Of course.' She was at least speaking to him. There had been an icy tension between them since he'd made his announcement. Poppy had been withdrawn – and with good reason. He felt a stab of disgust at his own behaviour.

'Goodness.' A fine powder was smeared across the sleeve of his jacket from the sheeting. 'It's dusty down here.'

'Give me it,' she said, and he took it off. He watched her fold the jacket and put it to her nose for a moment, then place it on the box. Tim felt ashamed. He should have thought things through properly before he upset her, he really should.

Tim crouched. 'Where did you lose it?'

'Over there somewhere,' she said, pointing.

Moving on his haunches, peering at the floor, he knew he had done her a terrible injustice, had caused her pain and uncertainty. He'd been unreasonable and selfish, a bloody idiot, frankly, and scared her for no good reason. All this stuff about going away was preposterous, a childish fantasy. The truth was, if he went away by himself he'd be throwing away the best part of him, his wife and child. He couldn't lose the love of his life, or his little boy. He'd let a few terrible weeks at work get on top of him. He'd get another job – he'd already had offers – and they would discuss the future together. Whatever they decided, it would be as a family. No, his behaviour had been inexcusable, and he'd do anything to make it up to her. Poppy wasn't perfect; she could be maddening – pushy, sulky, insecure and obsessed by material things. But he loved her and could never leave her.

'I can't see it.' He felt his legs stiffen. Instead of gadding about the planet, he needed to concentrate on getting healthy, losing a few pounds. Maybe they should get this basement converted into a gym after all.

Tim couldn't wait to get upstairs. He'd sit her down and tell her that he had been a stupid fool, an idiot, and beg for her forgiveness. Just as soon as he found this damned necklace.

She moved on the other side of the sheeting. Obscured by the plastic, he could just about see her moving to the wall.

'What about me?' she said, coming back.

'I'm sorry?' He hadn't heard properly. 'What did you say?' He lifted himself to his knees, stretched his spine.

'I said, who's going to look after me?'

The sheet moved in front of him and Tim had only a moment to register Poppy with the iron in her hand, and he didn't even feel it come down hard on the top of his head, didn't feel anything ever again.

57

Poppy gripped the edge of the sink, shoulders heaving, spine convulsing as she let out huge sobs. She was in shock: shock that she had actually gone through with it; shock that she had found in herself the cruelty to kill the man she had loved for many years.

Too late now. There was no turning back. She had set herself on a treacherous path and had to follow it to the bitter end. She didn't know if she could look John and Tanya in the eye ever again, let alone Gabriel. But she knew these feelings would pass. It would take weeks, months – possibly years – but a day would come when she would be able to live with herself, and she clung to that knowledge.

Her phone rang. Isobel's smiling face flashed on the screen. Poppy had arranged a sleepover for Gabriel at Issy's, a highly unusual occurrence for a weekday. She used the excuse that Tim had surprised her with the promise of a candlelit dinner as a late anniversary treat. She wanted to ignore the call. There could be plenty of reasons why she didn't answer, but it was vital that she carried on as if it was just a normal day.

Poppy pressed her fingers to her eyes. 'Hello, Issy?'

'Oh, Poppy,' said her friend, 'I'm so sorry to do this to you.'

Poppy heard the kids playing noisily in the background. She took the phone to the basement door and pressed her back to it, trying not to think of her husband's body in the darkness below. 'Is everything okay?'

'Bloody Duncan arranged to take Freddie to his mother's tonight and forgot to tell me about it,' said Issy. 'It's the old witch's birthday and she gets hysterical if people don't make a fuss, so I'm afraid I'm not going to be able to have Gabe tonight. Do you mind picking him up?'

'I . . .' Poppy was already trying to work out who would take him instead. There was no way he could stay here, not tonight. 'Really?'

'I know you and Tim were hoping for a nice evening.' There was an insistent edge to Issy's voice. 'But it really can't be helped.'

'I'll . . . come and get him,' said Poppy.

So she drove to her friend's house, the journey taking about ten minutes in the Galaxy, practising saying 'hi' in a perky voice in the mirror because it was vital that she didn't look downcast. She kept the phone in her lap so she could scroll down her list of friends, trying to think of anybody who would take Gabriel for the night at short notice, and getting nowhere. When she arrived, Issy was already with Gabe at the door, and didn't even notice Poppy's anxious greeting.

Issy smiled sympathetically. 'I hope I haven't spoiled your evening.'

'It's fine, really.' After a bit of strained small talk, Poppy pushed Gabriel towards the car and helped him into the back. She fumbled with the seatbelt, getting it all tangled. He took it from her and the belt clicked smoothly into place. Poppy climbed into the front seat, wanting to get away.

'I don't want to go,' he said, annoyed.

'Isobel says you're hot.' She pressed a hand against his forehead. 'You're obviously coming down with something. You need to go to bed.'

'She didn't say that,' said Gabriel. 'Freddie's got to see his grandma.'

'She said she thinks you're coming down with a fever, and I think she's right.' Poppy wrestled the car out of the parking space. 'You look very pale.'

'No, I don't,' said her son.

'We'll put you to bed as a precaution. A good night's sleep and you'll feel much better.'

'But I'm not ill!'

'Don't argue, Gabriel, not today.' She tried to smile. 'Please, let's get you to bed in case you're coming down with a bug. Then tomorrow, if you're feeling okay, we'll do something fun.'

'I'm okay now. When's Dad coming home?'

He looked so disappointed. She had brought him home from Freddie's and now he was being forced to go to bed early. It was bad enough he was going to be in the house; she had to keep him out of harm's way. When this nightmare was finally ended, she would devote herself to him. Try to put right what she had made wrong. She had to remind herself she had done what she had to do to ensure Gabe's life didn't change; so that he could grow up in a nice house in a good street. That's what all this was about.

'He'll be home later. But Gabe . . .' The dangling pine-tree air freshener swung crazily as she tried to meet his eyes in the mirror. 'Listen to me, Gabriel.'

'I'm listening,' he said, sulky.

343

'You must promise to stay in bed, promise you won't come downstairs. Whatever you hear, you must stay in bed.'

'I want to see Dad,' he said.

'He's going to be late.' She wished he wouldn't keep talking about Tim. 'And by then you'll be asleep. Promise me, Gabe.'

'I promise,' he said.

'Good boy.' Her nerves were shredded. 'I don't deserve you.'

'Who was Will?' he asked, and Poppy jolted. Her foot jerked on the accelerator so that the Galaxy lurched out of a junction, forcing an approaching car to screech to a halt. Its horn blared angrily. Poppy lifted a frantic hand in apology.

'I don't know who you—'

'The lady in the park talked about someone called Will and you shouted at her.'

'That strange lady was not well, Gabe,' said Poppy.

'You were angry with her,' he said.

'Because I was worried about you.'

'She had a nice smile,' he said.

'She was a crazy lady,' she snapped. 'With a nasty smile!'

Gabriel dragged his fingers through the fur of the dragosaur. Poppy just wanted to get home. Get him in the bath and off to bed. The coming weeks and months would be difficult for them both, but things would improve over time. She would devote her life to her son. Her every waking minute would be dedicated to making him happy, despite the tragedy that had engulfed him.

But as she turned into her street, Poppy's heart leapt when she saw two men sitting in a car on the corner. Sometimes taxi drivers pulled up on the street to wait for instructions, or to take a nap. But these men were too alert, too well dressed, and they watched her people carrier as it passed.

When they got inside the house, she put on the oven and went upstairs to run a bath for Gabriel. The water thundered into the tub. Poppy swished the mountain of bubbles around the surface. He didn't come when it was ready and she called his name. Terrified, she imagined him going into the basement. Poppy ran downstairs, trying not to sound panicked. 'Gabe! Gabe!'

To her shock, she found him in the hallway, near the basement door.

'Dad's here.' His eyes were wide. 'He's here.'

She took him by the shoulders, trying not to betray the terror she felt. 'What do you mean?'

'His coat.' He pointed to Tim's jacket, which she'd hung over the back of one of the chairs in the kitchen. 'Where is he?'

'He didn't wear that one this morning, silly.' Relieved, she pulled him into a hug. Over the top of his head she checked the basement door was shut. Gabriel had never shown any interest in going down there. The empty space with its stark bulb and long shadows, the rustle of the plastic sheeting in the chill air, had scared him when he was younger. 'Let's get you into the bath.'

She carried him upstairs, and while he splashed about, went out of the front door and walked across the street to where the two men sat in the car. When she rapped on the driver's window, it lowered slowly.

'What are you doing here?' she asked the two policemen.

The men looked at each other. 'We were told to watch—'

'I told DI Drake I didn't want anybody here. It's an

invasion of my family's privacy. Will you please leave? If you don't go, I'm going to make a complaint. This is harassment.' She slapped the roof of the car. 'And it's unacceptable.'

'I'm sorry, Mrs Mallory.' The man in the passenger seat leaned across his colleague. 'But we'll have to check.'

'Do what you have to do.' She looked up and down the street. It was getting late. 'Just make sure you go.'

She walked off without giving them the opportunity to respond.

Back in the house, she placed a lasagne in the hot oven. She heard water slap against the porcelain of the tub, and Gabriel chatting softly to himself as he moved his soldiers along the bath edge. She got his pyjamas ready and tidied up his room, throwing all his things into his big blue tub of toys, trying to distract herself from what she had done – and was intending to do. She threw the toys hard into the container, but each crack of plastic brought a different awful image.

Crack! The surprise on Tim's face when she swung the iron.

Crack! The rattle of the sheeting as he fell against it.

Crack! His staring eyes coated with concrete dust.

'Don't break my toys!' Gabriel shouted.

'Sorry,' she called.

There was one final thing she had to do, so she went into her and Tim's bedroom and opened the bottom drawer of a cabinet and took out a canister of pepper spray that had been there for years. She couldn't even remember who had given it to her – someone from her antenatal class years ago following a series of attacks in the area. She pressed the canister into the pocket of her jeans and went to the window.

The car was gone. The officers had left.

No turning back now.

'Mum!' called Gabriel from the bath. 'Where are you?'

'Coming!'

Poppy sat on the closed lid of the toilet and listened to Gabriel talk about his day. But she was distracted by thoughts of what was going to happen later. She had told Tatia and Joel to arrive at 8 p.m., and it was now 7.35 p.m. and she wanted Gabriel in bed as soon as possible, safely out of sight of that woman.

Placing his chin on the edge of the bath, her son said something.

'Sorry, darling?'

He blew foam from his hand. 'You're tired, Mummy.'

'That's true.' She rubbed her eyes. 'Mummy's very tired.'

'Perhaps *you're* sick.'

'It's very possible,' she said sadly.

'Daddy will look after you when he comes home.'

Poppy lifted a hand to her face to hide the pain she felt. 'Let's get you out.'

She wrapped a towel around his shivering body, lifted him from the bath.

'Can I read before I go to sleep?' he asked.

'Only if you promise to stay in bed,' she said. 'Whatever you hear.'

She made him brush his teeth, got him into his pyjamas and into bed, and then went back into the bathroom. Sucking down the revulsion she felt at the sight of the wretched person in the mirror, she took out her make-up and applied it with a trembling hand.

Concentrating on the familiarity of the actions, losing

herself in the rhythm of the small, precise movements, the reassuring click of the compacts, for a few precious minutes.

Until the doorbell rang.

58

Arriving back at the station, Flick went straight to Drake's office. While she'd been at Quartley's, waiting for Tatia Mamaladze to return, she'd tried numerous times to call Wylie to ask him about Drake's accusations that he was a copper, desperate to clear the air – but he didn't answer. The more she thought about it, the more she couldn't understand why he never mentioned it. There wasn't any reason on earth why he wouldn't have, and it played on her nerves. Now, when she tried to find Drake, he wasn't in his office or the incident room.

'Where's DI Drake?' she asked Dudley Kendrick, who was at his desk.

He peered over the top of his glasses. 'You just missed him.'

'Where's he gone?'

'No idea,' said Millie, walking past, 'but he left literally five seconds ago. You can probably still catch him.'

'I'll just see if I can,' she said lightly. As soon as she was outside the incident room, Flick flew down the stairwell as fast as she could, heading to the car park. She practically fell into the touch pad at the exit, nearly strangling herself with her lanyard when she pulled out her pass. The door unlocked with a hoarse buzz, and she ran outside. But Drake's car was still in the car park. She was about to go back inside, when a familiar dirty Mazda passed on the street.

Letting herself out of the gate, she saw Wylie's car stop further up the road and the passenger door swing open. To her shock, Ray Drake stepped forward on the pavement, hesitated – and then climbed in. The car roared off.

Back upstairs, Flick called Wylie's number. He wasn't the kind of man who'd have any qualms about answering his phone while driving, but it went to voicemail. Her anxiety building, she rang Drake's number. Again: no answer. Whatever was going on, whatever reason there was for Drake to get into Wylie's car, she knew no good would come of it.

Grabbing her coat and bag, Flick marched across the room. 'I'm going out.'

Millie stared. 'How long will you be?'

Everyone was working flat out, requesting Borough Operational Command Units across the city assign officers to the addresses written in Tatia's notebook. If Drake's theory was correct, they would find Carl Clarke's body at one of those addresses. But it was slow work, and the team would remain at work for a good few hours yet.

'I'm not sure.' Flick walked to the door before anyone asked any more questions. 'I'll be on my phone.'

Sitting in her car, she realised that she had no idea where to look for them. She knew so little about Wylie – still didn't even have a current address – and the fact that she had allowed him to get under her skin so quickly, seemingly to use her to get close to Drake, annoyed her intensely. But there was one place she had gone with him, and it was all she had to go on.

* * *

She drove to Enfield, with that feeling of disquiet growing inside her, arriving at the house just in time to see Astrid stepping outside. She wore a tight black dress, a pair of heels that made her tower over mere mortals and, despite the evening heat, a parka with a voluminous collar that framed her face in a cloud of fur. Slamming the door, she watched Flick climb out of the car. 'I'm going out.'

'Anywhere nice?' Hurrying to the step, Flick heard the dogs barking inside.

'The boys are staying at a friend's, so I'm taking the opportunity to get drunk and meet rich men.'

Flick smelled the sharp tang of spirits lifting off her. 'Sounds like a plan.'

Astrid looked at her, lips pursed in an angry pout. 'What are you doing here, Flit Crowley?'

'I can't get in contact with Sam,' said Flick. 'He's not answering my calls.'

'Well, well.' Astrid smirked. 'Welcome to my world.'

'I need to know where he is.'

Astrid gave an exaggerated shrug, nearly falling off the doorstep in the process. She held onto the knocker to steady herself. 'How would I know where he is?'

'He's with a colleague of mine.' Flick nodded at the door. 'It won't take long.'

Astrid sighed and unlocked the door. A pair of dogs ran around Flick's feet as she followed Astrid into the kitchen. Flick was sure there were three the last time she was here. Astrid threw down her bag and filled a shot glass from a bottle of tequila on the table. The glass overfilled quickly and liquid splashed the table. Flick saw the sinews in Astrid's long neck tighten when the alcohol hit the back of her throat.

'He's police,' said Flick. 'Is that right? A detective in the Met.'

Astrid half-heartedly tried to shoo the dog away from her legs. 'He was when we met, but now . . . I am not so sure.'

'You must know.'

'I don't ask him anything any more, I have learned that it's better that way for everybody concerned. Nobody gets hurt.' Astrid shrugged. 'But it would explain his interest in you.'

'Excuse me?' asked Flick.

'There's always an agenda with Wylie. He is a good father, I'll say that much for him, his boys think he is a god, but I have learned it is best to be wary. Look at me.' She ran her hands down her body. 'I am not so bad, even now. But I made the mistake of falling in love with Wylie and ended up here. In this house, living this life. This was never my destiny, Flit Crowley.' There was a knock on the door and she swept down the hallway and opened the door, told the man waiting outside that she was coming. 'My cab is here. Make sure you close the door properly when you leave.'

Flick rushed to the door. 'Where is he?'

Astrid laughed. 'Now you have a little taste of what it was like to be me. Never knowing where he is, what he is doing. We never used to see him. He would be gone weeks, months, with no explanation. You think you know him, but then you discover that you don't. You discover he is a man full of secrets.' She sucked her teeth. 'It annoys me intensely that I still love him so much. To be fair, he only ever lies when his lips move.'

'Help me,' said Flick. 'Tell me where he could be.'

Astrid looked her up and down. 'I'll be honest. I don't feel predisposed to help you. I am a bitter drunk.'

'I'm afraid,' said Flick.

'And with good reason. If Wylie wants something from your friend he will take it.'

She turned to leave, but Flick slammed the door shut. 'It's Wylie I'm afraid for. The man he is with is very dangerous. Wylie has no idea what this man is capable of, but I do. It would be a terrible shame if something happened to the father of your three boys.'

Astrid pulled her top lip slowly between her straight white teeth, considering her. 'There is a house, outside of the city. It belongs to an associate of his. I do not like to ask what he does there. He told me he was going there tonight. He has taken one of the dogs there already.'

'One of the dogs?' asked Flick. 'What for?'

'Oh, who knows what goes through that head of his? Wylie loves his theatre, his drama.' She wrenched open the door to see the cab drive away from the kerb. 'Now look. I was hoping to go somewhere classy, somewhere expensive, where I am able to meet a better type of person. But I don't have enough money, Flit Crowley. There is never enough money.' She sighed. 'Maybe if you and I take a trip to a cash machine and you slip your card into the little slot and do the thing with your fingers –' she mimed pressing a keypad '– beep, beep, beep, *beep*, it may help jog my memory about that address.'

59

The canister of pepper spray bulged in her jeans when Poppy came down the stairs, so she called to the people outlined in the stained-glass door, 'Just one moment!'

She went back into her bedroom and took a chunky cardigan from the wardrobe and placed the canister in a front pocket. 'Coming!'

'Mum?' called Gabriel behind the closed door of his room.

'Go to sleep!' Poppy said, running back downstairs. Straightening the cardigan, she pulled her fingers through her hair, a habitual thing she did when anybody arrived, and opened the door.

Tatia didn't wait to be asked, just walked in. 'Surprise!'

A neighbour drove past and Poppy pulled Joel inside, slammed the door shut. 'Welcome to my humble home!'

'I am so sorry.' Tatia turned in a slow circle, drinking in everything. She was dressed as usual in her ugly hoodie, cargo shorts and work boots. A torn polythene bag of clothes dropped from her fingers to the floor. 'We have no flowers. It has been . . . frantic.'

'It's perfectly fine,' gushed Poppy. 'I wasn't expecting anything.'

Tatia gestured at the room. 'May I?'

'Be my guest,' said Poppy, but Tatia had already darted next door.

Poppy found Joel's dull stare unnerving. If anything, her brother looked worse than the last time she'd seen him. His shoulders and neck were crooked, his knees bent as if it was an effort to carry even his own body weight.

'How are you, Joely?' she asked, but he didn't respond.

Tatia reappeared in the hallway. 'Your house is . . . exquisite.'

'I can show you upstairs later when you go to bed,' Poppy told Tatia quickly when it looked like she would climb the stairs. She eyed the polythene bag. 'You're staying, of course?'

'We would very much like to stay.' Stepping away, Tatia pressed a hand to her heart. 'Thank you.'

Unnerved by Joel's unblinking gaze, Poppy clapped her hands. 'Let's eat!'

Tatia walked around the kitchen and conservatory, looking closely at everything. Poppy feared she would never sit down. Closing the kitchen door so that she didn't have to see the door to the basement, which seemed to bulge towards her as if it was breathing, as if it was alive, she opened a bottle of red wine and placed it on the table with three glasses. She lit a candle and then put on oven gloves to take the bubbling lasagne from the oven.

'Let me help you,' suggested Tatia, but Poppy insisted she sit. The rich aroma of meat and cheese filled the room. Tatia folded Joel's slack fingers around a fork, but he barely moved.

'Are you not eating?' Tatia asked Poppy.

'I'm too excited.'

'Of course you are.' Tatia picked up her fork, but the knife was way too long and sharp, and she laughed. 'Ha ha, you have given me the wrong one!'

'Oh, I'm sorry,' said Poppy.

Tatia placed the long bread knife on the table. 'It is a very funny mistake.'

She made all manner of joyous faces as she ate, and satisfied noises, savouring every mouthful. Heaping food onto her fork, she lifted it to her mouth – and blushed, embarrassed, when she saw Poppy watching.

'You are so slim. But I cannot help myself. It has been a long time since I have eaten anything so delicious.'

'Please.' Poppy tried to smile. 'Enjoy it.'

Joel still hadn't touched his food when Tatia pushed away her empty plate and stood.

'What are you doing?' asked Poppy, alarmed.

'May I use the toilet?'

'Of course. Use the one down the hall.'

'I am so excited to meet your husband, and to see Gabriel.'

'They can't wait to meet you,' said Poppy. 'But I'm afraid they're out. They'll . . . be back later.'

'I am sorry to hear that, but we have the whole night ahead of us.' Tatia's smile was serene. 'And many years after that.'

'Yes.' Poppy watched her leave the room and walk along the hallway, pausing momentarily at the basement door. 'Not that one, the next one along!'

When Tatia went into the toilet, Poppy dropped her head, exhausted by all the tension. When she looked up, Joel was looking at her. She'd completely forgotten he was there.

Something about his blank, haunted gaze made her suddenly angry. 'What?'

He spoke in a drawl. 'Why are you doing this?'

'Doing what?'

Joel's shoulders were bent so low that his shallow breath almost ghosted the table top. 'Why are we here? You don't care for us. You left us all. Mum, Dad, me. You wanted nothing to do with us.'

Poppy snatched up the bottle of wine and poured a glass. She downed half of it in a moment. 'I'm just trying to do the right thing.'

'Are you?'

'I want you to be happy, is that so difficult to believe?' Conscious of Joel's gaze, she sighed. 'I was ashamed.'

His voice was barely a murmur. 'Of what?'

'Of what happened. Of how it happened. How could a family let such a thing happen to a child?' Poppy pushed the glass around the table by its long stem. 'Tatia's poison, Joel. Always has been, always will be. And now she's back.' She snorted with disgust. 'And using my downstairs toilet.'

'She loves me. She cares for me.'

'She's a *psycho*. I know what she did, Joel. I read the newspapers, I watch the news. Those people, Joel. What she *did* to those people.' She sneered. 'And maybe you did, too.'

'It wasn't Tatia.'

She hunched forward to challenge his stare. 'But she was there, right, Joel? Were you there when those people were murdered?'

She felt a sick kind of triumph when his eyes lowered to the table, and poured herself more wine.

'She would never hurt any of us,' he said. 'You lied. She didn't kill Will. When I see that cliff –' his hands lifted as if he saw it right then '– I don't see Sarah, I never see her.'

'Don't call her that. She's *Tatia*.'

'Why did you lie?'

She swigged from the glass. 'Leave it, Joel.'

'She wasn't near him.'

'Do you want to know the truth?' Poppy felt the alcohol hit her bloodstream, fuelling her anger. 'Yes, I lied, but Tatia lied, too. Because we had no choice.'

Behind Joel, Tatia came back into the room, and the bitter expression on Poppy's face made her freeze.

'Why shouldn't you know?' Poppy refilled her glass. 'You've tried to forget what really happened, you've made a super-human attempt to forget, but you always made sure to remember just enough to enable it to destroy you.' She gestured at him in disgust. 'Look at what it's done to you. Look at what you have become.'

'Poppy,' said Tatia. 'Please do not—'

'Maybe the truth will finally set you free.' Taking a long gulp of wine, she placed the glass gently on the table. 'The fact is, you're right. It wasn't Tatia who pushed Will off that cliff. Because *you* did it, Joel. You killed your brother.'

60

21 hours after Will:

For a few minutes the two girls were left alone in a room in the police station that was so cold Sarah could see her own breath. On the other side of the door they heard the murmured voices of their parents speaking to officers.

She did her best to comfort Poppy, putting her arms around her, but her sister didn't respond. Poppy stayed curled in a tight ball, heels up, arms folded tightly around her knees. Sarah wished her mother and father would come back soon because she badly needed the toilet.

Yesterday, when the emergency people eventually arrived at the cliff – the police, the medics, the officers in wetsuits who drifted in boats on the churning water – nobody had asked them what happened. Sarah wanted to be helpful, but she and Poppy and Joel were told to sit for many hours in a van further up the hill. Police officers spoke to them in kind voices and gave them soft drinks and sandwiches. Then, after a long day, the whole family was encouraged to go home and return to the station this morning so that the children could explain what had happened. Joel, still so young, was confused by events – Sarah wondered what he really understood about what had happened to Will – and Poppy was inconsolable.

'Please.' It broke Sarah's heart to see her like this. 'Let me help you.'

Poppy looked up sharply, but her expression softened, giving Sarah hope.

'I know . . . you do not like me very much, but I want to help you feel better.'

'I'm scared for him,' said Poppy. 'Joel is too young to explain what happened. I'm not even sure he understands what he did. He just ran past and . . . Will fell.'

'It was a terrible accident,' agreed Sarah.

'But I don't think Mum and Dad will see it that way. I'm afraid they'll never forgive Joel, because he and Will were always fighting. Mum and Dad will think he did it on purpose. He's not a strong boy – you know what he's like, he's quiet, sensitive – and I'm afraid they'll treat him differently from now on.' She sucked down a quivering breath. 'And he won't understand why.'

Sarah felt an aching sadness for her sister, and for Joel. She would do anything to turn back time and put right this terrible tragedy. 'Tell me what you want me to do.'

Poppy uncurled on the chair and, to Sarah's astonishment, took her hand. Her grip was hot and clammy, and her fingers slid willingly into Sarah's excited grasp.

'Don't you see? Will loved you.'

Sarah hadn't been near Will when it happened. She had been running around on her own, further along the edge, admiring the churning vastness of the ocean and the never-ending sky. When she heard Poppy's screams, she was already running up the incline. Sarah remembered standing at the edge of the cliff, smiling at the thought of seeing a seagull, a fish, or a cute seal rolling in the surf, and didn't even notice at first that Will was gone. It was only when she saw Joel's wide-eyed stare that she realised something was very wrong.

Sarah frowned. 'I do not understand.'

Poppy said, 'You could tell them you did it.'

'I was not, I did not—'

'If you help me, if you help Joel, I'll love you for ever.'

Sarah gaped in astonishment. Poppy had gone out of her way to make her feel unwelcome in their home. Sarah was her name now, and everyone in the family called her that – everyone except Poppy, who refused to accept the new name and still called her Tatia. Nothing Sarah did seemed to make things better between them. She had tried so hard to get her sister to love her – and now there was a chance that everything could change.

Her hot fingers slipping in Sarah's, Poppy glanced quickly at the door. The volume of the voices in the corridor lifted. The conversation was coming to an end.

'They think the best of you, they took you in. If you say you did it, they would understand that it was a stupid accident and forgive you.'

It tormented Sarah to see Poppy, usually a haughty and confident person, in such a wretched state. It was a terrible irony that their love and friendship would finally be cemented in such tragic circumstances. Sarah and Poppy would be united in grief, sisters in sadness. Together they would lift the terrible shadow that would hang over Joel's future. Sarah felt a stab of disgust at the way she craved Poppy's love and acceptance so much that she could even consider taking advantage of poor Will's death.

But Poppy had done a courageous thing. She had reached out to ask for her help and if Sarah was strong, if she could find it in her heart to do this important thing for Joel, then maybe some good could come of these awful circumstances.

She would finally have won her sister's respect, and the thing she craved most of all – her love.

'It is difficult to know what to do, I—'

'Please, *Sarah*,' Poppy whispered. 'Do it for Joel.'

Poppy's calling her Sarah – for the first time – was the most wonderful thing that had ever happened to her. Because it meant that finally she was accepted. Sarah shamefully wished the pair of them could stay there for ever in that small room holding hands, touching knees. Like sisters.

If only she didn't need the toilet so badly.

Poppy snatched back her hand just as the door opened and Patrick and Jill Bliss came back into the room. Their mother carried Joel in her arms. He was much too big to be carried, but she held him tightly, as if something terrible would happen to him if she dropped her guard for even an instant. A police officer followed them in, and stood at the back of the room.

Patrick Bliss leaned on the edge of the table opposite the two girls. His face was etched with tension.

'Can either of you tell us what happened?' His voice faltered. 'Poppy?'

Sarah rubbed her knees anxiously, knew that she had to make a quick decision. She could tell the truth or she could find it in her heart to take the blame for Will's tragic death, instantly lift from Joel's shoulders a lifetime of guilt – and win her sister's love for ever.

'Poppy,' repeated Patrick. 'Can you tell us what happened to Will?'

Poppy stared at Sarah, her eyes pleading.

362

Sarah whispered, 'It was an accident.'

Patrick turned to her. 'Sarah?'

'I am sorry, I did not mean to . . . he fell.' She felt everyone's eyes on her. 'I ran past him and I must have . . . I did not even know it had happened.'

After a tense moment of silence, her father said, 'Are you saying you are responsible, Sarah?'

'One moment he was there, and—'

'I saw Sarah run past and Will . . . was gone,' said Poppy quietly.

'It was an accident,' said Patrick Bliss. 'Is that what you're saying?'

Poppy looked away. 'If you like.'

Jill Bliss stifled a moan against Joel's hair.

'I am sorry.' Sarah reddened. 'I must have been clumsy.'

'Clumsy,' repeated Patrick.

'Clumsy me.' Her bladder swollen, Sarah shifted in her seat, but Poppy shot her a ghost of a smile, *thank you*, and she felt a treacherous happiness. 'I . . . need the toilet.'

The officer stepped forward and held out his hand. 'Let me take you.'

When Sarah left the room, Patrick Bliss rubbed his eyes and turned to Poppy. 'You saw this accident, is that right?'

Poppy looked at the floor. 'I saw *something*.'

'What?' asked her mother sharply. 'You have to tell us.'

'We're all sad and tired, Poppy,' said Patrick Bliss quietly, 'and it's very important you tell us what you saw.'

'But Tatia will know.'

This time, Poppy noticed, nobody told her off for calling her Tatia.

'What you say now will stay between us,' said her father. 'It will go no further.'

Poppy sensed that this was her moment, and she bit down hard on her lip to make her eyes sting with tears.

'I think . . . I may be wrong, but . . .'

'But what?'

'Just tell us,' said Jill Bliss shortly.

She met her mother's eyes. 'I think Tatia pushed him.'

'You're mistaken,' said her father.

'I saw her push Will off the edge.' Poppy made a violent shoving motion with her hands which made her mother shudder. 'On purpose.'

Patrick shook his head. 'No.'

'It's what I *saw*,' she said.

'I don't, I can't—'

'She wouldn't lie,' Jill Bliss said. 'Not about something as important as this. Would you, Poppy?'

'No.' She met her mother's eyes. 'Of course I wouldn't.'

They sat tensely for a moment, until they heard the sound of Sarah and the officer's footsteps returning down the hallway.

'Then we have to say something,' said Patrick.

'Not now,' said Jill Bliss, hugging Joel to her.

'We can't just keep this to ourselves.'

'You'll not say anything to the police, none of us will,' her mother said quietly. 'The way Tatia came to us is complicated. It's very possible there will be consequences, and your father and I could lose you and Joel. You mustn't say anything to anyone, anyone at all, until we decide as a family the best thing to do. We will resolve this situation among ourselves. Do you understand, Poppy?'

Jill Bliss hadn't realised she had called the girl Tatia, and not Sarah. But Poppy noticed, and it gave her a thrill of satisfaction.

'Yes, of course,' said Poppy, with what she hoped was a look of terrible despair.

61

Now:

Hunched forward, Joel was so still, for such a long time, that Poppy wondered if he had gone into some kind of catatonic state. But eventually he said, 'I don't remember what happened. All I know is that Will was there, and then . . .'

'You were very young,' said Poppy. 'And there are many aspects of it you've chosen not to remember. Let's face it, Joel, you've never been . . . sturdy.'

'What I did for you, little bear,' Tatia took his hand in hers, 'I would do all over again.'

'It's like I'm stuck,' said Joel to the surface of the table. 'I only see the cliff edge, the grass, the sea. Where he was standing, but he's not there any more. I'm sorry that I don't remember more. I'm sorry that I killed him.'

'It was an accident,' said Tatia, feeling his pain.

'But what I do know is . . .' His red eyes lifted to Poppy's. 'Sarah should never have been sent away.'

'No,' said Poppy. 'She shouldn't.'

'What do you want with us?'

'I just want you to be happy.' She picked up her glass. 'Is that so difficult to believe?'

'And Sarah?'

366

'Don't *call* her . . .' Poppy's fist flew to her mouth to stop herself saying the rest of the sentence. It sickened her that he had hitched his wagon to a certifiable maniac, a madwoman responsible for untold murders, but he dared to sit in judgement on his own flesh and blood.

'If our being here means anything,' said Joel, 'tell her what you did to her.'

Tatia shook her head. 'It is not necessary.'

'If you're so concerned about our happiness, tell her.'

Joel's head jerked forward suddenly, as if he was having trouble keeping it balanced on his neck, and Poppy knew her brother would probably never get better. She remembered seeing a movie once about a man who got smaller and smaller in size. His family did their best to care for him, but he eventually became so tiny they couldn't even see him. He was still in the room with them, but so microscopic that he was all but invisible. That was what was happening to Joel. He was diminishing before her very eyes as energy drained from his body.

He was a pathetic creature, but no more wretched than Tatia – or herself. None of them were the kind of people you'd want in your house, or near your loved ones. Poppy was as disgusting as either of them, maybe even worse, because she had killed in cold blood the man who loved her, and now she would get on with her life as if nothing had happened. At least Joel felt remorse. He had taken all the guilt about what had happened to their family and let it eat him from the inside out. If he wanted her to reveal to Tatia what she had done – well, she owed him that much at least.

Tatia squirmed on the chair beside her. It was grotesque

that she was in Poppy's house while her son slept upstairs. Poppy swallowed the acid that rose in her throat, and said, 'I owe you an apology.'

'*No.*' Tatia reached out to grab Poppy's hand. 'The past is past. Let us move forward. I have never been so happy as at this moment.'

'Sarah,' Joel said, 'she has something—'

'Please do not spoil things!'

Praying that it still worked all these years later, Poppy gripped the canister in her pocket tightly, just in case. 'It's best that you know.'

Joel's eyes drooped in their sockets. 'Tell . . . her.'

'I told my . . . I told our parents that you pushed Will off the cliff. I told them you did it on purpose. And that's why they sent you away,' said Poppy quickly. 'I told a terrible lie about you.'

'I know you did.' A pained smile twisted across Tatia's face. 'But it does not matter, not now.'

'I apologise.'

'Please do not.' Tatia shook her head. 'I forgive you for what happened. Please let us change the subject.'

'I did an unforgivable thing to you, and I'm sorry.'

'The past is over.'

'You took the blame for Will's death and I betrayed you the first moment I got and they sent you away. What I did is despicable.'

Tatia didn't know where to look. 'Please do not talk about it.'

'They sent you back to that disgusting place.'

'It is all past now.'

Poppy tightened her hold on the pepper spray. She knew

368

what had happened in those homes. People had been slaughtered. Tatia may be quite mad. Joel was sick, too, but in a different way. There was probably a cure for what Joel had, but there was no cure for Tatia's derangement. Poppy had killed, too, it was true, but her murder was borne of desperation and necessity – to provide a future for her son.

'This is lovely wine.' Tatia spun a glass in her hands, making the liquid race around. 'Look how ruby red it is.'

'I just want you to know,' said Poppy, 'that I'm sorry for what I did to you. I told our parents a vicious lie about you and they sent—'

'Stop it!' Tatia brought the flat of her hand down hard on the table, making the cutlery jump. 'Stop it, stop it, stop it!' Wine spilled onto the table, and Tatia cried out in despair. 'I have ruined everything!'

'No.' Poppy rushed to a drawer to fetch a cloth and dab at the stain soaking into the tablecloth. 'Look, see, it's fine!'

'Look what I have done!' Snatching the cloth, Tatia rubbed frantically.

'Please sit.'

Poppy tried to take it, but Tatia pulled the cloth angrily away. 'My life has been a hell on earth!' she cried as she scrubbed ferociously. 'Things have happened to me, things you will never be able to comprehend. I have *done* things. Terrible things, Poppy, disgusting things. I have been a bad person. But I had to survive. All I wanted to do was to come home. To you, to Joel. If you knew the kind of person I have been –' her eyes bulged '– you would not let me into your beautiful home, or near your lovely family.'

She fell into a chair. 'But . . . that was then, Poppy, and I am different now. You wronged me, yes, but you have also carried a terrible burden and it breaks my heart.' For one horrible moment Poppy thought Tatia would cry, but instead she sighed. 'But I am here now, and the three of us are reunited, and there is nothing now to stop us being happy. Everything that has happened has been worth it, all of it, because it has all led to this moment. We are a family again, finally. So, please, Poppy, I do not want to live in the past. Allow me to be happy now. We will never again discuss what happened, because it does not matter. I forgive you, I love you.' The sad smile returned. 'Do you understand?'

'Yes,' whispered Poppy.

'Call me Sarah.' Tatia's eyes pleaded. 'I am your Sarah.'

Poppy opened her mouth, but couldn't bring herself to say it.

'Please.' When Poppy didn't reply, Tatia looked away in embarrassment. 'I should go.'

'No.' Poppy pushed away her wine. 'Please stay.'

'I need to . . .' They looked at Joel, who was leaning heavily forward, nose almost touching the surface of the table, barely able to keep his eyes open. His voice was a slur. 'I think I need to go to sleep now.'

And Tatia cried out with joy.

62

They cut through the rush-hour traffic, the burnished red evening becoming night, onto the North Circular and then the M25, across the Dartford Crossing into Kent. Wylie bobbed his head to the burble of classic rock on the radio and told Drake what was going to happen. All he had to do, he said, was to keep watch while Wylie went inside a house.

'What kind of a house?'

'A big house,' said Wylie. 'Bigger than you or I will ever be able to afford.'

A house in the middle of nowhere, said Connor. *Your favourite kind.*

Drake didn't have to go inside, Wylie said, didn't have to go anywhere near it, just ensure Wylie was alerted in time, should – and if his intel was correct, this shouldn't happen – anybody approach the house.

'Because these are bad people. And if they find me inside, it would be . . .' Wylie shuddered for comic effect. 'Well, you get the picture.'

'Tell me what it is you're stealing,' said Drake.

'I'm not stealing anything.' Wylie jerked the car into the slow lane to overtake on the inside, then swerved back into the middle lane. 'Not technically. I'm taking back something that belongs to me. Not even to me, it wasn't mine to give in the first place. It belongs to my son. I'm breaking and entering, yes, but you know a little about that yourself.'

Drake felt his pulse accelerate. 'Tell me what it is or you pull the car over right now.'

Connor said, *Let's get this finished tonight.*

'Bloody hell, Ray, where's the trust?' Wylie sighed, disappointed. 'It's a dog.'

'You're stealing a dog,' said Drake.

'I'm taking it back from a man who shouldn't have it.' His eyes slid to Drake. 'I'm restoring balance to the universe.'

'How did you end up giving your son's dog away?'

'You know how it works.' Wylie rubbed his chin as he cut across two lanes towards a junction. 'When you go undercover, you have to know which buttons to press. When I first met him, one of the ways I gained the trust of this guy was to take along a puppy, because he's a big dog lover, and I thought it would impress him. I made up some cock-and-bull story about finding it, but it was my son's puppy because, you know, I could just borrow it any time.'

He's good, I'll give him that. He's really selling it.

'Trouble is, this guy, this gangster, demanded the dog. Wouldn't take no for an answer. So I gave it to him.' Wylie scratched his nose. 'Not the best idea in retrospect, because the bloody thing is chipped, and it would have led them right back to my home address. But it worked like a treat. The guy was all over me like a rash after that, and it wasn't difficult to gain his trust. My son wasn't so happy. He still misses the dog. My ex told me I have to get him back.' He reached into his pocket and took out keys and a chunky fob. 'I've got access to the house, and the burglar alarm code.'

'Don't you think he's going to notice the dog has gone?'

'He's got a lot of dogs. I'll leave a door open accidentally on purpose and they'll all run off into the night. It'll be no big surprise if one of them doesn't come back. He may not even remember it was the dog I gave him.' Wylie smiled. 'I really love our chats, Ray.'

Drake was disorientated. They had passed through the suburbs now, the distance between neighbourhoods getting longer, the junctions and roundabouts becoming more sporadic, the bends more twisting. And then the pretty country pubs with their thatched roofs and strings of coloured bulbs, and the new-build village estates were left behind, and they drove deeper into the countryside. Trees and bushes strained on either side of the road, pressing around the thin wash of light carved into the black tarmac by the headlights of Wylie's car.

'And what do I do, exactly?'

'Stand in the lane. It'll be pitch dark, nobody will see you. Let me know if anybody approaches. I'll be out like a shot.' He veered left and along a country lane, jerking the car up the verge when car headlights came out of the darkness, the high beams momentarily blinding Drake, and passed in the narrow space. 'I appreciate this, Ray. I just want to get my kid's dog back.'

'And then we're finished.'

'Yeah, we're done.' Wylie pressed his nose to the windscreen until he spotted a rutted track. Clumps of mud tapped against the windows as the car's suspension bounced angrily on the rough ground. Wylie drove too fast into thick woodland, only just missing the tall trees, ice blue in the moonlight, which lurched out of the darkness on either side. Twigs crunched beneath the wheels. Drake saw a pair of silver eyes reflected in the headlights – and then the creature darted away. Wylie pulled the car to a stop in a clearing and cranked the handbrake.

It was silent except for the tick of the car's cooling engine. If it was all so simple, so straightforward, if Wylie could slip in and out of the house in a heartbeat, Drake didn't know why he was there at all.

It's pitch dark and you're in the middle of nowhere. But at least you have me, Ray.

'Let's go.' Wylie climbed out, leaned back in. 'It's on the other side of these woods.'

Drake followed Wylie into the black void between the trees, his feet sinking into the soft, uneven ground. Anything could be waiting on the other side of the wood. An explosion of sound above made Drake jump. Something flapped from a tree into the night.

The Ghost Squad was known for its entrapment techniques. One trick was to leave drugs in an abandoned car for officers to discover and then wait to see if those same drugs ever arrived at the station property room. There was a chance that a night-vision camera was trained on him right now, following his stumbling progress through the wood in lurid green. Drake could take Wylie's phone – but that footage of him in the flat had more than likely been uploaded to a cloud or a remote server. Drake wondered who else had access to it – Wylie was unlikely to be working alone. Was it one person or a dozen? If this was a set-up, some kind of rogue investigation, it was an elaborate one.

'Everything good back there?'

The tension in Wylie's shoulders, the way he always kept Drake in his peripheral vision, was unsettling. He kept looking back and grinning as they walked further into the dark wood. Drake followed Wylie, his shadow elongating across the ground in the moonlight and climbing the trunks.

Something was happening here – but Drake had no idea what.

'It's just over here.' Wylie walked down a slope. They stood above a lane leading to a wide metal gate, looking up at a country house. Its dark mass rose up beyond the fence and a gravel courtyard. An L-shaped building with stables protruded on the right, its many windows black against the starry night.

'Won't be a tick,' said Wylie, and was about to leave when Drake grabbed his wrist.

'Five minutes.'

'Just don't fall asleep, Ray.'

Scrambling down the verge, Wylie lifted a fob and the gate began to trundle open on metallic casters. He slipped through the widening gap. Wylie lifted the fob over his shoulder and the gate began to close. Security lights popped on outside the house, illuminating the courtyard, when Wylie ran across the gravel. Drake heard dogs bark inside. Wylie went to the front door and a moment later disappeared inside.

I'll take it from here, said Connor, low. *Because you are weak and I am strong.*

Ignoring him, Drake stood at the end of the dark country lane winding through the woods. The courtyard lights went off. A breeze rustled the leaves on the trees. Somewhere high in the sky he heard the fading roar of a jet.

He waited five minutes and then ten – where the hell was Wylie? He said he'd be in and out.

Then he heard it – a distant moan. Saw a glint of light through the curve in the trees, the low throb of thumping bass.

A vehicle approaching the house.

63

Tatia laid Joel gently on the bed. His insubstantial body seemed barely to make any impression on the mattress.

'Is he okay?' asked Poppy at the door of the spare bedroom. For once Tatia barely noticed the tasteful decor – the white walls and curtains, the sleek wardrobe and cabinet; a simple black-and-white print on the wall; the soothing splash of light from a bedside lamp.

She stroked his forehead. 'He will sleep like a king.'

'I'll leave you two alone.' Poppy left, closing the door behind her.

Joel's half-closed eyes glimmered faintly from deep in his skull. Tatia knew he would be asleep within moments.

'We are the luckiest people on earth,' she whispered. 'We have been given a happy ending. What better place than Poppy's home for you to finally sleep?'

Tatia would cherish the memory of this night for ever, but knew if she stayed here she would bring shame on them all – so she had come to a decision.

'Tomorrow I will give myself up to Inspector Drake. Because then you and Poppy will be able to be a family again, little bear. They are only looking for me, Joel. I am ashamed of the horrors I have exposed you to. But I hope you will forgive me and that you will visit me in prison. I will think of you every day, have no doubt about that, and will forever be nourished by the thought that you are happy. Sleep well, my darling brother, and when you wake, I promise things will be better for you. You will be well, you will be stronger. You will live again.'

If you wanted something badly enough, if you tried your absolute hardest to make it happen, then dreams did come true. For one magical evening Tatia had been reunited with Joel and Poppy. Her memories of this night would help her through the difficult months and years to come. Prison and then, perhaps decades in the future, deportation.

Joel's mouth opened to say something, but she couldn't hear what. His jaw moved but he was so tired he was unable to articulate any words. She leaned her ear towards his lips, her hair brushing across his face like a shroud.

'What is it, my darling?'

'Do . . . n . . . tru . . . er.'

'Sleep.' She pressed the duvet around his shoulders. 'And we will speak when you are awake.'

A stillness washed over Joel. All the trembles and twitches that usually wracked his body left him. His head sank into the pillow. Sleep was coming any moment now to take him away – and no man had ever needed sleep more.

But he fought against it one last time. His fingers brushed her sleeve. 'Do . . . no . . . trust . . . Pop.'

Then his eyes closed and Joel fell, for the first time in months, into a deep sleep. Tatia held her hand to his mouth, needing the reassurance of his soft breath on her palm. When he awoke, he wouldn't be back to normal, but his slow recovery would have begun. She lifted a wrist to her eyes to stop herself from weeping over Poppy's crisp white sheets.

Then she turned off the lamp and left the room.

Downstairs, Poppy's strained features were reflected in the window at the sink as she soaked her glass under the tap. Tatia went to clear the plates.

'Leave it!' said Poppy, and then smiled quickly. 'I'll do it in the morning. Why don't you go to bed?'

'Yes. I am tired. I will sit with Joel so that I can watch him.' She held her hands together, as if blessing Poppy. 'Thank you.'

Poppy placed the empty glass on the draining board and took a deep breath. Her attention lingered on an iron on the sill. Tatia knew she was overcome with emotion, but it was understandable. They had all come a long way in such a short time. The past had finally been exorcised. Overwhelmed, Tatia flew at Poppy's back and enveloped her in her arms, kissing her ear. Poppy stiffened against the sink.

'I love you, my darling.'

Poppy shrugged her off. 'I have to be up in the morning.'

Tatia nodded. She was disappointed not to see Gabriel or Tim, but there was still time before she gave herself up to the police. 'Goodnight, Poppy.'

But just as she headed to the door, Poppy called: 'Wait!'

Tatia turned, alarmed.

'Did you hear something?'

Tatia hesitated at the door. 'No, I—'

'I heard a noise,' said Poppy. 'It sounded like it came from the basement.'

64

Drake took out his phone and called Wylie's number, stepping behind the trunk of a tree as the lights of the vehicle bumped along the uneven surface of the lane and came to a stop below him. Inside, the pounding bass of music, something loud, aggressive, shattered the uneasy silence of the night.

The phone rang and rang, but Wylie didn't answer. Below Drake, the steel security gate began to trundle open as the people carrier approached. The passenger-side window lowered – the music blared, Drake glimpsed men in the glow of the dashboard lights – and a cigarette butt was thrown to the verge, where it smouldered.

Once the gate had trundled open wide enough, the car swept into the courtyard, gravel snapping against the underside. The headlights raked the front of the house like a searchlight as the vehicle turned in a lazy curve and parked against the stable building. Then the engine died, the pumping music stopped. The headlights winked off.

Wylie's phone rang and rang.

Four men climbed out. Big men in suits. One of them – larger than the others, with a shaved head – said something. They stood around the car talking and laughing, ignoring the furious barking coming from inside the house.

The gate shuddered to a stop, fully open now, and one

of the men pointed a fob and it began to close again, metal screeching loudly on its runners in the dead of night. Three of the men finally walked towards the house – the courtyard lit up when the security lights were reactivated – and the big man leaned against the car, cupping his hands to his mouth to light a cigarette.

These weren't the kind of people who called the police if they found an intruder in the house. Drake knew Wylie wouldn't stand a chance. He listened to the phone ring and ring, weighing up his options.

And came to a decision.

He's making a fool of you.

Drake pocketed the phone and scrambled down the verge, swooping to pick up a branch from the ground, staying close to the shield of rolling metal as the gate closed, then slipping through the gap with only inches to spare. He kept low in the courtyard, trying to stay beyond the edge of the lights, until he reached the safety of the side of the stables. Looking around the corner, he saw the broad back of the man against the car, saw him put the cigarette to his mouth and lift his head to the sky to exhale a plume of smoke towards the stars. Drake smelled it drifting on the air.

A moment later he heard shouting in the house, and then gunfire – one, two, three cracks, faint blinks of light in the windows. Heard the dogs going crazy. Barking, yapping. The man stood bolt upright. The cigarette dropped from his fingers. Drake moved around the side of the outbuilding, his feet crunching noisily on the gravel – and the man turned, hand fumbling for his pocket. Drake swung the branch hard at his head and the man's heels lifted off the ground as he smacked against the bonnet of the car and slid to the floor.

Drake heard more shouting and the frantic barking of the dogs. He searched the man's pockets and found car keys – and a handgun – but no fob for the gate. He pocketed the gun and climbed into the driver's seat of the people carrier, which smelled of smoke and aftershave. He pressed the ignition and reversed, swinging the vehicle round to face the gate, its spinning wheels sending up a spurt of gravel.

He kept his eyes on the door of the house in the rear-view mirror, willing Wylie to appear, and searched the dash compartment for a fob to open the gate. If he had to, he'd jump on the bonnet and climb over. Whatever happened next, he wasn't going to go inside that house. Wylie was on his own. He'd give him a minute, no more than that – if he was killed, then all the better. There was no camera at the gate. Nobody had seen him, nobody knew he was there.

His phone rang and when he put it to his ear he heard Wylie's voice screaming something, and fragments of noise. Drake heard footsteps pounding on a wooden floor, the dogs barking and the crack of a gun again – saw the simultaneous muzzle flash in a window – and then the call went dead.

A moment later a figure burst out of the front door. Drake pushed his hand on the horn and Wylie veered towards the car, carrying something in his arms, nearly stumbling. He was near to the car now, but the three men came running out of the door behind him. Drake leaned over to open the passenger door and Wylie hurled himself inside, throwing something into the back. A small terrier jumped and turned in circles, yapping in Drake's ear. Blood pouring down his face, Wylie slammed the door shut. Drake pumped the accelerator and shouted for him to open the gate.

'Tell me who you are,' said Wylie, clenching the fob in his hand.

Drake didn't understand. The dog barked in his ear. 'Just open the gate!'

'Tell me your real name,' said Wylie, 'and I'll open it!'

And now you see, said Connor quietly.

'My name is Ray Drake – open the gate!'

'Who are you? Tell me now and we'll go!' Wylie slammed his fists down on the dashboard. 'Come on, man, tell me or we're gonna get killed here!'

Drake looked back. The men were running towards them fast, and the big man had climbed to his feet and was lurching unsteadily towards the car. They would be on them in seconds.

'Tell me who you are!'

Now you see why you need me. Connor was loud in his head. *Because you are weak –*

'Open the gate!'

Drake snatched at the fob, but Wylie held it out of his reach.

'Tell me!'

– And I am strong.

Drake took out the gun and stuck it into Wylie's cheek.

'Whoa!' Wylie reared back. The dog yapped, jumping in frantic circles on the back seat, its paws scrabbling on the leather.

'Just tell me – just—'

There was a loud crack and the rear windscreen exploded in a shower of glass, making them both flinch. The dog jumped frenziedly, barking, barking, barking.

'Open the gate or I'll shoot you now!' shouted Drake and

Wylie giggled, but it was a strangled sound. And then the driver's-side mirror splintered, parts of it bumping across thc bonnet. Drake glimpsed the man shooting at them reflected in the single jagged fragment of mirror remaining.

'Open the gate!' Drake screamed.

'Not until you—'

I'll take it from here, said Connor.

And Drake pushed the gun into Wylie's face and pulled the trigger.

65

'I heard scratching, like a rat or something.' Poppy didn't need to pretend to be frightened. Right at that moment she was petrified. 'Oh god, I hate rats.'

'They are tiny creatures,' said Tatia gently, 'who are more frightened of you than you of them.'

'I couldn't bear it if there's a rat, I won't be able to sleep.' Poppy lifted a finger. 'There it is again!'

Gripping the handle, Tatia put her ear to the basement door. 'I do not hear anything.'

'Please,' Poppy asked her. 'Do you mind taking a look?'

'Of course.' Tatia touched her arm. 'If it will make you feel better.'

'Take the iron with you, just in case.' Poppy walked back into the kitchen and picked it up, holding it low so that Tatia couldn't see the blood and gristle on its flat surface.

'I do not need—'

'Take it.' She pressed Tatia's fingers tightly around the handle. 'It'll make me feel better.'

The iron in her hand, Tatia opened the door and snapped on the light. Peering down the stairs, she could barely see as far as the plastic sheeting rippling in the draughty space. 'I do not see anything.'

'It's down there somewhere.' The distress in Poppy's voice was utterly convincing. If she had to, she would shove Tatia inside and slam the door, but she was terrified she would make a mess of it. To her relief, Tatia walked halfway down the wooden steps, looking over the bannister.

'Can you see anything?'

'There is nothing.'

'Look in the corners.' Poppy's hand hovered over the handle, ready to slam the door shut. 'I definitely heard a sound.'

Tatia continued to the bottom of the stairs. Lost in that excruciating moment, heart pounding, Poppy watched with a sick fascination as she walked to the curtain of plastic – and behind it. She saw Tatia's ghostly shape on the other side, looking down at Tim's body.

'Oh, Poppy.' She heard Tatia's sad voice, and then the iron thud to the concrete floor. 'What have you done?'

And then Poppy slammed the door and locked it. Crying now, real tears of terror and panic, she ran into the kitchen and heaved over the table, so all the plates and cutlery smashed to the floor. She kicked the bread knife, the one with Tatia's prints all over it, into the hallway. Fumbling her mobile from her jeans, she phoned 999.

'Emergency services,' said a voice. 'Which service do you require?'

'Police!' Poppy stood at the basement door, which seemed to jump in her vision as violently as her own thumping heart.

'How can we help you?' said the voice.

'She's here,' Poppy sobbed. 'That woman who killed all those people, she's in my house! She's crazy! She held us at knifepoint and, oh god, she's killed my husband!' Snot filled her nose and mouth. 'My son is here – my son!'

The woman asked for her address and Poppy told her in a terrified stutter. 'Are you and your child in a safe place now, madam?'

'I've trapped her in the basement,' she cried. 'She chased my husband down there, and now he's . . . gone.' Poppy wept at the thought of what she had done, and Tim's cold body. 'I don't know what to do, I'm scared!'

'Police are on their way,' said the operator, 'but it's important that you and your son get out of the house immediately, can you do that for me?'

There was a furious pounding on the basement door. Poppy jumped in terror, and the phone fell from her hand and bounced across the tiled floor.

'Poppy, open the door,' said Tatia calmly behind the door. The handle yanked up and down. 'I am not angry. Poppy, please open the door so that we may talk.'

And then Poppy remembered what the woman had said – get out of the house – and ran up the stairs. Gabriel was dead to the world as she lifted him from his bed, whispering, 'Come on, baby, let's go.'

His head lolled against her shoulder and his limp arms and legs thumped against her hips as she carried him downstairs, trying not to panic. Poppy flung open the front door and went to the car.

'Stand there,' she told him, 'just for a moment.'

She leaned Gabriel up against the car door – he was just about awake now, his legs swayed beneath him and his feet must have been very cold on the paving – while Poppy searched frantically for the car keys, whimpering when she couldn't find them. She remembered with horror that they were in the kitchen. She wondered momentarily if they should just go to a neighbour and lock themselves in, but she wanted to get as far from Tatia as possible.

Running back inside, Poppy heard something loud and heavy hammer against the basement door. Tatia was banging the iron against it. Thump, thump. Wood splintered off the frame.

Poppy snatched the car keys from a drawer in the kitchen and ran back towards the front door, but just as she reached the basement door . . .

It burst open.

She screamed when Tatia emerged, panting for breath, the iron in her hand.

'Your husband is dead.' Tatia nodded over her shoulder. 'Down there.'

Poppy cringed. 'Yes.'

'You killed him,' said Tatia. 'And you have said I did it.' Poppy shook her head, no, no, no. Dropping the iron to the floor, Tatia held up her hands in frustration. 'What did I ever do to you?'

Tatia walked towards her and, in a panic, Poppy ducked into the nearest doorway. Tatia followed her into the living room.

'All my life I have tried my best not to blame you for what you did to me. I told myself that you have always acted out of fear and not cruelty.' Tatia picked up a vase. 'But I see now that all you have ever done is disrespect me. All you have done is throw my love for you back in my face. Like this.'

She threw the vase at a mirror behind Poppy and it shattered. Shards flew into her face and bloodied her cheek.

'Tatia, I'm so sorry!' she cried.

'I lost everything!' Tatia's smile writhed across her face like a snake coiling in a bag. 'I lost my family, our family whom I loved more than you could ever know. I loved them – mother, father, Joel, Will – as I loved you. All I ever desired was your love, the love of my sister, but in return you hated me, and ruined my life. You have no idea, you selfish . . . person, of what I have suffered, of what it is like to be me.' She snatched a statuette off a shelf and it exploded against the wall above Poppy's cringing head. 'And the only thing that has kept me going was the thought that one day I could see you again, and that maybe you would like me, that I could make you *like* me!' She pounded her chest. 'Me!'

'Tatia, please.' Gripping the canister in her pocket, Poppy eyed the door behind Tatia. 'I'm so sorry, I didn't mean to . . .'

But then Tatia's hands lifted to her face and she stopped dead in the middle of the room, head bowed. Poppy saw her shoulders heave as she cried silent tears. This was surely Poppy's best chance to get away, and she was about to move when Tatia spoke quietly beneath her hands.

'I have done things. Someone like you – with your perfect life, your child and husband, your fine clothes and pedicures and supper clubs and Zumba classes and off-street parking, your farmers' markets! – you will not understand. I have lost so much.' Tatia's hands dropped to reveal a triumphant smile. 'But you have lost nothing. You have done terrible things, you have taken and taken and taken. But you have lost nothing of any consequence in your perfect life.'

There was something behind Tatia's smile Poppy had never seen there before. A loathing. A cold, implacable hatred.

'But I see you now. You are an evil person.' Tatia stepped

389

forward, eyeing the jade ring on Poppy's finger. 'And it is time you lost something of your own.'

'Take it,' said Poppy. She tried to pull the ring from her finger, but it wouldn't come off. Her hands were shaking so much and her fingers were slippery with tears. Finally, she managed to wrench it off. 'Please have it!'

Through the dark window, she saw her son standing against the car. Tatia followed her gaze. She'd never have a better moment. Poppy pulled the pepper spray from her pocket but it snagged against the fabric and Tatia leapt at her, nails digging into Poppy's wrist, viciously twisting her arm.

'Drop it!' She tried to wrench Poppy's fingers from the can. Poppy held onto it and they stumbled around the room, but her fear and panic made her weak. Tatia pushed her backwards, slamming her shoulders into the wall.

'I have done this before!' Eyes blazing, Tatia twisted Poppy's wrist towards the broken mirror, pressing it against a jagged piece. Blood popped on her skin and Poppy screamed, dropping the canister. Tatia snatched it up, swinging the back of her hand across Poppy's cheek, who fell to the floor.

Stunned, terrified, the room spinning, Poppy scraped back the thick curtain of hair hanging over her eyes.

'You are not my sister any more,' said Tatia sadly. 'You are nothing, and I am going to make you feel what it is like to be me. You are going to know what it is like to lose everything dear to you.'

Poppy sobbed. 'I'm so sorry, Sarah!'

'You are mistaken.' Her smile was triumphant. 'My name is Tatia.'

And she lifted the pepper spray.

66

'Damn you, Ray!' Wylie punched the roof as Drake's door opened and he was dragged out of the driver's seat. 'You're a very stubborn man!'

The men threw Drake across the gravel. He rolled in a cloud of dust. Before he'd even stopped moving, his body lifted when he took a kick to the stomach. He hit the ground, all the air exploding from his lungs, and was kicked again. The courtyard tipped sideways. In the back of the car, the dog's paws braced against the window as it yapped frenziedly.

Wylie came around the side of the people carrier.

'What a ride, what a blast! You didn't think we'd allow you to have a loaded gun, right? That would have been *really* careless!' He threw the weapon over his shoulder, let out an exasperated breath. 'All you had to do was tell me, Ray! That's all you had to do. How difficult was that?'

One of the men stepped in front of Drake and kicked him. His cheek stung, the world shifted out of focus.

'Oh, come on, guys!' Wylie pushed the man away. 'I told you, not the face. What are you people – animals? Step back, I want to speak to my friend.' He fluttered his fingers, like he was organising a disorderly queue, and crouched beside Drake. 'I'm disappointed, Ray, bitterly disappointed that you didn't tell me the truth. We could have been on our way home by now, and you wouldn't have had to get the shit kicked out of you. I imagine it's very demeaning for a man like yourself.'

Drake stretched out on the ground, the stars vibrating in the sky above him. 'My name is Ray Drake.'

The shaven-headed man lurched forward. 'He knocked me down.'

'Wait.'

The man pointed angrily. 'He hit me with a tree.'

'Tony,' Wylie said quietly, 'I told you to shut up.'

'This is how it works, these days?' Drake turned on his front, lifting himself to his elbows. 'This is what the Ghost Squad does to get a confession?'

'Tell me your *real* name and we'll all be on our way. Your name is Connor Laird.'

'My name is Ray Drake,' muttered Drake.

The shaven-headed man paced back and forth, impatient. 'Let me have a go.'

He knows and there's nothing you can do about it. Because you're weak.

'Shut up,' Drake told Connor.

'What did he just say?' The big man called Tony stepped forward.

'He's not in a good headspace right now.' Wylie held up a hand. 'Cut him some slack.'

But the man walked over to Drake and brought his foot down hard on the back of Drake's head.

Let me take it from here, said Connor.

And this time Drake listened.

The man called Tony lifted Drake to his feet and pushed him against the car. 'He asked you a question,' he said. 'What's your name?'

Drake's head flopped onto the man's chest. He put his hand on the back of Tony's neck to pull his face closer. Put his mouth to Tony's ear and whispered.

'*It's Connor.*'

And then, stepping to the side, he smashed Tony's head into the roof of the car. And when the stunned man's head bounced up, Drake slipped an arm around his neck, the crook of his elbow around his throat, and squeezed. Drake fell back against the car, straining with concentration as he choked the man. Tony's fingers clawed ineffectually at Drake's arm.

Wylie laughed uncertainly. 'Come on, Ray, where's this going to get you?'

Little *ack* noises came from Tony's throat. His face turned crimson and then no sound came out at all.

'Hey, Ray, you've made your point.' Wylie stepped forward, but Drake was wedged tight against the vehicle. The dog's breath clouded the inside of the glass as it barked. Tony would be unconscious in a matter of seconds – and if Drake didn't let go, dead within a minute. Tony's heels thudded against the gravel, sending up a puff of dust.

We'll show these people who we are.

'Let's back off now.' When Drake took no notice and Tony's eyes bulged, Wylie walked to the branch and picked it up. 'You're going to stop right now before poor old Tony becomes even more brain dead than he is already.'

Tony's body juddered, his eyes began to roll up in his head, and his body slipped in Drake's grasp.

'I'm going to count to three.' Wylie waved the branch. 'And then I'm going to hit you with this. Don't make me do that.'

Drake's lips drew back across his teeth as he choked the man, and Wylie sighed. 'Okay, then . . . three. I'm counting backwards, Ray, just so we're clear. Two . . . I'm going to hit you, Ray.'

But then headlights came down the lane. They heard the growl of an engine. Wylie squinted into the light, saw the number plate.

'Flick's coming,' he said. 'Do you want her to see this?'

Drake saw the car and pushed Tony away. The man fell to the ground in a heap, his legs still jerking involuntarily.

'Get him into the car,' Wylie told the others and they dragged him across the gravel. He kicked the gun beneath the car. 'I'm disappointed, Ray. That was totally uncalled for.'

Drake wheeled away, breathing hard. Flick's car pulled up at the gates and Flick jumped out.

'Let me in!' When the gate began to open, she slipped inside, walking quickly towards them. 'What's going on here?'

'Nothing's going on.' Wylie held up his hands. 'We've just been having a friendly meeting. Isn't that right, Ray?'

Flick went to Drake. 'Are you all right?'

'Yes, he's gone now,' he said, getting his breath back. 'But he was here.'

She frowned at him. 'Who was here?'

'Connor,' he told her. 'He's back.'

She stared at him for a long moment and then led him back to the car. 'We're going to get you home, okay?'

'I'll be in touch.' Wylie extended his fingers into a phone shape. 'Let's catch up later.'

'Stay away.' Flick leaned Drake against the car. 'From both of us!'

'But I like you!' called Wylie.

She laughed. 'Incredible!'

'We're great together, Flick.'

She stormed towards him. 'And I bet you stole that poor woman's money at the bar!'

'It was peeking from her bag.' He made a face. 'It would've been rude not to.'

'I knew it!'

Flick went back to her car.

'Wait,' Wylie called. 'Can I come around later?'

Flick placed Drake in the passenger seat and was about to pull the belt over him. Drake grabbed it, said, 'I can do it.'

She walked around to the driver's side and climbed in, considered the scratches on his face, the dust all over his suit. 'Want to tell me what just happened there? Who are those people? What do they want?'

'I don't know,' he said.

'What did you mean when you said Connor was there?'

She waited for him to answer while he clicked the belt into place, but then her phone rang and she took it out.

'Yes, Eddie.' His voice bled out of the receiver just enough for Drake to hear his urgent words. He heard Poppy's name, and Gabriel's – and Tatia's. 'I'll get there as soon as I can.'

Flick cut the call. 'There's been a development.'

'I heard,' Drake said. 'Let's go.'

'I can take this.'

'I want to be there.' He sat up straight, getting back some of his composure. 'Drop me home quickly so I can pick up my car.'

Flick stuck the gear into reverse to do a three-point turn. Stood silhouetted in the beam of the headlights, Wylie was still making that gesture with his fingers, *I'll be in touch*, as the car swung round on the tarmac.

67

'I don't know where she is, she just left! Why are you still here? Why aren't you looking for my boy?'

'We have officers all over London looking for Gabriel and they'll leave no stone unturned.' Flick saw Ray Drake duck beneath the police tape and stride towards the house. He had changed his suit, his shirt. Cleaned up his cuts. 'We have a very specific procedure called a Child Rescue Alert. It's triggered when it's believed a missing child is at serious risk of being harmed. It'll get Gabriel and Tatia's names and descriptions as well as the details of your car to the media and the general public. There'll be TV and radio news flashes. Everyone in the city will be on the lookout for them.'

'Then why haven't you done it already?' asked Poppy from the back of the ambulance. 'She killed my husband. What more evidence do you need that Gabe's in danger?'

'It'll happen very soon, I promise, but a CRA must be activated by a senior officer.'

'What if she's dumped the car?' Poppy scraped her fingers through her hair. 'What if she's already taken him somewhere?'

Her face was covered with tears and snot, and her red eyes were still swollen from where she had been attacked with the pepper spray. But she angrily waved away the paramedic who tried to press a cloth to her face.

'Mrs Mallory . . . Poppy.' Flick nodded at an officer to stay with her. 'I'm going to speak to DI Drake. In the meantime, perhaps you could think back again to what Tatia told you. Maybe she said something you didn't register at the time that indicated where she may have taken your son.'

Poppy shook her head. 'She said nothing.'

'Anything at all.'

'She was screaming like a madwoman when she attacked me.' Poppy pointed to her puffy eyes. 'She did this.'

'Excuse me a moment.'

When Flick began to climb from the vehicle, Poppy grabbed her hand. 'Please,' she whispered. 'Bring him home to me.'

Stepping onto the pavement, Flick ran to catch up with Drake as he approached the house. 'Poppy Mallory said Tatia and Joel Bliss turned up last night out of the blue – this was shortly after she sent our officers away – and they had dinner. The intention was to clear the air, apparently.'

'It didn't occur to her to call the police?' he asked.

'It was tense, she said. The atmosphere was intimidating. Tatia watched her like a hawk the whole time. Poppy said she pleaded with Tatia to hand herself in, and then Joel literally fell asleep at the table and they put him to bed.'

Drake stopped in his tracks to process this bit of information. 'Fell asleep?'

'When Poppy's husband arrived home, there was an argument, she said. Poppy threatened to call the police and Tatia went crazy and held them both at knifepoint. She chased Tim Mallory into the basement and killed him. Poppy says she locked Tatia down there and took her son out of the house. Tatia escaped and attacked her with pepper spray, then took the boy in Poppy's people carrier. She said she's going to kill him, Ray.'

'Does she have any idea where Tatia could have taken him?' When Flick shook her head, he asked, 'Where's Joel Bliss now?'

She nodded at an unmarked car parked further down the road. 'He looks in a bad way.'

'Was he attacked?'

'When the first responders got here he was upstairs asleep. It took a long time to get him to come around. It's difficult to explain, he has some kind of . . . condition. He's almost insensible, can barely keep awake.'

They walked the rest of the way to the house – Poppy's car was missing from the drive – and squeezed past a pair of officers standing in the doorway.

'Can we keep this entrance clear, please?' said Drake, and the two men moved quickly away.

Drake and Flick walked down the steps into the basement, where the body of Tim Mallory lay behind a hanging sheet of plastic. Flashes of light exploded up the surface of the sheet as a photographer moved around the body. Drake saw clear trails in the film of white dust on the plastic, and smudges on the fingertips of the dead man, where he had clutched at the sheeting as he fell.

Drake nodded at a video camera on a stand. 'Is that thing on?'

'Not yet,' said the forensic examiner, who walked up the stairs. Drake checked the equipment was switched off anyway.

'Poppy Mallory locked her husband in the basement with a killer?' Drake pondered out loud. 'Doesn't seem fair.'

'She said he screamed for her to save their son. She locked it in a panic. You can understand her thinking.'

He moved around the victim. The lifeless eyes of Tim Mallory stared blankly at the exposed beams on the ceiling. Flick stood on the other side of the body watching her DI at work. She had already seen the corpse and was preoccupied by the red marks on Drake's left cheek.

'What happened there?' she asked. 'At that house.'

'Wylie was trying to get me to tell him who I am . . . was.'

'How does he know about you? What does he want?'

'Good question.'

'What did you mean, Ray?' She put her hands on her hips. 'About Connor being there?'

'I didn't mean anything.' He didn't look up. 'I was confused. But whatever it is Wylie wants, it's all over now.'

They heard voices at the top of the stairs and someone began to come down. Drake's focus lifted to the sheeting. A figure approached on the other side of the plastic.

'Is it, Ray?' she asked quietly. 'Is it over? Because Myra's worried about you and I'm worried.'

'You don't have to.' He stood and his pale eyes met hers. 'I feel . . .'

'What?' she asked.

He smiled. 'Born again.'

There was something about the way he said it, the way those pale eyes flashed, that made her stare. For a moment, he didn't look like Ray Drake at all, but someone else completely. It was the same look she'd seen months ago when he had stood over Elliot Juniper.

And it made her afraid.

'DI Drake?' called Millie Steiner as she came around the side of the sheeting. 'DS Crowley?'

'Yes, Millie,' said Drake.

'Joel Bliss says he wants to speak to you.' Appearing at the edge of the plastic, Millie Steiner sensed a tension between her two superior officers. 'Sorry, did I interrupt something?'

'Just discussing murder, treachery, all the usual,' said Flick.

Drake followed them up the stairs. 'How long ago was the boy taken?'

'Over an hour and twenty minutes now,' said Flick. 'The vehicle was picked up on ANPR on the North Circular and the M25.'

'Which direction?'

'East.'

'The M25. Do you think she could be heading to Dover or Gatwick?'

'Or one of the addresses in the notebook, maybe?'

'It's possible.' He looked at the iron lying on the hallway floor. 'But she knows we have the book now, so I'd say it's unlikely. Where's the knife?'

'On the floor in the kitchen.'

'So Tatia had a knife in her hand but she dropped it and instead chased Mr Mallory downstairs, killing him with an iron she found in the basement?'

'Looks that way.'

'Let's go and see Joel Bliss,' said Drake, walking off.

They went back outside, Flick filling him in on more details as they approached the car. 'Poppy Mallory says he was asleep and didn't see any of it.'

A painfully thin man was hunched against the door of the car, his spine bent into the shape of a question mark.

68

The swirl of blue light hurt Joel's eyes. It was the middle of the night but everything was so bright – and loud. Lamplight reflected off the yellow jackets of the officers. Voices soaked in static erupted from police radios. He felt like a man who had been asleep for decades and awoken to find himself in a strange world of kaleidoscopic noise and blinding light.

A man and woman came towards him. The man was dressed in a black suit. When he stopped beneath a street lamp, shadows seemed to settle deep in the sharp contours of the policeman's face. Except in his pale eyes, which had a frightening, golden intensity.

'Joel.' The woman ensured everyone else moved away. There was an impatience in the way she organised the people around them, making sure they didn't crowd around Joel, and he was grateful she was there. 'I'm DS Flick Crowley and this is DI Ray Drake.'

'Do you understand what's happening?' asked Drake.

Joel nodded, only half listening. All he wanted to do was lie down on the pavement. He had waited so long to sleep – weeks and months. They just had to let him put his head down for a precious few hours. Once he had done that, he could help them.

'Tatia has abducted Gabriel, Joel, and we believe the boy

is in danger. You'll want to help us find him, I'm sure.' When Joel's head dropped, Drake snapped, 'Joel, do you understand?'

'She didn't do it.' He barely had the strength to enunciate his words and his voice slurred. 'She wouldn't.'

'What didn't she do?' asked Drake.

'Whatever they said she did . . . kill . . . Tim.'

'But Tatia's killed before, isn't that right, Joel?' said Drake. 'She as good as told me she murdered Carl Clarke.'

'That was different, she couldn't . . .' His weak knees nearly buckled beneath him. 'It was the only way to . . . he would have killed again.'

'The Langleys,' said Drake. 'Gareth Walker, Simon and Melinda Harrow. She was there when they died.'

'But Carl killed them all.'

'And what about you?' asked the detective. 'Were you there, Joel?'

When Joel shut his eyes he saw frightening images, spinning like fragments of broken glass in his mind's eye. He didn't know if they were memories or visions. Carl's arms thrashing in a wash of soft light, his face contorted in a frenzy; a woman's anguished screams; a man crawling across the floor.

'I saw what he did.'

'This is not the time,' said the policewoman quietly to her colleague. 'The most important thing is to get Gabriel back safely to Poppy. You want him to be safe, Joel, I'm sure you do.'

'Yes.'

'Then tell us where Tatia will have gone.'

The voice sounded like it came from very far away.

'Joel!' barked Drake, making him flinch. 'Where will she have taken him?'

And then he heard someone scream – and saw Poppy running across the road towards them.

'Where is she?' She twisted in the grip of an officer who took her arm. 'Where has she gone? She's going to kill my baby!'

'She didn't do it.' Ignoring Poppy's shouts, Joel spoke quietly. 'She would never kill your husband. Why would she? All she ever wanted was your love, but you wouldn't give it.'

'Where is she?' Enraged, Poppy tore out of the officer's grip and flew at Joel, knocking him into the road. She fell on top of him, shaking his shoulders. 'She killed him,' she screamed. 'She killed Tim!'

But before she could be pulled off, Joel grabbed the back of her head and pressed her face close to his. 'What have you done?' he asked.

Flick and Drake dragged Poppy to her feet.

'Get Mrs Mallory away from here,' said Drake.

But she struggled against the officers as she was pulled away. 'Where has she taken him?'

Flick helped Joel to his feet and he slumped against the car. 'I know where she is,' he told Ray Drake. 'I can help you, but you have to take me.'

'No deals, Joel,' said Drake. 'Not now. Gabriel is in great danger.'

'You don't understand. She'll only listen to me. I'm the only one.'

'Where is she?' Poppy wailed. 'Where has she gone?'

'Isn't it obvious?' Joel looked at them all in turn. At the

detectives and uniformed officers, and then at the sister he hardly knew. 'Back to the beginning, back to the place she lost everything.'

Poppy cried out. 'Oh god!'

69

'The wheels on the bus go round and round,' sang Tatia. 'Round and round, round and round!' Gabriel squirmed in the child seat behind her as the car plunged through the night, and Tatia had a joyous memory of Joel as a boy sticking out his legs to surge high in the swing. 'The wheels on the bus go round and round—'

'I want to go home,' whined the child.

'All day long!' Tatia laughed. 'Sing with your Auntie Tatia. You have the name of an angel and I would not be at all surprised if you sing like one, too!'

'I want to go home – I want Mummy!'

'We are going on a trip. Just you and me!' She gave him an encouraging smile. 'I spy with my little eye! Something beginning with . . .' She searched for something to spy but all she could see was the endless concrete ribbon of empty motorway unfolding in the dark, and the occasional bridge flashing above. They would be turning off soon and that was a good thing, because she knew the police would do everything in their power to find them.

'Something beginning with "C"! You must look very carefully, Gabriel!'

He rubbed his eyes, tired. 'I don't want to!'

'To the right, see if you can guess!' In the rear-view mirror, she thought she saw a blue light in the distance and her nerves shrieked. They were almost there, they were so close – the junction they needed was just ahead. Accelerating, she swung the car across two lanes so abruptly that the wheels skidded.

'It is gone now.' Tatia laughed. 'It is too late! It was a cow! I win, I win!'

It broke her heart to see him so unhappy, but with such a terrible mother – a treacherous lady, a sneaky person – it was no wonder. With a mother like that in his life – someone toxic, poisonous – his future would be blighted for ever. Tatia fully intended to save him from that woman.

'Let us listen to the radio, instead,' she said, as the people carrier flew up the slip road towards the mini-roundabout at the top. 'What songs do you like?'

She fumbled with the radio, desperate to cheer him up, but the controls in the car were so confusing. Pop music blared at full blast and the boy pressed his hands over his ears. When Tatia looked up the car was surging onto the roundabout too fast. She jerked the wheel but the side of the car clipped a verge.

'Sing with me!' she shouted as she wrestled for control of the wheel. 'Sing with Tatia!'

But the boy was crying now, big wracking sobs, and she felt awful. If she didn't have to drive she would climb into the back seat to give him a big cuddle.

'I am sorry, Gabriel,' she shouted over the din of the music, fumbling with the buttons on the wheel. The windscreen wipers scraped across the dry windscreen; water squirted against the back window. Finally locating the right switch, she managed to turn the music off. 'That is better.'

She let out a big sigh, and adjusted herself in the seat.

The vehicle, she had to admit, was very comfortable and responsive, a much smoother ride than the van she drove at work, and the interior smelled nice. An air freshener danced on the end of a piece of thread, making the compartment smell fresh. In more happy circumstances she would enjoy driving this vehicle.

She didn't recognise anything as she approached the country park, but there were plenty of signs. The last time she had been here was with her mother and father and Will and Joel – and *her*. Those first days of the holiday were the last time she was truly happy. Since then Tatia had kidded herself time and again that she could find peace – but events had conspired to keep her miserable. And one person was responsible for all the terrible things that had happened to her, and one person only – Poppy!

Tatia's teeth ground in anger at the thought of what she had done. But she would suffer, Tatia would make sure of that. Nice Sarah was a mirage, a fantasy – and gone for good. Tatia's own journey was coming to an end. She had nothing to lose. Poppy had taken her last shred of dignity, of hope. A person like that, cold and self-absorbed, didn't care for the feelings of anybody else, not even her own son. Tatia was doing a good thing, a compassionate thing, by saving Gabriel from a life in the shadow of that terrible woman.

Right at this moment, in a parallel dimension perhaps, everything was different. They were all sitting at Poppy's kitchen table. Tatia was loved and respected, a part of the family. Joel was there, looking fit and healthy, handsome and successful, and Gabriel was beside his father. A perfect hostess, Poppy filled the room with laughter and delight.

Her only desire was to make them all happy. And when everyone laughed at a funny joke Gabriel made, Poppy caught Tatia's eye and gave her a smile of such love and devotion.

Tatia closed her eyes, drinking in the scene. 'Oh, Poppy.'

'Look out!' cried the boy.

Tatia saw trees hurtle towards them and pulled the car back into the correct lane. Her dream had been so real that she had completely forgotten where she was. But now her attention snapped to a red light just above the trees. It seemed to hover there, and she was petrified that it was following them, even though it was still dark and the vehicle would be impossible to identify from the air.

'Tell me a joke,' she said.

The boy's head was bowed to his chest. 'Don't know any.'

'Of course you do!' Tatia lowered the window. The cold night air filled the compartment as the car flew down the road. The gale made her hair dance and blow into her eyes as she stuck her head out to follow the light – which had disappeared behind the trees. She smelled the sea air now, and the inky black sky began to reveal threads of purple. 'All little boys know jokes.'

The boy mumbled something.

'What did you say?' she asked above the roar of the wind. Watching the red light reappear directly above them, the steering wheel drifted in her hands.

'I just want to go home!'

'Tell me a joke,' she insisted, pressing down hard on the accelerator. The empty road curled and twisted ahead. Her eyes kept looking back to the rear-view mirror in appeal. 'It will make you feel better.'

'Don't want to!' said the boy, and he glared. 'I hate you! Mummy says you're mad!'

'Do not talk about her!' screamed Tatia. 'Do not ever mention her! Do not!'

Gabriel covered his eyes and sobbed, and Tatia was overcome with remorse at the way she had spoken. 'I am sorry,' she cried. 'I am so sorry!'

She hunched forward to look out of the windscreen. The red light was definitely keeping pace ahead. She expected police cars to appear behind them at any moment.

'Just one joke!' she said, desperate to cheer him up. 'A very funny joke!'

'Knock knock,' he mumbled.

'Who is there?' asked Tatia. 'Tell me, Gabriel, who is there?' He didn't answer. '*Who is there?*'

'Canoe,' said the boy.

'Canoe who?'

'Canoe help me with my homework.'

Tatia didn't understand the joke at first but then the penny dropped. 'Ha ha!' she said. 'Ha ha ha!'

She laughed and laughed until tears misted her eyes and her chest ached. Because it was the funniest joke she had ever heard. She couldn't get her breath. The road twisted ahead of them. Cats' eyes swerved on one side of the car, then the other. And the boy was screaming at her now, hurtful things, cruel things, and she wanted to tell him to stop, please stop, but she couldn't breathe. Her lungs felt like they were going to explode. Shapes popped in her eyes.

Out of the bend in front came a police car, its blue lights flashing angrily, and it headed straight for them. Tatia wrestled with the wheel, jerking it hard. She glimpsed the police vehicle swerve and fly off the road, smash into a tree, even as the wheels of the people carrier left the road and crashed down the verge. Hitting hard rock and tipping, it crashed and rolled through the undergrowth, the windscreen cracking in a thousand directions.

Gabriel's screams rang in her ears; she glimpsed his arms and legs flying above his body, felt her own tears whip across her cheeks as the airbag inflated. Her shoulder smashed against the door as the world rolled over and over, the screech of metal shattering the quiet of the night, until the vehicle came to a stop on its side at the edge of some trees at the bottom of an incline.

The engine hissed and ticked in the early dawn light, two wheels turning slowly – until they came to a gentle stop.

411

70

Beneath a sky still stained with the last bruised blue of the night, Drake's car made good time on the almost empty motorway. Disconnected voices burbled through the static on the police radio in the dark interior of the car. The array of lights from the dash washed his knuckles pink on the wheel. Flick spoke on the phone beside him. In the back, Joel's head lolled on his chest – he was asleep moments after getting into the car.

Flick braced her feet in the footwell every time Drake pulled up inches behind the bumper of the car in front to accelerate past, then returned to her calls, getting updates on the pursuit, reports from London. Sussex police had mobilised; Eddie told her that Poppy's car had been sighted on ANPR cameras on the M23; a helicopter was searching along the coast.

'Let us know as soon as you have anything.' She came off the phone and turned to Drake, whose eyes didn't leave the unfolding road, the white lines on the tarmac dancing towards them. 'They think she's keeping to side roads. There'll be cars on the approach to Beachy Head. She'll not be able to drive near it without getting picked up. How long?'

His gaze dropped to the glowing clock display on the dash. 'Twenty minutes, something like that.'

She turned to look at Joel in the back, his chin jumping on his chest with the vibration of the engine. 'You think he was involved in those home invasions?'

'As you said earlier, let's make sure the boy is safe,' said Drake, 'and then we can worry about that.'

They drove in silence for a while after that, speeding along a dual carriageway as the grey dawn bulged above the tops of the trees. Homes flashed past in the gloom, the road ever more winding. Approaching the Seven Sisters Country Park, and the chalk cliffs, they saw squad cars ahead. Drake slowed as officers flagged them down. A police car had crashed head-on into a tree; its bonnet was wrapped around the trunk. At the bottom of a slope a people carrier lay on its side on scrubby grassland.

'Let me out.' Flick unsnapped the seatbelt and opened the passenger door before Drake had even pulled to a stop. She slammed the door shut, and he saw her trot to an officer in a high-viz jacket who led her down the verge towards the overturned vehicle. A helicopter buzzed in the distance.

'Let me speak to her,' said a voice behind him.

He turned to see Joel was awake. He had forgotten he was there. 'You're going to stay in the car.'

'She'll be scared, upset. She'll listen to me,' he said. 'I'm the only one.'

'I can't allow you to get involved,' said Drake.

'She's not a bad person. She's . . . confused.'

Drake saw the officer point at a small wood, where torch-light whipped back and forth through the trees. Walking back to the car, Flick took out her phone to take another call.

'She wouldn't kill Poppy's husband,' said Joel. 'Why would she? All she wanted was for us to be a family again.'

'Poppy said Tatia hated your family.'

Joel's upper lip curled in a sloppy attempt at a smile. 'The only one who has ever hated our family is Poppy.'

Flick climbed back into the Mercedes, the phone still to her ear. 'We're about five minutes away, Eddie,' she said, killing the call and pulling the seatbelt across her chest. 'It's Poppy's car, but there's no sign of Tatia and the boy. They think she must be headed to the cliffs on foot.'

Drake pulled the Mercedes back into the road, as an officer tried his best to motion them slowly past the parked vehicles. He said into the rear-view, 'Is she heading to Beachy Head?'

'I – I don't remember. We were here . . . it was a long time ago.'

'Which cliff is she going to, Joel?' Drake gunned the engine, accelerating past the obstructions, thinking of the sequence of peaks, miles long, on the East Sussex coast.

Flick clutched the door handle for support and looked over her shoulder. 'If she doesn't go to Beachy Head, if she goes to any of the other cliffs, our people may not be able to save Gabriel in time.'

'I don't remember, I'm sorry. There's still so much I don't remember.' When Flick turned to face forward again, Joel said, 'Please let me speak with her. She'll listen to me.'

But his weak voice was lost beneath the roar of the engine.

71

Tatia dragged Gabriel down the incline, his legs stumbling on the uneven grass surface. She saw the police in the distance, at Beachy Head and the nearby Birling Gap visitor centre, but there was nobody this far along the cliffs. The sea churned on the horizon, a broiling mass as far as the eye could see. And then she saw the helicopter wheel in the sky and come towards them, imagined the people on board shout into their radios. She heard clearly the soft chop of the rotors, saw the glint of the early morning sun on its hard metal body. Tatia was terrified that it would suddenly swoop in front of them and men on wires would drop from it, brandishing guns or tranquillisers.

Running through a field of sheep, the bleating creatures scattering in front of them, she kept a tight grip on the boy's hand. 'The wheels on the . . . bus, they go . . .'

But she didn't have enough puff to sing and the boy kept losing his balance on the white chalk stones. 'Nearly there! The wheels on the . . . bus! Keep . . . moving!'

She was crying now, they both were. The wind this close to the cliff edge stung her cheeks, roared in her ears. And then the boy stumbled again and she wearily placed him on his bare feet. Tatia just wanted to fall to the ground herself. It felt like they had been running for ever, through woods and fields, ducking behind hedges when the helicopter passed near. But they were only a few feet now from the edge – where their journey would end.

'Wheels . . .' she panted. 'Bus . . . round.'

She had to save Gabriel from that woman. Because his life would be a perfect misery if she didn't. And – *and* – Poppy needed to learn a lesson. She needed to understand once and for all that actions had consequences.

Everything was so confusing in her head.

And now she saw half a dozen police cars bumping over the fields behind them – it made her shriek and pick up her pace – but then they stopped at a distance. Officers got out and ran towards them. The helicopter hovered over the churning water, the noise of it impossibly loud.

'Nearly there!' she told him in a panic. 'We are nearly . . . wheels on the . . . safe.'

She stumbled to the lip of the cliff, where the sea writhed hundreds of feet below. And then, just at that moment, the sun finally broke through the thick morning cloud, and its rays dropped to the rippling water to turn the waves a glorious burnished gold all the way to the horizon. She felt warmth on her face. They would soon be safe, both of them.

Nobody could hurt them ever again.

72

'They're at the cliff edge.' A uniformed officer hunched at the driver's window. 'The woman and the boy.'

Drake turned to Joel. 'Stay here.'

'I'm the only one who she'll listen to, I'm—'

But the two detectives had already climbed out of the car and were walking quickly down the incline, organising officers as they went. Doors slammed as vehicles arrived, pulling in at every angle – police cars, ambulances, a mobile chaplaincy unit. Emergency workers pulled on fluorescent vests. Radios chattered, the helicopter bobbed in the distance. Joel heard its flat whine in his head. Figures stood at the cliff edge. An officer approached when DI Drake pointed at the car.

'Please.' Joel opened the window a crack, the wind whistling through the gap. 'Let me go down there.'

'You're staying here.'

A winking light on the dashboard burned in Joel's head. The leather smell in the interior was too pungent. Feeling nauseous, he opened the door and heaved himself out of the car.

'I need some air!' Joel said, when the policeman moved towards him.

In this place, which he had revisited so many times in his head, he felt a sudden focus, a sharpness of the senses.

The grass beneath his feet was slippery. He smelled the brine tang of the sea, saw seagulls diving in the sky and the thin grey undulation where the ocean met the horizon. The wind blew up Joel's cuffs and beneath his collar, lifted his lank hair, chilled his burning face.

Someone called to the officer beside him, who walked to meet his colleague on the other side of the car.

Once again, those familiar addled memories, the colours at the same time oversaturated and sepia thin, fired up on the blank wall of Joel's mind like a projector bursting into life. Clumps of grass trembled on the lip of the muddy chalk cliff. An armada of cloud scudded across the horizon.

And this time, to his astonishment, Joel saw Will on the cliff edge.

The memories hit him with the force of a tidal wave, the sequence of events dropping neatly into place in his head. Will was standing there, he was crying, and there was someone beside him. He saw who it was.

He had to tell Tatia.

The officer was turned away from him, deep in conversation, and Joel took a step forward, expecting to be stopped at any moment. He took two steps – three, four, threading his way calmly through the vehicles, his tired legs picking up speed.

And then, at the edge of the cars, he didn't know how he found the strength – but he began to run.

73

What happened:

Will had been running across the grass, following Sarah up and down the edge of the cliff, when he stumbled on a stone and fell to the ground. Poppy, waiting for an excuse, rushed over to drag him to his feet and tell him to stop being a silly little boy.

Sitting on the grass further up the hill, Joel stood, curious to know what was going to happen next. It was the last thing you said to Will if you wanted him to behave – Poppy knew that as well as anyone – and he squirmed in her grip.

'Get off,' he said, and kicked her in the shin.

'Ouch!' She grabbed his shoulders and shook him. 'You little shit!'

'I'm going to tell Mum and Dad what you said!'

Poppy wouldn't let go. She kept telling him to calm down and stay away from the edge. It was dangerous, she said, but Joel knew she was just mad because Will had been racing about after Sarah all afternoon. Poppy scowled when Joel and Will came near her; she had reached the age where she regarded them as little kids. But what really annoyed her, what really made her mad, was when they chose to spend time with Sarah instead of her. It wasn't the first time Poppy had tried to stop Joel and Will playing with Sarah.

He saw Sarah further along the cliff, enjoying being at the very edge of the world, totally oblivious to what was happening. His parents had gone to the car to fetch the packed lunches – they said they would only be a couple of minutes, and had given Poppy strict instructions that no one should go too close to the edge.

Will tried to bite Poppy's hand and then spun away, ducking out of the way when she tried to grab him, running around her, making it all a big game.

'Come here!' Poppy commanded him, pointing to the space in front of her as if he were a little dog she was trying to bring to heel. But he wouldn't listen, repeatedly darting near and then running off, and Poppy was getting more and more angry.

Finally, she managed to grab the hood of his sweatshirt and swing him closer. Will's feet kicked out.

'No one likes you!' Joel heard him shout. Will knew just how to make Poppy mad. 'Everybody hates you! Mum and Dad hate you!'

'They don't!'

'Joel hates you!'

'Stop it!'

'I hate you!'

He yanked his hood out of her grip and stumbled. Waves crashed against the rocks hundreds of feet below. Seeing how close he was to the edge now, Poppy held up her hands, and calmly said, 'That's enough.'

But Will was in hysterics, jumping and hopping across the grass, worried that Poppy was going to snatch at him again.

She tried to keep her temper in check. 'I'm not going to touch you!'

'I hate you!'

Heart hammering, Joel looked back up the hill, wondering if he should fetch his parents.

'Stop it!' Poppy lurched forward.

But Will kept stepping back, stepping back. 'I won't!'

'You're a nasty little kid!' Poppy told him, and said a few other things, too, like how big his ears were and what a little crybaby he was. And that made Will cry big spluttering tears. He had to listen to her, said Poppy; he had to do what she said, because she was his big sister. Joel approached them from behind, locking his knees against the wind, but neither of them saw him there.

'You're not my sister,' shouted Will. 'Sarah is my *proper* sister!'

Poppy forgot immediately about trying to calm him down. Her face twisted in fury. 'She's not your sister, she's nothing!'

'I love Sarah – and hate you!'

'Don't call her that!'

'Sarah!' Will's face twisted in misery. 'Sarah! Sarah! Sarah!'

And Poppy screamed in fury and stepped forward, her arms pumping out.

Shoved him hard in the chest.

And he flew back.

One moment Will was there, and the next –

He was gone.

Clumps of grass trembled on the lip of the chalk cliff. An armada of cloud scudded across the thick line of the horizon where the sky met the ocean. But all that was left of Will was an absence where he had just been and now – in the blink of an eye – wasn't.

Poppy stood with her arms still stretched in front of her,

her back framed against the big ocean, which swayed and churned. Then she lifted her trembling hands to her face – and screamed.

Oblivious of Joel watching a few feet away, she ran back up the incline. Screaming in terror, calling for her parents.

Moments later, his mum and dad were running down the slope, their screams and shouts almost lost in the rattle of the wind in his ears. His mum's eyes bulged with terror, her legs almost buckling as she ran over the stony ground. His father roared for them to get back, step away from the edge, for god's sake, get back.

And when Joel looked again to the edge, Sarah was there. Hands planted hard on her knees to stop her toppling, hair twisting and tumbling around her pretty face in the fierce gale.

His dad's voice was hoarse as he charged towards them: 'Get away, get back!'

'Will! Will!' shrieked his mum.

And Sarah glanced over her shoulder, suddenly aware of all the commotion, and her eyes fell on Joel.

This big smile on her face. 'What is it? What did you see, Joel? What have I missed?'

74

Now:

Tatia stood on the edge of the cliff, the boy's hand gripped tightly in hers, only inches from where the ground dropped away. If she took a single step back, she and the boy would plummet over the side. Or the ground could crumble beneath them at any moment. These cliffs were notorious for erosion and sudden landslips, Drake knew, and whole sections of rock regularly smashed into the water.

He drifted forward until he was maybe ten or twelve feet away. The boy wriggled in Tatia's anxious grasp and for one moment his whole body swung off the edge, and she had to use all her strength to pull him back upright.

'Hello, Tatia. I'm Detective Inspector Ray Drake.'

'Yes, sir.' She darted nervous glances at Flick and the other officers behind him. 'I recognise your voice.'

'Would you rather they weren't here?'

'It does not matter,' she said. 'It is too late now.'

But Drake gestured for the men to go back up the incline.

'I did not mean for those people to die,' said Tatia. 'It was not my fault. I was there, but I could not stop him. He was ill, you see, poor Carl.'

'It's good to see you again, Gabriel.' The boy stared, bewildered, at the detective and at the helicopter. 'Let's get you both somewhere safe, Tatia, and then you can tell me everything. I'm looking forward to getting this whole situation resolved, and Gabriel back home safely.'

'Her husband,' Tatia said. 'You need to know that it was not—'

She stopped, flustered by the loud drone of the helicopter. Drake gestured at Flick, who spoke into her radio to get it sent away.

'You were saying, Tatia.'

'It was . . . I did not—' She shook her head, confused. 'I forget now.'

'You must be exhausted. It's been a long night. Look at Gabriel, the poor lad can barely stand. He needs to be in bed. This isn't his fault, none of it has anything to do with him. Let my colleague take him, Tatia, and then we can talk.'

'No!' she shouted, and pulled the boy closer to her. 'I killed Carl, I did that, sir, but I had to . . . those people, you see . . . he would not have stopped. We just wanted to be free.'

'We can talk about Carl, and about what happened at Poppy's, but do me a favour.' He moved closer. 'Step away from the edge.'

'Please, sir, get back, I insist!' She let out an exasperated breath. 'She always gets what she wants, she always ends up with everything, and I end up with nothing. She is not a good person, sir, she is not. But people,' she shook her head in wonder, 'they believe her.'

'I'll listen to you, Tatia.'

'But you will not *believe*.'

'I can't make up my mind until you tell me. Let the boy come to me.'

'No, it is too late.' Over her shoulder, waves crashing into the cliffs sent up violent spumes of foam. Tatia's shoulders drooped. 'I am saving this poor little fellow, sir, from a terrible life. We are going now.'

'Tatia,' said Drake. 'No!'

Tatia gripped the boy's hand tightly and was about to step off the edge when her attention was grabbed by something happening over Drake's shoulder.

Joel was stumbling down the hill towards them, police officers quickly closing in on him.

75

He ran down the incline, his weak heart clattering in his chest, his knees buckling beneath him. Joel was aware that he was moving painfully slowly, and when he finally fell, his foot snagging in a hole, his palms skidded across the ground. He smelled the grass on his hands, the iron tang of mud smeared on his palms. An officer grabbed hold of him.

'Sarah! Sarah!' he called, but his voice was a hoarse croak.

'Joel,' Tatia screamed at the cliff edge. 'Joel!'

The officer pulled him up, but Drake trotted towards them. 'Let him go!'

Joel could hardly hear himself think beneath the churning rotors of the helicopter, which had dropped so low that it flattened the grass against the hillside.

Drake shouted to Flick. 'Get that bloody thing out of here!'

He took Joel's arm and led him down the incline. Joel was exhausted from the run, but it had been a long time since he had felt so – awake.

'Can you talk to her?' Drake asked, leading him towards Tatia and Gabriel.

It was all he wanted. 'Yes, yes.'

'Joel!' Tatia cried, as he approached.

'You left me,' he told her. 'You said you would never leave me.'

She smiled sadly at him, framed against the vast grey churn of the sea. 'I am sorry, little bear, but it was for the best.'

'You can't go.'

'You look so well,' she told him. 'You will get better without me. I am not a good person.'

'You can't leave me by myself,' he said. 'Not again.'

'She took everything from me,' said Tatia. 'And from you, and she cannot keep getting away with her unkindness.'

'Let Gabriel go. You're not punishing her, you're punishing him.'

'I am setting him free.'

'I don't care about her, she's nothing to me – *you're* my sister.' He thumped his chest. 'I need you. Don't leave me, Sarah.'

She shook her head, in tears now. 'There is no Sarah, only Tatia. Please stay away. We are going now, Gabriel and I, to a better place.'

'I remember what happened to Will, now. I see everything. I'll tell people and it'll change everything.'

'What happened?' She shook her head. 'I do not understand.'

'I'll tell you,' he glanced at the boy, 'but first you must let Gabriel go.'

Joel didn't know what to do or say, because her familiar smile was twisted into something full of agony and indecision. Joel knew if he took one more step forward she would leap, and take the boy with her.

She swayed in the whipping wind. 'Poppy took my life from me!' she cried. 'My happiness! And now I am going to take something from her.'

427

'I can't let it happen again,' Joel said. 'I'll tell them what happened to Will, what really happened.'

'I have never been so happy as when I first came here. I remember standing on this cliff and looking out at the sea and thinking how my life had changed. I had a family – parents, brothers and a sister – and a home. Everything that I could possibly want. But then I turned, and Will was gone and in an instant, everything was changed. Poppy made me say I was responsible for Will's death and I agreed. But she tricked me, little bear.'

'I saw what happened, and I should have said something,' said Joel. 'But everything was so confused in my head, you all said one thing and I saw something different, it was just easier to . . . blank out what really happened. But I remember now, Sarah, and I'll tell the police.' Joel glanced at Drake. 'They'll know the truth.'

'She said I did it on purpose.' Tatia's chest heaved with sobs and Joel didn't know if she had even listened to him. 'But I did not. All I wanted was to help you, and for her to love me.'

'I *know* what she did. Please, Sarah, come away from the edge.'

'I am not Sarah! Sarah was a dream, a fiction. I am Tatia, I have always been Tatia.'

'You're my Sarah.'

'She said our parents would forgive me, but then she told lies about me – she made them hate me. They said I had to go back to that place, just for a short while, but that they would come back for me one day. I waited and waited. For months, for years, but nobody came.' Her face crumpled. 'Nobody came, Joel.'

'You must listen to me. I *know* what happened to Will, and I'm going to tell the world, and when this is all over we'll be together again. I'll wait for you, I don't care how long it takes, we'll be a family again.'

'I am sorry.' Tatia's smile was dismal. 'She took my life and now I must take something from her. It is not fair, it is not right, but it is the only thing I am able to do.'

'Ring-a-ring o' roses,' Joel sang suddenly.

'We are going,' said Tatia, confused.

'Come on, you and me, Sarah, one last time. Ring-a-ring o' roses, a pocket full . . . Come on, Sarah! Sing it with me!'

'Do not call me that,' she said with a weary smile. 'It is too late.'

'One last time with me.' He stepped closer, hands out. 'Just one last time.'

'Joel!' barked Drake. 'Don't.'

'Shut up!' Joel told him. 'This is between me and my sister, my only sister.' He turned back to Tatia, who teetered on the edge. 'Ring-a-ring o' roses . . .'

And she sang softly. 'A pocket full of posies.'

'A-tishoo!' Joel nodded grimly at Drake. 'A-tishoo!'

'A-tishoo!' she sang. 'We all—'

Joel lifted his arms into the air, and Tatia did, too, letting go of the boy.

'Fall down!' Joel rushed towards her. Flew into her body, his arms folding around her neck in a tight embrace.

Together Joel and Tatia flew off the edge.

One moment they were there, and the next –

76

If the attendance at his funeral was anything to go by, Tim had been a popular man. Friends and colleagues turned out in droves to pay their last respects. And there was also a crowd of people, fascinated by the intense media coverage of the story, who gathered at the edge of the graveyard hoping to get a glimpse of the beautiful widow and her brave boy.

The press was there, of course. The telephoto lenses of countless photographers were trained at a discreet distance on Poppy Mallory née Bliss. However, only a single journalist was allowed to attend the ceremony. He stood behind the family, making sure rival reporters didn't attempt to approach Poppy until her tragic story had exclusively appeared in his newspaper, as stipulated in the terms of the contract.

The widow looked very sad and stylish in her simple mourning dress with its classic V-neck and tall black heels. Her hair was worn up and her make-up understated, the exception a slash of bright red lipstick. She had never looked more vulnerable – or more striking. Gabriel stood beside her in a suit and tie, and everyone agreed he looked a fine young gentleman. John and Tanya Mallory stood on either side of their daughter-in-law as the priest spoke at the graveside.

Ray Drake joined the procession of people paying their respects to Poppy. Clasping hands and receiving kisses, she nodded her thanks to mourners who offered commiserations. John and Tanya stayed close, ready to intervene if the situation became too overwhelming. Drake knew that as soon as the funeral was over the family was flying to Portugal, where a famous PR friend of John's was joining them to explore possible media projects. A book was planned and a US television network was interested in making a miniseries. The public was fascinated by what had happened. Poppy had been a victim of a terrible sequence of events. Her husband had been murdered by a vengeful psychopath and her beloved son abducted and saved in the nick of time. But with all kinds of lurid speculation appearing on the internet, the family was keen to ensure the public heard Poppy's account of what had happened. After all, she was as much a victim of mad Tatia Mamaladze and her feeble-minded brother as her dead husband.

Her darkest nightmare had become a terrible reality. Poppy had lived in fear of the return of Tatia since the murder of her own little brother, which had been covered up by her own parents many years ago. Everyone agreed that it was a miracle that mother and child had come through their ordeal unscathed.

Nobody could comprehend such terrible suffering. Poppy would live with the scars of her experience for ever. Tim, the love of her life – her rock, her anchor – was dead. But, thank the lord, her son had been saved when Tatia plunged to her death. At least Tim's family would be there to look after her. John and Tanya Mallory were devoted in-laws, who would care for Poppy in the difficult days to come.

Ray Drake, the man who had pursued the so-called Goldilocks Killers, pushed to the front. Positioning Gabriel in front of her like a human shield, Poppy gracefully accepted his sympathies. When he shook it, her hand was limp and cold.

He smiled down at the boy. 'Hello, Gabriel. It's nice to meet you again.'

'Hello,' said Gabriel.

'Thank you for coming,' said Poppy and the people around them pressed forward to listen. 'I owe you my son's life.'

'It's your brother you should thank,' said Drake. 'Joel saved his life.'

Poppy nodded sadly at her poor brother's sacrifice – hundreds of yards away, camera motors whirred – but her attention was caught by the arrival of an investment banker colleague of her late husband.

'There are a couple of aspects to the investigation I'd like to talk about when you're ready,' Drake said. 'Some irregularities we'd like to clear up.'

'Of course.' Poppy smiled bravely. 'Whatever you need. Now if you'll excuse me.'

She moved quickly past him, John and Tanya making sure to step between Drake and Poppy as she greeted the tall, handsome banker.

'Poppy.' A mutual friend introduced them. 'This is Tim's friend Lee.'

The sad smile stayed in place, but Poppy's eyes sparkled momentarily. 'Thank you so much for coming, Lee.'

The man took both her hands in his and she made no attempt to remove them. 'I'm so sorry for your loss,' he said. 'Tim was a good man.'

Tears glistened in her eyes. 'It means so much to hear you say that.'

'I'd like to help,' he said. 'In any way I can.'

She pressed her lips together, overwhelmed by his heartfelt offer.

Drake walked back to his car to find someone pacing up and down beside it, thumbs moving up and down on his phone as he played a game.

'I love a funeral,' said Wylie, not looking up.

'Who are you working for?'

Wylie held up a finger, wanting to finish the game. Drake put his hands in his pockets and waited, tired already of this particular charade. Then Wylie pocketed the phone, grinning. 'Made it to the next level.'

'Who are you working for?' said Drake.

'Lucky for you, I didn't have to arrange a funeral for my friend Tony. Wow, Ray, you have a temper on you. We're going to have to watch out for that.'

Drake repeated the question.

'I work for an interested party.' Wylie watched everyone leaving the graveyard. 'This person saw a photo of you in a newspaper, and got a tingly feeling. It was really bugging them. They said you reminded them of someone they knew a long time ago, and they really, really wanted to confirm who you are, who you really are, *Connor*. But, I have to say, you are a far more interesting character than I ever imagined. Dangerous, unpredictable.'

'Who knows me?' asked Drake

'I heard about that poor woman.' Wylie nodded in the direction of Poppy. 'Those home invasions. Bloody awful business. Flick's not talking to me, you probably know that. I'm gutted because I really like her. But I hope we're still friends, Ray. I really enjoyed our night out. Except that bit when you tried to blow my head off, that wasn't much fun. And there was poor Tony, of course. I really thought he was a goner.' Wylie frowned. 'You really would have killed me. I thought we were mates.'

'Who is it?' asked Drake.

This is never going to be over.

'All in good time. Get on with your life, catch your breath, pursue a few bad guys. Our mutual friend will be in touch when they're good and ready. Personally, I'm looking forward to it. Life's so much more *fun* when you're around.' He winked. 'Be seeing you.'

But you have nothing to worry about, said Connor.

Drake watched Wylie walk away. He leaned up against the car.

I'm here and I'm going to protect you, whether you like it or not.

Drake saw Poppy and the banker walking together alone, gradually separating from the throng. Her son stood forgotten in the middle of the crowd of people, stood as his mother fell into deep conversation with the banker about the future.

Because you are weak and I am strong.

77

3 days before Will's death:

She was woken by the throb of a car engine, and the flash of the motorway lights in her eyes.

It took Poppy a moment to realise where she was, squashed in the back of the car – hunched stiffly against the door, cheek numb against the cold window – on the way to Brighton. Joel was pressed against her, his head lolling against hers, but Tatia on the other side of him had plenty of room. Somehow, she had managed to hog all the space on the back seat, and was curled comfortably, using a coat as a pillow. Tatia always got what she wanted, it seemed to Poppy, and had Mum and Dad wrapped around her little finger.

'She's settling in well,' Poppy heard her father say quietly over the drone of the engine. 'Will loves her to bits – and Joel.'

Sitting in the front, her parents were mostly obscured by their headrests. All Poppy could see was a grey sliver of her father's unshaved cheek and the knuckles of his left hand resting on the steering wheel. Her mother, directly in front of her, was completely hidden. Will lay on her chest, his head rested on her shoulder.

It was typical that the first thing she heard when she woke up was a conversation about *her*. Everything was all Sarah this and Sarah that, saying how nice she was and how clever – and how kind. But Poppy would never call her by that name. Hell would freeze over before she called her Sarah. She wasn't Sarah, she was Tatia, and always would be.

Her mother said, 'Poppy doesn't like her.'

Patrick Bliss lifted his fingers from the wheel. 'Poppy has got to learn that the world doesn't revolve around her.'

That familiar anger surged like hot lava inside her. She wanted to scream at the top of her lungs that she would never accept that girl in her home. Tatia might fool everyone else, but she didn't fool Poppy.

They had all been happy before she came, they had been a proper family: Mum, Dad, Poppy, Joel, Will. Why did her parents have to ruin everything by bringing a stranger into their lives? She was an intruder in their home, someone who didn't belong, and her mum and dad had given no consideration to how their own children felt about it. They were expected to just accept it. Nobody had asked Poppy whether she wanted a sister. Nobody had given the slightest consideration to *her* feelings.

She felt a rage that made her shudder so violently that Joel's head jolted against her shoulder. Poppy was the only person who could see what a freak Tatia was. Joel didn't see it; Will was too young to understand. And Poppy didn't see why, if her parents wanted to save the little children, they should ruin her life in the process. It made her want to scream at the unfairness of it all.

When she looked up Will's eyes were open. Poppy didn't like the way he was staring at her over his mother's shoulder, as if he knew what she was thinking, and she poked out her tongue.

She decided then and there that she would make Tatia pay for coming into her life and ruining everything. She didn't know how, she didn't know when. Sooner or later, a situation would present itself and Poppy would make the most of it. She would rid herself of that little bitch.

'Things will calm down. Poppy will get used to the way things are, and sooner than you think.' Patrick Bliss placed a hand on his wife's arm. 'And in the meantime, we're going to have a lovely holiday.'

Poppy lifted her head again to look at Tatia sleeping on the other side of Joel, head burrowed into her coat, the smile on her face briefly illuminated by a cascade of light dragging down it.

Smiling in her sleep. Normal people just didn't do that.

God, how Poppy hated that smile.

ACKNOWLEDGEMENTS

Just give me one more page to mention some lovely people who helped bring this book to life!

Thanks to Inspector Kevin Horn, Mick Gradwell and Bob Cummings for patiently putting up with my avalanche of questions about police procedure, and Senior Paramedic Jason Eddings for providing the medical guidance.

My gratitude to Mobile Network geeks Jo Purdue and Steve Dyett for their hi-tech expertise; to Dr Neil Stanley for speaking to me about sleep disorders; and to Vicky Mackinnon for discussing adoption procedure back in the day.

I'm indebted to Jamie Cowen, my amazing agent at The Ampersand Agency, and Rosie and Jessica Buckman at The Buckman Agency, for all their wonderful work.

Ed Wood is my brilliant editor at Sphere, and I've been lucky to work with other incredibly talented people at Little, Brown. I'm talking about you, Thalia Proctor, Charlotte Chapman, Ella Bowman, Tom Webster, Emma Williams and the Sales Gang. And let's not forget Bekki Guyatt and Sean Garrehy for the terrific cover.

Much love to Fiona and Archie for their unwavering support and patience when I'm writing – and when I'm not. I'm hugely grateful to friends and family for all their encouragement, and also to everybody who's read *It Was Her* and taken the time to comment.

And finally, my everlasting thanks go to my English teacher, Mrs Patricia Tighe. Many years ago, she planted the seed of an incredible idea into the head of a mediocre student: that maybe, just maybe, he could one day write a book . . .